About Margaret Cahill

Margaret Cahill's day job is publishing MBS books through her company The Wessex Astrologer. She started writing a blog to keep in touch with friends during treatment for lymphoma in 2013; the blog led to her first book, *Under Cover of Darkness: How I Blogged My Way Through Mantle Cell Lymphoma* as well as invitations to write about complementary support for cancer patients by various organisations including Bloodwise.org. She's now completely addicted to writing; this is her first work of fiction, but her love of cruising might just peek through the storyline. She lives with her partner and three cats on the sunny south coast of England.

You can reach Margaret through the blog at
www.margaretcahill.wordpress.com.

It Could Only Happen at Sea

Margaret Cahill

Bookworm Press

Published in 2018 by
Bookworm Press an imprint of
The Wessex Astrologer Ltd
4A Woodside Road
Bournemouth
BH5 2AZ
www.wessexastrologer.com

Cover Design by Jonathan Taylor

A catalogue record for this book is available at The British Library

ISBN 9781910531242

Acknowledgements

I don't believe a book can ever be a purely solo adventure – and indeed it *is* an adventure because you don't truly know where you will end up. There are so many other people in the background who provide invaluable support in one form or another, ranging from proof-reading until their eyes are nearly bleeding, to a simple phone call just asking how it's going. Or indeed, *if* it is going. There were times when it wasn't. So here's a non-exhaustive list of some lovely people I'd like to thank.

Barnaby – you know why. Lyn and John for being the bestest besties ever, and for encouraging me all the way by being such inspirations. My niece Talya, whose experience working on the Domestic Violence Unit of the Metropolitan Police gave me an invaluable sounding board. To the un-named women who have shared their experiences of domestic abuse with me: thank you from the bottom of my heart for your bravery. If we all pull together on this there can be some progress. To my long-suffering and ever-supportive partner Stephen for doing the shopping, the cooking *and* the washing up while I was totally engrossed in writing, for being my muse, for reading the manuscript God knows how many times, for helping me when the story-line floundered, and for always being sure I could do this. You're the best.

And here are a few people who don't know they helped but their contribution is immense: Eden – you're one in a million and I hope your clients appreciate your astounding optimism and total determination to make your dreams come true. We can all learn from you. Jonny Geller of Curtis Brown Literary Agency. Sadly your agency didn't offer a blinding deal for my manuscript but your TEDx Talk was a massive inspiration for me. Lindsey Kelk, Milly Johnson and Jojo Moyes: thank you for writing books that are perfect examples of how to discuss a difficult subject while including laughter and tears along the way.

And finally... a massive shout-out to all the hard-working crew on the cruise ships, especially P&O and Cunard. You're all brilliant, and thanks a million for enriching our lives with your good humour and amazing service.

"We shall not cease from exploration and the end of all our exploring will be to arrive where we began and to know the place for the first time."

T.S. Eliot

Chapter 1

Gulp.

Dragged violently and rudely back to reality, I stop typing, fingers freezing over the keyboard so I can listen properly. Fight or flight? Old habits take over as, heart pounding, I lift up quietly out of my chair and tiptoe as far as the hallway before I remember the front door is locked and bolted.

Safe. As always, these days. Stop being paranoid.

I can't. So just to be sure, I go all the way out to give it a tug. Yup. Imagining it.

Aaaaaargh.

I lean back against the solid wooden door in relief. My poor heart calms down to something approaching normal, but as it does so a solitary tear trickles down my cheek and drips off my chin. This has got to stop. I'm turning into some kind of emotional wreck. Sliding downwards, I end up sitting on the floor, arms wrapped around my legs, face resting on jean–clad knees. Trying to think rationally about what's just happened, then realising I've failed miserably as more tears arrive uninvited to follow their buddy. Before very long I'm deeply into a massive release of sadness and anger, a volatile combination at best. And I know all about volatile.

Someone knocks on the door, making me jump.

"You okay, love?" It's my lovely neighbour, Ellie.

Noooo! I'm not okay! I'm falling apart... screams the voice in my head.

Deep breath, false bright voice like nothing's wrong. "Yup, all good in here, Ellie. Just having a moment, but thanks for asking," I call through the door. She's so sweet.

"Just wanted to check. Always here for you," and I hear her going back to her flat and the door closing.

Sobbing is a messy and exhausting business, so heaving myself to my feet, I'm just plodding wearily to the bathroom for a nose blow and a splash of cold water when the landline rings, making me jump again. I stare at it, willing it to stop. Finally it does. Friends and family all text before calling, and as there hasn't been one there's no way I'm answering it. I finally make it to the bathroom and can't help noticing that even after a shockingly cold face wash I'm doing a good impression of what my Grandma would have called 'death warmed up'. Surely there's still a little bit of the old me left inside, isn't there? Leaning on the sink, I move in closer towards the mirror, looking vainly for a sign of the happy person that used to beam out at me, way back when. Um, nope. Not at the moment, it seems.

The phone goes again.

My frazzled nerves have made me all jangly and irritable and now I'm cross at the continued intrusion into what, up until a few moments ago, was my nice calm day. I don't need this. Storming out of the bathroom, and across the lounge I wrench the handset out of its cradle, not giving a shit who might be on the other end.

"WHAT?!"

"Good evening Madam, and how are you today?"

"Ex–*cuse* me? Who the hell are you?"

"Well actually I'm calling about your personal computer."

"Oh, just fuck off! This is the last thing I need," I shout, slamming the phone down.

All this emotional stuff is wearing me out, and I'm just making my way to the kitchen for a restorative cup of coffee when it suddenly dawns on me that he said, 'Good evening'. My spirits lift as the oven clock reveals it is in fact wine o'clock. Result! Everything suddenly seems a little bit brighter. I've just poured a glass of perfectly chilled Chardonnay when the phone rings.

Again.

And no text.

Again.

What the hell is going on?

Maybe it's the first caller again and it's someone I know and they're in trouble – and for some reason they can't text me. Maybe I'm over-thinking all this. I really need to splash out on one of those caller display phones for the sake of everyone's sanity.

"Hello?" I answer cautiously, having already let a satisfying amount of anger out on the computer bloke. Poor guy. He didn't deserve that.

"Caitlin! Sorry – my phone's dead so I couldn't text. Tried earlier too, but it just rang so I figured you were busy." It's Jules, my totally nuts best friend. She's like a mobile party and everyone warms to her on sight. Just at this moment she is a balm for my soul.

"Yeah, busy having a nervous breakdown."

"Aw… sounds like it was a good thing I called then – and sorry not to have texted first. Are you around tonight? Some of us are going down to Mojive at the British Legion Club. Do you want to come along?"

Jules and I go back a long, long way, to those youthful days of staying out ridiculously late and falling out of taxis without a care in the world. It would be fair to say that she has moved on quite substantially, whereas I – um – haven't, especially in the relationship department. When I finally escaped from this most recent and particularly damaging one – the kind where all your friends say, 'well, thank God for that!' – she dragged me along to the local Mojive class on the flimsy excuse that she needed to escape from Simon and his DIY. Having only ever danced around my handbag in the past, I was quite chuffed to discover I'm not a bad dancer after all. Jules has taken to it like a duck to water and is now like Mojive Mummy to the new arrivals, probably due to her day job as childminder extraordinaire.

"Hmm. Feeling a bit fragile actually. And I'm on a deadline." I'm looking longingly at my glass of wine. I absolutely cannot drink and dance. Tried it once and nearly fell over, which was deeply embarrassing. Or drink and drive, obviously. Hmm. And I could really do with a drink after my emotional outburst. This is a tough one. Wine…dance… wine…dance. Love them both. What to do?

"Well, the offer's there if you want to come. But I completely understand if you're not up for it."

She's so hard to refuse. And she knows if I don't go along I'm likely to sit like Billy No–Mates and drink a whole bottle of wine on my own.

"Blimey. I can almost hear the cogs turning. I'll just sit down while you have a think. No pressure," Jules chuckles.

"Haha. Sorry. It's just that I'm not feeling very sociable, to be honest."

"You wouldn't be thinking of standing me up for a bottle of wine, would you?"

"Nooo!" Well yes, actually. And it has to be said that after a tough day at the 'office' I feel somewhat brain-dead in the evenings and am thus forming an ever closer bond with Miss Chardonnay. And then episodes like earlier don't help a lot either.

"Okay, I have a plan."

Jules always has a plan – she has to. It's part of the risk assessment she has to carry out for every single activity, every time she has an under-five in her presence, and she can't seem to switch it off with adults. I was amazed to find out that even eating a cake is risky for small people. You honestly couldn't make some of this stuff up.

"How about I pick you up at seven-thirty? If it gets too much, I promise I'll take you home."

She's so sweet that I have to give in. "M'kay. Guess I should. Hope it's a good one."

"Brilliant – it will be, and the music will help you relax. Now get your arse in gear and I'll see you in a bit."

Okay. So that's about an hour and a half to find something to eat (no garlic – one of the Most Important Rules of the jive class), and have a wardrobe crisis. And have a go at making my blotchy face a bit less scary. Loads of time then. With a final, longing look at my wine I pour it back into the bottle.

"Let's take it from the top ... and 5–6–7–8!"

Once I get in there, I love it. The energy of the class always lifts me up if I'm tired or down, and I end up being really glad I made the effort. I read somewhere that dancing helps release happy hormones, so this is the best therapy ever.

Half an hour later the beginner class finishes, and after a tiny break people are belting back onto the dancefloor as the evening moves on to the freestyle section. This bit always reminds me of a merry-go-round, because as each track ends there's a rush of dancers leaving the floor to find the next partner, then it all starts up again; a whirlwind of bodies moving to the music. It's thirsty work.

"Phew. It's warm tonight. I'll get some water," says Jules, fanning her rosy face. That's another thing. Dancers are usually really healthy, and when they make for the bar, more often than not it's for a pint of water. No wonder so many dance halls go out of business.

"Let's both go. I could do with a bit of air, actually." We grab pints of water from the bar and make our way outside onto the balcony that runs down the side of the building. There's an empty table over by the railing, so we plonk our glasses down and lean over, watching the people wander by below. People who are completely oblivious to the fact that their every move is being scrutinised from above. As I follow their progress along the road, it occurs to me that they've all got their own little dramas going on too. Everyone has. We never know what's going on in other people's lives, do we? I'm lost in thought, then guiltily realise Jules is talking to me and I haven't heard a word.

"Ooh, sorry – I was miles away. Watching all those people going about their lives and just wondering..."

"Oh that's funny – not a million miles away from my question then. I was just asking how the latest book's coming along. It's another one of Ivy's, isn't it? Are they sobbing in the aisles yet?"

Big sigh. "Am I that predictable?"

"Well, Lovely, to be honest, that kind of *is* your job, isn't it? I mean, turning very put-downable manuscripts into beautiful heart-breaking romances. Not that you aren't capable of a lot more – in my humble opinion of course – but hey! If there's the market and the money, why not?"

"Yeah. Why not indeed?" I mumble. "But I don't want to get stuck in a rut, Jules. I don't want to wake up one day and realise that life has passed me by, and I haven't done anything more than this. I'm sure I can do something a bit more serious. I'm finding my way back to the light after a lot of shit, and to be honest, this is all starting to look a bit naïve."

"You can say that again. The shit bit, not the naïve bit, by the way, as I think you'd be a fabulous writer whatever the subject. I'm just glad you've escaped physically intact – emotionally... hmm. Work in progress, I think, looking at your face." She leans across to give me a hug which is so unexpected I need to choke back a wave of emotion, as tears threaten again. A couple escape down my cheeks and I brush them away in annoyance.

And I thought I was doing so well.

"Ooh, sweetie, I'm so sorry. Didn't mean to set you off. Tough day?"

"Didn't start out that way. Just... you know... stuff. There always seems to be 'stuff'." The tears are flowing freely now, much to my embarrassment, so I shove my fingers into the corners of my eyes, willing them to dry up. I'm OUT, trying to have FUN, for fuck's sake. Jules stands with her arm around my shoulders while I sniffle indiscreetly into a tissue and try to mop up my eyes. Thank God I'm facing out into the night rather than in towards the dance hall.

She gives me a squeeze and leans her head against mine. "You *will* get through this you know. It might not feel like it, but you will."

Then turning back to the table, she passes my glass. "Here, have some water. Sorry it's not wine."

She's so in my head it's untrue.

"Seriously though, it's going to take a while to get over what you've been through – it's not going to happen overnight. There's going to be good times and bad times, so just be kind to yourself, huh? And I'm sorry to have dragged you out when you didn't feel like it. Would you like me to take you home?"

"No. Because that would mean he'd won. And I'm stronger than that." If I say it often enough, maybe I'll start believing it.

"Well, if you're sure. We can carry this on over a coffee if you want to. Do you want to go back in yet?"

I nod and go back via the Ladies in that time-honoured fashion to powder my nose. Although to be honest a cooling cucumber eye mask would be a lot more help at this point.

Jules was right. It was a really good evening despite my little wobble, and several hours later she drops me back home.

"I didn't mean your writing isn't good, you know."

'Mmm. I know. But you've made me think. I'm not exactly Jane Austen, but maybe I could try something a bit deeper...'

"Why not do it alongside? It might exercise a different part of your brain."

"So funny."

"I was just thinking you could jot a few ideas down, you know… for future use. I have no idea why I'm even saying this. What do I know about writing? My world revolves around nappies and baby wipes!"

That much is true as Jules isn't a writer, but she has a unique take on life, being a childminder to several under-fives. She reads avidly as her antidote to long hours spent with small people with short attention spans – which would drive me insane – but it makes her a good sounding board for just about anything. She always says that spending so much time with small children means she can only think simple thoughts and talk in short sentences. I beg to differ, as size isn't always everything, and she is usually right on the nail.

Safely inside my flat with the door bolted once more, I realise that the dancing has worked its magic. Just the right amount of tired and definitely ready for bed.

So yay! A night off the wine. That's a bit of a miracle then, going on recent history.

Chapter 2

viouselincnlyeayiz.fgwudsczddzbbbbbbbbbbbbbbbbbbb

"TITAN! You brat! Get OFF!"

My ginger office assistant has arisen from his 'desk' (my laptop bag) and is busily stomping over my keyboard while I'm thinking about how to tweak this particular love scene. It's all a bit ironic if you think about it, that as a person in a (currently) single (and fragile) state I'm editing warm, fuzzy, old-fashioned romances. It must be so good to have someone – truly loving – in one's life. Someone to choose a card specifically for you in advance rather than at the last minute. Or not at all. Perhaps to accompany a present that hasn't been bought at the market the day before as an afterthought. Dark memories crowd in for a moment, then I grab Titan and plonk him on the floor before he does any more damage. He's a relatively new addition to my small but perfectly-formed household, and was also somewhat unplanned.

My very charming and musical kid brother was collecting his car on the way back from a gig, at some ungodly and decidedly chilly hour, when he spotted a carrier bag by the ticket machine in the car park. It seemed to be moving and making a pathetic mewing noise. Who in their right mind could ignore it? Aiden carefully untied the bag and discovered a weeny ginger kitten inside, very cold and hungry and very scared. He took him back home to the B&B in Glastonbury where he lives with Mum and her partner, Michael. Although they obviously took pity on the tiny kitten, it quickly became obvious that the B&B was not the place for him; once he recovered from his inauspicious beginnings, he was a nightmare. The B&B is on a busy road and with guests coming and going, it became harder and harder to keep him safe. The request for a transfer of residence happened in a late night phone call.

"Caitlin?"

"Mmmm. Why are you waking me up at this time? Normal people are asleep now."

"You know the kitten?"

"Of course I know the kitten. What's he done now?"

"Mum said he's got to go. He's too much trouble and they can't watch him all the time."

"Oh."

Silence.

"And? The reason you're calling me is…?"

"Will you have him, Cait? Please? After what happened to him I can't bear never to see him again. At least if he's with you I'll get to see him from time to time, and I could come and cat-sit for you if you go away. I mean, not that you go away, but if you do I can come and be with him. Please?"

"Whoa there! Let's just back-track a bit shall we? Don't go making rash promises you can't keep."

"But I will. I promise."

"Like when we had the pet rats and you never once cleaned them out. Or the goldfish that never got fed? And the time you left the front door open when you went out? Do you think I would really trust you to look after a cat *and* my flat?"

"I've changed, Cait. I'm a lot more grown up now. I'll be twenty-four in February, and I've got to start taking responsibility at some point. And I love that cat."

Did I want a cat? No. Am I a cat person? No. But how could I let the little guy down after the way he'd started life?

"Oh God, okay then. But you owe me big time. And I might just start going away if I know you'll be here to look after him."

"Ah, thankyouthankyouthankyou!" It was worth giving in just to hear Aiden's happiness exploding down the phone. "When shall I bring him?"

"Tomorrow, I guess?"

"Yep. I've got a gig in the evening but I can bring him down early and stay for a bit to help him settle."

"That's probably a good idea, as I haven't got the slightest idea how to look after a cat."

"Oh you'll be fine. He's such a friendly little chap. Can you promise me something though?"

"Possibly. I know you too well to promise something in advance."

"Please don't change his name. Please can you leave it as Titan?" Aiden is nuts about astronomy and he named the kitten after Titan, one of Saturn's moons – a hugely impressive name for what is turning out to be a very small cat.

And so Titan joined the household, and now I wouldn't be without him. Working from home has a whole load of benefits, like I can stay in my pyjamas all day if I want to, get the washing done when it's sunny, and drink my own coffee, but by far the best thing is having the little ginger ninja for company. His favourite place is without doubt my laptop case, but if that isn't available he'll slump down as close to me as possible, as if he knows I need some gentle company. Love him to bits.

Incoming text.

"Are you up for coffee? Have unexpected free time, yay :-)" Jules is hardly ever free.

"Absa-fuckin-lutely! Where and when?" This is brilliant. I've reached a complete plateau with Ivy and her love birds and could so do with a break.

"Debenhams 2.30 will get a table xx"

"Yessssssssssssss xxxxx!"

"Yoohoo!" Jules stands up and waves as I wander into the restaurant. I hate going into places like this on my own, as I feel such a lemon looking round for the person I'm supposed to be meeting, or not meeting, as has happened in the past. Jules always sweetly caters for this by arriving early and jumping up and down like a lunatic to attract my attention.

"You nutter," I say, giving her a hug. "Thank you. I see you've already secured a stash."

She knows my weakness for cream cakes, and as I had lunch quite early I think this is a perfectly acceptable time to start afternoon tea.

"Absolutely, dear heart. What else are girlfriends for?"

"Sobbing all over, going by recent events? Sorry about that." Rule number one of being my friend: if you're too kind to me when I'm down, I'll almost certainly cry all over you at some point. If you can't stand the heat… But I always apologise afterwards.

"It's fine, you know that. But why were you so close to the edge? It looked like you'd been crying when I picked you up."

"Oh, just me being silly and jumpy. I still feel very vulnerable. Can't believe it's really over and that he won't be back. I was busy working and it sounded like someone tried to put their key in the door – and I just panicked. I mean, he could have copied the key before I finally got it back. I'm not even sure I really heard anything, but I just freaked out – a whole load of horrible memories swamped me and I lost it. Leaned against the door and howled a bit, then Ellie knocked – which made me jump out of my skin – but she was really sweet and said she was just checking on me... It was so embarrassing. And then again at jive. I can't keep doing this Jules, it's wearing me out. My emotions are all over the place, going from laughter to tears in seconds. I'm frightened of my own shadow and don't even know who I am anymore."

Jules nods. "I can understand that. I mean, I didn't go through it, but I'm not surprised. But he's gone now. He's really gone."

"I know. And when I first got him out I was so relieved, but now it's like I've become a different person because of him. I haven't got the courage to say 'Boo!' to a toddler, let alone a goose." I manage a small smile.

"Oh, trust me, a toddler is the way scarier proposition. So what can we do about this? Apart from getting that lock changed, which I'm sure Simon will do for you. Can't believe we haven't sorted that out yet."

Just the way she says 'we' helps. And makes me well up. Oh FFS get a grip.

"I dunno. Maybe get a software upgrade, then reboot?" I try to smile at my pathetic joke through the tears now trickling down my cheeks. Realising I've lost the battle, I lower my face into my hands and try not to sob too loudly.

Jules drags her chair round to my side and sits holding me until I calm down. With amazing foresight she'd chosen a corner table, so for the second time in a week I'm relieved to be facing away from other people.

After a couple of minutes it looks as though the storm is subsiding.

"Cream cake?" she asks, offering me the stacked plate with a silly wide-eyed grin on her face. She knows this will make me laugh, and indeed I do start to chortle through my tears, which is possibly the more frightening spectacle for any witnesses to this whole sad debacle. Fortunately she snaffled a huge pile of napkins along with the cakes (I'm sure she knew this was coming), so I can dry my eyes and blow my nose and try to look a bit more like a grown-up.

"You know, the old you is still in there. She's just had a bit of a battering. In fact when she comes out again she's going to be even stronger, because she absolutely won't put up with any kind of shit like that again. No Sirreee!" Which fortunately makes me laugh, as her sweet words were about to set me off again. "Do you think counselling would help?"

"Not sure I can face talking about it at the moment. Or possibly ever. There's a certain sense of embarrassment that I allowed myself to get into such a bad situation. I'm not stupid, but it happened so subtly that I was in up to my neck before I realised, by which time I was too cowed down to do anything about it. And on the outside I tried to pretend everything was okay so I didn't look a complete failure."

"And you didn't fool us for a minute. But no amount of people telling you to get out of the relationship would have done it. And we did try. But I think it's one of those things you have to realise for yourself, or you slide back into it again. So you see you were strong, even if you think you weren't. NO! Quick – have a cake." Jules clocks another storm brewing and practically shoves a mini cream doughnut in my face. "These aren't just for decoration you know."

It does the trick, and after at least one more cake and a vat of tea I'm feeling a bit more human, and possibly a tad sick.

"So, Lovely. What would help you to feel better? Obviously not a knight in shining armour just yet. A bit of retail therapy? A spa break. Ooh, how about a holiday? Really get away from it all for a while."

"Mm. Can't see it happening, to be honest. Nice idea, but I haven't got much money, and also there's Titan to worry about."

"Wouldn't Aiden come down to look after him?"

"I wouldn't trust him. Not being funny, but he does stuff like leave doors open and lights on and taps running – so I would really worry while I was away."

"I can keep tabs on him if it would make you feel better. And Ellie will too. He would have enough people to call on if there was a crisis. Which there wouldn't be."

"Thanks, but it doesn't solve the money issue. I've probably got enough for a budget break to Ibiza as long as I don't eat while I'm there. And I haven't got anyone to go with."

"Woah – what's with the turning into Ms Neggie? Thought you were a 'can do' kind of girl."

"Yeah, well, I used to be, but being randomly screamed at and told you're a useless piece of shit doesn't do a lot for one's confidence."

"That was then, and this is now. You can do this – you just need to keep telling yourself you can. And possibly eat more cake."

Shaking my head, I hold up my hand in a 'I will be sick if I eat any more' kind of gesture. "Maybe. I've also got a lot of work on."

"So just *supposing* Aiden can come down, and *supposing* you had enough money, and *supposing* you got all your work done. What then?"

"Haven't got anyone to go with. And I wouldn't go alone. I'm kind of assuming you wouldn't be free."

"Much as I'd love to, I'm up to my ears in little ones and haven't given the mums any notice. But you know I would if I could. I really, really think you need a holiday though. Just to get away from everything, even if it's just for a week. Ooh!"

"What? Have you just magicked up a travelling companion and a big pile of money?"

"Might have an idea on the companion front. Maybe you do have a knight in shining armour after all."

"Um, nope. Not to my knowledge. In fact I'd say there's a whacking great vacancy in that department right now."

Jules just looks at me, a wide grin spreading across her face. Then she nods. "You *do*! C'mon, think! Make that clever brain of yours work. Someone you love to bits and completely trust. And don't see anything like often enough."

I look at her blankly for a moment, then the penny drops. "Oh my God. You mean James? As in *James* James?"

"Is there another? Could there possibly be another James?"

"No way. He's got his own life in London now, working at that swanky social media company. And probably loads of boyfriends he can go on holiday with. If he wants a holiday. Which he might not."

"Have you talked to him recently? Does he even know what's been going on with you?"

"Yes, but not in moment-by-moment detail. We do catch up on Facebook from time to time, but I don't really want to unload it all on him."

"Well I think you should at least talk to him. You two have been friends for ages and he would want to know about all this shit you're going through."

That much is true. James is my gay best friend and we go back a looong way to when we both worked in a local bookshop. Jules knows him through me, and we both love him to bits. But a holiday with him? Really not sure about that.

"Nah. They say the best way to lose a friend is to go on holiday with them, and I don't want to lose him. And I've got no idea what he's doing. I can't just randomly ask if he'll come on holiday with me. That would just be... too weird."

"For fuck's sake, Cait." There's a few glances in our direction as her voice rises in frustration, so she leans in closer. "These are extenuating circumstances and he is one of your best friends. Don't you think he would want to help? Do you want me to ask him?"

"NO! No. That would be even weirder. I just need to think about how to approach it – so it doesn't gross him out."

"I don't think it will. You two go back yonks. And you're not alone in this, you know. We all love you and want to help you through it, whatever it takes, but you have to let people in. If you don't, we can't do anything."

Jules helpfully passes me a napkin as my eyes threaten to leak again at her words, but it looks like the fountain has dried up for the moment.

Well thank God for that.

Back home, completely stuffed with cake and feeling a bit more cheery, I'm wondering how the hell to ask one of my bestest friends if he wants to come on holiday with me. Like, that is so weird. But I'm pretty sure that Jules will call him herself if I don't, which would make me look even more pathetic than I've been feeling of late. So with butterflies flitting about in my stomach I get on Messenger hoping he won't be online. That magic green light shows me he is.

Oh bollocks. Convincing myself the worst he can do is say no, I ask if he's free for a chat. Seconds later my mobile rings, so he's obviously bored or the office is empty.

"Hey, you okay?"

"Um, is the bush telegraph that fast?"

"Not really. Jules just mentioned you might call."

She's a one. It's been all of two hours since I left her.

"She's really quite scary you know."

"But she's an excellent friend. I promise she didn't say anything else. So what's up?"

"Oh God this is going to sound completely random and I have no idea how to say it."

"I usually find just opening my mouth and pitching in works for me."

"Shit. Okay. So. In a nutshell, I had a bit of a meltdown the other day, well, several actually, and the lovely Jules has been picking up the pieces again, bless her. She suggested a holiday to get a proper break from everything, but I said that I've got too much work on and I also don't have anyone to go with as she's busy as hell and can't get any time off from the kids. Then she thought of you. That's about as far as we got. No pressure. Just wondering. And feel free to say I'm nuts, or… 'ew no?'"

Oh God, I'm gabbling. And the butterflies are having a fine old time.

"Ooh. Interesting. Wasn't expecting that, but it could be fun, couldn't it? Hmm."

That went better than expected then. "Really? I don't hear you laughing."

"Why would I laugh?"

"Just worried you might. Because I'm used to being laughed at or getting a 'why on earth would I want to do that?' stony-faced response. So thank you. But what if we argue? They say the best way to wreck a friendship is to go on holiday together."

"Well, I think we'd be fine. In fact the more I think about it the more I like the idea. I haven't had a holiday for ages. Any idea where, or when?"

"Soon as possible and cheap as chips, as I don't have a lot of money. Warm would be good if the budget can stretch to it."

"Okay – I've got an idea but it's going to take a couple of days. Can I get back to you? That's not me putting you off, just so you know. Just need to speak to someone and also check my holiday leave. Which I'm sure will be fine as I never go anywhere. I PROMISE I'll get back to you. And I'm gonna have to go now as the manager's back."

In spite of myself I'm grinning stupidly as we finish the call and a little bit of my stomach unclenches. Swooping a surprised Titan above my head, I jump around singing, 'Yay-o-yay-o-yay-o-yay!' just the once before he sinks his claws into my wrists.

Oh yeah, forgot only Aiden can do that with him.

Chapter 3

It's a sunny and beautiful morning. Think I'll go for a run before lunch, then settle down to another session of editing some more of Ivy's book – part of the incredibly popular (and why, exactly?) modern romance series published by Hearts and Flowers. Actually, it's more like ghost-writing, if I'm honest. But it does have its funny moments.

On days like this, with a slight wind blowing and a clear blue sky, I just love to run. Not far, admittedly, because I don't do pain or discomfort, but I do want to push the distance a teeny bit. Actually, today I want to try to run to the beach and back without stopping, which will be a first, if I can do it. Living at the top of a very steep hill isn't a lot of help in this. Heading out the front door, the fresh air hits me full in the face. It smells amazing and just the vibrancy of being outside helps me to unwind and relax. At the bottom of the hill I go left and start up another very long hill, which is what usually wears me out. Just before the peak comes the point where I'll cross over for the road that leads to the beach – or not. Historically it's always been 'not', but I'm not going to get better that way. Getting closer to the turn-off point. Yes – no – shall I? Yes. But my legs are aching – no. If there's a gap in the traffic I'll do it. Looking over my shoulder I see an unusually empty road.

Bugger.

No traffic.

I cross over and start down the much longer road that leads to the beach, severely doubting my ability to get there and back and then run home along the usual route. Definitely a wimp.

Once the shock of trying something new and harder has worn off, I start to enjoy it. Wow. Running is my respite from the turmoil of the last few years and it's also good grounding time, which, believe me, is SO much needed, as I live in my head most of the time. Apparently some people don't. That's weird. It's also good to enjoy nature when I manage to remember that it's actually out there. Settling into an easy rhythm I'm at the beach before I know it, and get such a huge surge of pride that I DID IT that I suddenly realise I'm running along with a big grin on my face. Hanging a left at the end of the colourful beach huts and starting the long loop home, I'm so lost in the moment it takes me a while to realise that people are smiling back at me. This is *fun*. My smile widens, and even passers-by who are pre-occupied break into a grin when they see me. What an amazing day, and what a difference a smile makes! The run back is indeed long and slow, but I collapse triumphantly onto the grass outside the flat with a great big 'Yessss!' as I made it all the way back without stopping. It's as though I've broken through some barrier and it feels amazing.

It's back to work after a shower and a quick lunch, ginger ninja at his desk, me at mine. That bubble of happiness is still intact and my body's buzzing with happy hormones. I discovered to my huge delight that a specific type of endorphin is only released during two activities: sex and running. Fancy that. So I figure if I'm not getting it one way at least I can participate in the other. Still grinning, I open up the manuscript I've been working on. This particular one, *Walking on Air*, is the story of a woman who falls in love with a pilot. And although the story line is interesting, the author's grasp of grammar is somewhat doubtful, as is her sense of passion. This is where I come in – to basically turn a sow's ear into a silk purse. Well, at least I try. Honestly though, I do enjoy tidying it up so the book reads smoothly. If you like that kind of stuff.

"Walking over to the window, she sat down suddenly in the chair that was placed there for that reason. She looked longingly up at the sky, wondering when her pilot would return."

Some authors keep track of every comma, but Ivy is a bit more flexible so maybe I can push it a bit.

"Moving slowly across the room, she sank gently into the chair placed right by the window. From here she could watch the sky for hours. When would her pilot return?"

Hmm. Not bad. Let's see how the rest of it unfolds.

"Rosie met her pilot when she was at an airport hotel at a business conference and his crew were also staying at the hotel because they were on a stopover before they went back home. She saw him when he was sitting at the bar and their eyes met. She was a bit embarrassed and tried to look away but when he got up and walked past on his way to the bathrooms he smiled at her. When he came out again and walked past again he turned round just before he sat down and smiled again. She smiled back."

Lordy. A bit of romance and atmosphere needed here. And possibly a bit less smiling?

"Rosie had met her pilot when she was attending a work conference at an airport hotel; he and his crew – who flew for an extremely upmarket airline – were staying there for a few days on a stopover before they headed back home. Rosie's group were sitting in the lounge, quietly chatting, when she had the feeling she was being watched. Turning slightly, her eyes followed the feeling to the bar, where a gorgeous man caught her eye and smiled. She felt a hot rush of emotion rise up through her body. Slightly embarrassed by the reaction, and not knowing what to do, she turned back to her colleagues. Moments later the man walked past on his way to the bathroom. God, he was lovely. On his return journey he treated her to another dazzling smile before taking his place back at the bar."

Better. Guess the smiles can stay.

Actually, I'm fascinated that these books have such a wide audience. They are really basic stories, the usual boy-meets-girl stuff in a million different scenarios, all completely detached from reality – which is exactly what everyone is trying to escape, aren't they? Any woman who gets picked up in an airport hotel bar by an itinerant pilot is just asking for trouble, as far as I'm concerned. But however these stories unfold, there's never any sense of the woman being a cheap slapper or the man being a complete bastard; loveable rogue, maybe, but never really nasty. And that's sort of sweet. Undemanding, harmless, dreamy fun.

I know I'm taking a bit of a risk with this, but I'm really excited about getting these two together – and yes, I know I need to get out more. I've been working with Ivy on and off for several years and she is a sweetie. She's an 'older' lady who has an old-fashioned air of innocence in her writing. Although she's set the story in current times it's almost harking back to a bygone era, when values were different. For instance, I'm pleased that she doesn't have Rosie and Ross (which turns out to be the pilot's name) belting back to one of their rooms for a quick shag at the end of the evening. Or even halfway through it. (Er-hem.) It turns out that Ross is from the USA and has some leave before flying back home with a different crew; he spends the next evening with Rosie, then as her course has finished, on the following day Ivy has them taking a trip into London for some sightseeing, then cocktails at a bar in Covent Garden, followed by some expensive wine and a candlelit meal. Obviously. Par for the course with this kind of book.

Helping Ivy draw the two characters together in such a touching and romantic way leaves me with an unexpected frisson of excitement, followed by an equally unexpected pang of loneliness. At nearly thirty I'm trying to ignore the loud ticking of that good old biological clock, but I'm beginning to wonder if I'll ever meet the right man. God, what a cliché. Well at least I can get these two together.

Thankfully there are no scary noises today, and Titan and I carry on working until finally he stands up and stretches. His movement alerts me to impending disaster, as of course I'm miles away, and I only just catch him before he tramps across my keyboard.

"Oooooh no you don't!" I say, gazing into his beautiful amber eyes. "Are you trying to tell me it's dinner time already?"

Apparently he is, as he struggles free and belts out to the kitchen, where I find him sitting politely in front of his bowl, tail wrapped neatly round his paws. Cracks me up the way he does that.

And the best news is that his dinnertime means it's also wine o'clock. Yay! Pouring myself a celebratory glass as reward for a good afternoon's work, it's time to seriously consider my own menu options. Which to be frank, are limited. Looks like pasta again then.

Several glasses of wine and a bowl of cheesy pasta later (I did say 'limited'), it seems like a good idea to get my lovely mum's wise words on what is turning out to be a rollercoaster of a time, with more ups and downs than a full-blown episode of PMT.

She leads an 'interesting' life in Glastonbury – certainly busier than mine (pleased for her, sad for me). Mum (Rosalind) and Dad (Bob) split up about five years ago. Well, I say 'split up' but as the oldest I saw the writing on the wall way before that, TBH, as they couldn't be more different from each other if they tried. I think their sole purpose in life must have been to produce two kids, as they really have nothing in common at all except for being our parents. Dad likes any kind of sport, taking part as well as watching, and took early retirement so he could do even more of it. Now they're apart, he also enjoys pottering around with his friends and disappearing for long holidays on swanky cruise ships, having a fine old time.

Mum, on the other hand, took exactly the opposite direction and journeyed inwards, taking up spiritual practices like meditation and yoga. She always loved Glastonbury, but Dad completely took the piss out of its slightly edgy, hippy culture. And he was definitely against her walking up the Tor to celebrate the Solstice. So now they're apart, and happy, which is much easier to live with. Dad stayed on the coast and Mum moved to a rented flat in Glastonbury, fully intending to buy a small cottage and work in one of her friend's shops until 'The Right Thing' came along. Funnily enough, The Right Thing turned out to be not a thing but a man called Michael, a local market gardener she met at a yoga class, and in no time at all they'd fallen in love and opened a small B&B together near the Tor. It was all a bit of a whirlwind romance, but Mum looks so, so happy. Michael has laughter lines around his eyes and one of those faces that is welcoming and friendly, and we all love him to bits.

Hoping she's free of incoming guests, I call their landline as she hates talking on mobiles as much as I do. "Hi Mum, how's things? Is this a good time for a catch-up?"

"Perfect, actually. I've just made a cup of tea. So what's been going on with you? You've been on my mind a lot recently."

Not like she's on the ball or anything.

"All over the place, to be honest. I thought I was doing really well, but now I feel like I'm turning into some kind of emotional wreck. One minute I'm fine, then the next I'm sobbing my heart out. So fed up with it. I saw Jules yesterday – I've been crying all over her recently and she wanted to find something, possibly anything, that would pull me out of this, bless her. She thought maybe a holiday would help."

"Good idea – get you out of your cave for a while. Would you go with her?"

"No – she's too busy, but she suggested James, and then she said that if I didn't call him, she would. So I had to."

"Haha. Love that girl. And?"

"Well, funnily enough, he seems really interested – and then he said he had an idea and would get back to me. So I'm a teeny bit excited. But also anxious. What if we argue?" In recent history, holidays have always meant arguments.

"I think you just need to relax and see what he comes up with. You two have known each other long enough that I'm sure you'd be fine. And I agree with Jules that you need to get away from the usual triggers, and everyday life. Even if it's just for a week or so. It's amazing what a break can do. If you're not at the flat then you'll have the chance to unwind. The old you is under there somewhere and she just needs the chance to come out again."

"Yeah, had a few conversations with her about that too. It's all got a bit ridiculous lately."

"It will come back, love. You went through a really horrible experience, but just see it for what it was – an experience. Don't wear it like a badge or let it define your future. You are so much more than that."

Gulp.

She's good at silences, my mum.

"I mean it. Leave it behind. It's hard, but you have to do it."

"Yeah. You're right. Do you get some special training for all this stuff when you have kids?"

"Ha! Wish. You wouldn't believe how hard it is to watch your children go through difficult times."

"I think I can imagine. So I guess a good start would be thinking seriously about this holiday."

"Absolutely. I'm sorry sweetie, someone's just come to the desk so I need to see to them – but let me know how it goes."

"Will do."

Aw. Love my mum.

Chapter 4

So another totally awesome thing about working from home is that I can stay in bed a bit longer if I want to, but I really must make the effort to get Ivy's work done just IN CASE James comes up with something. Just to show willing I did a bit of research yesterday too, but only came up with some last minute all-inclusive deals to Majorca and Ibiza, nothing exactly jaw-dropping. But then beggars can't be choosers and just to get away would be good. Heaving my unwilling body into the shower, I stand for a good long time under the slightly feeble flow. Must get that sorted. What I want, what I really, really want is one of those lovely rain forest showers. Dream on with that one then...

Half an hour and a good coffee later I suddenly notice my phone is flashing like crazy.

A message from James. "Think I might have something. FB me when you're free."

Ooh. That would be now, then. It's been a couple of days since we spoke and I've been SO patient. Not an easy task. I fire up FB. "I'm here!"

"Have a def possibility. But there is a drawback."

"Can a holiday have a drawback?"

"Depends on your pint of view :-) Haha *point"

"Are you going to actually TELL me or have I got to drag it out of you?"

"Ooooooh. Spiky! OK, do you want to go on a cruise?"

"YOU ARE KIDDING ME! YESSSS! But aren't they expensive? Was thinking cheapie to Majorca."

"No need to shout. Yes. Usually they are. But this one isn't."

"And the drawback? Do I have to do the washing up or something?"

There's a lot of jumping up and down of the little icon that shows James is typing away, so I take the phone to the kitchen to make some more cafetière coffee, which is my morning treat, wine of course being my evening treat. Still no beep from the phone. Could I really be going on holiday? Wow. I'm just pouring the coffee and wondering what kind of essay James is writing when my phone chimes and I nearly spill it in excitement.

"No."

What? I waited all that time just for a 'No'? I'm just typing something sarcastic when another message appears.

"Can't talk freely now or I'd call you. Have to be patient while I type this."

Lol. Does he know me or what?

"You don't have to work. Have a friend who is a hairdresser on Titania, can get us cheap last minute holiday. Had to wait for her to get to port to ask her hence delay. Anyway, they have space. Have to share cabin. OK?"

His little icon has stopped jumping around so I guess he's waiting for a response. Then my mobile goes and it's him.

"Free now. The boss is hanging around so I have to be quick."

"Oooh. Wow. That would be amazing." I'm gushing a bit with the excitement. "Wait. You said Titania. That's funny. Titan/Titania. Haha. Wonder if the ship is as big as he is small. Obviously it won't be ginger..."

"Haha didn't think of that. But Titania is queen of the fairies, isn't she? Maybe there'll be lots of people on there for me."

"Oh Lordy. I wish I hadn't gone down that route. So – do we have to share a bed? Do you snore?"

"Um, no? They have single beds if you request them. Which I have. And no, I don't think so. And I'm very clean and tidy. And we can get changed in the bathroom so there don't have to be any bare bums or anything."

God, I hadn't got as far as that thought, thank you very much.

"Would you be hogging the mirror?"

"We could set up a rota. Haha. Well? Are you up for it? Do you want to know what the drawback is?"

Ah. "Yes? Guess I'd better."

"The reason I could get it is that it's late availability. Very late availability."

"HOW LATE? WHEN IS IT?"

"You're shouting. Saturday."

"Sorry, I'm excited. WHAT THIS SATURDAY AS IN THREE DAYS TIME?"

"Yes. Can you stop shouting? I'm trying to make out this is a business call and you're not helping."

"Sorry," I whisper, quite unnecessarily. "Is this quiet enough? How about food and stuff?"

"All included in the price. Except for wine I believe."

"And where is it going? Do we have to fly anywhere?"

"I'm sending you the link right now so you read all about it, and no, we go from Southampton so no flying. Have to go now."

"Ooh okay, and yesyesyesyesyesyes please! Wherever it's going!"

My phone pings to tell me James' link has arrived, and as I open it up the list of ports appears in front of my incredulous eyes. OMG. After a bit of excitable jigging round the room, at which point Titan sensibly takes cover, I suddenly realise I have SHITLOADS of stuff to sort out – Ivy's editing being top of the list, and I need to see whether Aiden can come down, and… what the hell am I going to wear? That's obvs gonna need a call to Jules. And Dad, actually as he knows cruises inside out.

No time like the present. "Hi Dad, how are you doing?"

"Just fine love. How are you? Haven't seen you for a bit. Are you still buried in that laptop of yours? You should get out more, get some fresh air and stuff."

"Well, I do run a few times a week. And sometimes I go to jive. But, yeah, pretty much buried in the laptop. But that's why I'm calling. I'm going on a cruise with James!"

"Hey well done! At last! But with James? How did that happen? Is there something you need to tell me? You will absolutely love it, I promise you."

"We're so excited! James has a friend who works on the Titania so we got a really cheap late deal. And we go on Saturday! ON SATURDAY!!!! As in THIS Saturday."

I can hear Dad laughing. I have been known to get a bit excitable from time to time.

"I was hoping you could give me the lowdown on life on board and also what to wear. Think I'm gonna have to do a bit of shopping."

"You'll like Titania. She's a family kind of ship that's not too posh, although there will be a Captain's Reception and a couple of formal nights that you might want something special for. Otherwise it's fairly casual."

"And is the food really included?"

"Yes. On a 24-hour basis, so I promise you, you won't starve. There's a couple of what they call 'speciality' restaurants where you pay a bit extra for different food and a different atmosphere, like an Indian or Italian – but otherwise it's wall-to-wall free food. Oh and take your cafetière. I know how much you like your coffee and on that ship you'll have a kettle in the cabin. The ordinary coffee isn't up to much."

"How do we pay for drinks?"

"At check-in you're given a cruise card and that's your key to everything – literally. The ships are cashless and you sign for everything and it gets charged to your credit card at the end of the holiday. So keep a bit of an eye on the spending as it can mount up pretty quickly. Oh and tips. They get added to your account unless you specifically ask them not to be. Some people do that but I find it easier to just include it, and hopefully the right people get the money. The other thing is the excursions, which are usually pretty expensive. You can just get off at most ports and do your own thing. Where are you going?"

"Hang on a minute. James sent me the details just now." Fumbling in excitement, I open his link on my phone. "Malaga, Barcelona, Villefranche, Naples, Rome, Cartagena and Gibraltar. It's for two weeks going from Southampton."

"I'd go online and check out port reviews, see what you can do without going on a tour. You must be docking at Civitavecchia for Rome, which is amazing. You can go by train on your own – now that's an experience I'll never forget."

It's an absolute revelation talking to Dad like this. I don't think I've ever heard him so interested and engaged – he's always been a bit distant, as though he's thinking about something else and wants to get off the phone as fast as possible.

"You know, I'm really pleased, love. It's been a while since you went off and had some fun and you really deserve it. I'll let you know if I think of anything else."

We chat a bit more then I hang up and do another crazy jig around the room. It's a long time since I've felt this good. But I DO need to concentrate on Ivy, then I can think about clothes. Oh. That's not going to take long, then. I haven't exactly got anything new or special to take. The most dressed up I get these days is to go to jive, and that's hardly cruise wear. And my undies are pretty disgraceful. And I'll need a decent nightie or something if I'm sharing with James. And do I even have a bikini anymore? So – yay! A bit of a shopping trip then. But I need to work now and maybe call Jules later.

Knowing Jules will be up to her eyes in little ones all day, I'm very good and do loads of work. When it hits wine o'clock I grab a glass of Chardonnay, feed Titan, then text her.

"OMFG you will never guess what. Need to talk!"

I'm just wondering if she got the text when the phone rings.

"What? So glad to get your text. I was up a ladder supporting a sheet of plasterboard with my head, while Simon nailed it to the ceiling. The plasterboard, not my head. Not fun. What?! Good news?"

I gabble out what's happened as I haven't spoken to anyone all day – not since Dad.

"Ooh you lucky lady. Sounds like you need to go shopping then. Can I come? And have you got a passport? And what about Aiden? You need to make a list!"

"You can absolutely definitely come! I have no idea what to buy any more, so I need your special skills. Think I might need to start from scratch actually."

"I can fit you in tomorrow in between one bunch of children and the next – sadly not for a whole day, but we'll do what we can."

Haha. That's probably good news as I'm not sure my bank balance could survive a whole day with Jules, whose expertise and stamina in the shopping department are legendary.

Time for a top-up methinks.

Chapter 5

Next morning I'm panicking. Aiden's sorted and looking forward to spending time with his still very small rescue cat, but I do need to get some food in for him and make up his bed. I jot that down on a handy piece of paper and add PACK at the bottom. What I really need is a wardrobe inspection in the cold light of day.

It's not pretty and it doesn't take long. I've never really got to grips with the whole idea of putting things away for the season because a) I never do anything season-related any more, actually, never have and b) I work from home and can slob around in anything I want. It turns out that a rough shopping list would be:

DECENT UNDERWEAR
Some pretty/bright/pink?? flip flops
Floaty skirt ~~or two~~?
Several T-shirt/light tops
Cardi/sthg warm for evening
Will I need a wrap or sarong?
Long hippy dress ~~or two~~
Sthg smart for Captain's Do
New handbag, definitely
Shoes obvs
Bikini DEF
Hair removal cream
Book manicure?

Ooooh. This is going to be fun. And expensive, looking at that list, so I think it's going to be Primark then. To be fair, having accompanied Jules on a few of these trips, it isn't all about spending money; it's also really good girlie fun. I do have a credit card but it is definitely only for emergencies, in which case I had better investigate just how much I actually have stashed away. The ginger ninja follows me to my laptop and sits patiently next to my keyboard. Bless him, he thinks I'm starting another day at the office BUT I'M NOT :-)

This whole logging into my bank account thing is completely doing my head in though, and I could seriously lose the will to live by the time I've got through all the passcodes and warnings and messages about saving links to my bookmarks. I JUST WANT TO SEE HOW MUCH MONEY I CAN SPEND!

Shit.

That can't be right.

Someone must have paid a chunk of money into the wrong account as I definitely haven't. Mystified, I click on the details of my current account, and find a credit from one R.J. Powell.

What?!

"Dad?"

"Hey love. How are you?"

"I'm brilliant, thank you, but ever so slightly confused. I've just gone into my bank account and you seem to have put some money in there. Er…. Why? What's going on?"

There's a huge amount of chuckling going on at the other end of the line.

"Dad!"

"Sorry. Couldn't resist it. I've been waiting for you to come out from under your cloud, and I couldn't believe it when you said you were going on a cruise. Go. Have fun. Spend a bit of money. You've had a rough time recently and you deserve some fun."

"Oh my God. Are you serious? Really? Really?"

This is all a bit much. First a lovely holiday, now spending money; I feel like I've gate-crashed one of Ivy's books. Things like this don't happen to me.

"Are you sure? I mean… Thank you. Thank you! Wow!"

"Just pleased to be able to help out, love. And surprise you. That's the best bit. I was so excited – and impatient. I was trying to think of a way to get you to check your account but now you have. You are gonna have SO much fun. I'm excited just thinking about it!"

I can feel a bit of a happy jig coming on. This is getting to be a regular thing, and I like it a lot. "D'you know if they have dancing on there? Be good to have a bit of a jive."

"The night club is more of a really loud disco so I didn't actually stay in there for more than about ten seconds. But they do have line dancing classes and sometimes ballroom. They also have a spa so you can get your nails done and stuff, and they have special offers on massages on port days so keep your eyes peeled and you might get a bargain."

Hmm. Nails. Was wondering about that. Mine are shocking, but with the money Dad's given me maybe I can get them done on board. Now that would be luxury. Maybe sort my hairy legs out too rather than use that yucky smelly cream that shouts out to the world, "Hey, I've just got rid of all my hairy bits." Actually, no, as I'd be covered in a post-wax rash on the ship and that would look awful. Better try and get that done today or tomorrow. Eek. Sometimes it's really complicated being a girlie – the men have no idea. Well James does, obvs.

"I'm building up a bit of a to-do list here, you know! I'm beginning to feel as if I've been living in a cave for years and I'm just emerging, blinking into the daylight. And it's fun! Thank you so much, Dad. That money has turned the whole cruise into something really special. I mean, I was excited enough before, but this has made it amazing."

"Well – enjoy the excitement and the cruise. The doorbell just went so I need to go. Going out for a ramble along the coast path with some people. Bye love, speak soon."

This is weird. He's been chatty twice now, has given me money and is going for walks with friends. After all those years of being distant and unapproachable something is definitely afoot. Maybe there's a new lady in his life. Hmm. Hope so.

And next is a call to Aiden to check a few things as I'm totally paranoid about leaving him in charge of Titan and my flat for two weeks.

"So you'll find Titan's grown quite a bit. I mean he is still really small for his age, but he is bigger than he was. Obviously."

"I know. I see all the pictures on Facebook."

"That's cos he's so gorgeous I just can't resist posting them. So what are you doing about food? Shall I get some stuff in? Jules says she'll leave you a big cake to keep you going too. And of course she is on call should you need her." Jules certainly knows the way to Aiden's heart.

"Ah brilliant. Her cakes are wicked. And yes, just the odd pizza to get me started then I'll go out and shop. And can I have a barbeque if the weather's good? Thought I'd ask some old friends round."

Oh no. I was really hoping he wouldn't mention that. He isn't the most reliable person in the world, but he *is* doing me a massive favour in coming to flat-sit. Hopefully. So long as there aren't too many spills or breakages.

"Before you say no, you can check with Mum. I've been really good recently. I'm closing windows and keeping my room clean and helping in the B&B and even locking up at night. I really, really promise you can trust me. Why would I mess it up? If I did you wouldn't ask me again so it's not in my interest, is it?"

Wow. He's thought that one through to the end.

I take a deep breath and crossing my fingers frantically, say, "Okay... I can't believe I'm saying this, but I'll leave it out for you. And I'll even get some burgers in for you and a few bits and pieces so you don't starve. And Ellie is only next door if you need anything. And of course you have Jules' number in case you run out of cake."

Ellie's an amazing neighbour – one of those people who gives incredible support when you need it, but never intrudes or pokes her nose, even when she must have heard every word of the screaming rows with Mr Not-So-Charming. Sometimes I go in to share a bottle of wine with her in the evening. Well actually, she drinks lager so I have all the wine. Moving on… She is on secret standby in the event of an emergency, which is a huge relief.

"You know, once you're on the ship you won't be able to worry. For one thing you won't have any signal, so I really will have to cope on my own."

"How do you know stuff like that? You've never even been on a rowing boat!"

"Jem's mum goes on them all the time. And he stays and looks after her dog, so I do know a bit about it. Sometimes I think you think I don't know anything."

"That's because you're my little brother and you're not supposed to know anything."

Lol. Aiden and his friends are all growing up fast and becoming lovely young men. Some of them even have proper jobs, whereas Aiden's absolute determination to break into the music industry has meant he's taken no end of unlikely jobs just to stay afloat. He really isn't interested in anything else – there is no Plan B as far as he's concerned, so he often doesn't have any money. It'll be good to leave him a few treats.

"Dad's offered to take me to Southampton and we're leaving around 11. See you sometime before that?"

"Yep. I'll text you when I'm leaving. Then I'll text you when I'm half-way, then I'll ..."

"Stop taking the piss or I'll spike the burgers," but I'm laughing as I say it. Now there's an idea...

Chapter 6

I don't usually answer calls from unfamiliar numbers on my mobile but this one's local. Hmm. Maybe it's important.

"Hi, is that Miss Powell? This is Julie from Nailed It." Julie sounds ever so slightly harassed.

"Ooh. Yes! Sorry – didn't recognise the number."

"No worries. Can I just talk to you about your appointment tomorrow?"

"Yep. Is everything still OK?" I've managed to get an appointment for legs AND nails tomorrow – unbelievably enough – as I don't want to waste time indoors with all that lovely sunshine happening outside once I'm on the ship. And as it is literally years since I've had a proper manicure I'm looking forward to it a stupid amount. Not so much the waxing, obvs, but needs must and all that.

"Our usual beautician has just left without notice. We've managed to get a young girl in to replace her but I must stress she is just out of college. Will that be okay for you?"

"Of course – we all have to start somewhere, don't we?"

The relief from the other end is obvious as Julie brightens considerably. "Oh, wonderful. As she's just from college we can offer a discount, so the entire package will be just £25 instead of £45. Is that okay too?"

Result. And she can't be that bad if she's just out of college. I mean, I expect they do have to do some work experience. Hopefully. Whatever. If the kid is any good she'll get a great big tip to encourage her on her way.

I'm officially over-excited, even by my standards. In less than 24 hours I will be on the ship. And I am supremely well organised.

1. I have masses of new clothes thanks to my amazing trip with Jules. Hell, that girl can shop. It could be a whole new career for her once she gives up childminding.

2. I've got food in for Aiden.
3. And Titan.
4. His bed is made (Aiden's).
5. The barbie is out and clean.
6. I've got my holiday money.
7. Just need to pack. Must also remember:
   Cafetière
   Coffee!!!! Haha
   Phone charger
   Sun block
   Passport! Hmm. Not sure where I put that.
   Stuff to stop my hair frizzing

So otherwise I'm ready. Aiden comes early tomorrow, Dad will be here at 11 and then we are OFF!

With a happy little smile I open the door to the nail salon, and announce myself to the receptionist who asks me to take a seat for a moment as the therapist is still with the previous client. Well that's good. At least the manageress hasn't managed to put everyone off. I become so engrossed in a surprisingly up-to-date magazine – loads of brownie points for that important detail – that I don't notice someone standing in front of me.

"Hi Miss Powell, I'm Eden. I'm sorry to have kept you waiting."

I look up to find an elfin-like girl in front of me, who must be all of fifteen. Her black hair is scruffed artfully off her face (how do these kids do that?), she has huge eyes, perfect skin and is immaculately turned out in black trousers and a black, sleeveless top with a white lace Peter Pan collar. If she's out to make a good impression, it's a ten from me.

"I'm so sorry! I was completely engrossed. Magazines in these places are usually about two years old so it was lovely to find a new one." I stand up to shake the tiny hand Eden is holding out – very, very carefully as I'm a bit worried about breaking it.

"Yes, good isn't it? The manageress has them on subscription so we always have new ones out. Come on through." She leads the way through the salon to a treatment room and beckons me up onto the couch, then assembles the waxing kit. "Shall we get this bit over with first? Then we can have fun with your nails."

I like her style. And the waxing isn't as bad as I expected. Probably cos I'm fascinated that such a tiny person has the strength to rip the waxing sheets off my legs. Less said the better about that bit I think.

Once I'm bikini ready, Eden carefully moves a footbath into position. "Pop both feet in there to have a bit of a soak while we choose a colour."

Oh. The colours in the basket she offers me are all red or pink and I was hoping to try something new. After all, new experiences demand a new colour and these aren't it. Not being the most forthright of people in these circumstances, I'm gutted. What if they haven't got the right colour? Do I get up and leave? That would be awful. Aaargh. Big breath, be brave. Go on.

"Hmm. I was hoping to try something a bit different, like blue, maybe?"

"No worries. Let me see what we have out the front." Eden belts out of the room at the speed of light and is back in a moment. "How about these?" Pale blue, spearmint green.

"Erm, no?" Maybe it would be easier to give in and go for one of the pinks after all. But my heart sinks and suddenly this isn't fun anymore.

"Ah, purple! There was a purple out there. Hang on!"

Again, she is back in a flash. Good grief. If she does this all day she'll be exhausted and there's already nothing of her. The purple is LOVELY and Eden has saved the day. Back down to Defcon 1 as my stomach unclenches. And this colour is a perfect complement to my new clothes. Did I mention I have some delicious new clothes? I especially like the slinky hippy skirt and matching vest Jules talked me into.

"You've got a gorgeous figure Cait – flaunt it! You've been holed up too long with your cat, and you have no idea how GORGEOUS you are. In fact my mission is to stop you turning into some crazy old cat woman," she'd chuckled as we stood facing the mirror in the changing room.

"That will be perfect, actually," I tell Eden. "I've got some new clothes that will look really good with it."

"Ooh, sounds exciting. Is it for some special occasion?" she asks, carefully removing one of my feet from the bath and starting the pedicure.

After I've bored her shitless with exactly why I want the manicure (she hides it well), we have a good old chat. Which is a huge relief as an hour and a half is a very long time to spend in close and intense proximity to a complete stranger. I discover that Eden is in fact nineteen, and that she is still at college for three days a week doing the hairdressing module, even though she really prefers beauty therapy. She is only able to work at the salon for two half days and a Saturday, as apart from college she also has two cleaning jobs. I'm seriously impressed.

"I'm seriously impressed. You must be knackered by the end of the week."

"Not really, 'cos I'm working towards something – it will all be worth it in the end."

"And what will that end be? What do you really want to do, no holds barred?"

"Really? You mean, really, really?" Eden's eyes twinkle as I nod.

"A Disney princess. There, you can laugh now!"

She is actually right on the button, as except for the fact that she would have to be a miniature princess, she is cute beyond belief.

"Wow. I mean, I didn't expect to hear that!"

"Nobody does. I've got my CV out with all the Disney World parks but they want an acting qualification so I probably don't stand much chance. I've been obsessed with it since I was tiny."

Haha. You mean you were smaller than this? Of course I don't say that.

"I've still got pictures on my wall of Disney princesses and if I got the call I would go at the drop of a hat. But if I can't do that I want to have my own spa on a really swanky island somewhere hot. Only of course I wouldn't be doing all the treatments on my own. I'd have other therapists to work for me."

This kid sure knows how to dream big. Dynamite, all wrapped up in a very small package. Imagine if she was full-size. She'd be unbelievable. All of a sudden, and in the face of such certainty, I realise I'm not even sure what my dreams are any more. "You're amazingly positive for someone so young. What's your mum like?"

"Oh, she's great. She's a reflexologist. And she says I came out like this. She says I'm like a little rainbow, which is sort of sweet – I try to cheer people up along the way. Always have done. I mean, why not make the best of life?"

Such an old head on young shoulders. "And how about your name? Eden's really unusual."

"Ah, that's 'cos around the time I was born, my mum was reading a book that had two female characters and the prettiest was called Eden. So when I turned out to be a girl that's what she called me."

What a brilliant kid. She's like a massive dose of feel-good medicine, all wrapped up in this sparkling little package. The perfect prelude to the cruise.

"There you go – all done!"

The time has passed by in a flash, and I find I'm actually a bit sad to leave. And, looking down at my beautifully manicured purple nails I feel genuinely refreshed and happy. Bearing in mind the extra discount I've been given, I pay the bill and give Eden a fiver for herself.

Her eyes light up. "Are you sure? That's so generous. Thank you! I've only been here two days and I seem to be doing really well."

I bet she is. I watch as she adds the money to an already substantial pile of coins on her work tray. "That's because you're so good, and I can't wait to come back again."

"Ah thanks. Have a fabulous holiday and I'll see you again." Talk about feel-good factor, I feel amazing.

Chapter 7

"Leavin now shld be coupla hrs. Will text when close xx"

"What do you mean, leaving now? Thought you left about 2 hrs ago!!!!!!" No kisses. I'm cross now. I wanted to spend a bit of time with him before Dad arrives and do a bit of a handover, but it seems we will literally be passing each other on the threshold. My lovely brother, as ever, has probably tried to fit far too much into his day already, and now, at 10.00 he is only just leaving.

"Soz. Tried to do too much as usual. Don't be mad. Yr goin on hols :-) xx"

Don't know why I expect him to be on time and organised. He's never gonna change. At least he's coming.

"Soz back. So glad you r coming. Drive safely xxx"

Trying hard not to worry about what could happen while I'm away – to the ginger ninja and my flat – I have to pinch myself to believe this is really happening. When in doubt, retreat to a list.

1. Suitcase (new) packed and ready in the hall.
2. Passport – definitely, checked three times – in my handbag (new). Meeting James in the terminal reception at Southampton and he has the tickets. I hope.
3. Phone charger in hand luggage (new).
4. Pool attire (new) as suggested by Dad also in hand luggage.

For the first time in my life I've got co-ordinated luggage; this is partly Jules' fault, as I would have been quite happy with my beaten up suitcase, but she was having none of it.

"Is this you, or what?!" she'd laughed as she rushed over to the pile of pink and black striped luggage. "Smart but kind of nuts. Got your name written all over it."

I have to agree it is stunning. In fact the whole shopping trip was amazing and quite a revelation. Where have I been all this time? The shops were filled with the most beautiful clothes; hippy-style dresses and skirts, feminine tops and loose cardigans, soft baggy harem pants and t-shirts – in fact it was as if the designers were in my head and brought out this range just for me. Bearing in mind the sheer amount of clothes I needed, we did actually head for one of the more affordable shops in town. There were seriously big changing rooms, and plenty of room to strut up and down in front of the floor-to-ceiling mirrors. Its motto is that the customer should take in at least two items of clothing to try on that they wouldn't dream of wearing. It worked a treat. Jules was loving it and was rushing back and forth with an ever-increasing pile of clothes for me to try on anyway, "just in case."

Must admit I was a bit amused by all this attention, and also a bit surprised. Apart from whacking on the odd bit of eye shadow for jive, I don't generally spend much time in front of the mirror.

"Are you coming out yet? I've got a few more bits."

"Hmm. In a mo. Not sure about this one."

"Well come out here and we'll help you decide."

Gulp. I stepped out of the cubicle to be faced with a mini audience. The changing rooms were a bit quiet for a few minutes so a couple of the assistants were also looking on with interest.

"Jeez. Which bit aren't you sure about? Cos from where I'm standing you look amazing!"

I turned to face the huge mirror and did a double take. I was having an unusually good hair day, and for once my crazy curls looked rather good, even if I say so myself. Hmm. Not bad. And despite the long hours in front of the computer, the running and walking by the sea seem to have paid off; the misty blue shade of the long, slightly clingy dress (that's the bit I wasn't sure about!) highlighted my runner's tan and made my hair look quite a pretty auburn colour. I liked the way the fabric fanned out slightly just above my ankles, showing the pretty sandals Jules had picked out. I walked up and down a bit in front of the mirror, feeling a tiny bit proud that I still have a flat stomach, then suddenly remembered that I had an audience.

"Wow. I like it! I mean, I feel like a new me is crawling out from the shadows. I didn't think I had the figure for this sort of stuff."

"Well, hallelujah, girlfriend. A sight for sore eyes, I can assure you! And you weren't even going to try it on." Jules handed over another pile of clothes. "Now give me what you're keeping and try this lot on."

And so it had continued. I smile at the memory and feel lucky to have a friend like Jules. Who, as it turned out, didn't really need much for herself after all, in spite of saying she needed to shop too. Jules is, in fact, the best-dressed childminder in town. No idea how she does it being permanently overrun with other peoples' children, but that woman has some seriously classy clothes.

"The thing is," she replied, when I queried her extensive wardrobe, "you never know when you might need this stuff. I mean, we do manage to have the odd holiday, and it's nice to have a few bits and pieces ready. So if I see something I like, I buy it."

The 'somethings' on this trip happened to be some dark navy cropped pants with discreet buttons up the side and a matching jacket. Jules sure knows how to shop.

Breaking away from my happy memory, I suddenly realise I'd better let Dad know there will be an Aiden-induced delay in our departure. I'm just reaching for my mobile when the front door bell rings. Oh no. I'm too late and he's here. He always likes being a bit early. Just a shame baby bro isn't anywhere close yet.

"Dad, I was just …" I say as I open the door. "You utter brat! You…. grrr! You are such a wind-up!"

And there, of course, is my brother, with a massive grin on his face. I launch myself at him and we share a massive hug.

Aiden gently pulls away, his eyes twinkling with laughter. "Haha! Too good an opportunity to miss. Now you're even happier to see me…. Ah, my boy…!"

This is directed at Titan, who, awoken from his slumbers by all the excitement, is sleepily making his way into the hall. Aiden picks up the little cat and holds him in the way that only Aiden can. I know if I try I'll be savaged. Sort of sat in his hand and high up. Not at all like anyone usually cuddles their cat, but Titan seems to like it. He obviously remembers Aiden even though it's been a while, and is busily purring contentedly, enjoying the attention.

"I'm sure he'll love you being here. He is such a cute little thing. Little being the operative word. He has a huge personality packed into that teeny little body, although he eats enough to feed an entire cattery. I'll show you where everything is."

We head into the kitchen and I watch Aiden's eyes glaze over with boredom until I come to all the goodies I've got for him, and then the doorbell goes again. This time it really is Dad, who also excitedly leaps at Aiden.

"Wow. You're really here!"

"Just why does everyone think I'm always late and you're amazed when I turn up?" Aiden's wearing his hurt little boy face.

"Erm, experience? When did you ever get anywhere on time? But you *are* here and we love you for it."

"Not without winding me up a treat first," I add. "But this is my baby brother and I should be used to it by now."

"And seeing as we're all here now, baby brother thinks you two should just piss off to the port so he can get settled in and enjoy the peace and quiet. Yes, my mobile will be on, and no I'm not going to burn the place down, and yes I will remember to feed Titan and lock the doors and close the windows and wipe down the shower. It's only for two weeks. Go!"

Chapter 8

We're waved into the correct lane for drop-off at the cruise terminal by a brightly smiling man, then as Dad leaves me with a big hug and kiss, my suitcase is taken away by another lovely smiling man. In fact all the staff are smiling. How weird. Imagine spending the entire day right next to a ship you're not going away on. A ship which is, incidentally, absolutely enormous from where I'm standing.

"Are you going to stand and look at it all day or are we going to get on board, Ms Powell?"

"James!!!!! Aw, you look amazing! You're looking especially like a young Julian Clary today. I'm soooo excited." I leap at him and do my jumpy kind of jig.

"I'd never have guessed. And thank you, and no I don't, and you look totally amazeballs yourself. Come on, let's get checked in and on the ship. Mia said we should be able to get on early as she's put a note on our booking. She said we need to go into the Priority Boarding line."

I've never been in a Priority anything line so I'm well impressed, but not half as impressed as when the (smiling) check-in lady tells us we've been upgraded to Superior Balcony and can go straight through to board. WTF?

"Just how good a friend is this friend? I mean, she must be able to pull some heavyweight strings to do this."

"Just told her I was bringing a dear friend on a much-needed holiday. All this is her doing."

Cue hugs and a bit of mistiness as I get overwhelmed at all this kindness. I definitely feel like I'm in one of Ivy's stories now. "Well the lovely Mia is going to get one massivo hug from me, I can tell you. In fact loads. What a treasure."

"Absolutely. And at the risk of not seeming gentlemanly, are you OK pulling your own overnight bag as the pink and black stripes are a bit much even for me." Twinkly smile.

"James McGrew, I do believe you are turning straight."

We get through security and start walking down the funny bendy corridor towards the ship.

"Never in a million years sweetie, but I do have limits and a reputation to protect. There are some seriously fit dancers on this ship. Mia told me." Very Big Smile.

"Oh goody, I could do with some diversions. Joking. Don't think they'd be interested in me somehow. On the other hand…you just never know."

By now we've gone round the last bend and are walking on the dockside itself. The only thing between us and the ship is a drop-dead-gorgeous photographer who waves us in front of a sort of screen with a picture of the ship itself on it and snaps a picture of us. And then another as I had my eyes closed. And then another as James says he wasn't smiling properly. Perleeease! Can we just get on the ship? I'd say we went up the gangplank, but it's not a gangplank in a pirate ship kind of way. In fact it's not a plank at all. It's a wide gangway which has a little disinfectant dispenser before you even step onto it, attended by a charming (and smiling) but ruthlessly efficient lady in a really crisp white uniform who is there to make sure we get the required squirt before boarding the ship.

And then, we're here! Loads more smiling faces, and a stunning atrium with the most beautiful staircase and a sense of being in the most luxurious hotel in the world. And I honestly can't tell it's floating. Now there's a thought. I'm assuming I don't get seasick. Oooh. I will definitely be fine.

"Mia!" James is busily hugging a lady in a very white and very smart beautician's outfit. "Cait, come and meet Mia!"

Mia turns towards me with a wide grin and a welcoming hug. Aw.

"So good to meet you, Caitlin. You're going to have the time of your life on here. I'm based in the beauty salon in the Lotus Spa, so you can come and find me there if you need anything. I've got to stay here at the beauty stand now to help welcome everyone on board, but come along later and I'll show you around. See you guys!" And she's off to meet and greet the constant stream of people coming on board.

And we're off in another direction, as a kindly gentleman in a snappy white uniform is asking whether we've been on board before and whether we know where we're going. So that's a double 'No', then. Fortunately the cards we've been given with our room keys have a fold-out map, so we decide to go and explore and find our own way around the ship as our cabin won't be ready for a few hours. Now that feels weird. I never expected to be saying 'our cabin' when the 'our' bit is with James. This is going to be interesting.

Bearing in mind the hand luggage, we get a lift straight up to the Lido deck where there's apparently a barbeque going on; plus I want to see the pools and look down onto the dockside from the vast height of the top deck. The lifts are crazily busy, so we decide wherever possible in the future to walk up and down all the flights of stairs. It will also be an attempt to work off some of the huge amount of food we are planning on eating. Having not been away for a long time it's going to be the ultimate luxury not having to shop or cook.

'Cook' is obviously more of a blanket term to describe opening packets rather than any genuine culinary activity, in my case.

We finally squeeze into a lift and in seconds are poured back out and through some whooshing doors to the Great Outside. Wow. The British Summer is really showing off today and the first thing we see is the pool, its water sparkling in the sunshine. Along one side is a great long snaking line of tables covered in immaculate white cloths and on those cloths are trays and trays of delicious looking food. All the staff are dressed in immaculate white uniforms and are wearing huge smiles and the whole thing is dazzling. These people must get through a ton of bleach.

"Good afternoon, ma'am, sir, welcome on board! Can I offer you a glass of Prosecco with our compliments?"

"Absolutely," smiles James, reaching for two glasses from the proffered tray. "Thank you so much. Do we just help ourselves to the buffet? And is it really free?"

"Oh yes, sir. Please do have as much as you like. Relax, enjoy the food and the sun and our beautiful ship. You are on holiday now."

Woah. I can definitely get used to this. And we haven't even left port yet. We manage to get a table near the pool and sit down, grinning at each other stupidly.

"To my dear and very lovely friend Caitlin amazeballs Powell!"

"James McGrew, you have truly outdone yourself here. Cheers."

Glasses duly clinked we drift off into our own worlds. I don't know where James has gone in his head, but I sit here slightly dazed, wondering how I managed to be blessed with such a special friend. Gay men are so totally excellent at creating an occasion. James has done it time and time again – even going out for a coffee with him is an experience that is so different from being with, say, Jules. He is totally outrageous and can get away with saying things a woman never could. He seems to be the best blend of male and female emotions, psyche, can't put my finger on it. And there's no danger of our friendship being spoilt by sexual attraction (as with a straight man), and no competition in terms of who looks best or gets most attention from the opposite sex like there could be with a female friend. My (pretty appalling) experience of straight men has been that they are either socially gauche, or want to appear macho and so miss the sensitive touches a woman wants (well, I do), or try to do what they think I would like and fail miserably because their motives aren't genuine. Sigh. James is actually the perfect companion, but in the darkest recesses of my mind, I can't help wishing he was attracted to me.

We had a massive conversation about that once. When I first met James I thought he was a dead ringer for Julian Clary. And so did a lot of other people apparently, which irritated the hell out of him. I told him he should be pleased because Julian Clary is drop-dead-gorgeous. Then followed it up with the incredibly insensitive comment that it was a shame he's gay as there are so many women absolutely gagging for him. I can't believe I said that. I like to think it was because I was so young at the time, but I'll never forget the look on his face.

"Why is it a shame he's gay? You're implying that's a waste of a person. So that's also like saying I'm a waste too, just because I'm not straight. Why can't he – or I for that matter – be appreciated just as we are, regardless of our sexuality? Don't you think a gay guy will look at him and think he's gorgeous too?"

"I'm so sorry James. That came out before I thought about it – nothing new there then!"

My pathetic attempt to backtrack and make him laugh failed miserably. It was true, I hadn't thought about it. James had only recently come out, although he'd known for a long time that he was gay, so this was all very raw for him. It made me realise for the first time that a straight man might think about meeting the right woman, falling in love and having kids, and they all live happily ever after (maybe that is a bit too influenced by Ivy), but it couldn't be more different for James. He said in the early days he wished he wasn't gay and that everything could be as straightforward for him as it would be for me. Well, through the years, things haven't turned out to be straightforward for me, but they haven't been nearly as complicated as for James.

I drag myself back to the ship and my drink and this lovely man sitting opposite me. Jacket off, sleeves rolled up, shades in place, looking round the deck, taking it all in.

"First selfie?"

"Reckon so!" James is the king of selfies.

He is my absolute 'go-to' on these occasions as he always looks completely normal in his selfies, whereas I gain baggy-eyes and exceedingly unflattering cheek jowls in a matter of seconds. He tells me this is because I always look down at my phone, so grabbing his, he comes round to my side of the table so we get the pool in the pic too. Raising the phone waaay up high, we both look up at it and grin massively. These cats have definitely got the cream. When we look at the picture, it's perfect. How does he do that?

"Share?"

"Oh yes! Especially while we've got free wi-fi. Dad says it's really expensive when you get to sea."

"Yeah, so did Mia. She says as soon as the crew are allowed off the ship when it gets to port they know exactly where to go to get free wi-fi. So we'll just follow them!"

This is the perfect place for people watching, something I never tire of. An extended family of several adults and a gazillion children have just descended on a bunch of sun loungers and set up camp like it's their second home. They seem to get organised and into their cozzies at lightning speed, and within seconds the kids are heading for the pool, which has a very obvious sign saying 'NO JUMPING'. The massive splash caused by their team jump lands all over my pale blue sundress, leaving unsightly dark blue marks.

"Time to move, I think. How does Jules work with kids? Total saint in my mind."

"From what you tell me, it's because she's got rules and they do as they're told."

"Yes, well, that's a huge leap in the right direction. They know exactly where they are with her. Like if they don't eat their lunch they don't get their treat. Simple as that, in her mind. I wish I was a bit more like that – you know, consistent. I've been called 'consistently inconsistent' in the past. And you know those multiple choice personality tests – um, Myers-Briggs? I've tried them several times online, and depending on how I'm feeling, I get a different type each time.

I can't believe companies actually use those to help them recruit staff. In fact I heard that one very high profile chain store choose management staff from applicants who are some way up the psychopathic scale. Or was it sociopathic? Whatever, they don't really care about other people or any of that team-building shit. More a case of, sorry your cat's died, but if you're not performing, you're out."

"Oh God, yes." James worked at a big supermarket over Christmas one year and experienced it first-hand. He also discovered he hated working in a supermarket. As well as the psychopathic management issues, he looked rubbish in the lime green uniform, and TBH James can look amazing in a brown paper bag. I mean, who could possibly look good in a lime green uniform? Are they trying to make their staff feel as uncomfortable as possible?

Actually, as a bystander it was hilarious. During the summer he worked at a holiday park, in a role that was full-on entertainment for the punters, which also involved a massive amount of grinning and looking deliriously happy even if you were feeling horrible. Which is very hard for James as his feelings tend to be really obvious. I digress. So this was seasonal work which meant at the end of October he had to join the ranks of the great unwashed, at a time when everyone else was hunting for Christmas work too. Pretty tough to actually get something, but this particular year he found the job in the supermarket with the lime green uniform. He was happily in his own little world filling shelves when an old friend spotted him.

"Hey James! How ARE you mate? Good to see you're working!"

"Hey, hi! Yes, just a Christmas job here, you know filling in till the spring."

"Doesn't matter mate, at least you've got a job. The uniform really suits you, haha."

"Um, yeah, but like I said, this is just over Christmas. I do have a proper job, much cooler uniform, but it doesn't start until the spring."

"Really, it's OK mate. Doesn't matter about working here. Your secret's safe with me. See you around!"

So the next year he had a complete change of scenery and went from lime green to sort of pinky with a fill-in job at Lush, who make all those amazing smellies. Much more his thing.

We vacate our table just in time to avoid another cascade of splashes, and pick our way slowly along the buffet until we both have plates piled high with beautiful looking food. Fortunately we find another table at a safe distance from the pool.

"Some wine to go with your lunch, Madam?" A waiter in dazzling white uniform has appeared like magic, just as I was thinking I should have some water, what with the warmth and the bubbly.

"Hmm, I think I just might be tempted...."

Chapter 9

Several glasses of wine and a LOT of food later, we realise we haven't even strayed from the Lido deck to explore the rest of the ship. This could get to be a habit, especially as I don't even have to move from my chair to get the Chardonnay. These waiters appear like magic. "Come on McG, we should go for a wander. Maybe our cabin is ready."

"Not sure I can move after all that. And we've got another meal tonight! Where are we going to put it all?"

"That's why we need a bit of a walk. If the cabin's ready we won't have to drag our bags around everywhere. I'm much too full to think about changing or going for a swim now."

According to our little map, we need to go down four floors and along the port side – so not too much of a schlep in our overstuffed state. The lifts are still crazy-busy with new arrivals so James does the honourable thing and overcomes his aversion to my bag, which he carries down the eight flights of stairs for me. As we find the right passageway I spot my stripey case a mile off and run towards it. "Come on! I just cannot wait for this, but we have to see it together."

The door swings open as James inserts his card key and we peer in eagerly. Then stare at each other in disbelief. The cabin is huge, with its own sofa area and two beds covered in dazzling white linen and floor to ceiling windows that lead out to our own balcony, which is graced by two reclining chairs and a table. There's something on the table by the sofa and as I get closer realise it's a bottle of bubbly in a wine chiller.

"Is this Mia too?"

"Actually, no, that was me. Just wanted to say happy holidays to my best friend, and thank you for coming along with me. I've wanted to do this ever since I've known Mia, but I've never had the right person to go with." James turns to me with a shy smile.

"Aw, you're just amazing. And thank you so much. I kind of assumed you had loads of friends in London and were having a really good old time." We wander out to the balcony as we chat and see that we're on the side that looks out over the dockside; porters are busily loading cases onto a conveyor belt, which then disappears into the bowels of the ship.

"Um no. Actually. Not that great, to be honest. I've had a couple of 'encounters," James makes those silly inverted comma signs with his fingers at this point and carries on, "which turned out to be absolute disasters, and it's quite hard to meet people in London. Well, people who aren't just out for a bit of action in the toilets or round the back of the nightclub. And even if I did have someone, I wouldn't feel comfortable on a cruise with them. I mean, we can't hold hands in public, or hug, or kiss like you guys can – it's like living half a life. I know that some people do, but I don't like to be that obvious. So you can understand that it's easier with you as we don't do those things anyway. Well, apart from the odd hug."

James isn't that happy with hugs at all, actually, but at this point I decide he needs one as he is looking a teeny bit sad, so I wrap my arms round him in a very matey and non-sexual way.

"Well I'm sad for you, but ridiculously happy for me – how lucky can a girl get?"

"You've got a point there. If we both had partners we wouldn't be having this experience, and that would be terrible. Just think, all these people would be deprived of our sparkling wit and delightful company."

I look up and he's smiling again so I think it's safe to let go. Which is timely as there's a polite knock on the door, which turns out to be our steward, Marco. Fortunately he has a) an easy name and b) a name badge which is really handy as I'm likely to forget it in the next two minutes. Marco makes sure we know how the lights operate and shows us where the Room Service menu is and tells us we will need to attend the Safety Drill at 4.30 in the Marquis Bar, which will be just before the Sailaway party. Ooh. That sounds fun. Not so excited about the Safety Drill, but having read what happened on the Costa Concordia I can see the sense in making it compulsory. He also shows us the little card with our restaurant details on and says we have Freedom Dining, which means we can turn up to our designated restaurant (the Pyramid) at any time and we will be accommodated as soon as possible. I seriously think I'm going to run out of wows on this holiday.

We unpack ridiculously quickly because we want to explore. I personally hate both packing and unpacking and could quite happily let a butler do it for me, like in some of Ivy's books, but clearly that's not an option at the moment.

I'm enjoying being a bit girlie for a change so the dress stays on (water spots have dried, thankfully), but the sandals are swapped for my brand new Primark ballet pumps on the basis they'll be easier for walking about on deck. They're also beautifully colour co-ordinated with the dress (not Primark) so it does all look rather smart if I say so myself. James changes into some pale chinos and a white baggy shirt which along with some deck shoes looks too cool for words. We had a very late night phone conversation to colour co-ordinate our wardrobes before packing, just so we didn't clash horribly. Fortunately we're both into the blue/grey/purple/white/pink (yes even James) side of the spectrum as I couldn't tolerate walking around with someone wearing orange. Or lime green, but I think he's served his time on that one. We also decided to be a little bit smart even though Dad said we didn't need to be, and I'm glad we did. Clearly other passengers didn't have the same discussion with their co-travellers as quite frankly some of their colour choices make my eyes bleed, and there is an awful lot of flesh on show.

Anyway.

The food is starting to work its way down now so we brace ourselves to walk from the cabin back up to the Lido deck, which isn't actually too taxing. That's it. No more lifts for us for two weeks! We find our way back to the Lido only this time walk on past the pool area, which is where the Sailaway party will be, through the Lido restaurant itself, then out the doors at the end to a quieter and more enclosed pool which looks as though it has a roof that pulls over in bad weather. This ship is endless! A quick shifty at some of the details in the room reveal that three laps round the deck equals a mile. Think I'm going to need that based on the food I've just eaten. It would be nice if I can actually get into the new clothes I've brought along before my waistline expands beyond belief.

Thank God for the map and that we have one each, because if we get separated I'm quite sure I might never find the cabin again without it. We wander happily around discovering a late night cocktail bar (empty obvs but we will be back), a bridge room (not sure I'll be doing that!)

and a stunning Sky bar which does what it says on the tin – gives wrap-around visibility from every seat. This is going to be amazing.

"Ooh look! The Spa! Funny, and we weren't even heading there." I'm also interested in the gym and the classes held therein, so I drag James past the beauticians touting their wares by the entrance to explore.

Within minutes I've got the timetable for the classes as I definitely want to try Pilates and maybe yoga, as I haven't really done them properly, and maybe the morning stretch class, if I'm not hungover.

"How about you James?"

Silence. That's funny, he was here just now. Then I spot him loitering in a doorway outside the gym, presumably talking to someone I can't see. He turns and looks in my direction and waves.

"I found Mia! Come on over."

Mia is still bubbly and bouncy and immaculate, and you would never have guessed she has just welcomed about three thousand people on board. She takes us on a tour of the Spa, which has its own hydro massage pool and sun lounger area – Yay! Child free! – then shows us the treatment rooms where we can have anything from a hot stone massage to osteopathy, to... well almost anything. It all smells divine and really is an oasis of peace and I'm clearly going to need a month on here. Or maybe I could just live on here and work from my cabin. Or the Lido. Now there's a thought.

Mia turns to me. "So – tomorrow night is the Captain's Reception. I was just saying to James that I'd really like to get my hands on your hair and do something amazing for the occasion. You can get dressed in your posh togs, have your photo taken, and wow the world. How about it? Oh and it's his treat."

Crikey. Wasn't expecting that. I look uncertainly at James. It's so long since I've been made a fuss of that I'm almost embarrassed.

"Absolutely – go for it. You're going to look incredible. I mean, you're already lovely, but Mia will work miracles on your hair. Oh shit. Your hair is lovely too and I didn't mean that the way it came out. Anyone got a spade?"

I'm laughing now which relieves the sudden tension in my stomach. Too many years with the wrong bloke has completely messed with my mind. "Aw, thank you, James. And Mia, I would absolutely love that.

Anyone who offers to tame my hair is a saint as far as I'm concerned. What time shall I come up?"

Appointment booked, we make our way back to the cabin to collect our very fetching orange buoyancy aids as it's nearly time for the safety drill. I guess orange and pale blue won't look too bad, just for a short while.

"Thanks. You know I can't believe all this attention, and I don't quite know what to do with it. I'm scared the bubble will burst and I'll suddenly wake up and find it's all been a dream and someone's laughing at me for being so gullible. That sounds stupid, but I do feel like that, way down inside."

"That's because you were with a bullying arsehole who doesn't know how to treat a woman. Even I know how to treat women – and I'm gay!"

Ouch. He wasn't like that when I started going out with him though, he was Mr Charming or I wouldn't have been sucked in. OK he had a touch of Mr Stingy about him that wasn't very attractive. Like never buying me a coffee when we were out ("I don't want one"), and making me drink tap water in a bar when I really wanted sparkling mineral water ("I'm not paying for water – it's free and it comes out of the tap"). And then the first Christmas when I bought him a digital camera and he bought me a shite skirt from a market stall. The signs were all there really, but by that stage I didn't want to be alone again so I carried on, hoping it would get better. Then Mr Angry started to make an appearance, and I realised I could actually be in danger if I tried to throw him out. Or in danger if he stayed. Messy.

"Well, you're right, you know. And now I'm on holiday, a million miles away from the memories of all that shit, so at the risk of appearing completely crass," at this point I burst into that very well-known song. "The only way is up, babeeeeeee," just as the safety drill is announced at mega-volume through the cabin speakers. No chance of anyone missing that!

"Thank God for small mercies."

"Cut off in my prime, you cheeky brat," I say, giving James a playful slap. "Come on, let's go and inspect our fellow passengers. Should be pretty spectacular, en masse."

The stairways are packed, and each one is marshalled by members of the ship's crew looking important and serious in their orange floaties and baseball caps bearing the word CREW – obviously in case we're not sure who they are. All the recent smiles and friendliness are gone as they focus on the task at hand, which in this case is getting thousands of people down the stairways who would really prefer to be up in the sunshine. Memories of footage from the Costa Concordia rise up in my mind as they must be doing with the other passengers, and en masse the mood turns a bit more sober. If this was the real thing it would be terrifying.

Safely herded into the theatre, we find out seats and get the chance to have a good look around. The auditorium is a riot of colour as smart check-in outfits have been exchanged for bright holiday clothes, most of which clash like hell with the bright orange of our floaties. Euuw. But then I realise that if we need to use these for real at some point I'm going to be worrying about an awful lot more than colour coordination.

It's actually quite fun sitting in here. I smile at the odd person who meets my eye, and can sense there's a kind of camaraderie building up, because this is all we have for the next two weeks. Each Other. In fact nearly three thousand 'Each Others'. Wonder how that's going to pan out then.

A lady wearing a blindingly white uniform bounds onto the stage. With one of those around I can't see we'd need an orange floaty, TBH.

"Ladies and gentlemen, good afternoon and WELCOME. Now don't WORRY, you will soon be back out in that beautiful sunshine, we just have to cover some safety information first. What the stewards are going to do NOW, is they are going to show you how to put on a buoyancy aid. Now please DON'T put yours on yet as there will be time for that later and you need to watch how to do it first. Er – Sir! Sir! Yes, sir, you."

Everyone turns round to stare at the guy who has started to put his orange floaty over his head.

"Can you please take your buoyancy aid OFF and sit down and watch the demonstration. We will wait until you are comfortably seated BEFORE we continue."

Oooh. Bossy when they need to be, then.

So after a lot of instructions we finally get to stand up and put our aids on, check that the light works and remember NOT to blow the whistle as that would be unhygienic. Yuk. I bet Kate Winslet's whistle was totally pristine in *Titanic*. She probably had it written into the contract. I don't want to even think about that, especially as I hear a few illegal 'peeps' behind me. And then we're free.

Next up is the Sailaway Party on the Lido Deck, and our cabin just happens to be on the way. How handy. The lifts are now back in use after the drill, but only take about half the people they would usually due to the buoyancy aids we're all dragging around (with the ties safely AWAY from the floor please). There's good deal of grumbling amongst some of the passengers who look as if they haven't climbed even a single stair in a very long time, and I can't help wondering what they'll be like by the end of the cruise if what I've heard about the food on cruise ships is for real. I decide at that moment to walk the mile course around the deck at least once a day, even if we're going off the ship. And maybe have a run on the machine in the gym, and of course to always walk up the stairs from now on.

"Actually, that was quite tough," pants James as we finally make it to the Lido, eight floors and sixteen flights of steps later.

"Big pansy. You'll get used to it. Ooh look, glasses of bubbly!"

Chapter 10

These people know how to party. The band are playing and the wine is flowing, and the waiters are immediately attentive to our every whim. Thanks to my dad's generosity and the fact I didn't blow all his money on clothes, I realise I can afford to get absolutely lashed every night if I want to.

I'm about to order another glass of bubbly when I realise that James is being quite abstemious. "Have you turned over a new leaf without telling me?"

"Haha. Not really. Just trying to take it a bit more slowly. I've been overdoing it somewhat in London under the mistaken impression that alcohol will help ease the loneliness."

Oh. I thought that's what alcohol was for. Actually, no, just joking. I do agree actually, as I've been doing the same. I remember a friend saying that she never drank alone. Which of course she could say, viewed from the lofty heights of being in a relationship. If I stuck to that I'd hardly drink at all. Anyway, I've got Titan, so I'm not alone.

"I totally admire your willpower and I'll do my best to cut down too. But as we're at a party and this is so ridiculously exciting, I AM just going to get another glass of bubbly. Can I get one for you too? Sorry, didn't mean to tempt you, but it would be rude not to ask."

James shakes his head slowly and we collapse into giggles.

Our drinks arrive in no time at all and we raise our glasses to each other.

"To cutting back on the old happy juice tomorrow!" Way to go.

We can really feel the ship's engines now, and along with a whole load of other passengers we move over to the port side to watch it edge carefully away from the dock. I wouldn't want to hang a U-turn in this thing. It is really, really big and very, very long and we are all deeply impressed.

The entertainers have taken over from the band and are giving it their all round by the pool – and before we know it we're joining in with 'Knees up Mother Brown' and 'My Old Man' and all the party songs that would usually send me running screaming in the opposite direction. The British Summer is still on its best behaviour for us, and as the ship heads out of the port area and off down Southampton Water towards the Isle of Wight, we fade out the music and spend ages just looking over the back, mesmerised by the sunshine sparkling on the wake we leave behind. God, how much more gorgeous can it get?

"Can I just get a Sailaway photo of you two lovely people?"

We turn around to find Mr Drop-Dead-Gorgeous photographer waiting to snap us. I wonder if this is how the Kardashians feel.

"Oh, yes please. Where do you want us?"

"Just where you are is perfect. Sir, if you would like to move a bit closer and put your hand over her shoulder, and Madam, just turn slightly towards him and look at me. Fabulous. Thank you. You'll be able to see them tomorrow in the photo gallery outside the Pyramid Restaurant."

Well that was awkward.

"That was awkward. How are we going to handle that kind of stuff? How could he not clock that you're gay and we're not a couple?" Oh bollocks. There I go again. Me in my mouth-in-gear-before-brain-engages mode. Talk about ruining the moment. I'm surprised to see that James is laughing.

"What?!"

"I think we can have a lot of fun with this. The poor photographers must have to deal with so many people that they just get into a spiel and don't even think about the relationship between the subjects. They just want a good picture so we buy it. And anyway, does it matter? Gorgeous bloke, by the way. One of yours or one of mine, d'you think?"

"Good question. No doubt all will be revealed, erm, in one way or another." Shut UP. This is definitely the bubbly talking. "So how are we going to have fun with it? Pretend to be a couple?"

"I think we should just act as if we are. I mean, obviously no kisses or strolling along hand in hand, but I honestly don't mind closing in for a photo where required, and I think there might be a few of those based on today. And anyway, you're a gorgeous woman and I'm proud to be with you."

Shucks. "And you're pretty lush yourself, so I'm up for it if you are. Guess we should go and change into our finery for dinner. If you can face more food."

The food turns out to be a bit further away than we expect. Firstly because the restaurant is on the same level as the theatre, so it's back down all those stairs (as per our new regime) and then about a five minute walk to the other end of the ship in my smart (but uncomfortable) spiky-heeled sandals which are from an earlier, not-so-happy time. I do still like them but they're on a final warning. And at the moment they're hurting. Ouch. And secondly there is the queue. When we hear the maître d' asking people waaaay up at the front of the queue if they are happy to sit with Other People, I turn to James in panic.

"Um, I'm not very good at small talk and being with strangers, especially over dinner. Do you mind if we ask for a table for two? Sorry. Maybe I'll get a bit braver as we go on." Another result of being with Mr Not-So-Charming, as I think I used to be quite confident in public.

"No worries at all. We can sit and stare into each other's eyes and confuse the hell out of everyone." James approaches the desk, as the queue has moved surprisingly quickly, and requests a table for two. In return he gets one of those buzzy monitor things and we're despatched to the nearest seats – which just happen to be in a bar – to await the buzz. So what we decide, as he drinks a glass of red wine and I drink some excellent Chardonnay, is that we will get separate bottles at the table and ask if they can be kept over for tomorrow night. If we manage to leave any of course. And I do think there's a chance of that tonight actually, as I'm possibly approaching my supposed weekly quota in just one day. Even I have limits.

The restaurant is like a merry-go-round with waiters moving at breakneck speed between tables, somehow never crashing into each other. After quite a wait at the bar we're shown to our table, which is thankfully safely away from anyone else, and within seconds our Head Waiter Sebastian introduces himself and hands us some menus. What a lovely guy. And another name I can remember. Yay! He introduces us to the wine waiter who is called something like Srelleck so I settle for Star Trek because his name badge is too small for me to read properly. He establishes that Madam likes the South African Chardonnay and Sir will go with the Chilean Merlot and that we would like to (try to) keep the bottles over for tomorrow. So all good and pretty amazing then.

I try to imagine having to get used to a whole new load of people every few days, and realise very quickly that it would completely do my head in. And all that smiling. I wonder if they have a smile check before they start work, and get sent back to their cabins if they're not wearing it. I remember James saying that at the holiday park there was a huge SMILE sign on the back of the door between staff and public areas to remind them to paste it on before going on show. I so couldn't do that all the time and neither could James in the end, which is why he left.

And we do actually manage to save some wine for tomorrow, probably because the delicious four course meal followed by petit-fours (new one on me) and peppermint tea have filled us up beyond the point of being able to drink any more of it. Hoping to stave off imminent indigestion I suggest a walk.

Waddling out of the restaurant we discover that the restaurant is only two decks below the Promenade Deck, which is excellent as there is no way I can face too many stairs for a while yet. It's really hard to push the door open, and when we do make it out onto the deck we're surprised by the strength of the wind. I'm just thinking this is going to be a very quick walk as a) when I came up with this bright idea I forgot I had my spiky sandals on and b) I didn't think to bring a jumper with me, when James very gallantly offers me his jacket. I take my shoes off and walk barefoot, so job done. It really is a beautiful night and we wander slowly all the way round the deck, stopping occasionally to look over the side, just marvelling at the way the ship cuts through the water. I haven't been on a proper ship before (the school trip to France doesn't really count) and it's hard to believe this will be our home for the next two weeks. It'll take that long to find out where everything is. Peering through the windows I notice we're on the shopping deck – result!

"A little bit of retail therapy before bedtime?"

"Anything as long it's warm!"

"Ah, sorry! You should have said! I'll remember my jacket tomorrow, or at least a wrap."

Fighting our way back through the door I give James back his coat and put my shoes back on, as I'm not sure barefoot would go down well here. The wander through the Duty Free shops doesn't take that long as we're overcome by tiredness as soon as the warm air hits us; Aiden's arrival and driving to Southampton seem so long ago now, but it has been a fabulous day.

A massive yawn threatens to break my jaw. "Guess maybe I'm ready for bed now. Can't really do these shops justice. How about you?"

"I'm definitely feeling like snuggling down for a very good night's sleep. Is it the sea air? I'm knackered."

"Yep, me too. Shall we see how far we get with the steps before we need the lift? Only eight flights of stairs." I pull a big smiley face.

"Did you notice that last sentence contained the word 'knackered'?"

"Er, yup. Shall we at least give it a go? Slowly?"

"Aaargh. You. Will. Be. The. Death. Of. Me."

"No, I absolutely promise not, especially after you organised all this."

Gently bantering we start the long climb to bed. It's easier than expected as we pause for breath every so often, and it isn't long before James is opening the door. The cabin has been transformed in our absence. Curtains closed, lights low, chocolates on the pillow, WAIT. Chocolates on the pillow? I have definitely died and gone to heaven.

"Would Madam prefer the curtains open or closed?"

"I prefer them open actually – I like to wake up with the daylight."

"Good. So do I. That was easy then. Window open or closed?"

"Erm, open? Not sure if we can do that with the sliding door though."

"I'll sort it out while you use the bathroom."

And just like that James eased us into spending our first night together. I think I was probably asleep by the time he'd finished in the bathroom, but I know the last thing I heard was the sound of the ship cutting through the water, gently lulling me to sleep. Heaven.

Horrible feeling I might have snored though...

Chapter 11

I wake up after the best night's sleep ever, which is due somewhat to the lack of Titan scratching at the door for breakfast. The silence is astounding, as is the sublime smoothness of the dazzling white sheets on my lovely snuggly bed. I glance across at James, who is still in the land of nod. What a guy. I can't get over yesterday, and him arranging all this and the bubbly and the hair appointment. I want to find a way of thanking him without being obvious, because he really is the best friend ever. Maybe book him a massage? I will sneakily investigate. My bed is closest to the balcony, so I creep out of bed and try not to wake him as I open the door. I fail. His eyes ping open and a huge grin spreads across his face.

"Mornin!" He stretches luxuriantly. "We're on HOLIDAY, yay! We made it!" Grabbing the huge fluffy (dazzling white and complimentary) dressing grown from the end of his bed he wraps himself up and joins me on the balcony where I'm now gazing out to sea.

"Wow."

And indeed it is a wow moment. The early morning sun is shining down on us across the sea, and we stand there, just lapping up the warmth as the ship moves smoothly onwards.

"Coffee. We need to sit out here with a mug of my extra-special home brew coffee."

So I make it and we do. According to the daily newsletter that was left on my bed last night by Marco, we have a packed day ahead, so it's really a matter of choosing what to fit in and what to leave out.

"I really fancy line dancing in the Atrium at 10. Anything special you want to do? Ooh there's also Cha-cha-cha classes today. I'm thinking you don't want to join me…" I've never seen James dance and never even talked about dancing with him, so I have no idea what kind of reaction I'm going to get, which is a bit scary. Then I remember who I'm with.

"Okay. Can't hurt to give it a go. The line dancing anyway."

Result. "Really?! Cool!" I'm so surprised he's actually agreed that I don't push the Cha-cha in case it spoils the moment. I'm hyper-sensitive to spoiling moments as Mr Charming used to turn to Mr Nasty in a nano-second due to me apparently doing so.

"That's brilliant. I've never done it before but it looks fun. There's a few films on today too, table tennis by the pool – not sure I can fit the yoga in as well as the dance classes though …." Too many options. "And of course we've got to eat, and factor in the time to walk up and down all those stairs. And my hair appointment is at 4, mustn't forget that."

I look up guiltily as I've been hogging the newsletter. James is quietly chuckling at me.

"What?"

"Doing nothing. You've forgotten to schedule in doing nothing." Monster grin. "And sunbathing and reading and swimming."

I smile happily. "True. You do have a point. Isn't it amazing? All this stuff to choose from, and we don't have to do any of it if we don't want to. Not sure I can cope with all the choices."

"I suspect after a few days of this you'll be happy to just flop by the pool like any normal person. Shall we go and explore breakfast? We could try the Lido restaurant – maybe we can sit outside there."

James uses the bathroom while I have a wardrobe crisis. I've just decided on one of my floaty hippy skirts with sparkly pink flip-flops and a vest and a wrap in case it gets chilly, when I realise that particular combo – lovely as it may be – probably isn't any good for line dancing. So the skirt is swapped for some cropped trousers which will look okay with the jazz trainers I cleverly remembered to pack.

By now James needs the changing area so I nip into the bathroom, thinking this cabin sharing is all working out rather well. The bathroom smells gorgeous. James has carefully organised all his man stuff on one side of the sink. Jeez. He's got loads more than me. Never knew a man could use so many products, but then he always looks as if he's just stepped out of the shower and always smells amazing. Guess all that takes effort. Tucking the jazz trainers into my cavernous tote bag bought for the express purpose of carrying 'things' around the ship, I'm now officially ready for business.

"Shall we, Mr McG?"

"I think we should, Miss Powell," opening the door. "Please, after you."

Eight flights of stairs later we're at the Lido restaurant, where cabinets of food seem to extend in every direction. Amidst the general confusion and bustling bodies it's strangely comforting to see a familiar face.

"Hey, Star Trek! How are you?" It's a very tired looking version of our wine waiter from the Pyramid restaurant the night before. Just thinking it's a bit early for wine, even for me, when I realise he's on hand sanitiser duty.

"Madam. It is lovely to see you. Did you have a good evening?"

"Beautiful thank you. So I see you have a day job too?"

The tired eyes twinkle. "Oh yes, Madam, many! Please, help yourself to food from the buffet and sit wherever you choose. There are also tables outside in the sunshine. Enjoy." Having applied sanitiser to our hands he nods us forward so he can get on with the big queue of people behind us.

There is a LOT of food at the buffet, and people seem to be piling an obscene amount of it on their plates, like they're not going to be eating again for a month. People who, TBH, should really be munching on a few lettuce leaves instead. I mean, who needs cake for breakfast? I like the odd croissant, but big, sticky cakes, and waffles with chocolate and maple syrup? Really? Being more into the savoury stuff, I make a bee-line for the bacon and eggs section, where there's a Chinese chef working his socks off making eggs to order. As the fried eggs look a bit chewy I hedge my bets and ask him for a poached egg.

"Of course, Madam, but just the one? Can I make two for you?"

"Ooh, go on then. Just as well I'm line dancing later!"

"Please do go and get the rest of your breakfast and I will have the eggs ready for you in a moment."

I return with a plate laden with mushroom, beans, bacon and tomato and just about find space for the weird shaped poached eggs Chinese Chef has ready for me. They're in little white sacks rather than all spread out like when I cook them. Interesting. Must find out how they do that. Casting around for the tea and coffee area, I see James is already in the queue.

"Shall I grab a table while you get coffee?"

"Er, how the hell will I find you in this?"

"Good point. I'll hover over here."

My hovering point turns out to be the fresh fruit cabinet, which is stuffed with all the fruit I love but can't be arsed to prepare for myself at home. By the time James has the drinks I've managed to accumulate some melon, pineapple and mango on another plate which is precariously balanced at the edge of the tray. It really is heaving in here, but with a bit of clever manoeuvring we manage to escape to the relative peace and quiet of the al fresco dining area at the back.

"Phew. That's a bit of a bun fight. Are you sure you've got enough to eat?"

"Sarcasm will get you nowhere. Where did you find that cheese and ham?"

"I'll only tell if you reveal where you got the fruit."

We chuckle at the ridiculous amount of food on our plates, despite still being full from last night. It's pleasantly warm out here and quite empty. Most of our fellow passengers seem to have stayed inside, probably because they can't carry their groaning trays any further.

A man fights his way through the doors and lays his breakfast out carefully on a table near us. He's just about to sit down when he realises he's forgotten to get a drink. That's a bit of a bugger. I watch as with an irritated sigh he leaves his pretty impressive array of food (and I thought we'd done well) to go back into the fray and fight for a coffee. I've been so involved in the little scene unfolding in front of me that I don't even think to say something to the harassed waiter who starts clearing away the table. They're fast, these guys, and within seconds it's cleared and pristine and ready for a new occupant. I look in panic at James. He's clocked it too, but by the time he's swallowed his mouthful the waiter has turned around to go back to the kitchen, straight into the owner of the disappearing breakfast. We're all shocked into silence.

"That's my food. You've just taken away all my food."

"Sir, I'm so sorry."

"Well, just take it off your tray and give it back to me!"

"I can't, Sir, it will be contaminated by leftovers."

Well that's true, as I can see a half-chewed roll on there too. Euuuw.

"I will go and get another breakfast for you immediately, Sir, I really am so sorry."

By which time the man's drink will be cold... and I can see it unfolding all over again in my mind. But actually the waiter returns almost immediately with what appears to be exactly the same choice of food, and the man is soon happily munching. Amazing. How did he do that?

Our breakfast continues in companionable silence and eventually we both sort of stretch and realise we should at least try to move. Line dancing is in half an hour, down sixteen flights of stairs and at the other end of the ship. We wander back through the pool areas, noting that the back one is definitely busier; it looks like the families from yesterday have set up camp good and early and there's already a lot of high-spirited jumping going on.

On the other hand, the middle pool is much calmer with only a few people dotted around on sun loungers, but they don't pay us any attention as their noses are buried in their Kindles – which is incredibly frustrating as I can't see what they're reading. Which probably explains the rise in housewife porn like *50 Shades of Grey* – nobody can see what anyone's reading. Spoilsports. Give me an old-fashioned book any day.

"I think I'd like to go back there later for a bit of a sunbathe," James is saying, as we find the inner staircase and start the long descent to Reception level.

"Yep, absolutely."

My mind is on the line dancing which I'm really excited about but a bit nervous, as I haven't done it before. I'm glad James is with me, as having done the entertainment job at the holiday park he doesn't get embarrassed about anything. When we finally reach the Atrium it's heaving with people who have either come to dance or just want to sit and watch us all make idiots of ourselves. In fact some of them are sitting right next to the dancefloor, with their feet actually on it. I mean, why? That gives us even less space.

Just changing into my jazz trainers when someone asks me how long I've been dancing. Eek. I tell them it's just jive and I'm new at this, at which they look relieved and say they're new too. I'm discovering the nice thing about cruises is that people actually talk to each other, something I've missed with my solitary existence. And we're all in the same boat (haha!) in that none of us know many people. We squash onto the dance floor and I wonder how on earth this is going to work. How are we not going to tread on each other? The woman next to me asks me to 'move up please' in a stage whisper, to which I reply in a normal voice that I can't as we're all rammed in.

At that moment our teacher appears. A ridiculously immaculate member of the entertainment team, dressed in the sharpest, whitest white shorts I have ever seen in my life bounces up onto the stage, with an ear-splitting, "HALLO everyone! I'm LAURA and it's lovely to meet you. ARE YOU HAVING FUN YET?"

Oh lordy. Please not Butlins. But Laura turns out to be really good fun, especially once I discover she's wearing bright pink trainers and pink and white stripey socks. Anyone who wears pink is okay by me, and I especially like to see a bit of individuality amidst the sea of white. An image of one of those socks getting into the white wash and all the crew ending up wearing pastel pink sneaks playfully into my mind. I'm just about to relay this to James when Laura starts with the first few steps of "The Lemon Tree".

With her back to us she calls down the mike. "SO, everyone. We are taking a step to the RIGHT, then a small step back with the LEFT, then another step to the RIGHT, then cross in front with the LEFT, then a step to the RIGHT, then weight back onto the Left which is called RE-COVER, then cross in front with the RIGHT." She turns around and surveys the crowd. "HAVE WE GOT THAT? So AGAIN everyone…"

It's like a solid mass of people all moving in one direction then back again like a wave on the beach as we return to the starting position and build up the dance. Once I start to relax I realise I'm actually enjoying it – jive seems to have helped and I seem to be picking up the steps quite quickly. The masses descend into confusion once we get to the quarter turn when people seem to have a problem turning to their right. I come face to face with Mrs Grumpy who hisses at me to move up. I hiss back that I can't and that she is facing the wrong way, which doesn't help our budding relationship. After another five walk-throughs we move to the final stage which features POINT, CROSS, POINT, CROSS, POINT, POINT, POINT. Mrs Grumpy has decided to do the whole sequence in a mirror image to me, which means she is pointing and crossing towards me with a vicious look on her face just as I'm moving towards *her*. Some people take this so SERIOUSLY.

At the next walk-through I mutter this to James who instantly swaps places with me. And then to my utter amazement, as soon as she goes wrong he whips her round the other way and guides her into the right steps. Whaaaat?! When did he turn into an expert line dancer? And she LOVES him. She's literally morphed into a giggling teenager. I've noticed that happens a lot actually. When we worked in the bookshop, female customers would often take me to one side and ask 'a bit more about him'. I mean, couldn't they see he's gay?

"SO ARE WE HAVING FUN YET? I CAN'T HEAR YOU!"

I leap up and down like a lunatic, as YES! I am in fact having fun now. We do a full dance through with the music and I feel amazing. With a happy grin on my face I walk back to my Mary Poppins bag and slump down into a chair to change my shoes.

James' new admirer is busily chatting to him over the other side of the floor, but he graciously extricates himself and walks back over to me with a huge grin on his face. "Eee. Just like the old days at the park."

"Well, Mr Golden Bollocks, look at you. That was bloody amazing. So please tell me you taught line dancing in your entertainment job."

"Okay, I taught line dancing in my entertainment job."

"Did you really?"

"No, but I helped with the classes."

"Well strike me down with a feather, you kept that one quiet."

"You never asked."

True. "So are you a closet Latin World champion too? I'm expecting a blinding Cha-cha from you this afternoon."

"Ah, no. Really, honestly haven't done any Latin, but I'll give it a go."

Just look at that. I seem to have a dance partner. This is turning out to my best day ever and it's only 11 o'clock on the first day of the holiday.

Chapter 12

It's 3.30 and I'm just getting out of the shower, which is so much better than mine at home. (How does that work? This is a *ship* for God's sake.) It suddenly dawned on me in the Cha-cha class at 2.30 that if my hair appointment is at 4 o'clock then obvs I need to shower before rather than after, so it's suddenly turned into a bit of a rush. After the line dance class I belted back to get my swimming cozzie on (new) and had some chilled time in the pool and a bit of a sunbathe until lunchtime (yes, more food). James took himself off to explore the ship and even managed to find me again, but then he has a much better sense of direction than I do. TBH I was too scared to move as I can get lost in a brown paper bag, even with a map. The dance class was nuts and very busy, but we loved it. I was glad to see he isn't any better than me, lol. And now he's having some pool time while I get my hair done. We're meeting back in the cabin at 5 o'clock. Hopefully.

I'm going all out with the slinky midnight blue dress Jules lent me as it should look good with Eden's handiwork. It has slashes of silver fanning out into a gorgeous sort of fishtail shape that I worry makes my bum look big but apparently it doesn't. I take comfort in the knowledge that if I look rubbish in it there will be no witnesses to tell on me apart from James, who I can definitely trust not to take the piss out of me at some point in the future. I'm cautiously excited because it's so long since I've been to a really posh evening out, and my personal history on that front hasn't been great, but also a touch nervous as I've only had my hair chopped around a bit by friends in the last couple of years, so it's probably a real mess.

Having navigated my way to the Spa successfully, I find Mia waiting in reception. Giving me a warm hug she leads me into the salon, which is really busy; only to be expected I guess, with it being the Captain's Reception for half the ship – the other half have theirs tomorrow night.

"I am *so* looking forward to this. Your hair's amazing and it will be a welcome change from the usual clientele." She gives a subtle wink and nods at a row of older ladies in various stages of being cut-and-blow-dried.

"Now. Do you trust me to make you look un-put-downable and completely gorgeous?"

Gulp. "Er – yes! Even better, can you find someone who doesn't want to put me down?"

"I will do my absolute best," she grins at me. "You never can tell on a ship this size. Now I know we only booked a wash and blow-dry but there's a serious bit of sorting out to be done here, so I'm just going ahead with it, okay?"

Just as I suspected then. Hair has been the last thing on my mind for ages. I'd sort of stopped making the effort as there wasn't anyone to notice whether I did or not, so I really don't look in the mirror that much anymore.

Over at the basin I'm busy appreciating just how nice it is to have someone else wash my hair. TBH I just whack shampoo and conditioner on in the shower, and that's it. Job done. This experience is something else completely.

"I'm using a nutrient mask that I'm supposed to try and sell you but I'm not going to, because I just want to make you look lovely and not bankrupt you on the first day."

Aw. That's sweet. The massage she's giving me is amazing, and I realise how tight my scalp is. Aaaaah.

Back in front of the mirror now, we chat away as Mia snips and I discover she met James at a private gym he goes to in London. Ah, so that's how he looks so good. He kept that quiet too. She tells me she got very bored with having the same clients all the time and when a friend of hers left to work on cruise ships, she decided to give it a go as well.

"Yes, it's hard, being away from home, but I'm honestly having such a good time. I don't have a boyfriend or kids or anything, so why not? When I've seen as much of the world as I can, I'll be ready to go back and settle down as the wanderlust will have been satisfied. Probably."

"It does seem an exotic lifestyle. Is it really? Do you get much time off? Are you allowed to have relationships on board?"

"There's no rule about having relationships with each other, just not with the guests. The main thing to realise is that it's all temporary, although some people do stay together and end up working on the same ship. We're a lot better off than some of the crew though. The catering and housekeeping staff work so incredibly hard, but, and I have to say this carefully, they have different reasons for being on the ship. People like me have come on for a good time, and when that good time comes to an end or I get bored or I miss home too much, I'll leave. They usually have families back in India, or the Philippines, and although their wages seem meagre compared to ours, they are wealthy in local terms. Yes, they're away from their families for nine months at a time, but the money they send back seems to more than make up for their absence."

"That doesn't surprise me, because although we've only been on here for just over 24 hours (really?!) I've already noticed that different nationalities seem to do different jobs. And some of them look so tired. Like our wine waiter from last night was on sanitiser duty this morning. Do they get much time off?"

"If they get all their work done first – like cleaning their allocated cabins – they can go ashore on port days. On sea days nobody gets any time off. Especially the entertainment crew, who are at it all day and all night."

"Oh, we did line dancing today, and Laura was amazing! I had SO much fun. At first I was thinking, oh God no, this is like Butlins, but she won everyone over except for the old bat who was next to me. But that was okay too as James sorted her out."

"Good. And yes, Laura is a sweetie. Always bubbly and always amazing. Don't know how she does it. Don't know how any of them do it – they don't seem to have an 'off' switch in the entertainments team. Maybe that's a prerequisite for the job!"

Mia puts down her scissors and ruffles gently through my hair. I've been too busy chatting to notice exactly what she's been doing but, hey, hair grows, doesn't it? No biggie if it's a bit short for a while.

"Trust me?"

"Well, I guess the photographer will be around tonight, so I'm sure you want me to promote your skills." I'm grinning.

"Absolutely! So. Are you looking forward to the Reception and meeting the Captain and having a really posh night out?"

Oooh. Gulp. Surprisingly difficult question. It must have shown on my face.

"Sorry. Didn't mean to intrude."

"Um, no. Really. There have been times when, possibly, the effort I made wasn't appreciated. Or, maybe appreciated by the wrong people. According to the person I was with. Or maybe the person I was doing it for didn't care." I'm gabbling. "Or I thought the posh night out was brilliant right up to the point when I got home. When suddenly it wasn't. Apparently."

Suddenly there are hot tears pricking my eyes. Shit.

"Ah sweetheart. That sounds horrible. So the fact that you're here with James means you escaped from that particular situation. Good. You are worth so much more than that."

How do hairdressers do that? They fanny around with your hair at the same time as asking what appears to be a really simple question and somehow find out what's going on inside your head too.

Surprisingly, I want to talk about it, tears or no tears.

"Everything seemed to be great in the beginning. Then there were little things, like a sulky silence because I'd done something he didn't like and I hadn't realised it. Or I didn't notice if he actually did something useful, like the washing up. Or if I was wearing the wrong thing, which didn't co-ordinate with him. So I tried to make sure I did the right thing all the time as I couldn't stand the silences. Then the silences turned into raging outbursts. I mean, not physically, just shouting at me for things he'd twisted to make out I had done something wrong. Like ignoring him when I wasn't, or apparently being really 'up myself' and thinking I was amazing and he was shit. Which never happened – as far as I remember. He really messed with my head, so I never knew where I was. So we'd be all done up to go out on a night like tonight and he'd be okay, then at some point during the evening he'd suddenly change, and not look at me or talk to me. So I'd be completely wound up wondering what I'd done, and then when we got home, all hell would break loose and he would just scream and scream at me, and I used to worry I'd be thrown out of my flat as the neighbours would complain. Sorry. Didn't mean for all that to come out." It did feel good though.

Mia is gently moulding my usually frizzy hair into corkscrew curls. Amazing what an expert can do.

"No wonder you're a bit apprehensive about tonight. Thing is, people like that get into your mind and then you start to believe everything is your fault, when in fact it's them that are warped and twisted. And you know what? They are actually sick – you can't heal them."

"Oh, God, yes. That too. He'd had a horrible, unloving home life, so I wanted to make him feel safe and secure and happy and give him all the things he hadn't had. Even like cuddles. His mum never cuddled him. How sad is that? But that was wrong too as he told me to stop touching him all the time. Or I wasn't holding his hand right."

"Yes, it *is* sad, but relationships are supposed to be equal, aren't they? It's not about being a therapist for your partner, is it? Because if you're busy looking after him, who's looking after you? Ooh hark at me!"

Mia laughs as she pulls and curls my hair round her fingers as I watch, mesmerised. I would never in a million years have thought a) my hair could look like this and b) that I'd be pouring my heart out to a hairdresser on a cruise ship.

"You sound like you know what you're talking about."

"I'm just interested in people, to be honest. Doing this job gets me talking to all sorts about all kinds of stuff. And for some reason, hairdressing opens up something. Guess because for women it's more about self-esteem than the actual hairstyle. I bet if you put identical women with identical hairstyles together, the one who is standing in her power will look a million times better than the one who isn't. That's my pet theory, anyway, so if I can help my clients by listening and maybe discussing things, then I think I've done a good job. And hopefully their hair looks better too. Haha. Sure beats asking what you do for a living. So anyway, what *do* you do for a living?"

She's brilliant and I absolutely crack up.

"Well, this is the ridiculous irony. I'm an editor, slash, ghost writer for a publisher of women's romance novels."

"You're kidding me. So life isn't exactly imitating art here, is it?"

"Hardly. If only!"

Mia stands back from the chair, arms folded, a huge grin on her face.

"Oh my God. How the hell do I do this for myself? It's amazing. *You're* amazing." I've been so busy unloading my troubles that I really didn't notice what she was doing

The person sitting in front of the mirror, which at the last check was me, has gorgeous corkscrew curls cascading round her face and down her back. I'm speechless.

"You go out there and rock it, girl. You're nothing short of beautiful."

We have big hugs, a few snuffly tears of gratitude (me), and I bounce my way back to the cabin.

James looks up from his reading as I open the door. "Holy fuck. That was definitely one of my better ideas. You look like the girl from *Brave*. Did you have a good time?"

"A-maz-ing! She's like a therapist, as well as being a brilliant hairdresser. I can't believe she got my hair to look like this." I spin around in front of the mirror with delight. "And she got me talking about stuff I've kept bottled up for years."

"Yeah, she's good like that. She used to work in the salon at the gym I go to and there was always a waiting list for appointments with her. Her clients were gutted when she left."

"I bet. She just seemed to get right inside my head and I ended up telling her loads about what happened with You-Know-Who and she understood straight away. And she also made me realise that it wasn't my fault. That's the trouble, people like him make you feel it's all your fault. But I don't want to think about him now because I'm all cheered up and ready to rock. How was your sunbathing?"

"Yeah – really good. Nice to sit quietly and just read. It's been a busy couple of days! I'm all showered and ready to get changed. Shall we go for it?"

"Yes indeed. I'll go and make myself smell gorgeous and totally irresistible while you get dressed."

Once in the bathroom, I whirl round again a few times, chuckling quietly to myself. Who'd have thought I could have hair like this? Double wowza. And I like what Mia said about women being in their power – it sounds strong, and grounded and all the things I haven't been while I've been busy wallowing in how bad it's all been. A bit more weight tumbles from my shoulders as I realise it doesn't have to be that way any more. Which is of course what people like Jules have been telling me for ages. But maybe it needed a complete stranger and a fabulous hair makeover to make me realise it.

So James, of course, looks film-star stunning, but to be honest, I wouldn't expect any less of him. He always scrubs up well and this evening he has excelled himself. His rich golden hair is gelled into little peaks and the little bit of sun he caught today brings a glow to his cheeks, which sets off his dress shirt, which must be new to be so incredibly white. His dinner suit is spotless and his bow tie matches the dark blue of my dress. Heaven knows how he managed that one.

"You look just *gaw-jus,* sweetie. Maybe now you'll start to have some faith in yourself. Just wait until that photographer sees you!"

"Or you!" I reply. "We don't know yet, do we?

Chapter 13

We're taking a graceful (that means slow on account of my shoes) walk down the stairs rather than wait for the lifts, which all have massive queues. Presumably other people's shoes are uncomfortable too and they're just more sensible than me. Whatever. Anyway, I'm enjoying swishing along feeling like a million dollars. Jules' dress does in fact look amazing with my nails and James has assured me my bum doesn't look big in it, so I'm allowing the fledgling nub of genuine excitement to grow. As we get closer to the Atrium the noise level increases. I was worried we'd be early, but in fact we're far from it. Happy cruisers are wandering in and out of the Duty Free shops in their posh togs, clutching glasses of wine and bubbly. Now that's the way to shop. A waiter passes by with a tray of red and white wine, so I say, "Don't mind if I do," and we join them. Mrs Grumpy and her husband are loitering by the expensive-looking designer handbags, and she literally can't take her eyes off James.

"Thank you so much for your help today. Will you be doing the class tomorrow?"

"You're more than welcome. And that probably depends on the hangover, actually." He turns to look at me, grinning. "Doesn't it?"

"Cheers to that one!" I say, taking a slurp of wine, and we all laugh; and find out this is their fifteenth cruise which is to celebrate their fortieth wedding anniversary but that the service isn't as good as it was before and the food portions are smaller and that the cruise lines are cutting corners and costs now by doing things like spending less time in the ports. Crikey. I'm sure she must have a happier side buried somewhere in there. I hope so for Mr Grumpy's sake. It's all getting a bit intense when fortunately we spot the queue to have a photo taken with the Captain, and make our excuses (they don't get their photo taken any more as it's all too expensive and a rip off), and go over to join it. The Captain seems a jovial kind of chap, and our time in the queue passes swiftly due to a) being kept topped up by exceedingly attentive wine waiters, b) watching Drop-Dead-Gorgeous photographer tease people into flattering poses for their pictures and c) wondering what the hell we're going to say to the Captain as I'm rubbish at small talk. James, however, isn't, so I'm relying heavily on him.

An exceedingly glamorous lady wearing a name badge which includes the words 'Cruise Director' (the rest is too small to read) bears down on us and asks our names to present us to Captain Fernbank. And I am stunned that she remembers them correctly when she does so. The Captain shakes our hands and asks if it's our first cruise and we all turn to DDG photographer and pose and smile, and then move on swiftly so he can meet the hundreds of people queueing up behind us – so it's over in seconds, which is a big relief. Oh good, they're bringing out the canapés now. This wine is making me really hungry.

After a bit of a mooch around the shops where I spot a watch I quite like, there is an announcement that the Captain is about to start his speech. The Atrium opens out so that there are actually two floors looking down on it, and they are all crammed with people waiting for him to start. No pressure then. But it turns out that Captains don't just steer the ship – this one is going to have a fabulous career as an after-dinner speaker when he retires. He gives us some facts about how many passengers and crew there are and that there will be three weddings and a renewal of vows during our cruise and that it will mostly be 'the youngsters' sailing the ship as he likes to let them have a bit of a go, but that he will be on hand for any tight three point turns should the need arise. What a wag. Apparently the Bay of Biscay is still as a millpond and the Med is hot, so we are all set for a lovely holiday. Then he finishes by bringing on the heads of the various departments all of whom look freshly pressed and sparkling white, and some of whom look frankly scary. I wouldn't want to get on the wrong side of the Housekeeping manager for instance. He is tall, Nordic-looking, with piercing eyes (can't tell the colour from here but I bet they are icy blue) and his level of immaculate-ness makes the rest of the immaculate crew look scruffy. Eek. I can imagine the cabin stewards hiding behind the door when they hear him coming.

I manage to snag another glass of the surprisingly acceptable wine just as the waiters are starting to clear away, and notice that a crocodile of people are moving towards the lifts and stairs in a kind of slow-mo rugby scrum to get to the restaurants. They're obviously worried the food will run out as they're not hanging around either.

I lean in so James can hear me. "Are we going to join the stampede to get our buzzer, or shall we wait for a bit?"

"I'm thinking we should probably get a buzzer, or you risk falling into your food if you continue at this rate."

"I have NEVER fallen into my food...."

James is nodding slowly and I think that oops, I may have had one too many a couple of times in the past. And it would be sad not to see Mrs Grumpy's eyes light up when she sees James tomorrow morning at line dance class. And there is a real danger of that if I do in fact carry on drinking at this rate.

"C'mon then, Captain Sensible," I say, cradling my last free glass of wine. It's the 'free' bit that does it for me, I think. I mean, why not take advantage of it while it's there? I pick my way carefully to the stairs (obvs the lifts are heaving with people who have apparently lost the ability to walk; mind you, who's talking?) and negotiate them with only a small stumble or two.

We're greeted at the restaurant desk by Franko, the charming maître d' who remembers us from last night, which is an impressive touch. How do they do that? Do these people have photographic memories or something?

"Good evening Madam, Sir. A table for two again?"

"Oh, yes please. Will we have much of a wait?" I'm seriously hungry now.

"Actually no. Most people are dining in groups so there is already a table free. You were with Sebastian last night, yes? Well you are in his area again." And with that we're led through the sea of black dinner suits and gorgeous evening gowns to the same table as last night – yay! I liked those guys.

Sebastian is with us in moments, wielding tonight's menu. He stands in front of the table with a twinkling smile, and looking at me, declares, "Madam, I have to say you are looking spectacular this evening. I will leave you to look at the menu." And then he's gone.

"Haha. Mia's bribed him..."

"Cynic. It might actually be that he's telling the truth, you know. The dress is amazing and you're kind of glowing – although that might be the wine. Joking. Whatever Mia said to you has worked wonders. Long may it continue!"

We go to raise our glasses but find that my free one is now empty so we clink our empty water glasses. This brings Star Trek belting over, bearing our bottles of wine from last night. He looks even more tired, were it possible.

"Madam, Sir, have you had a good day?"

"Yes, lovely thank you. But what about you? Did you have any time off?"

"No Madam, not on a sea day. There is much to be done. But I am fine and I will be going off the ship at Malaga for a few hours with some of my friends. Please, enjoy your wine and just ask for me if you need more."

Totally in my head, as I clearly didn't leave *quite* as much last night as I thought I had.

"A photograph of you both perhaps? Be a shame not to." It's DDG photographer, who has appeared at my side as if by magic. I raise an eyebrow at James.

"Yep, I think we should just to record the hairdo if nothing else." James comes round to my side and squats down next to me, his gorgeous aftershave wafting over me. Haha. As I realise what I'm thinking, I wonder whether I've been working on Ivy's books for too long. But he does smell pretty special. I whisper it in his ear, and just as he turns to grin at me DDG gets the shot.

"Oh, stunning. That's gonna be a keeper." Then he winks at us/me/ James and goes off to the next table.

James is back at his seat now and we giggle at what's just happened.

"He's definitely one of yours. He was flirting with you."

"Never, it was you he was winking at because of your hair."

"We are gonna have to find out. We could ask Mia – aw thanks!" Our main courses have arrived, which I'm looking forward to as the starter didn't touch the sides. Well, I think it's the main course. My 'salmon' is actually about five flakes carefully balanced on something green, and there's a matching sauce and a tiny dollop of what should be dauphinois potatoes. And, well, that's it. But I'm still really hungry.

Sebastian is by my side in an instant, as if he's been watching my thoughts unfurl. "Is everything alright, Madam?"

"Um, there doesn't seem to be much here. Any chance of a big pile of veg or something as well?"

He snaps his fingers and another waiter scurries up. "A bowl of green vegetables for this table please. Now." Turning to me, "Madam, it is no problem at all. We will make sure you get a bowl of freshly cooked vegetables every night."

And he's away to the table next to us where another couple have just taken their seats. The man looks like a retired academic – bristly eyebrows and glasses – and Wifey looks scared of her own shadow. Interesting. Cruises are so good for people-watching. Star Trek approaches their table with the wine menu but is briskly waved away.

I try to eat really slowly, but I've nearly finished the last mouthful of this five-bite dish by the time the waiter returns with a big bowl of broccoli and green beans. His arrival is followed immediately by Sebastian who whisks away my empty plate and replaces it with another portion of salmon, all in one smooth movement.

"Aw, crikey! Thank you!"

He grins and belts away, having probably spent too much time on us already.

"Jeez. Think I might have to treat you to another session with Mia! They're falling at your feet. Totally brilliant. I love it. Don't you?"

I'm still in shock at all the attention. It's been quite a day, and the conversation with Mia has opened up places in my mind that haven't seen the light of day for a very long time.

"You deserve all this, so don't go telling me you don't."

"Um... thanks, but I'm a bit on edge – like the bubble's going to burst. Don't you mind?"

"Mind? Of course I don't mind! Why would I mind?"

"Because they aren't paying attention to you? And you're looking pretty gorgeous, too."

"Well, firstly, I don't want the attention, and secondly, thank you for noticing. I do try to make an effort," he grinned.

Star Trek has appeared to investigate our wine status, and we decide we do in fact want more. This carrying it over to the next evening malarky is most handy.

"Why don't you want the attention? Mr Nasty always did."

"He was an insecure idiot. Strong men don't need to put a woman down to make themselves feel good. Truly strong men rejoice in having a strong woman by their side, and do all they can to support her. What?!"

Over to my left I'm aware that Wifey may have overheard that comment so I lower my voice a touch, and indicate the same to James.

"You've really changed since you went to London. In a good way. I mean, you're much calmer. And wiser. And sort of quieter inside. Thanks, Star Trek – brilliant."

Wine glass duly topped up, I carry on. "But what's been going on?"

"Life, I guess. It's become more important to me to be with the right person rather than just putting myself out there so I appear to be having a good time. Which isn't really a good time at all. It just leaves me feeling empty and lonely – and a little bit used. I didn't choose to be this way, but I am, and I have to find a way of dealing with it. They say nobody is 100% straight or 100% gay, and I guess the percentage of me that is straight craves what a regular straight guy would also want."

"You know I never heard that percentage thing before. But have you talked to any of your friends about this?"

"God, no. At least, not the gay ones. They would throw up their hands in horror that I'm not proud to be gay. I'm not. I'm a man who happens to be gay – I don't need to wear it like a badge."

I don't think we've ever gone this deep before, and I'm not sure it's sitting well with Mr Academic, who has just shot a look in our general direction. Where is crazy James? The party-loving animal who used to get completely rat-arsed, then fall totally head-over-heels for somebody, only to be cruelly cast aside in the blink of an eye.

"So – okay. What would be special about 'the right person' for you? Which part of the percentage would they fit into?"

"Doesn't matter. Their mind and personality would be more important than their gender."

"So if those two factors are right, you don't mind whether it's a man or a woman?"

"No. Although I haven't actually had a relationship with a woman, I wouldn't rule it out if I was attracted to her and the chemistry was good. In fact it would be quite a learning experience as I'm not sure how all the bits fit together."

I can't believe we're talking about the merits of straight and gay sex over dinner. "Um, didn't you do sex education at school?" I can't help noticing that Mr Academic and Wifey, who hadn't even been making eye contact up until now, are having a very hissy and intense kind of conversation.

"Yes, but having only been with men, it looks a lot more complicated with women. I mean, bits get in the way and stuff, don't they?"

Sebastian approaches with my pineapple brulée. James went for good old-fashioned apple crumble because he's still got a bit of space left. I'm quite glad of the diversion as I'm not really sure how to respond to his comment. Well, not in polite company anyway.

"It occurs to me that if it's the right person you could have a lot of fun finding out!" I grin widely. "Because good relationships are all about exploring each other and helping each other grow, aren't they?"

James snorts into his wine and nearly chokes, which lightens the atmosphere considerably.

"You have got such a smutty mind."

"I know. I like to think it's one of my better traits."

At which point Mr Academic rises to his feet, throws down his napkin and stomps off. Wifey gets up too, gives me a sneaky thumbs-up and a grin, then follows along in his wake. Oops.

We stare at each other in astonishment then collapse into giggles. I'd quite like to come back to this restaurant so I try to get myself under control. "OK, peppermint tea or more wine?"

"Ahhmmm. More wine. Definitely. Can't imagine what we could have said to upset them."

"Stop it. I'm trying to behave." Star Trek appears to be otherwise engaged, so I top up both glasses. "Shall we have a wander? See who else we can upset? How about the Sky Bar right at the top? That looked amazing. If we take our wine up there it'll save us buying more."

It turns out we have to transfer our drinks into a different sort of glass if we want to take them away as these are for restaurant use only, and having done so we head on our merry way up to the very top of the ship. On this occasion (and only on this occasion) I give in and take the lift (much to James' delight), as I've possibly had a wee bit too much to drink to walk safely up around twenty flights of stairs in these heels, especially carrying a glass of wine. Not a good combo. It looks as though everyone else in the lift has the same idea, as they too are clutching their wine. At least I don't feel such an alcoholic cheapskate.

The Sky Bar is fabulous. We find seats in a corner, away from the lights of the bar, and spend a while quietly absorbing the events of the day and gazing out of the huge plate glass windows into the endless darkness beyond.

I haven't laughed so much and had such a good time in a long while. All is good.

Chapter 14

Ow. Blargh, mouth like the bottom of a budgie's cage.

Later.... Ow. BIG headache. Why did I do that? I open my eyes very carefully. I'm facing James' bed which is empty and the cabin is very quiet. Turning over ever so gently I can see the balcony and James isn't on it.   Oh.

Even later, I hear the cabin door open and panic that it's Marco come to tidy the cabin. But no, it's a very fresh and smiling James, bearing a tray, bless him.

"Thought you might need a bit of Vitamin C to get you going today, so I got pineapple, melon, orange and mango. And a freshly-baked croissant to go with the coffee I'm going to make us. And Star Trek was on sanitiser patrol again. He asked after you and I said you were having a lazy morning. Hope that's right?"

"JamesJamesJamesJames. James. You are totally wonderful! Did anyone ever tell you that? Well even if they did, I am even more appreciative than they could possibly have been." I haul myself up in bed and realise I'm still wearing my underwear from last night. I look down at my bra and up at him.

"You were having a bit of difficulty getting the dress off, so I helped you. It's hanging up safely in the wardrobe. Didn't think I should get any further involved," waggling his eyebrows and grinning.

"What a gent. Thank you. Was I really that bad?"

"No. Well, yes, as in not being able to get undressed very successfully. But not badly behaved. Promise. Why don't you get your dressing gown on and sit on the balcony? I'll bring the food out."

I blow him a kiss and go out onto the balcony where I instantly realise it's way too hot to be wearing my big white fluffy complimentary dressing gown. Take two, only with bikini and sarong is much more comfortable. The sun is shining straight onto us and as it's already quite high in the sky, time must be cracking on. Well, the line dancing was never going to happen for me today, but I thought James wanted to go.

"No, not bothered. Mrs Grumpy would eat me alive. Anyway, it'll be nearly finished now."

Blimey. I never sleep this late. But 'sleep' is a pretty loose description. More like passed out. We spend the rest of the morning on the sun-kissed balcony, in a pleasant coffee-enhanced blur along with the odd vat of water to relieve my dehydration. James had sufficient grey cells left to think of putting the 'Do Not Disturb' sign on the door so we're left in peace, and it really is peace. It's just what the doctor ordered and by lunchtime I'm starting to feel a bit more human. As the sun moves off the balcony we take our swimming stuff up with us to lunch in the Lido so we can stay by the pool afterwards. And yes, I do climb the stairs but it is a slow and delicate process.

It's pretty busy by the middle pool, so James leads me up the maze of outside stairways he discovered on his wanderings, until we are virtually at the top of the ship, where there's a terrace of completely unoccupied sun loungers. Bliss. I spend the afternoon reading then sleeping then reading again until I'm so hot I have to go down all those stairs to the middle pool for a swim.

I'm having a hair crisis. My beautiful curls are still in place and I don't want to waste Mia's work by putting my head under the water and swimming properly, which is what I would usually do. Nothing for it – gathering it up into one of the million or so scrunchies I usually have about my person it ends up more of a 'lunchtime swim' with my head above the water – there's no way I'm ruining this hairdo. Should be able to get at least another evening out of it.

Pootling back and forth across the pool it seems like most people have cleared off and it's gloriously peaceful down here. I guess because tonight is part two of the Captain's Reception, and they're off getting prettied up for the main event. Must admit I fancy trying the Lido for the evening meal tonight. It's lovely having Sebastian and everything but I'm still slightly in recovery from last night and thus in need of a bit more peace and quiet. And I'm definitely not over-indulging in the happy juice tonight. In fact I might even abstain completely. Hah! Really? Sometimes even I can't take myself seriously.

Pootling finished, I drip up the outside stairs all the way back to James, who is peacefully sleeping with his book on his face. Ahh. Sweet. I flop down on the lounger and stretch out to dry off in the sun, my absolute favourite thing.

I'm just turning over to dry my back when a shadow falls across the sun lounger. A waitress bearing a big smile and an empty tray has climbed all the way up here to see whether she can get us anything. We have water in my Mary Poppins bag, so I am about to be good and say no, but thank you, when James wakes up and says he fancies a cold beer. So on the basis that he shouldn't be drinking alone, I order a large glass of Chardonnay – which I think is very public-spirited of us, as otherwise she would have climbed all this way for nothing. But then, because we *have* ordered something, she has to go all the way down then all the way up again. So maybe we haven't done her a favour at all. Sometimes life seems so complicated.

It's amazing up here. Our drinks arrive and we say "Cheers" and sit contemplating the empty and endless horizon for a few moments.

"You know the waitress that just came up here?"

"Yes."

"Do you think it would have been better if we'd have gone down to the pool bar to get a drink? Then she wouldn't have had to climb all the way up here, and then down and then up again."

"It's her job, Cait."

"Yes, but we could have helped her by not ordering. I mean, hindsight is a wonderful thing but if it happens again I might refuse."

James looks at me, shaking his head. "It's her *job* to come up and see whether we want a drink. She would only find out if there's anyone up here by coming up here. Yes? And then by coming up here maybe she gets lots of orders from other people, so lots of brownie points, and possibly a good tip. Do you spend a lot of time worrying about this kind of stuff?"

"Well, yes, pretty much. I like to be considerate. I mean those waiters must get so tired. And hot."

"You know, I think that's really sweet, but I can also see how it might lead to you totally compromising what you want just to make someone else happy. And you don't even know you're right. Maybe she likes walking around up here because it's away from everyone else. Maybe she likes the exercise 'cos it keeps her fit. She looked pretty fit to me."

Shaking my head, I grin at him. "Nothing wrong with your powers of perception – for either sex!"

"Haha. Just sayin.'"

We chuckle and sit in companionable silence for a while. It's completely quiet up here and the movement of the ship is having an almost hypnotic effect on me. Or maybe that's the wine. I think it could also be a tiny bit too much sun as my skin is kind of prickly. It's lovely having auburny highlights in my hair, but the down side is burning to a frazzle pretty quickly if I don't whack the factor 30 on. Which I didn't.

James sits up on his lounger. "I think I have a solution."

"To what?"

"The Waitress Problem. If we go down to the nearly empty pool we will be near the bar and the jacuzzi, which I really fancy. Yes? And then if we happen to decide we want another drink she won't have to schlep all the way up here, will they?"

"Clever man. Come on then." My glass appears to be empty, but honouring my earlier thoughts I bring it down with me so someone doesn't have to climb all those stairs to collect it. And funnily enough, about halfway down the long flights of endless steps we pass our waitress again.

"Hi there. We've brought our glasses down with us, and it's empty up there – just in case it saves you a trip." Luisa (I clock the name badge) smiles sweetly and thanks us, saying she really appreciates it. So it's always worth thinking these things through to the end, isn't it?

In fact both pools are empty so we go to the back one which is still getting the sun. Thankfully, the Illegal Jumpers have been taken off to tea or whatever they do at this time, so we have the place to ourselves. Despite my best intentions I find myself sitting in the jacuzzi, a fresh glass of Chardonnay carefully placed on the ledge beside me. This is, in fact, the life.

"I'm still having to pinch myself that we're here, you know. Thank you so much, again, for organising this. If you get bored of me saying that, just throw something. I feel like the cat that's got the cream."

"Haha. So do I. Mia said we'd love it, but I didn't realise just how much. We have another sea day tomorrow, then we get to the first port – Malaga. Do you want to do a trip or shall we just wander? Actually it probably depends on what's left. How's your Spanish?"

"Absolutely non-existent, but I would imagine there will be more Brits than Spanish people, it being ex-pat heaven. We could have a look once we're changed – I think they have the excursions on one of the TV channels. But I don't mind either way, to be honest."

"Ooh, look! A library!"

I drag James over. A proper old-fashioned library on a ship. Who'd have thought it? We're on our way to the Excursion Desk, but I am completely side-tracked by this vision of peace, this gorgeous room filled with wooden bookcases and squishy chairs. I am rendered helpless in the presence of books. Even though I've worked in a bookshop and my day job is ghost-writing, I am physically incapable of walking past a bookshop without going in. Which isn't that often, actually, as they're closing down at an alarming rate or turning into gift shops with a token bookshelf lobbed in a corner. Viva Amazon! Anyway, it's very rare to see somewhere as beautifully laid out as this little treasure.

Within moments I'm scanning the shelves and have picked out several new biographies I've been lusting after, and I can't resist going looking for Ivy's books, as James has heard about them but never actually seen one. And there they are – well – two of them. Good to know they're getting into such places. Snatching them excitedly from the shelf and sidling across to James – who's got his nose buried in a horror story or something blokey – I give him a prod, which he ignores. There is a rule of SILENCE PLEASE in here, so having prodded him again and finally got his attention, I point at the books and point at myself and nod vigorously.

He looks at me, looks at the books, shrugs at me and mimes, "What?"

I point again at the books and me, with a big grin on my face.

With a completely straight face he shrugs his shoulders again and shakes his head, so I smack him in the stomach hard because he's deliberately winding me up. Somebody clears their throat very loudly next to my right hip and I look down to see Mr Academic frowning up at me. I guess it's one more penalty and I'm out, lol.

Our 'Highlights of Malaga' excursion successfully booked, we wander out into the Atrium and I get a massive sense of déjà vu as it's thronged with people in their posh togs and waiters circulating with trays of wine because we have caught the tail-end of the Captain's speech. I successfully snaffle a red and a white – result! – and then remember that our photos should be out on display somewhere on this floor in the photo gallery. Clutching our glasses we make our way through the Art Gallery, the Speak Easy Bar, past a 'pay extra' restaurant and then finally discover the wall of photos, all neatly labelled with arrival times on check-in day, then the Sailaway, then the Captain's Reception.

"Aw. I like this one. Don't we look excited?" I'm jigging about in front of the first photo. We do look incredibly good together and very cool, even if I say so myself. "Might have to have that one."

James has clocked it and moved further down the display. "And how about this? The Sailaway picture looks good too. Shall we have it?"

"Aw, yes!" And I leapfrog past him to the Captain's Reception. The picture with the Captain is kind of okay, but what I'm really excited about is the one of us at dinner. It is unspeakably gorgeous because DDG photographer absolutely caught the moment when I whispered to James.

"Woah. Look at us!"

James comes over. "Wow. We scrub up well, don't we? And your hair..."

"... is truly amazing," chips in DDG photographer who is obviously free of his Captain's Reception duties and is now standing behind us. If this was one of Ivy's books she would have the characters whirling around to face the intruder into their private moment, and that's exactly what we did. We were literally in our own world, marvelling at the way he'd caught the mood.

"I'm quite proud of that one – I said it was good at the time, didn't I?"

No ego in this one, obvs.

"You just have to wait for the shot, then – bang – there it is," he adds, looking at me and winking.

A slight flush rises in my cheeks at his brazen flirting, then, bugger me, he turns to James, and pushing him slightly on the shoulder, says, "And mate, you need to go into modelling. Come over to the desk if you want to buy them and I'll give you a bit of a discount." And wanders off, leaving us flushed (me) and open-mouthed (James) to talk to some other passengers.

"Fuck me, maybe he wants a threesome." James recovers faster than I do and is now grinning at me. I look around anxiously in case there are any fellow passengers close enough to upset. He raises his eyebrows at me.

"Don't even think of going there. That's just plain weird, I mean what's wrong with just two people? Everyone knows three is a crowd, so there's always going to be someone...STOP IT. You will NOT lure me into THAT kind of a conversation in public again. In fact you are so naughty you need to get me some more wine to make up for it."

That worked out well, as we now have several people staring at us. Blushing furiously (me, again) and laughing his head off (James) we exit the photo gallery before we get thrown out.

"You know, considering the inauspicious start, it really has been an amazing day."

We're up in the Sky bar again, which I suspect may become our favourite evening haunt.

"Do you think they'll let us back in the restaurant tomorrow night, now we've given them a break? Not sure I like the Lido in the evening."

That said, the plus side is that in helping oneself from the buffet one can obviously take massive portions, which one might just have done with the curry.

James stretches and yawns. "Reckon so. I like it better too. And after such an exciting day, I'm ready for bed. Must be all that sea air!"

"Well it certainly isn't the exercise! Tomorrow I'm definitely doing the line dance class and whatever the other one is. And walking round the promenade deck." Yeah, I know I said it before, but let's just see. Tomorrow's another day.

Chapter 15

Final day at sea – Yay!

I like being on the ship, but even I'm looking forward to a change of scenery. We've got a table at the back of the Lido and are enjoying breakfast outside, not a million miles away from where we witnessed the disappearing breakfast episode on the first morning. James is off to get coffee top-ups and I'm revelling in the sunshine, which is really hot now, even though it's only around 9. A good slather of after-sun lotion last night helped my redder-than-they-should-be bits, and some sun block today should see me through without too much discomfort, although I'm possibly not going to laze in it all day. Maybe a dance class or even a run in the gym if I can stir myself... I'm jolted from my reverie by someone apologising as they nearly trip over my Mary Poppins bag.

I look up and apologise, then realise it's Mr Disappearing Breakfast.

"Oh, hi! No worries, it's my fault. Sorry! Massive bag. Have you got your drink this time? If not, I promise I will defend your breakfast better than last time."

Mr Disappearing Breakfast looks slightly puzzled, then laughs.

"Oh, it was you! Yes, that was funny. Although I didn't think so at the time. And yes, thank you, I do have my coffee. I think I'm getting a bit better organised." He puts his tray down on a nearby table then comes over, extending his hand. "I'm Nick, by the way."

"Caitlin. Oh and this is James," as he returns to the table with our coffees.

They shake hands, then Nick says, "My wife Sarah might turn up shortly. Or she might not. She's in the gym, so it's anyone's guess. Hence me learning to manage my food on my own." Tight smile. Hmm.

James doesn't seem to notice. "Ah, good to meet you Nick. If you need anything, anything at all, like your breakfast looking after, you couldn't be in safer hands."

We all laugh and chat for a bit across the tables, then Nick retreats to his breakfast and his book and we discuss our plans.

"So, are you line dancing today? Haven't seen Mrs Grumpy around, so you might be safe."

James pauses. "Hmm. Yes, I'll come to that, but I'm not bothered about the waltz class. Do you mind? Honestly not interested in that sort of dancing. I'll just mooch by the pool or something if you want to go."

"Yep, no worries. I'm really happy on my own – and I'm a bit burnt after yesterday, so staying out of the sun would be good. And it would help to shift a bit of the weight I must be putting on. Dad said it was four pounds a day on average, but I think I must be over that already."

"Stop obsessing about your weight. If you just concentrate on relaxing and having a good time, you'll be fine."

"Yeah – happy and FAT! I don't think I could do more than two weeks on here you know. They'd have to hoist me off with a crane. Having said that, I think I've got time for a croissant and another coffee before the class. They really shouldn't put such temptation in our way. Well, not mine, anyway!" As I go back into the restaurant I collide with Star Trek, who recognises me and grins.

"Ah, Madam, how are you today? Are you coming into the Pyramid restaurant tonight? We missed you last night. It was a lot quieter without you." His eyes twinkle so I know we're not really in trouble.

"Yes, we are. We missed you all as well. Not the same up here, is it? Would we be allowed to ask for that same table? Do they do that?"

"Oh yes, just ask for table 121 and if it is busy they will buzz you when it's free. And I will make sure to bring your wine up so it's ready for you."

Oh yeah. Didn't think about that last night so we just bought wine by the glass in the Lido. "Good shout Star Trek, we'll see you later." Chuffed to bits with that, as I like our little area and the waiters that look after us.

When I finally get to the Atrium, having had to belt back to the cabin for my jazz trainers as I had literally everything in my Mary Poppins bag *except* for them, it's heaving again and people are fighting for every inch of floor space. I spot James and he beckons me over to the square foot of carpet he's defending as the dance floor is full.

"I've had to guard this patch with my life!" he exclaims. "Talk about aggressive!"

I squeeze in between him and a very large lady who doesn't seem to have any sense of personal space. Well, not mine anyway, as she is sort of halfway across me already and we haven't even started moving yet.

And then into that non-space squeezes Mrs Grumpy, beaming brightly at James.

She says, "Ooh, I missed you yesterday. Can I be next to you in case I get lost? Excuse me dear," and pushes past me to be next to James.

What?!

He looks at me in a 'not my fault!' kind of way, then our silent communication is broken as Laura bounds on stage with a big, "HALLO! Are we having FUN yet?"

And we all shout, "YES," even though I want to shout, "I'm fucking not. I can hardly breathe, let alone MOVE!" but obviously I don't.

Then Large Lady to my leftish looks across at Mrs Grumpy and says, "Ooh, is that the lad you told me about? 'Scuse me." And she pushes past me too, so I'm now two people further down the line. I'm tempted to respond in a way which would belie my good upbringing, when I realise that actually I'm better off and have a bit more space here, whilst James is all cramped in with his 'Babes'. Haha.

"So TODAY we are doing the ELECTRIC SLIDE, which is nice and easy but also a lot of FUN to dance. SO, everyone, we are starting with a GRAPEVINE. Step RIGHT, then BEHIND with your LEFT, then RIGHT then TOUCH. SHALL WE DO THAT AGAIN? OK, AGAIN."

We manage that successfully and even manage to do it to the left. And REPEAT.

"So now we're going to walk back THREE steps starting with the RIGHT. ONE, TWO, THREE and TOUCH." Which ends in chaos because quite a lot of people don't know their left from their right.

"SO. I'm going to HOLD UP MY HAND AND THAT IS THE FOOT YOU WILL USE, OKAY? We can DO this."

And so it continues. It becomes like a heaving mass of people and a case of move or die in the stampede. I'm getting hot and fed up with being cramped, so after a bit I move away to the edge and just watch them. James' Babes appear to be having lots of fun as he hams up the moves, and when he sees me watching, he grins and shrugs his shoulders. He's clearly loving the attention, and I love that he is loving the attention. He is so good at this stuff, and the light in him that seems to have faded somewhat since he got all kind of mature, reignites. I grin back and shake my head.

Some while later we're out on the Lido deck after having lunch. Yup, more food.

"D'you feel like a walk around the Promenade deck? I fancy a bit of peace and quiet. Had enough of packed bodies so I'm not that bothered about the class."

James thinks for a bit. "Only if I can come back up for tea time. I want some of those cakes I saw them putting out."

"Oh, you have got to be kidding!"

"Well, they did look nice. And holidays are about treats." Big smile.

"Your cakes, your waistline. Shall we go?"

We walk down the sixteen flights of stairs to the Prom deck only to discover there's a massive sale going on in the Atrium. How did I miss that in the Newsletter? Tables are filled to overflowing with scarves, handbags, watches, you name it, it's there. I'm faced with a massive dilemma. I want to see whether the watch I liked is in the sale but don't want to fight through all the people.

"I think we should walk first to calm you down, then go in and have a look. They're not seriously going to run out, are they? A bit of exercise and sea air and you'll be able to face them." James convinces me and we push open the heavy sea door to the Promenade deck. "Which way round?" he asks. "Clockwise or anti-clockwise?"

"Anti-clockwise – easier for your heart."

"I was actually joking, but now I'm interested. Do tell me more."

"I read it in one of my running magazines. Apparently the major vein in the heart – the superior vena cava - goes from the left to the right and the action of running anti-clockwise helps the process of pumping the blood, whereas going the other way is literally against the flow. So running clockwise is harder work. And I don't do hard." I double-blink at him, like, 'I'm cleverer than I look, mate,' and grin.

"Well. I never knew that. Impressed-dot-com."

And we start off anti-clockwise around the Promenade deck, happily enjoying the sunny side, then noticing how cold and windy it is on the other side. We need to do three circuits to walk a mile, and after some brisk walking we actively look forward to the shady side as it's a chance to cool down. We also look forward to it as the sunny side is filled with smokers and I belt through them as fast as I can, holding my breath.

We make it round the back of the ship to fresh air and James looks at me weirdly. "What were you doing back there?"

"Did you ever see *Looney Toons* 'I wish I was in Happy World Land' where they hold their breath through the tunnel? I've always done that, which probably isn't so good if I'm the one driving, but that's what I was thinking about. And doing the equivalent. Walking as fast as I could, so I didn't have to breathe in their smoke."

James just looks at me.

"Yep. I know. Love me, or hate me… it's the way I am."

"So… do you have to turn around three times before you open a door or something? Or tap your head before you pick up a pen?"

"Yeah, so funny; and no, actually."

"But you do count the number of stairs."

"Well, yes. But that's so I know how many more we've got to go."

"And what if you didn't know? Say we didn't actually know which floor we needed?"

"I would be very troubled by that, actually. I'd have to check before we set off. I do need to know the end point."

"And if there isn't one?"

"Do people really live like that? Like, totally random? I don't think I could do that. Could you?"

James pauses in his interrogation. "I feel a bit like my whole life is random. No idea, at all, where I'm going. I don't have that whole thing of find a woman, get married, have kids; kids grow up, we retire. Can't see that happening really, so, yes, it's all up for grabs. Not sure I like it, but that's the way it is. For now, anyway. But. We have officially done our three laps and I'm knackered. Are you ready for some retail therapy? Then can I have some cake?"

"You are something else."

"I like to think so," he grins, pushing ahead manfully to open the door.

You would honestly think these were the best bargains in the whole world – ever. Okay, I'm interested in a watch. But there are women clutching four or five handbags, and scarves, and perfume, and like, woah! We haven't even got to Spain yet. I have a rummage for watches and decide the one I wanted isn't that great after all, so we go into one of the concessions for a bit of fun. Bearing in mind there is no alcohol involved at this point, I'm surprised to discover that I am genuinely relaxing.

I hold up a truly disgusting green slinky top. "James, James. Is this good?"

He is absolutely on the case. "No, sweetie. I think the orange would be better. Really. Go on, just slip it over your shirt. Let me see."

I slide it over my head.

"Oooh. No. Take it off. Now. With that hair you can't do orange. Sorry – my bad."

And sliding over to some navy and silver evening jackets, which I wouldn't be seen dead in as I'm about fifty years too young, "Whaddya think of this one then? With my white trousers?"

"No. Well, yes, the jacket, but black or navy trousers. Definitely not white. Too cheap."

At this moment a tall, whippet-thin lady appears, making a bee-line for James.

"Er – excuse me. Sorry to intrude, but you seem to have a good eye for colour and clothes. Do you think this would be a good idea?" She's holding a dark green fitted shirt under her chin, which really suits her colouring.

James swivels round and does that down-up-down thing men do.

"Hmm. Yes. With some tapered black trousers. Like over here."

As if by magic, he chances upon a whole rail of black evening trousers. "I know you can't try them on, but I'm sure this good lady," indicating the slightly bewildered sales assistant who's just joined our happy group, "will let you exchange them if they don't fit."

Sales Assistant snaps to attention. "Erm, of course!"

"Thank you – you're so much more use than my husband." She moves to the till to complete her purchases, just as 'Where's my breakfast?' Nick walks in.

"Ah, here you are. Are you having fun?"

Oooh. This must be his wife. Spikey.

"Yes, no thanks to you. This lovely man obviously has an eye for clothes." She turns to James. "Don't you? Sorry, I don't know your name."

"Ah, yes, it's James, and, um, I met your husband earlier, at breakfast. Nick, isn't it?" James expertly brings Nick into the fold.

Awkward.

"And I'm Caitlin – you must be Sarah."

A sharp look from Sarah to Nick. "Have you been talking about me?"

"Only to explain why I was on my own. I just mentioned that you were at the gym and might be along in a few minutes."

"Well I actually care what I look like, so I take the time to work out."

Well, that was rude.

"And how about you, James? Have you been to the gym on here yet? It's very well equipped and the instructors are excellent."

That guy really is a babe magnet.

"Er no, actually. Not yet. I've been concentrating on relaxing and eating, to be honest. But I expect I'll get up there at some point." James flashes his dazzling grin.

"Exercise stimulates endorphins which help you relax. And it also helps to work off the extra food some people seem to be stuffing." She looks pointedly at Nick.

Crikey. She's a barrel of laughs. Her and Mrs Grumpy should get along just fine – maybe we should introduce them. A malicious smirk creeps on to my face, which clearly doesn't go un-noticed.

"And how about you, Caitlin?" Eek. She's moved her razor-sharp focus to me. What is this, an inquisition?

"I usually run, at home. And I was thinking of taking a yoga class or something on the ship. And we're walking up and down the stairs all the time. And dancing – we've done lots of that. And we've just walked round the Promenade Deck three times, so James can make room for all the cakes he wants to eat."

Haha. That's moved the attention back to James, who can cope with it, whereas I can't, and it's a good way of getting rid of her. Bet she won't go within a million miles of the cakes James has his eyes on. In fact she probably doesn't even eat.

"Ooh yes! Thanks for reminding me!" says James, with no sign of the relief he must be feeling. I know I am. "They'll be serving tea now. Nice to meet you Sarah. Hope the clothes fit. See you around!"

We both nod to them and make a beeline for the stairs to start the long haul back up to the Lido.

"Wow. Poor Nick. And he's on holiday with her. Like, no escape. He must have some way of dealing with it without murdering her. Or maybe he's planning on pushing her overboard? Or leaving her behind at one of the ports?" We giggle like schoolkids as we reach the Lido level and make our way through a ton of flesh to get to the cakes. "I hope the greedy buggers have left us some!"

"Oh, so you've got room, now, have you?" James has his hand on his hip and puts on his best bitchy voice.

Oh yes indeedy I have, but I'm not going to admit it. I'm just going to have a small cake now though, to keep James company. He's busily piling his plate with all kinds of goodies and we waddle outside to eat in the sunshine as there seem to be loads of tables free. Within about ten seconds we realise the reason the tables are empty is because the sun is so hot that it's melting all the cream. We make it inside in time to save them from completely disintegrating, and by some miracle manage to find a cool spot by the window.

"So – did you get a chance to look at any of the ports, or the excursions? I know it's the last port but I was looking forward to Gibraltar."

"I did manage to do a bit of research, and it looks like the shops there might be good." James can leave Jules standing once he gets going. "Apparently the exchange rate is really good at the moment - d'you want to come?"

Hmm. "Monkeys. I'd like to see the monkeys, as I've recently had a shopping fest. But I could do that on my own if you like."

"I think we could do both as we've got the whole day there. We can get the bus up to see the monkeys then shop when we come down. Well, you can help me shop. Would that work?"

"Good idea. I wonder if we can walk into town from where the ship docks. Otherwise we'd need to book the coach."

"Next time we're near the excursions desk we can check. Maybe before dinner tonight?"

"Blaaargh. I don't know how you can mention food when you've just stuffed all those cakes. C'mon, let's go and find somewhere to crash and read until I feel capable of attacking the stairs."

That doesn't happen though, because just as we're gathering the strength to stand up, along comes Nick with his coffee and a cake or two.

"Hi. Mind if I join you?"

"Of course not. As long as you're not expecting any intelligent conversation – my brain doesn't work when my stomach's this full," I joke. "In fact did you know that your gut is known as the 'second brain' as it can function independently from the one upstairs?"

I turn proudly to James who is looking surprised at my second outburst of knowledge for the day. "So actually, neither of my brains are working very well at the moment."

Shut UP.

Nick smiles. "Haha. No, I didn't, but that's the kind of thing Sarah would come out with. In fact that's why I'm here – I wanted to apologise for her behaviour." He catches me looking over his shoulder in case she's about to creep up on us again. "It's OK, she's having a massage. Safely out of the way for an hour."

What on earth do you say to that? Yes, she's an utter bitch… Or, why did you marry her then? Or, you're not wrong there, please don't inflict her on us again. Any of the above, really.

"You've certainly got your hands full there, mate," chips in James, thankfully, in a blokey kind of way.

"Well, yes. That's true. Bit of a strange story, to be honest. We booked the cruise in one of our better moments during what was a very bad time for us. Further down the line we decided to separate – in fact, we have – but neither of us could find someone to inflict ourselves on for two weeks, so we chose to come on the cruise together rather than lose the deposit. All I can say is, thank God she's got the gym and I've got my books. And food, of course. Most of which I eat on my own." At this point he breaks into a grin.

"I think you're pretty safe on that one," I say. "Does she actually eat?"

"Not much on the ship, if she can help it. Food for the masses an' all that. First cruise for you two?"

And so we get into the joys of cruising and discover this is a first for them too, but apparently Sarah's already decided the food is shit and she can't wait to get home, which is a bit sad as Nick seems really easy-going and just wants to relax and enjot the cruise. Much like us really. We tell him what we do for a living and he tells us he's an IT consultant which isn't as boring as everyone thinks it is, as he handles security for the computer systems used on trading floors around the world.

"Is that the same people who hack into our bank accounts and stuff?" I hate online banking with a passion.

"That's one side of it. The finance world is a constant target so we have to keep up to date with what those pain-in-the-arse hackers are doing."

"I don't get that," says James. "Why do they do it? I mean why create viruses anyway? Even the ones that email all your contacts with porn pics or dangerous links."

"It's usually a peer thing amongst clever programmers who have gone off the rails at some point along the way. They get kudos as soon as something they've done, like disrupt social media or something, hits the news and they revel in the attention it gets. Then there are the hackers who do it because they're disenchanted with an organisation and want to cause a lot of disruption, especially with national security agencies and even institutions like NASA. And of course there are the ones that want to steal. And they're pretty dangerous if you think about the amount of money that changes hands on stock exchanges around the world."

"It sounds really exciting, actually," I pipe up. "Do you get to see some amazing places?"

"Theoretically, but I'm usually zooming in, working totally ridiculous hours, staying in a faceless hotel for a few nights, then coming back home to collapse."

Ah. Not so exciting then. I'm not giving up though. "And do you actually catch anyone? Are there late night covert operations with the police swooping in on the suspect?"

"I'm not really involved in that bit – my job is to make sure the systems are impenetrable, which is of course almost impossible. But of course I can't tell you what goes on, as then I'd have to kill you." His eyes twinkle at me and we both burst out laughing.

"But, hey, I'm keeping you. Think I'll have a bit of a swim before I go back and get changed for dinner. Good to talk to you guys – see you around!"

We wander thoughtfully over to the nearest sun loungers and plonk ourselves down. Nice man, shame about the ex-wife.

Chapter 16

We're woken really early by a lot of banging and grinding and shouting coming from below. After a lovely meal and just a touch of wine last night (pleased I can actually be good if I need to), we retired at a sensible time in order to be fresh as daisies for our first port day. We have to be in the Marquis Theatre for 8.30 to get checked in for our excursion but the banging has woken us up way before our alarm call. We wrap up in our dressing gowns to investigate from our balcony, which is freezing cold as it's facing away from the sun; it's also facing away from the quayside so although we can see Malaga across the water, we're none the wiser, so we scurry back inside to the warm.

"Better go and join the scrum for breakfast then. I should think it's gonna take a bit of time to get everyone off." I'm excited because a) I haven't seen Malaga before and b) I'm a bit bored of being at sea, so I belt into the bathroom and am ready in the blink of an eye. This strategy was cleverly planned last night and included the whole (somewhat scary) hair-washing thing before dinner. It doesn't matter if it looks a frizzball at home, but this looking good and getting a bit of attention thing is new and feels strangely nice, so I'm trying to keep the standard high.

The best news is that the water on here is so soft that my hair does in fact fall in pretty spirals without me doing a lot. Result! The rest of the clever planning included choosing my new pink tie-dye maxi dress and some pretty hippy sandals I picked up in Primark. We're doing a bit of walking up to the fortress so heels are a no-no, plus I can't walk very well in them even on the flat. I can't stand seeing women totter along on high heels with their bums stuck out because the shoes are impossible to walk in – not planning on joining them again. Been there, done that.

The shopping trip with Jules included buying a small purple ruck-sack into which go a bottle of water, shades, my wallet and phone. It's beautiful and I didn't need a lot of persuading to buy it, TBH. Oh and a wrap, although the newsletter from last night said it's going to be a rather warm 25 degrees today, which is plenty hot enough for me. Actually, some sunblock wouldn't go amiss, as we're going straight from breakfast to the theatre to join our excursion.

I manage to whip off my dress, whack a bit of sunblock over the more vulnerable areas and get it back on before James is out of the bathroom. Sharing with him is really easy as we seem to glide between the bathroom and the dressing area like a well-rehearsed dance. No embarrassment or awkwardness – so lucky.

My phone starts bleeping like crazy from inside my rucksack as it connects to the local mobile network. I get all excited, heaven knows why, fumbling to get it out, then realise that all the texts are to welcome me to Spain and to tell me how much it will cost to download data, which of course I won't be doing. Oh. Bored with that, so it gets stuffed back in the bag. James is all ready to go when suddenly it bleeps again with the WhatsApp tone. Ooh. I must have wifi. Scrabbling to untangle it from my sunglasses, I finally get to see it's a message from Aiden. In fact it bleeps several times more and they're all from him.

Panic.

"There's loads of messages from Aiden! He must have burnt the flat down, or maybe there's something wrong with Titan."

James has been watching all this unfold from the doorway, with a bemused look on his face. "I'm sure it's all fine. He's probably just keeping in touch and saying happy holidays."

"No! It IS Titan…listen. 'Hi sis just need to tell you about the cat.' See? Aaargh. That's all. Hold on, here's the next one, it's a picture actually, of Titan all curled up on my laptop bag. Ahhh. He always loves doing that – it's his office. And the words under it say, 'He's loving having me here and is fine.'"

"I'm sure they're both fine. Shall we go on up?"

"No, wait, there's another picture. Oh. It's the lounge, all tidy. Oh."

"Cait? Can we?"

"Just the last one. Ah, look. The bathroom. Clean."

"And that's all in one piece too?"

"Wait – there's a selfie of Aiden – smiling his socks off. And underneath his pic it says, 'See? Told you I could do it. We are well and don't miss you at all, as I am remembering to feed Titan and giving him lots of cuddles. The flat is fine. I am also fine. Have a HAPPY HOLIDAY and FORGET about us. OK? Big hugs xxxxxxxxxxxxxxx' Ah." I have a bit of a misty eye moment as I realise that I have actually been worrying about them in some teeny part of my brain that isn't absorbed in eating, drinking or sunbathing.

"Thank heavens for that. Can we go now?"

The Lido is busy, as predicted, only there's a certain edgy undertone as people are obviously panicking about shoving enough food down their throats to last until the next free meal, but still make it to the theatre on time. Chinese Chef recognises me from a distance, holds up a thumb and raises his eyebrows. I stick my thumb up too and nod, and I know that by the time I've got everything else together my eggs will be ready. I'm gradually downsizing my breakfast as having bacon every day is a bit much, and there's loads of other stuff to try. So this morning it's slices of cheese and some grapes, a croissant, a few slices of melon and mango, and then to go with the eggs, just some mushrooms and beans and a tomato. 'Just'. Wow. I'm going to miss this when I get home.

We're queueing for coffee as one of the stewards wheels a trolley up to sort out the orange juice machine. He's got a whole crate of tetrapaks of juice, and somewhere further back in the queue behind me I'm aware of a hand reaching out to grab one of the packs. Oh no. I bet I know who that belongs to. I dig James in the back, just as a voice pipes up, designed for the whole world to hear. Or at least everyone in the Lido buffet.

"Will you just look at this shit? Are they kidding? Orange juice is the fourth ingredient, for God's sake. Behind water and glucose fructose syrup. Then sugar. No wonder everyone is stuffing their faces on here, they're all having massive blood sugar dips. They don't stay full for more than ten minutes drinking this stuff. Jeeeesus."

Ducking our heads we manage to get our coffee without making eye contact with anyone at all, and belt out to find a table. We adopt the same policy while we're eating, and pray to all the gods and goddesses there are that Nick and Sarah aren't on our trip. Shame, as I think I could get to like him.

A crocodile of passengers are making their way down the stairs to the theatre, as obvs the lifts are over-subscribed again, but it is a happy throng as we're all excited to get off the ship and explore. Clutching our tour tickets we finally approach the desk in the lobby and are assigned an orange sticker with a number, which is our tour reference, and we're instructed to put it somewhere prominent so the guide can see it easily.

I'm deeply troubled as we leave the desk.

"You understand I can't put this on a pink dress, don't you?"

"Cait, you are so precious. If you stick it high enough up you won't be able to see it against the pink."

"But I'll know it's there and it will be a horrible clash."

"Well they make them that lovely fluorescent colour so we can be spotted. I mean, if you lose a passenger it's much easier to find them if they're wearing bright orange or green, or something, isn't it?"

Grumbling somewhat, I place the sticker almost under my ear so I can't see the horrible colour. We take our seats as directed and I nudge James. "But I can see other people's stickers. Look at that woman. She's wearing pink too. And red actually, but that's her sunburn – ooh that looks sore." This is coming from one who has only just escaped being fried too, BTW. "But it still clashes with the orange."

James gently takes my face in his hands and turns it towards him. This is strange as we generally have a non-verbalised 'no touching' agreement, apart from the odd hug. He looks straight into my eyes with his very gorgeous deep brown eyes. "Cait. Stop it. Let go. Just allow it all to be, and relax. This isn't about colour coordination today. This is about Malaga. Now just concentrate as they're calling the numbers and we don't want to miss ours."

Oh. Am I really that bad? This is possibly what Mr Angry would've called 'so fucking irritating.' My heart sinks. Maybe I am that bad.

Suddenly there's a massive uprising, and a great gathering together of bags and paraphernalia, and James grabs my arm. "C'mon, that's us! Good job one of us is paying attention!" But he smiles as he says it, which helps to dispel the little bubble of doubt and sadness that was rising up from within. He pushes me into the queue ahead of him, which is now snaking up the stairs from the theatre, then down to the next deck where we're being disembarked. Then all of a sudden our cruise ID cards are being scanned, and we're out! Yay!

We scuttle down the gangway and at the end is the ever-present

DDG photographer waiting to snap us in front of the ship. After quickly striking a pose for him we belt off to find our coach amongst the tens of them lined up on the quayside. It's amazing how many people are pouring off the ship, as it doesn't really feel that crowded on there most of the time, but within minutes we're loaded onto our coach, counted and ready to go. They certainly have this off to a T. Thankfully the air conditioning is already on, as I can't believe how hot it is even at this early hour. Our tour guide is a cute little Spanish lady with twinkly eyes and a killer outfit of teeny skirt, leggings and boots. Yes. I guess they are used to the heat or something, as she's also wearing a leather jacket over her shirt. It looks amazing.

Driving through the city is a revelation, as it's surprisingly pretty. Being a classic 'Brits Abroad' holiday destination I (wrongly) expected Malaga to be a kind of ex-pat haven and a characterless city, but it isn't. We head on upwards to the 11th century Alcazaba fortress, then get off the coach ready to explore on foot. The walk leads up through the entrance into the steep winding internal cobbled street, and our guide stops at key points to point out the astounding architecture and impart some of the rich and varied history of the area and the building. Every viewpoint is framed by an exquisite archway, or a fountain which captures the slant of the sun, and I'm in awe of these people who knew how to design and build something of such beauty, which also functioned as a symbol of power. I could literally stand for hours absorbing the atmosphere and the views, which are truly spectacular, but all too soon we have to go back down to continue our tour; James has to physically drag me away so we can get to the next point of interest, which is Picasso's birthplace.

We're allowed up the creaky stairs into the two storey townhouse where he lived (NO photographs please) for just the first ten years of his life – so although it's filled with photographs of his childhood, it doesn't actually *feel* like there's a real connection. Once we're done in there, we file outside to a leafy square which features a bench with a statue of the seated artist; when the crowds have cleared we take pictures of each other sitting next to a stony-faced Picasso, then follow the tour guide on to the next stop. I need to come back. A beautiful city with so much more to offer.

The final part of the excursion is a refreshment break in the garden of a hotel a short walk away from Picasso's place. Thankfully the seating is under a massive sun shade, as it's seriously hot now. A smiling waiter brings us glasses of the local sweet wine. I take a teeny sip – blah! Too sweet. James catches my look and summons the waiter back, and bless him, orders me a glass of chilled Chardonnay, while he manages to drink both mine and his own sweet wine. Mr You-Know-Who would have just told me to stop whining and drink it as it's free, so this is all a bit of a treat.

Grinning at James, I mouth 'Thank you'. He smiles back. What a gorgeous guy. I so want him to find the right person, someone who appreciates his sensitivity and beautiful manners.

This 'being-looked-after-but-not-by-a-boyfriend' kind of thing is so calming and relaxing, especially after so many years of living with my stomach in knots. I guess it's because it doesn't have the unspoken shades and nuances and twists and turns of an intimate relationship that can go tits-up at the drop of a hat. I think he's enjoying it too, because he seems to like looking after me and I am deeply appreciative. Maybe we should just stay together forever.

We're driven around some of the city's landmarks then deposited safely back at the ship; after squirting the ever-present sanitiser on our hands, and climbing wearily up the gangway, we're enveloped by the cool, air-conditioned interior. Aaah. It's good to be home. And this was only a half-day trip!

The first thing I want after all that heat is a cooling dip in the pool. My hair's piled up again in the style of a 'lunchtime swim', but the rest of me is blissfully under water. The ship's virtually empty as a lot of people are still on trips, and we have the pool area pretty much to ourselves. I spot a couple sharing a bottle of chilled white wine, and just at that point a waiter wanders slowly by, all ready to be hailed. They're good at this stuff.

I reply to his polite question as to whether Madam would like a drink. "Ooh. Don't mind if I do!" James also succumbs to the heat and orders a cold beer. This swanning around in the sun drinking Chardonnay is totally addictive, and after we've had a bit of lunch on trays from the nearby buffet, we stretch out on sun loungers to enjoy the peace and quiet.

"James?"

"Hmmm?"

"Do you think I'm really controlling?"

"Hmmm?"

"I mean, the colour clashes, and the counting stairs, and timing and organising everything. Why do I do that?"

"Maybe because you're worried about what will happen if you don't?"

"But who'll organise stuff if I don't? Someone has to!" Maybe I've been around Jules too long.

"Well, the sky isn't going to fall in, is it? Suppose you had a whole afternoon of just taking every moment as it comes, not planning anything. Just be guided by whatever comes along. Be open as opposed to setting an expectation, then being all worried in case it doesn't happen the way you want it to. I think that's the bit that makes you stressed."

"Hmmm. So I shouldn't be lying here thinking about what time we need to leave and get changed so we can get to dinner."

"Nope."

"But thinking about the alarm call for tomorrow is good, yes?"

"Well obviously, because we don't want to miss the Barcelona trip."

"James?"

"Hmmm?"

"We haven't actually booked the trip. We just talked about it when we booked the Malaga one. So as of this moment we don't have a trip to get up for."

"Shit. Good point. We'll book it when the Desk opens."

"So sometimes my thinking ahead is a bit useful then. I like to think so." And with that I snuggle back into my towel and fall asleep, which seems the only sensible thing to do after a few glasses of Chardonnay at lunchtime. Such a light-weight.

Chapter 17

We slowly become aware of people moving around us. The other excursions are returning and there's a bubble of excitement as the Sailaway party will be starting soon. James decides his lunch has gone down sufficiently to go hunting for cream cakes while I guard the loungers; we've got a spot quite close to the back so we can get a good view of Malaga as we slip out of port, but as soon as he gets back I'm secretly planning on getting a few treats myself.

"It's heaving in there, so I got stuff for you too. There wouldn't have been any left if you'd waited."

Did I mention how much I love this guy?

"Ooh – chocolate eclairs – thank you! They didn't have those last time." I tuck in extra fast as the chocolate's already starting to drip, and I'm in danger of wearing it rather than eating it. A familiar shadow falls across my food and I look up to see our waitress from the other day, Luisa.

"Can I get you a glass of Chardonnay ready for the Sailaway, Madam?"

I look down at my selection of cakes and cup of tea. "Hey – well, be rude not to I guess. Thank you! And a beer for you, James? It's not good for me to drink alone, you know." Fiendish grin. "And by the time the drinks arrive we'll have finished this little lot."

He grins and nods, knowing resistance is futile.

"Good afternoon, ladies and gentlemen, this is the Captain speaking. I hope you've all had a lovely day in Malaga. In fact some people are still in Malaga so we are a few passengers short of a full set. It seems one of the coaches has broken down and the breakdown service has been called, so we will be here a bit longer. Please just relax in the sun, and I'll let you know when we're ready to go."

Such a turn of phrase, that guy. But in spite of his apparent good humour, there are serious consquences when passengers are late back. The tour guides are absolutely adamant that the ship must sail when it's due to sail, and anyone who's left behind will have to make their way to the next port to re-join it. Surely they couldn't do that with a whole coach-load though...

We finish our cakes just as Luisa delivers our drinks, so we take them over to the starboard side to look out for the missing coach – of which there is no sign.

"I guess they'll just have to welly it a bit more so we make it to Barcelona on time, then. I wonder if they get fined for staying too long," I wonder aloud.

"Yes they do, actually." It's Nick, who's just appeared behind my left shoulder, which is a pleasant surprise. What's even nicer is that he appears to be alone. "I looked it up as I wondered the same thing, and they get hefty fines if they don't leave when they're supposed to. And I've also heard tell that the port fees are the reason we don't get as long in port as in previous years. But hey, I was ready to come back anyway." He grins at me. "How about you guys. Did you get off?"

"Yes, we went on the Best of Malaga trip, which took in the amazing Alcazaba fortress. Didn't think I was going to like it, but it's really special. The Moors were so clever with their architecture. There's one bit where you look back down the passageway and all the arches line up one within the other. They have everything so balanced and pleasing to the eye. Like it matters that the buildings are aesthetic as well as useful." Where did that come from?! "I'd like to come back and spend more time here, for sure. How about you? What did you do?"

"Oh, we've been here before as it's an easy hop across from Southampton airport – so, basically wandering round the shops in Sarah's case, and sitting drinking coffee and reading, in mine. The perfect day really, just good to get off the ship for a while."

I'm expecting him to be wearing a sarcastic expression, but actually he isn't.

"No, really, it was. I don't mind a bit of shopping, but I'm not on Sarah's level, so I really enjoy just sitting and reading and watching the world go by. I don't get to do enough of that."

"Oh, I've got a friend like that, Jules. Her shopping trips completely exhaust me. She is a serious shopper. As is James."

James hasn't heard any of this conversation as he's been busy leaning over the side of the ship, watching the very bored port personnel walk up and down. Presumably there's no word of the broken-down coach. Suddenly there's a flurry of activity and it comes hurtling round the corner of the Duty Free building and screeches to a halt right next to the gangway. What happens next has to be the fastest unloading in the history of tourism; with one attendant at each door of the coach, front and back, the happy cruisers are literally man-handled from coach to portside and up the gangway in the blink of an eye. All the fancy bunting and safety cones have already been removed and the gangway slides back into the ship on the heels of the last passenger. Wow. Seriously impressive – the cruise line must be charged by the second.

And then moments later. "So, good afternoon again ladies and gentlemen, this is the Captain speaking. Our final passengers are now safely onboard and we will shortly be pushing away from the side. One of the youngsters will be handling the reversing and exit from the port, but there is no need to worry at all. I believe they've had quite a lot of work experience, so I'm pretty confident they know what they're doing by now. So enjoy these last views of Malaga and have a lovely evening. Our next port of call will be Barcelona, where we will be docking at around 5 AM."

Haha. So funny. Obviously in training for his next career as an after-dinner speaker. The entertainers are on the stage above the pool and soon everyone's belting out timeless hits like 'Hi, Ho, Silver Lining', which I wouldn't usually be caught dead singing, but the atmosphere is fabulous, and the sight of the sun twinkling on the wake the ship leaves as she turns to head out to sea and towards Barcelona is nothing short of spectacular.

Nick's clocked what we're drinking and catches a waitress to order some refills, as well as a Merlot for himself. I'm going to be utterly wrecked by dinner time if I carry on like this. Better slow down a bit.

"Are you going into Barcelona, or taking a trip?" he asks.

"We're hoping to go up to Montserrat to see the Black Madonna, but we forgot to book the trip. We're going down after the Sailaway to see if there are any spaces left. How about you?"

"Ahm, we're booked on the Highlights of Barcelona tour, but to be honest I think Sarah prefers the gym to just about anything else at the moment. Which is kind of handy as it gives us a bit of breathing space."

He's not kidding. Having been on countless holidays with Mr Nasty – who could kick off at any moment, maybe much like Sarah – I really don't envy him. Who wants to be walking on eggshells on their holiday, FFS? I'm fast coming to the conclusion that in any 'slightly difficult' relationship there will be one person that compromises and one person that probably doesn't give a shit. And they know that the other person will just soak it up because they don't have the courage, or bad manners, to have a fight in public and put the other person in their place. Or leave them. I suspect Sarah is the one who doesn't give a shit, and Nick is just trying to get by and keep the damage to a minimum. Tricky.

The entertainments team have left the stage so it's a lot more peaceful up here now. People are sitting around in groups chatting, just enjoying the lovely weather, and nobody wants to break the spell.

James spots a vacant table. "Shall we move over there? More comfortable than the sun loungers. Nick? Would you like to join us?"

"Sure, thanks. I suspect Sarah will be some time yet."

"Crikey. She must be so fit. Is she training for something?" James grabs the stuff and I take the glasses to the table.

"Not really, although she runs the odd marathon. It's more that she's training in order to keep stuff at bay. She's a lawyer, which is obviously very stressful, so she exercises to work off the adrenalin. And of course in this environment it gives us time apart, which is helpful. I'm sure she could, and probably will, give you a lecture about this at some point. In fact the only passion I think she has in life apart from law, is health.

I'm about to say I really can't wait for that moment when fortunately Sarah appears through the doors over the other side of the pool.

"Ah – and here is the lady herself." Nick waves to get her attention and I fervently hope she's in a good mood after her workout. Just as she reaches our table Luisa wanders by, and to my absolute shock Sarah orders Chardonnay for herself and top-ups for the rest of us. Well, me of little faith. I wasn't expecting that.

"Aaaargh! That was tough! Some solid retail therapy followed by a massive workout. It's gotta be chilled white wine as far as I'm concerned. James, you would have loved the shops in Malaga."

"I love shops anywhere, to be honest," he replies, laughing. "And I haven't had a really good root round on here yet. I overheard someone saying Cartagena is good, so I might let it rip there. Oh, and Gibraltar, of course, after we've seen the monkeys, or apes, or whatever they are. Oh, Cait, we mustn't forget to buy the tickets for tomorrow."

"Yup. After this one. Cheers!" We clink glasses and the next half hour passes more companionably than I would ever have imagined.

"She's a tricky one," says James, sprawled on his bed.

We're collapsing before dinner, having made it to the Excursions Desk and bought the tickets we want for tomorrow and also for Pompeii, which I've always wanted to see.

"You're not kidding. Nick seems so nice and she's so, I dunno, sharp. Not really very feminine, is she? I can't imagine her being supportive or loving. Or gagging for sex. Whoops."

"Thanks for that little image, Cait. Just what I needed. But seriously, don't you think some people are just like that? You can't just round their edges and make them all loving and happy and horny if deep down, for whatever reason, they're not. Or maybe he thought he could heal her. Make her happy so she wasn't so hard on herself and everyone else. We can't know these things."

"Well I do understand that bit, actually. Because that's how you feel when you think you love someone, isn't it? That's why I stuck with Mr You-Know-Who way after we should've split up. I thought I would be the one to fix all his problems."

"And instead of fixing him, he almost destroyed you. Thank God you got out of that one."

"Yeah. Me too. Jules told me she thought it looked bad, but she didn't want to intrude. And I probably wouldn't have said much even if she'd tried to get me to talk about it while we were still together, because it would have seemed disloyal."

"See that's where it all goes wrong. How could you be loyal to someone who treated you so badly? He knew you wouldn't say anything – or if you did that nobody would believe you because he would just deny it all. Aaargh. Makes my blood boil. Sorry. That's not very helpful, is it?"

"It's okay, honestly. I need to hear those things because it helps me get my thinking straight. In the better times I wondered whether it could actually work out – if it was just one of those relationships you had to put some effort into. Then in the bad times, which were getting more frequent, I was worried for my own safety and I couldn't figure out what to do. And I didn't want to let anyone know how bad it was. It was like I had to keep up this façade of everything being okay, but underneath I was falling apart."

"Did you ever think of reporting him to the police, or trying to get him thrown out – and a restraining order or something?"

"Didn't think they'd be interested. Their funds are so tight, they've got an awful lot more to be doing than sorting out a domestic, especially when there's nobody being smacked around. And what would I have said? 'He's shouting at me?' 'He makes me feel useless?' I think that was part of the problem actually. There were no cuts or bruises, so I didn't have a clue who to turn to. And I was worried about what would happen if I tried to throw him out. And it had to be that way round. I couldn't leave because he was in my flat, so disappearing into the night was never an option and that made it all the more complicated. Although at times I worried that we'd get thrown out because of all the shouting. From him. I never shouted back – not that I could ever get a word in edgeways. I just tried to calm it all down."

"So what was the final straw? How did it finally finish?"

"A truly awful holiday, when he was acting so weird. I overheard him talking to himself in the bathroom one evening, saying really vicious things about me in such a strange voice. I wondered whether he was schizo or something, but I knew at that point he had to go – and as soon as we got back. I really didn't feel safe being alone with him. I didn't feel safe with him anyway once he started to show his true colours – he had such cold eyes – but this shocked me so much, it made me absolutely positive of what I had to do and gave me the courage to carry it through. He didn't know I overheard him, but he knew the holiday was terrible – massive bouts of screaming at me, telling me how worthless I was, how everything was always about me and how great I was, and how I was sex-mad but had no idea how to act like a woman – that even he realised at some level that we were over and it couldn't go on. So when we got back we had a very civilised conversation, which was a huge relief as I don't know what I would have done otherwise. I started trawling through websites looking for flats for him, as he'd look in the local paper once a week, find nothing, and end up staying yet another week. He showed no sign of wanting to give up the comfortable lifestyle I was providing, so I literally drove him out to places I found online and made him sign up for one. I even helped him move in, to make sure he was really gone, and that was it – I got back home and collapsed in a big heap from the relief that he was finally out of my life. I had a lucky escape though, as I heard that his next girlfriend had to get a restraining order on him."

"Aw Cait. I'm so sorry you had to go through all that."

"Yeah, so am I. But now I understand why to outsiders it appears that women won't, or can't, extricate themselves from abusive relationships; it's much more complicated than just walking away. It was all really embarrassing and I was always covering for his bad behaviour and rudeness, then in secret, I couldn't believe I'd got myself into such a mess. So maybe one day I'll use it in a book, or do some voluntary work or something.

The thing is, it had to come from deep within me. I can see that now. I had to find that strength, for myself. It wouldn't have worked if someone had just come and spirited me away. Men like him wear you down so much and they make you feel worthless and spineless. It's like I lost the ability to decide anything for myself, let alone carry it out, in case there was another explosion. So it's about helping women to be strong. Getting them to have the courage to tell someone what's going on and accept help if they can't do it alone. And if friends pick up on something that doesn't add up they also need to have the courage to ask. To probe further. It could literally save a life, of that I'm sure."

James is sitting up on his bed now, cross-legged, and concentrating on me. "You're one special lady, Caitlin Powell, and I'm so proud of you for coming through it like this."

At which point his stomach gives a massive rumble.

"'Talk about bad timing!" At least he has the grace to blush.

Chapter 18

Well thanks heavens for that. We're safely docked – which is what woke me up in the wee small hours – and I am un-hung-over. These Sailaways are deadly. The whole party starting at 4.30/5.00 in the afternoon thing means me and Miss Chardonnay are well acquainted by dinner time, but last night I moved on to water with my dinner, as Barcelona without a pounding headache would be good. Plus if we eat in the Lido there's less attention from waiters and it's all a lot calmer. Maybe tonight we'll go back down to the Pyramid, as I do miss seeing them all.

Being mindful of the revoltingly bright tour stickers we're likely to be given I'm playing safe with a navy vest, pretty floaty hippy skirt and my Primark pumps, which are turning into a godsend as it just isn't practical to stagger around in heels, and certainly not today. Maybe I'll make a bit more of an effort to dress up tonight if we go to the restaurant instead of the Lido. James, of course, has no such wardrobe issues and looks stunning as ever in long navy shorts, sandals and a big billowy white shirt and shades. We honestly didn't plan this but we do look amazingly co-ordinated for a non-couple. (Unlike some of the *actual* couples who clearly don't even look at what the other one is wearing. Moving on...)

We're planning on getting up to the Lido nice and early today, so there's a bit of time to relax and enjoy eating breakfast sitting out in the sun. How the gods laugh. As soon as we walk through the doors (no Star Trek on sanitiser – wonder where he is), it's obvious that everyone else has exactly the same idea. No worries though; the chefs are working their socks off to get all the hungry punters through in time, and Chinese Chef gives me a wave and a thumbs up from a distance as if he has all the time in the world.

"You know, I could really get used to this. And you look like you're relaxing a bit more." Having just taken on enough calories for, oh, a week, James stretches out his long frame with a contented sigh. "I love the way we're transported from one place to another, and get spoilt rotten all the time. All I've had to think about is where and when I'm eating next and whether I've got a drink to go with it. Heaven, then, actually."

"Have to say I agree with you. I've stopped counting the stairs and I'm not worried about the stickers, and I'm sure we won't miss the coach… and all is good."

Eventually it really is time to get moving and join the other passengers going down the stairs (forget the lifts) to the bowels of the ship to get our stickers. Barcelona is one of the most popular ports, it seems, as everyone who isn't in the Lido must already be down here, and it's full to the rafters. If ships have rafters. People are spilling out into the areas around the theatre, but the whole thing is managed really well by the Entertainments team who are happily handing out stickers and bottles of water, and reminding ladies they will need a wrap to cover their shoulders if they're going into any of the churches. Hah! I've made sure I always have a wrap as I don't want to get caught out. I'm certainly not going to need it for warmth as it's absolutely baking out there already. Pretty soon we're wending our way down the stairs to disembark, our party wearing a beautiful pink sticker, which goes perfectly with the navy. See? Relax, and things work out.

The coaches are lined up by the ship and we're loaded onto ours and scooting off almost before we can draw breath. I do an excited jig in the seat next to James, who's got the aisle seat due to his long legs so I don't have a lot of space for it, but no matter. Contained is good.

"We're off!! It is SO exciting being taken around to see everything. I mean, I do want to do some stuff on our own, but this is really exciting."

"I'd never have guessed," grins James, then our attention is taken by our tour guide, Monica, as she starts the introduction to Barcelona, which is looking pretty stunning from where I'm sitting. The countryside changes as we leave the city and soon we're speeding through lush green countryside and upwards towards the mountains.

Monica tells us that, according to Catholic tradition, the statue of the Black Virgin of Montserrat was carved by St. Luke around 50 AD and brought to Spain. It was later hidden from the Moors in a cave (Santa Cova, the Holy Grotto), where it was rediscovered by some shepherds (in 880 AD) who saw a bright light and heard heavenly music which they eventually traced to the grotto and the statue. The Bishop of Manresa, who was there when it was discovered, wanted it taken to Manresa, but the small statue was so heavy that it couldn't be moved – the Madonna was obviously saying she wanted to stay where she was! Word spread of the statue and the miracles that were witnessed in her presence, and increasing numbers of pilgrims visited her to pray for miracles. The monastery itself grew from the humble individual churches that had existed on the site and in 1592, the Grand Basilica of Montserrat was consecrated.

By the time we get out to stretch our legs and queue for the rack railway, I'm so entranced by the story that I can't wait to get in there. There's a bit of a bun-fight – which definitely involves elbows – when the train arrives, as everyone wants the back carriage because it has the best views, but I can't be bothered to fight – like – why be so aggressive just to get a view? James and I head for one of the front carriages where it's all a lot more civilised. Besides, we'll see the amazing views when we get out.

And when we do get out I'm rather pleased I brought my wrap. Okay, so I forgot the 'jacket suggested' part of the instructions, but I'll survive. The views are astounding. We're halfway up a mountain and some very enthusiastic hikers get out all ready with their gear – presumably to hike to the top – but I'm happy to stay right here and take in the scenery. We join a queue which threads its way towards the Basilica then through it towards the special area where the Black Madonna is sited. The Basilica is beautiful and totally awe-inspiring. I'm not religious, but I absolutely pick up on the purity of this place and feel like I could stay here for hours.

Nudging James, who's shuffling along in the queue beside me, "Like it?"

"Pretty amazing, isn't it?"

"Maybe when we've seen the Madonna we can come back and find a quiet corner?"

"Yup. I'm up for that."

Our slow shuffle continues until at last we reach the stairs. James pushes me gently ahead of him up to face the Black Madonna in her protected bubble, by which time my heart is thumping with excitement. Something special is happening here. She holds an orb in her hand which symbolises her reaching out to the world, and the edge of the orb is sticking out of the protective cask so we can touch it; some people are kissing it, euuuw! No. No way. I do stroke it though, because I can't come all the way here and not touch it.

Touch, yes, kiss, no.

The statue is really dark, which is apparently just a natural process of the wood she's carved from, and the varnish used to protect her – it isn't some massively political or cultural statement, which is a surprise as I assumed it would be. I get a genuine buzz from stroking the orb, then somewhat reluctantly move aside so James can follow on behind me. We both stand there for a moment, transfixed by being in the presence of an icon that is centuries old and literally humming with power.

A polite cough from behind reminds us we're not alone, and that in fact there are probably a few hundred people queueing up for just that experience. With an apologetic smile, we follow the crocodile of people outside then circle back, and avoiding the queue for the Madonna this time, head instead to a quieter area of the Basilica. I sink into the corner seat of one of the pews and take several moments to gather my thoughts. James slides in next to me, equally pensive. What's going on here? The humming, buzzing feeling seems to be in my whole body; it's not uncomfortable, just strange, as if I'm plugged into something. Then it gradually seems to draw in on itself until it's centring on my throat area, resting like a warm, healing scarf around my neck. Something deep inside me releases, and as it does so, a wave of emotion rises up and bursts out of my mouth in a great sob that I have no hope of controlling. Aargh! Please! Not here!

James reaches out and gently pulls me into his side as the sobs continue and tears pour down my cheeks in torrents. By now I'm beyond embarrassed and just have to go with it.

When the storm finally subsides – and after heaving a great sigh that seems to take in my whole body – I turn to look at him and realise there are tears running down his face too. Jeez. I don't even trust myself to speak.

Some time later, when we're both a bit more composed, I notice there's a votive stand over in the corner, so on slightly wobbly legs I wander over and pop a euro in the box. Using the light of the big candle by the side to light my own, I place it gently in one of the holders.

James has followed me. "Who's that for?"

"It's for me," I whisper. "The new me. The strong me, who isn't going to ever let anyone have power over me again." And somewhere in my chest area, there's another release of something I seem to have been carrying for so long. But thankfully no more tears. James' eyes widen and he too reaches for a votive, lighting it from the big candle on the side.

"And you?"

"It's for me too," he whispers back. "I want to release my past and be free of it."

We stand in a few moments of contemplative silence, thankfully undisturbed by the hordes heading in the direction of the Madonna.

"So what happened in there, d'you think?"

We've found a quiet seat outside the Basilica which looks down the mountainside. I feel like my mind has been turned upside down and my heart's been blown wide open. In a good way.

"Something raw, and honest and, I dunno – completely unexpected."

"Why did you say you wanted to release your past? I mean, you don't have to answer if you don't want to."

"I don't mind, funnily enough. It was liberating. For some bizarre reason I suddenly realised how the underlying religious influence of my childhood has made me feel guilty that I'm gay. That I've been programmed to believe I will rot in hell, and all that horrible imagery we have of people doing bad things and being roasted alive for eternity will come true. And now I feel that's maybe not the case. Maybe I don't have to believe all that."

Gulp. "That's really sad – you've never said anything like that before. I know you said you weren't happy being gay, but is this a big part of it?"

"Definitely. There's a bit of me that feels guilty for something that isn't my doing. That I should be 'normal' – but I don't know what normal is, or how to be it. I can only be me, can't I? But after being in there, and I know this sounds nuts, I feel stronger rather than weaker, and I do feel sort of free."

"Doesn't sound nuts at all. I had the same feeling. Suddenly I felt, like, 'Fuck you! I can and will be strong'. Like throwing off an old coat

I'm sick of wearing. Bored with that, bored with the way it's been for so long. Wow. I'm using that word a lot on this cruise, I know, but, wow! Something really has shifted, hasn't it?"

We turn to face each other on our bench and have a massive, heart-warming, soul-embracing hug.

We've been allotted an hour and a half at the monastery and Basilica, but spend the remainder of it wandering around in a kind of daze; taking in the view here, sitting there, chatting for a while. When Monica calls us, we walk slowly back to the rack railway and are oblivious to the pushing and shoving that goes on as people rush to get the best view.

Our guide comes into the carriage with us, and watches us thoughtfully for a moment. "You had a good experience in there, yes?"

I try unsuccessfully to string a few words together. "Um, yes. Unexpected."

James fails completely and just looks at me and shrugs.

"Some people are touched very deeply and get strong healing in there. You never know who, or when, but people come back again and again because it is a very special place. I'm pleased for you. I will leave you to your thoughts." At which point she turns towards our fellow passengers and chats with them until we get back down to the coach.

The atmosphere in the coach is muted on the journey home. We're hardly a raucous bunch, but I suspect some people got more than they bargained for in the Basilica, us included. There's another few hours before the ship leaves, so we ask to be dropped in the city centre so we can wander back on our own. Neither of us feel like getting back on the ship for a while, so we wander down Las Ramblas – because that's where everyone talks about – and eventually end up in a little coffee shop because we're still not ready to go back.

"How are you feeling now?" asks James.

"I'm still thinking about it, but it felt like a huge lump was removed from my throat – like all the words I'd bitten back because I didn't dare speak my mind, and all the anger and frustration I've had to swallow has been released. I feel lighter, and freer – and different inside. So I guess that in itself will create little changes that I might not even notice; then one day I'll realise I'm completely free of that horrible period and it won't ever sink its claws into me again. And that will be amazing." I smile at him, with a feeling of real joy in my heart. "The first thing I'm going to do is start writing for me, instead of tarting up other people's work. Now, that will be fun. Well, obviously I'll have to carry on for a while to pay the bills – until I'm world famous and getting blinding book deals of course. Tee-hee!" I kind of wriggle in my seat with excitement at the thought. "And how about you?"

James pauses for a moment. "I think, like you, there won't be any outward change immediately. I feel like I've been given the freedom to explore myself," at which he sniggers. "No, I mean, find out who I am outside of the conditioning I grew up with. We're all conditioned, aren't we? That's what happens in family life, and that's why each family has its own weird rituals and habits and ways of being. Like the sign I once saw in a shop, 'Just remember, to the outside world we're a normal family'. None of us are normal, and maybe I've got to learn how to be who I am outside of all the family stuff. I'm not any clearer about my sexuality, but I'm sure that will come. Who'd have thought a simple day trip would bring all this up? Hmm. Are you ready to head back to the ship? I think I can face them all now, and I fancy a swim."

We avoid the Sailaway party and have a gentle, cooling swim in the middle pool instead. Just as we're considering leaping into the currently empty jacuzzi, Luisa appears – how does she do that? Is she stalking us? Always nearby with her big smile and an order pad, knowing exactly what we want. Amazing. Either that or we're totally predictable because a) we never say 'No', and b) having given in and said 'Yes', we always have the same thing. Think I know the answer to that actually. And the experiences and revelations of the day clearly deserve some recognition.

"Cheers, Mr McG. Thank you for being such an important part of my astounding day, and I wish you great joy in exploring yourself." I raise my glass with a snigger.

"And cheers to you too, Miss Powell. I would just like to say how much I look forward to watching you grow into the woman you are supposed to be. Which will be the size of a house if you keep on eating and drinking at this rate."

The perfect friend indeed.

Chapter 19

And so, indeed, there is more food. We're queuing up outside the Pyramid and Franko seems genuinely pleased to see us when we get to the desk. Either that or he's a really good actor and he does it to everyone. I like to think it's the former.

"Madam, Sir, I'm so glad you decided to eat with us this evening. Would you like your usual table? I think it has just become free."

See? Today is working out just *perfectly*.

"Thanks, Franko. We missed you too," says James, the cool dude.

Sebastian gives us a big grin as we arrive at our table, and it's just like being with friends in our favourite restaurant. "Madam, I must say the sunshine suits you – you are looking very well this evening."

Well, I must admit I made quite an effort and the 'new' me thinks she looks pretty damned good too. "Aw thanks. I'm loving all of it – the sun, the ship, oh and of course the food – haha. How could I forget the food?"

"Of course, Madam," he chuckles. "And did you go on a trip today?"

"Oh, yes! Oh. My. God, yes. We went to Montserrat. Have you been there?"

"Ah. It's a very special place, isn't it? I have only visited it the once but I will remember it forever."

"That's how I feel too," says James. "I think all the other ports will pale in comparison to this."

Sebastian smiles. "Tomorrow is Villefranche, which is very different. If you don't have a trip you can just get the tender to the quay and have a wander around. It's a very pretty town. Very hilly, so quite hard work. But you will have a lot of time for thinking, if that is what you want. And I suspect you will." With that knowing comment he hands over our menus, then goes off to look after the other tables.

"Nice to know other people think it's special too. Ooh Star Trek, haven't seen you for a while. How are you? Did you get off today?"

"Thank you Madam, yes I did. I love Barcelona so I am very happy. Would you like your usual Chardonnay? And Merlot for you, Sir?"

"You are too smooth for words. How do you remember all this stuff?" I ask.

"Habit." He grins, and walks away.

I'm even more impressed when a big bowl of green veg appears with my main course, without me saying a thing. I've ordered fillet of beef, but as I'm getting wise to the way they serve the food on here, I'm not surprised when it arrives. Three fine slices of meat curled around some asparagus with a cute little path of drops – I assume it's horseradish – leading to some tiny tomatoes.

"Praise be for the greenery, huh?" I chuckle.

Sebastian wanders by, eyebrows raised at me, as in 'shall I get you another one?'

"No, really, I'm fine. I've got all this to get through too," I wave at the huge bowl of veg, "but thank you." Sweet. James, on the other hand, seems to have struck gold in choosing the rack of lamb, which is as ridiculously huge as my fillet of beef dish is unbelievably small. "And you've got the cheek to say I'm gonna be massive by the end of the holiday. Pot and kettle, perchance?"

James swallows the mouthful of lamb he's just been chewing and waving his fork at me, says smugly, "But *I* have a large frame to fill so I can cope with it – and besides, we can walk a bit of it off after dinner. Do you fancy a turn around the deck later?"

"That would be really good, actually. A bit of thinking space. And something completely unrelated that I meant to mention earlier – do you fancy trying breakfast down here tomorrow? It would make a change from fighting with everyone else in the Lido, and we haven't got a trip, so we'll have a bit more time."

"Oh my God. How can you even think about another meal when we're in the middle of this one?"

"That would be because I'm not stuffing my face with half a lamb, Mr McG," I say sweetly, arranging my knife and fork elegantly together on my empty plate. Touché.

Several thousand calories later, by my reckoning, we drag our stuffed bodies out onto the Promenade Deck. After eating the miniscule portion of beef and a massively impressive pile of greens, my several thousand extra calories arrived in the form of a pineapple crème brûlée or two, thanks to Sebastian, who was clearly feeling bad about the weeny main course. That guy will be the death of me, but I also love him very much. James, on the other hand, was suffering from over-exerting himself with the lamb and had a very tame little scoop of sorbet. Thus we are definitely only up for a slow saunter.

It's lovely to be out on deck, and I'm getting good at being ready for anything. The ballet pumps make it easy to walk, and the requisite wrap is always in my bag so I don't need to deprive James of his coat again. Can't help remembering how Mr Nasty sulked for an entire evening because I hadn't taken a jacket and he felt obliged to offer me his... ANYWAY, we've come out on the smoking side, but the deck seems to be empty – and the moon is shining across the sea, right at us. So beautiful.

"Look at that – it's shining right at us. How does it *do* that?"

"Something to do with the angle of our perspective in relation to the moon, and the fact that the light is reflected off all the waves. If it was a really still night it wouldn't be so obvious. But, ahem, don't quote me on that as my physics is rubbish." James beams a dazzling, know-it-all smile at me.

"Well, smarty-pants, this sea air is obviously causing an outbreak of intelligence in both of us. Which is surely a good sign, as the amount of alcohol I'm taking in is surely killing a few brain cells! But do I care? No."

Our light-hearted, happy banter is interrupted by a door swooshing open somewhere behind us. An irate voice precedes its owner outside.

"Well if you weren't so fucking rude, maybe we would get better service! What is wrong with you for God's sake?"

Ooh. Spiky. We continue looking out to sea as if nothing is happening. Clearly the sea air has different effects on different people.

"I don't see what's wrong with pointing out that the service is rubbish."

"Rubbish? The poor guy is obviously new, and okay, he made a mistake. No need to come down on him like a ton of bricks! You are such an arrogant shit sometimes."

James and I exchange glances and walk on away from where the angry couple are continuing their row. Don't need that after our beautiful day. We stop further along the deck and hope they won't follow. The sound of the ship cutting through the water seems much louder at night, and we lean over the side, completely captivated by its gentle rocking motion. There's a feeling of travelling onwards, ever onwards.

"Just wanted to say how much I'm enjoying this, and being with you." James breaks into my reverie. "And I've come to see that it's about enjoying the moment with whoever I'm with. It doesn't have to be romantic, just right."

Gulp. Wasn't expecting that.

"Thank you. That's so lovely. And so true. Have you ever had those times with someone when everything should be perfect – candles, picnic, music, whatever – but there's an empty ache inside, cos it just doesn't feel right? Then they're all cross because they made the effort, and you're not falling all over them with gratitude for creating something so perfect? I once had a boyfriend who took me on a surprise day out, which turned out to be a picnic beside the river. Beautiful spot, amazing food, chilled bubbly, all the stuff that other girls would have died for. And all I wanted to do was howl because it felt so empty."

"Yep. Been there, done that, and it's horrible. That's why it's good to feel so relaxed on here. No pressure, just genuine fun and chilling."

There's another couple walking towards us, and although they don't seem to be having a full–blown domestic, she's not looking happy, TBH.

"So – let me get this straight. You want to go to the casino, right now, and just dump me for the evening."

He's trying to be reasonable. "You don't like the casino, so I thought you'd like to see one of the shows."

Poor attempt, mate, in my opinion.

"Why would I want to sit and watch something on my own, like Billy No–Mates, while you're busily gambling away our money? Is there anything about that that suggests being together? Or is it an alien concept to you?"

Ouch. Definitely not winning. I grab James' arm and lead him away from them too, towards the back of the ship. Crikey. Is anywhere safe tonight?

"Must be that full moon that's setting them all off," I say. "Either that or they can't cope with being together all the time."

Apparently nowhere *is* safe as within seconds we notice a couple walking towards us at great speed. The woman is clearly unhappy as she is gesticulating wildly, and the man is just listening. Either that or he's under attack and is sensibly keeping his mouth shut.

"Oh gawd, it's Nick and Sarah, obviously having a row too. Can't we escape? Jump overboard?"

James is more sanguine. "We can just nod and walk by and let them get on with it. It'll be fine."

We get within hailing distance of them.

"Ah, hi!" calls a surprisingly smiley Sarah. "We're belting down to see the comedian, and this is the quickest way – too crowded in there. Have you seen him? Apparently he's amazing. You're welcome to join us."

Well *that* will teach me, won't it? "No we haven't. You up for it?" I look up at James.

"Absolutely!"

We arrive at the theatre just in time, and manage to get four seats together in the back row. That was lucky! Sarah goes in first, followed by Nick; then James, being the perfect gentleman he is, lets me in next. Actually it's because he wants the aisle seat for his long legs, but he is a gentleman too, without doubt. As we sit down I realise it's the theatre where we had our safety briefing; it looks a lot different now with the audience in their glad rags, rather than clutching their buoyancy aids, and most people are looking a lot browner and a lot more relaxed now they've had a few days to unwind. I suspect there are a few simmering rows, but on the whole they look a happy bunch. I smile at a few vaguely familiar faces like Mrs Grumpy – who isn't actually looking grumpy at the moment, so I only just recognise her. Maybe the cruise is doing her good too. Sitting back ready to enjoy the show, it becomes clear that the seats are very, erm, compact and that there isn't room for both Nick and me to share the armrest. There's a bit of embarrassment (from me) as our bare skins touch when we both go to lean on it. Ooh. Makes me realise I haven't had any bare skin contact in a long time, apart from jive, which doesn't count.

"Oops. Sorry!" I whisper, as the Cruise Director comes on stage to introduce the act.

"No worries, be my guest!" whispers Nick.

We're in the late show, and presumably the comedian, Lee Comet (that so *has* to be his stage name), has ramped up the content to take advantage of the child–free audience.

"You must be wondering why I'm called Lee Comet. Who's thinking that's my stage name? Come on, be brave. You can tell me in complete privacy – no-one's listening."

And so it goes on, in a very predictable but hilarious fashion. It is incredibly smutty but I haven't laughed so much for ages. He really is good. And then I notice that we've all shuffled about in our seats, rocking forward and back as one does when having a jolly good laugh and going, 'Noooo! How can he say that!'

And I also notice that Nick's leg is almost but not quite touching mine, and the next time we all laugh, it actually makes very gentle contact, but almost immediately moves away and he whispers, "Sorry!"

"No worries," I whisper back, hoping it happens again.

Chapter 20

I'm awake bright and early, despite the fact we can actually relax a bit today and go over to Villefranche on the tender when we're ready. James is still asleep so I sneak out onto the balcony in just my nightshirt, as it's plenty warm enough. The ship is moored in the bay, which according to our newsletter separates Nice and the extremely swanky Cap Ferrat, which is the bit I'm looking at now. Apparently it's the home of millionaires and the world-famous Four Seasons Grand-Hôtel du Cap-Ferrat, where suites go for so much money I can't even imagine it. Oh for some good binoculars, cos I'd love a good snoop at who just happens to be having breakfast on their balconies. The tenders are obviously going off from the other side as nothing is happening down below, from what I can see.

"You're up bright and early. I've put the kettle on for some of your lovely coffee," James pokes his nose out of the patio door. He is pure gold and I decide to keep him all to myself forever. "Last night was brilliant, wasn't it?"

He has no idea just how brilliant it was, but I'm keeping that delicious little snippet to myself. At least, for the moment. Is it pathetic that a bit of unexpected and probably meaningless physical contact sends tingles up my spine? Possibly.

"You're a treasure, and yes, it was. I haven't laughed so much in ages. *So* smutty but so funny. I've come to see that one of the benefits of getting older is being able to appreciate really filthy humour without being embarrassed by it. Did you see those youngsters in the theatre, probably in their late teens? Did you see them squirming? So funny. Nearly as funny as the comedian."

A few minutes later we're settled in our chairs with mugs of coffee, falling into a comfortable contemplative silence. The show didn't finish until late, so we piled out of the theatre and came straight back to the cabin, where the extreme emotions of the day took their toll and I think

I fell asleep in seconds. That's pretty unusual without the help of a vat of wine.

My mind wanders through the memories of the day. Touching the Madonna seems to have started a whole new ball rolling in my life as in 1) I definitely felt some kind of buzz when I touched her and that was weird, and 2) doing so had the effect of picking my emotions up and dropping them from a great height. I haven't even started to rearrange them yet. And 3) Nick. Is it all in my head?

"You're very thoughtful. Are you thinking of your stomach again?"

Bless him for unwittingly giving me a get-out. "Hmm. Guess so. Shall we try the restaurant instead of the Lido then?"

After an extremely civilised breakfast we're down on the lower deck, queuing to get onto a tender. The floaty hippy look has been swapped for practical cropped trousers and t-shirt, and pink trainers. Watching the way the tender is bobbing around, I'm also glad I've got my rucksack (water, phone and wrap safely stowed) securely on my back – this operation definitely needs two hands! We're helped into the boat by two very smiley crewmen, and I immediately lose my balance as it bobs up and down. Chuckling, I stagger to a free seat where James literally falls in next to me.

"Haven't quite got my sea legs yet," he laughs.

And he's right. Although the sea looks really calm from about eleven floors up, once we get down here the waves are actually quite big, and people are falling all over the place. There's a surprising number of passengers in the boat. I was assuming it would only take about 50 but the sign up on the stairs says 'Maximum Persons 100'. Where do they get that horrible 'persons' thing from? It's *people*, people!

Anyway, we're jammed in like sardines now, so nobody is moving at all as the tender is released from the mother ship and starts its journey to the quay. As we pull away James and I crane our necks to look up at Titania; she's imposing, magnificent and sparkling white as she floats majestically on the choppy seas. Funny to think she's the centre of our lives at the moment.

The journey to land takes about twenty minutes as it's a lot further than it looks from the top of the ship. The lady squashed in to my left seems to be on her own and is looking a bit concerned, so I start chatting to her. She tells me she booked the cruise because her recently departed husband insisted she was to carry on having a life if anything happened to him. Bless her. That can't be an easy task. Her name is June and she has the most beautiful white hair, and really gentle, smiling eyes with crinkly little lines around them. She would be absolutely at home in one of Ivy's books so I make a mental note to include her at some point.

She's relaxing a bit more now. "It isn't as bad on my own as I thought it would be, actually," she says. "I booked with our local travel agency and this is one of their escorted cruises. They have two reps on call all the time; we can meet up with them at specific times for get-togethers, and they organise where we sit for meals so we don't feel alone. I've got a few trips booked too – always wanted to see Pompeii, so I booked that one straight away. It's all turning out quite nicely. Thought I would be a brave adventurer and try this port on my own though," June smiles, probably with more bravery than she actually feels. "I love your Brandenberg amethyst," she adds, pointing to the chunky crystal hanging from a chain around my neck.

"Ah thanks. My mum gave it to me a while back, when I was having a bit of a rough time. She said it would help me to forgive and forget the past and give me healing at a very deep level. Oh, and help me to be calm and centred. Not sure how successful that bit is, to be honest, but I do love wearing it."

"Your mum is very wise. It's considered to be one of the most prized crystals and it's very powerful."

"It's funny you know, she's always been into crystals, yoga, meditation, and all that stuff, but I think I'm only just beginning to appreciate how wise she is. Strange what you get to know about your own parents."

"What, like they're people too?" June chuckles.

"Yes, definitely. She moved to Glastonbury a few years ago and she runs a B&B with a lovely guy she met there, and she's really happy."

Suddenly I miss her and realise I want to tell her about yesterday while it's still fresh in my mind. Hopefully it won't break the bank if I make a quick call when we get ashore. Talking with June has made the time speed by, and we're already pulling up to the quay, where, guess who's waiting?

I nudge James, who's been chatting to an older guy on his right. These boats are really very good for passenger relations.

"Look. It's your mate." I say, pointing at DDG photographer who is busily snapping pictures of people once they have clambered off the tender and rearranged themselves. We decide to have our picture taken in front of the 'Welcome to Villefranche' canvas backdrop he has thoughtfully arranged for us all in case we forget where we've been. Not because we really want the pic, but because I can't resist being in his gorgeous presence again, even if it is for just a few moments. And I'm nosey.

"Well, hello beautiful people! How's the cruise going?"

"Loving it, thank you. You might have to throw me off at the end, as I'm quite possibly loving it a bit too much." I turn to James." And you are too, James, aren't you?" For which I get a sharp dig in the ribs. "Does the fact that you're always there to take the pictures mean you never get a day off in port, then?" I'm on a roll.

"Oh I do. There's a few of us so yes, we do get port days off occasionally. Just that I always seem to be here when you two are getting off. Shall we?" There's a bit of a queue building up behind us, so he gestures towards the fetching backdrop, takes our picture as we pose in front of it, then with a cheery farewell moves on to his next victims.

"And what we found out from that was…. precisely nothing," says James. "Obviously plays his cards very close to his gorgeous chest."

"Talking of playing, I gather from Mia there's a 'no messing with the passengers' rule. But he clearly enjoys a bit of a flirt. Must be one of the perks of the job. And I guess it makes us feel good, so we buy the photos. Were you allowed to play with the clientele at the holiday park?"

"Ooh no. Strictly verboten. People still did in secret of course, probably like they do on the ship. But I never did – not really into that stuff."

As we wander away from the quayside towards the western side of the bay, I tell James about June, and how our conversation made me think of Mum.

"You should call her. I can have a wander, maybe find a coffee shop for us."

So I do. Hoping that she's finished the breakfasts for the guests and can talk, I wander over to a bench in the sunshine (obvs) and call the

B&B landline. I'm ridiculously happy to hear her voice.

"Mum! It's me! I'm in Villefranche. Can you talk for a minute?"

"Sweetie! Yes, I can talk for a bit. How's it going? Must either be very good or very bad for you to be calling me," she chuckles.

"You wouldn't believe how amazing it all is. The ship is gorgeous, our cabin is lovely, James bought some bubbly for us, and he paid for me to have my hair done by the friend that got us on the ship. And she cut and scrunched it and I can't believe how good it looked." I'm gabbling, but then she must be used to it by now. "And then yesterday we went to Barcelona, on a trip up to Montserrat to see the Black Madonna, and Oh. My. God."

Mum is laughing her socks off the other end. "I'm so pleased. I haven't seen the Black Madonna, always wanted to though."

"Oh she's something else. I really wasn't expecting that. The rack railway was fun, but the feeling when you get to the Basilica is out of this world. We queued up to touch her – there's just a tiny bit of her hand holding an orb, sticking out of the case – and I got such a buzz. Then we went over to a quiet bit of the cathedral and just sat down to think about it and I ended up sobbing my heart out. Even James was in tears. It was so powerful. Then I lit a candle for myself – my 'new' self – like, what's that about?! And now I feel as if a huge weight has lifted."

"Beautiful. I'm so pleased for you. Maybe touching her kicked off a deep recognition that something had to change. Sounds like you were ready for it and she was the catalyst. Sometimes just the knowledge that something is powerful is enough to give you an experience of the divine, or whatever you want to call it. That's why people go on pilgrimages, or to churches and shrines – to visit places that have built up enormous power because the people who visit them through the centuries believe they are powerful. As well as having been built on ley lines and all that stuff of course. The ancients knew a thing or two about sacred geometry." She laughs.

"Well, I'm stunned. And James had a good experience too. He's been so lovely and we really are having the best time. Is everything okay at home? Have you spoken to Aiden?"

"No, but I'll call him tonight and have a sneaky check. I'm sure he's fine, and probably loving having the place to himself. You'd better go now sweetie, or you'll be paying this bill off for months."

She's right of course, and much as I could prattle on for hours, we say our goodbyes and hang up.

James has found a table in the shade outside a coffee shop just across the road, and he's got coffees, and what look suspiciously like a couple of French pastries on a plate.

"Had to. Minimum spend for credit card," he shrugs helplessly.

I see straight through him. "You're just a greedy-guts. I happen to know you have a stash of Euros in your wallet."

Then I realise there's only one and a half pastries on the plate, and picking up the whole one, sink my teeth into a stunningly mouth-watering confection of almond paste and delicious pastry.

"Mmmm." I know it's rude to talk with my mouth full, but needs must and all that. "Wow. How do they do that? Good shout. I take it all back."

James nods in recognition and takes another mouthful of his; we sit in silence looking out over the bay, just enjoying this perfect moment.

Reality rudely intrudes with a cold, sharp breeze – the first of the cruise, actually – raising goosebumps on my bare arms. Grey clouds are now scudding across the sky at an alarming rate, and looking down at the quay, it seems the crew are having a difficult time docking the incoming tenders.

"Well that came up suddenly. I wonder what happens if we can't get back to the ship. Just look at the weather – it's really turned."

James drags himself back from the ecstasy of his coffee and pastry.

"Shit. That looks bad. No idea, actually. Think maybe we should join the queue to get back on, don't you? I'm not bothered about staying if you're not."

"Yep, good idea. Looking at those clouds, it's only going to get worse. And then we can just collapse on the ship and relax ready for our big day out tomorrow. *So* excited about that!" I chuckle to myself as I realise that I seem to be 'so excited' about everything at the moment. And what an unusual feeling that is.

We join the queue and observe with increasing concern the difficulty the crew are having manoeuvring the tenders up to the quay. The tenders coming in seem to be empty, so presumably people have been stopped from leaving the ship. We get into conversation with a couple behind us who say they had a real problem on one of the Caribbean islands, when a storm hit unexpectedly and the ship had to move to another bay in order for the tenders to dock safely. So I guess there is usually a way to get back to the ship. Hopefully. Must say I'm not that confident when it comes to our turn to board, as with the boat jumping all over the place, the crew are having a struggle getting people from shore to tender. After what seems an age we're finally loaded and move away from the quay, which is when the waves really hit.

"Woaaahhh!" I can't help shouting out as the tender tilts upwards into what feels like almost vertical, and the woman across from me lands in my lap. She's just apologised and I've said it's fine, when suddenly the tender reaches the crest of the wave and plunges straight back down in the opposite direction, and I go hurtling into her. The window at the end is open and a whole load of water pours through, soaking those closest to it. As we move further out towards the ship we're also hit by the cross-wind, which throws us every which way. The lady next to James is starting to panic and saying she'll be sick if it carries on like this.

"You'll be fine," he's saying, in an easy, chatty manner, with the confidence of experience that I absolutely know he doesn't have. "They have to cope with this sort of stuff all the time."

Like, how the hell does HE know? It's working though, as she has fallen for the McGrew charm and gone back down to Defcon 1.

There are more voices piping up.

"Are we going to be alright?"

"I'm gonna be sick!"

In amongst the growing panic and being thrown all over the place, I can also hear sobbing as more water comes in through the window.

"What if we sink? There's too much water coming in!"

"Hey, we're not going to sink." It's James, being very confident again. "It's brilliant that we've got fresh air coming in, which will help us not to feel sick. Come on, a nice big breath in, hold a second, then out through your mouth….. And again…. The crew don't need us to be panicking, do they?"

And bugger me, they're doing it.

The atmosphere in the tender calms down considerably, even though the weather outside most definitely has not, and after what seems like an eternity we draw close to Titania. The crew take the boat around the other side from where we disembarked, as there is more protection from the wind. After several failed attempts we finally pull up to the boarding platform and are helped off by the crew when there's a break in the swell. As I stand up I realise I am a lot more wobbly than I expected, and grab James' arm to avoid going arse-over-tit as another wave hits us.

Safely back on the ship, a bunch of people are congregating on the other side of security which is odd as they usually belt straight to the lifts, lazy lot that they are. Then as we get through ourselves, they head en masse for James, the women hugging him and the men shaking his hand.

"Thanks mate – got a bit scary out there!"

"Cheers – thanks for that. Are you crew?"

June (didn't notice her on the tender) gives James a big hug then turns to me. "Amazing man you have there. I'd hang onto him if I were you." Oh, if only I could…

Chapter 21

After the first few flights of stairs my legs start to regain a bit of strength, and by the time we've climbed all twenty flights up to the Lido I'm feeling a lot more me, if a touch out of breath. All things are relative, aren't they? Like, one would think that sitting in my flat is a lot more homely and stable than being on a cruise ship. But then sitting with a glass of restorative Chardonnay in the Lido is one hell of a lot more comforting and stable than being on the tender. Oooh yesss!

"So. What other surprises do you have in store for me? You conjure up a fabulous cruise in three days flat, turn out to be a line-dancing and ladies' fashion superhero, then single-handedly calm down a load of panicking tourists who think they're gonna drown. What's going on?"

Unusually for James, he's quietly cuddling a glass of Merlot. He's normally a cold beer man at lunchtime, but then the sky has turned very dark and everyone has moved indoors away from the pool as it looks like there's a huge storm coming. So not cold beer weather at all.

He grins, and looks over at me, then down into his Merlot.

An enigmatic silence follows and for once I'm patient.

Then he speaks. "The calming down bit was easy. We had a few tricky situations at the holiday park. We get trained for emergencies. Granted, not quite like that one, but it's basically the same."

"It's more than that though. You're thoughtful. And all kind of calm. And different. Not the you that went to London – that was the party animal – so something has changed. Do you want to tell me about it?"

"Well, maybe. I'm still thinking about it all, to be honest. When I first went to live in London – and I was so ready to do that – it seemed like one big party. The people at work are so cool and really sociable and I like making new friends, so it all went swimmingly for a while. I moved up late summer, so it was all about sitting outside bars drinking beer and wine after work, having this amazing social life, while living in one of the most exciting and vibrant cities in the world.

Then as the evenings drew in and people went straight home from work, usually outside London, and the parties and good times faded into distant memory, I realised I was really lonely. And that my life, which had seemed so exciting and debonair, was actually very shallow. It's a ridiculously expensive place to live, so money was tight – and any money I did have I didn't want to spend on going out to get wrecked. Assuming I could find anyone to go out and get wrecked with. So I stayed in and got wrecked instead, and got more and more depressed."

I'm so sad to hear this, but James never let on that he was having a rough time. "Why didn't you tell me what was going on?"

"Too proud to ask for help. I wanted to manage it all myself – without running back to friends because I couldn't cope. I wanted to find my own answers, for once."

"So what happened?"

"It got to Christmas and I crashed. I told Mum and Dad I wasn't coming home for the holiday as I didn't want them to see me like that. Said I was doing some charity work or something so they thought I was amazing, but actually I just stayed holed up in my little flat having a private meltdown, which involved an awful lot of alcohol, and definitely no turkey with trimmings.

Then by some miracle, the weather on Boxing Day was lovely. That, at least, I did notice. I wandered out into the sunshine and ended up at Battersea Park, which is a bit quieter than the other parks. I sat down on a bench for a while, just enjoying the unexpected warmth of the sun. After a while I became aware of a group of people sitting quietly under one of the trees. Not chatting, just sitting cross-legged, and I assumed they were meditating, as people do all kinds of crazy things outdoors in London. Then I realised that other people were joining them, one by one. Some were wearing brown robes, others just ordinary clothes, but they all sat quietly, eyes closed, sending out a massive sense of peace."

I'm about to blurt out something like, 'Woah, you've joined a cult!', but I have an unexpected attack of sensitivity and hold back. This is obviously a huge thing for James. "And….?"

"Well, I just sat on that bench for ages, and closed my eyes too. Didn't have a clue what I was doing, but it felt good. Good to be with people. And good to be with people who weren't drinking themselves stupid or just up for a quick shag. Eventually one of them – I assume it was one of the monks – sounded a bell, and they gradually got up and stretched. I stayed on the bench, not wanting it to end because for the first time in ages I felt calm, and not lonely. Then a guy from the group came over and asked if he could sit down. We got chatting and I ended up telling him the whole sorry story. Turns out he had a similar one, and he also got right to the end of the road before he found something that made sense. He told me about the meditation group he was going to and invited me along. So I went."

"And was it all... weird and culty?" Really hoping it's not, as then I'd definitely have to be sarcastic.

"Not in the least. Just ordinary people trying to understand their crazy, mixed-up lives."

That's a relief then. "And how do they do that? Just by meditating?"

"That's a very big part of it. Meditating starts with watching the breath, like I was getting those people to do on the boat. It's a very powerful technique you can use anywhere, and I've found it really helpful. If my breathing is all out of synch then the rest of me is also off balance, so I'm learning how to use my breath to calm myself down. And will always be learning. It isn't something that you can ever come to the end of, which appeals to my low boredom threshold. Haha!"

"I'm so pleased for you. And it explains why you have been so different from how you were when we last met in person – which was ages ago, thanks to the wonders of the internet."

Luisa's shadow falls across the table. I've been so engrossed in James that I haven't been aware of anything for a while.

"Madam, I could see you have been very busy talking, so you must be very thirsty. Can I get you both some more drinks?"

Love her. James nods and thanks her and she disappears to the bar.

"And where does all this fit in with what happened at Montserrat?"

"It's another piece of the puzzle that is me, I guess. I realised that I'm changing and learning all the time, and by going back to the breath I can keep a sense of balance in the midst of all that. It was a massive relief to realise that I don't have to be defined by my upbringing, but I've got no idea how it will affect me. Maybe I just need to keep on keeping on and see what happens."

A whole bunch of people pour in through the doors, as presumably several more tenders have managed to dock. By the colour of their faces it looks like things have got a whole lot worse out there.

"Ladies and gentlemen, this is the Captain speaking. The remaining passengers on tours will be returning early, and the ship will depart as soon as they are safely on board as we want to be ahead of this storm if we can. Consequently, and also for safety reasons, the Sailaway party will take place in the Sky Bar for those passengers capable of remaining upright. It is going to be choppy out there once we get going, but the ship has stabilisers so we hope it won't affect you too badly. I will give you further information as we have it." Such a wag.

Luisa arrives with our drinks, and I get the bright idea of going out to look over the side and watch the tenders docking.

"Really? I'm nice and cosy in here." James isn't excited.

"No worries, I'll go out on my own. Just want to see what's going on." And I scoot off, leaving my drink in his care, pretty safe as I know he hates Chardonnay.

Wandering out somewhat naively through the sliding doors I'm smacked full in the face by a wind which is so strong it's hard to get my breath. Woah. Huge waves are building up in the middle pool as the ship rocks from side to side, and literally as I'm watching they start to spill over the edge and onto the deck. And this is with stabilisers?

Fuck.

That's scary.

Determined to have just a teeny look over the side I fight against the wind towards the handrail where I can hang on for grim death and look down. Several tenders are circling, taking it in turns to disgorge their passengers, which is no easy task. Not just all sunshine and smiles then for the crew – they must have some serious skills for times like this, as it really wouldn't look good if they lost anyone. One lady almost falls into the gap as a massive wave suddenly lifts the tender but thankfully they manage to drag her across to safety. She's gonna have one hell of a story to tell her grandkids. Finally beaten by the sheer force of the wind and being face-lashed by my hair, it's another fight back into the Lido and to our table, where James is talking to Sarah.

Oh.

"Hi!" I say, breezily (haha) as I make my way back to my wine and my seat. "It's a bit nuts out there, isn't it? They just nearly lost someone getting onto the ship from the tender. But only nearly. She's okay, I think."

"Yes. I only went off for a bit of a look around, which wasn't really worth all the hassle. Thankfully I don't seem to get seasick – some poor souls were looking very green on our tender."

I'm wondering where Nick is, but don't want to ask.

"They were starting to panic on ours, but James talked them down. He's our resident Zen master." I grin mischievously at him, and he shoots me a 'shut up!' kind of look.

Sarah looks questioningly at him.

"It was nothing really. Just if you distract people when they're panicking it helps to calm them down."

I could do with some of that as I'm still wondering where Nick is. For some reason my heart is skipping around a bit.

"That's interesting. What exactly did you do?"

Oops. I'm going to be in trouble for this.

"Just talked to them and told them we weren't going to sink and got them to focus on their breathing."

"And they did it," I interrupt like a proud parent. "Some of them were really starting to lose it and he calmed them down."

At that moment, June appears beside Sarah, looking very petite and sweet compared to Sarah's tall and highly toned frame.

"Don't want to interrupt, just wanted to say thank you dear. And if I could book you as my personal escort that would be amazing." She beams at James, which lights up her whole face and makes her look so lovely. "Just joking," she chuckles, "but you were excellent on there, and the world needs more people like you. And now I'm off to a room where some very brave souls are going to try and teach me bridge. I may be a while!"

Aah. How kind. James looks touched and somewhat surprised and Sarah sits down at the table with an attitude of 'I want to know more'.

"James, I've just noticed they're serving tea. Shall I go and get you a plateful of cakes? Sarah?"

Oh no, of course, she doesn't really eat. And where's Nick? It's usually the other way round – she's safely away somewhere and Nick's wandering free.

"Ooh yes please – the usual," says James. "As much cream and chocolate as you can get and a cup of tea."

Sarah shakes her head. "No, I'm off to the gym soon, but thanks for asking."

Phew. I know she was better than I expected last night, but I freely admit to being completely intimidated by her – so I'm relieved she's on a timetable for something and we won't be stuck with her for ages. How could anyone (i.e. Nick of course) fall in love with someone as hard as she seems to be? Totally lost in thought, I pile straight into someone as I'm heading for the cake counter at the other end of the buffet. Hands grab my arms to steady me and as they do so I look up into Nick's lovely brown eyes.

Gulp.

Straight out of one of Ivy's books. Per-lease.

"You okay? You were miles away. What were you thinking about? Looked important."

How I don't like your wife and I wonder if you are really separated and did you mean to touch my leg and also where you were. "Um, oh, just the journey back on the tender and stuff. Ours was pretty hairy. Did you go off?"

"No. Sarah wanted a look around over there, but I just wanted to stay on the ship and relax, read – oh and drink coffee obviously. Glad I did in the circumstances! You're on the cake run? Need a hand?"

And we end up walking very companionably to the cake area, where we snaffle a big pile of treats and some coffees and a tea for James. I tell Nick that Sarah is talking to James but that she is off to the gym, so he just gets her some water.

"At least she's cheap to run," I quip, and instantly regret it.

He laughs. Phew. "Thankfully I'm not involved in those details anymore."

Ah. So they really ARE living apart. Could I be over-thinking this? Has been known, on occasion.

Back at the table Sarah is just standing up, ready to go. She spots Nick and me walking back together and her eyes flicker from him to me to him. Ooh.

"Great timing, I'm just off."

And she goes, just like that. What was that about?! I look at Nick.

"Don't worry about it. Being on here is more difficult than we expected, so we're having as little 'together' time as possible. That's why it's easy to be with you two – not that we're stalking you, promise. Just that you're not all lovey-dovey like quite a lot of the others. Oh. Whoops! Sorry – that was really intrusive. I sort of assumed you're just friends. Like we're trying to be. And failing. Oh shit. You are just friends, right?"

James and I look at each other and burst out laughing. It's the first time anyone has actually asked anything about our 'relationship'. I gesture to James, as in 'you go for it, mate, whatever you say is fine by me'.

"Honestly, it's fine. Don't worry. Cait and I have been friends for years, grew up in the same town, then I scuttled off to London to work last year. We stayed in touch, and it seemed she was in need of a swanky holiday so I rode to the rescue on my white charger, scooped her up and delivered her to the cruise ship."

Nick looks at me, like, 'really?'

"Yep – what he says." And I just look back at him until I can't stay serious anymore and start laughing again. "No, really. I was a bit low..."

"A LOT low," James interrupts.

"… true, very low, and a friend made me realise that what I needed was a holiday, only there wasn't anyone to go with. So I mentioned it to James and a few days later he booked *this*. He happens to know someone who works on here and called in a favour to rescue me from my desperate plight. Sorry, a bit of the day job sneaked in there."

He's got no idea just how much of the day job is sneaking in right now.

"So you only knew about this last week?"

"Last Wednesday, to be precise."

"That's really exciting – must be so much fun to do that. We've been, erm, 'looking forward' to this for about four months, and from my point of view, with a certain amount of dread. In some ways I wish we'd just cancelled or that one of us had come alone. It was a real spur of the moment thing, booked and deposit paid when we seemed to be making a bit of headway. Thought it would give us something to look forward to. Then very soon afterwards we had the most massive row ever, and I left."

"Oh, I'm so sorry." I genuinely am. I don't even like writing about rows and upsets. Why can't people just be civil to one another, even if the relationship has come to an end? Because some people just aren't very nice, I remind myself, thinking of Mr Nasty.

"Don't be. It's been on the cards for a very long time and we probably should have been brave enough to face it before. Thankfully there's no children, so it's just our own mess to sort out."

"Good afternoon, everyone, this is the Captain speaking. I'm delighted to say that all passengers are now on board, so we have weighed anchor and will shortly be leaving the shelter of the bay. There will be a strong crosswind, so the ship is likely to pitch a bit, despite the stabilisers. In anticipation of this the Promenade Deck and other passenger walkways on the outside of the ship have been closed off for your own safety. However, we are hoping to outrun the storm before too long, so you should be able to go ahead and enjoy your evening as expected. I will of course update you should conditions change."

We all look at each other.

"Not that I was planning to go for my constitutional around the Prom Deck of course," I say to break the ice, feeling just a bit troubled by that little snippet.

"Well, we didn't get sick in the tender, so I'm sure we'll be fine with this," adds James, cheerily. "Where shall we go to watch? Or do you think we're good here?"

"I reckon here – plus there's food if we need it." And drink, obvs.

Nick has been watching this exchange, shaking his head slowly. "You two are nuts. Like a comedy act."

"We do bring out the worst in each other," I agreed. "We upset some fellow diners in the restaurant one night because we were having a discussion about the merits of gay and straight sex. Which, I have to say, wasn't started by me. It was him," nodding at James.

"Well the waiters were loving it – it was just some of the punters got up and left….WOAH!"

We've obviously hit that 'crosswind' as the ship tilts sharply and our now empty plates and mugs slide en masse across the table. Not my glass though, which was clearly the priority here, as my lightning fast reactions have saved me losing my last mouthful of Chardonnay. This is going to be fun.

Chapter 22

Actually, it wasn't fun at all, I'm thinking, as we speed our way towards Rome on the train. I wasn't seasick but it was pretty scary watching the ship pitch from one side to another. Chairs were sliding around the Lido at an alarming rate, so James and I went back to our cabin to read, where it wasn't so noticeable. I suspect Nick went anywhere *but* his cabin, poor guy. A bit later on we made it down to our usual table in what was a decidedly empty restaurant, where Sebastian told us with a big grin on his face there have been much worse storms, and this was really nothing to worry about. Nevertheless, the atmosphere around the ship was very subdued, with several shows being cancelled as it would have been too dangerous for any dancing on stage.

So we had a very quiet and civilised evening holding tightly onto our wine glasses, made it through the night in one piece and without being sick, and today we're being intrepid explorers; some speedy research before we came away (prompted by talking to Dad), confirmed it's perfectly possible to get to Rome under our own steam. And hopefully a lot more fun. Even if we can't get into the Vatican museum, at least we will be able to have a wander round and maybe look at some of the landmarks used in *Angels and Demons*. Yes, I know. Sad. Visit one of the most amazingly beautiful and historic cities in the world, the heart of the Roman Empire, and spend my time going around locations mentioned in a novel.

"Isn't it incredibly ironic that while the Catholic Church banned filming in the Holy See due to the 'blasphemous nature' of the book, both it and the film have probably been responsible for a massive increase in tourism? And therefore, it was actually good for them?" I see I've disturbed James from his snooze. "Oops. Sorry."

"I'm awake now. If they were banned from filming how did the film get made? It looked as if they were really there."

"Ah. I read a bit about that. The producers were really clever. They sent a team of people who mixed with tourists and took thousands of photos and a lot of video footage. That helped the special effects department create CGI images which recreated the Square right down to the shadows cast by the statues and monuments. Then they used the crowds they'd filmed as the cast for the hundreds shown in the square. Smart work-around huh? I like that kind of thinking."

"Yes?! I would never have believed that in a million years as it's so realistic – especially the antimatter explosion scene – d'you remember that?"

"Never fear you're not a proper bloke, James. You really are such a blokey bloke. Only a bloke would say, 'oh, do you remember the antimatter explosion scene? Yes, I do, actually. And it was totally brilliant, as is the entire film. So even if we're visiting the sites and the filming didn't really happen there, I still think it will be amazing."

"Where are we starting from then? Don't tell me you've researched that too."

"No, not really. It's just that I was so inspired by the book that I'm more interested in Rome than I might otherwise have been. Probably like several million other people, so it might be a touch busy."

"And when you say, 'not really', just how 'not really' is that?"

"Um, well," I say, getting a couple of neatly folded sheets of paper out of my rucksack, and opening them out to show a map on the first page, "I think we should get out at San Pietro station, rather than Termini which is the furthest point, so we can get to St Peter's Square more easily. I don't think for a minute we'll have time to queue for the Vatican Museum, but we will be able to have a mooch around, then maybe make our way across taking in the Pantheon – which by the way is a miracle of engineering, having the largest unreinforced concrete dome in the world, and is apparently totally awesome – and some other stuff, and lunch of course, then we'll have plenty of time to get the train back to the port from Termini."

"And you managed to research that as well as shop and pack and get your nails done all in three days."

"Needs must, an' all that," and what I hope is a beatific smile spreads across my suntanned features. I know this because I noticed in the mirror this morning that I'm actually starting to look quite tanned and healthy. Not healthy as in lots of exercise, as that so hasn't been happening. No gym, no Pilates, no pounding up and down the pool. More 'healthy' as in eating a lot and drinking a lot and relaxing and enjoying myself properly for the first time in absolutely ages. Having said that, I really do want to get to the gym ASAP. It *must* be good if Sarah is practically living there.

"Jeez. I'm impressed. But then why am I not surprised?"

"You mean I'm doing that control-freaky thing again?"

"Mmmaybe? Just an observation. But actually I'm very glad you did as I must admit I didn't think of it. So thank you."

Very shortly the train pulls into San Pietro station and we don't even have to look at my printout – we just join the stream of tourists who all appear to be heading in the same direction – and suddenly we're in St Peter's Square.

"Oh. My. God. This is way bigger than anything in London. I mean it's HUGE. Look at all the columns, and statues, and… and…" James is clearly impressed.

As am I. It is as grand and beautiful as I was hoping it would be. If the architects intended to intimidate the humble little person on the street into insignificance with these buildings, they certainly succeeded. What confuses me is that the square is actually set within what appears to be a circle of buildings. Maybe that makes it a squircle. Lol. We stand there for quite some time, just literally staring at the absolute grandeur of it all.

I turn to James. "Don't you think it's interesting that they designed such massive buildings? They must have had something to prove to the rest of the world. Well, clearly they did cos they took over most of it, didn't they?"

"So, like the speed merchant who belts around in his souped-up sports car probably has a really small penis? That kind of thing?"

"Haha. I see you reached about the same level in history as I did!"

"Yes. And at times like this I wish I'd paid more attention."

"Aha!" I wave my sheets of paper in his face. "Here we have it. Well, at least the history of Rome according to Dan Brown."

We're about to move on when a stream of tourists following their guide cuts across our path. They're heading towards the entrance to the

Vatican, which is guarded by some guys wearing the weirdest clothes ever. I know I've seen *Angels and Demons,* but they still look like court jesters to me. I catch some snatches of English from the group as they pass by, so when they pause to listen to the guide I move over to be just on the edge and out of her eyesight. How handy is that?

James joins me, and we listen carefully as she explains that the jesters are called the Pontifical Swiss Guard, whose history goes back over 500 years, and they are actually highly-trained bodyguards from the Swiss army. So not unlike our guards at Buckingham Palace then. I'm just wondering what the Swiss army are doing in Italy, when she explains that in medieval times they had a fearsome reputation of being virtually unbeatable. They were also highly valued as they never switched sides (chuckles at that from the crowd), so were highly sought-after to guard European royals. Ah. That all makes sense now. And it seems that their job isn't just ceremonial, as they very efficiently kept the Vatican safe from the Nazi invasion in World War Two, and would without doubt repel any threat in the current day. There are only 135 of them and their uniform, in the colours of the House of Medici, has remained unchanged since it was designed in the early 1900s.

I like this guide. Much more interesting than someone spouting a load of dates and figures. Unfortunately we can't take advantage of any more free information as she leads the crocodile towards the museum entrance, where of course we can't follow.

"I want to come back here and do the whole tour thing with a proper guide," I say to James, leading him out into the middle of the squircle towards the Egyptian Obelisk. "It's fascinating. And imagine this square packed with people to hear the Pope's Christmas message. Or Easter message. It must be so powerful. Just remember how we felt at Montserrat and magnify that thousands of times."

"Don't think I'd like being with all those people. And what the hell is an Egyptian Obelisk doing in the middle of Rome?"

"Apparently there were thirteen of them at one time, brought from Egypt by various different emperors, although this one was moved from its original site." I look up from my papers. "And this circle we're standing in is called the Wind Rose, because it has relief sculptures of angels blowing wind from each of the sixteen compass points.

In the book, Langdon arrives here looking for the one representing the West, which is the next clue on the Path of Illumination. It was here, under the obelisk, you'll remember, that the second cardinal was murdered – his lungs were punctured and he was left to die in the middle of crowds of people."

"Yes – have to say all the murders were pretty grim… Even though they were played out by actors in front of a green screen. Very effective. At this rate you'll be offering your own tours. And we won't make it back to the ship before she sails."

"True. We'd better crack on as I'm starting to feel a bit hungry and we absolutely have to have pizza while we're here. Let's head for Castel Sant'Angelo which is where there's supposed to be the secret tunnel leading to the Vatican. In the book it was also the lair of the Illuminati, and it was the passageway that enabled Langdon to get back to St Peter's Square in record time for the anti-matter explosion scene. It's about a 15 minute walk from here."

We follow the route suggested on my map that takes us over the Ponte Sant'Angelo Bridge, delivering as promised an astounding view of the castle, which we duly photograph. Walking across the bridge itself is somewhat spooky as it's lined on both sides by statues of angels. I get that distinct feeling their eyes are following me and I hurry across as fast as I can.

"Are you doing that funny holding your breath thing again?" calls James, who is left behind as the slow saunter is suddenly upgraded to a mad dash.

"Nooo. It's just these angels. Don't they give you the creeps? Reminds me of that *Doctor Who* episode, 'Weeping Angels', where they move as soon as you blink, or take your eyes off them. I keep thinking one of them is suddenly going to appear inches in front of me."

"Ah. Yes. Thanks for that, Cait," and James ups his speed too, arriving at my side in seconds. "We'll run when we go back across, okay?"

The castle itself has a pretty gory history having been everything from a mausoleum to a fortress, jail and place of execution. I'm not especially eager to go inside, which is just as well as we don't have the time.

"OK, been there, done that. We can't go in and I'm hungry now. Shall we walk on to the next one and find a restaurant on the way? I'm getting a bit worried about the time. I'd like to see the Fountain of the Four Rivers, which is in Piazza Navona, about another 10 minutes from here. That's where the fourth Cardinal was drowned. But as he wasn't really, we can appreciate what is supposed to be a beautiful fountain. After that, the Pantheon is just round the corner, then we can go on to the train station."

As it happens, we pass a restaurant which isn't ridiculously overpriced as it's a bit off the main drag, and collapse gratefully at a table in the shade. It's way hotter in Rome than I expected and even being out of the sun doesn't really help as the heat builds up under the awning. But a glass or two of chilled Pinot Grigio does. When in Rome... lol. The pizza is pretty magnificent too when it arrives. Our waiter suggested a huge Quattro Stagione to share and it was definitely a good shout. This is on a light pastry base with lots and lots of topping, and melted cheese, and it's dripping with olive oil. Oh my word. James and I grin at each other over our greasy chins. This *is* in fact the life and home seems very, very far away. It's a brilliant feeling.

Happily fed and watered we're back on the road, and with the help of our waiter's directions are very soon standing in front of the fountain where the fourth cardinal died in the book, but was rescued in the film. Confusing. I thought it was a really dramatic scene actually, all the more impressive considering they didn't actually film it all there.

I shuffle through my notes. "The square itself is reputed to be one of the most beautiful in Italy. It was originally built for races, sporting events and bloody gladiator competitions (why *were* they so bloodthirsty?) but the key feature is now the Fountain of the Four Rivers with of course, a whacking great obelisk in the middle. The four male statues represent the four major rivers of the four continents that papal authority had spread through – the Nile for Africa, the Danube for Europe, the Ganges for Asia, and the Rio de la Plata for the Americas."

"Crikey. Nothing like a bit of showing off, is there?"

"Oh, there's shitloads of symbolism – and the shenanigans that went on behind the scenes is mind-blowing – but I didn't print that off, so I can't bore you with it." I chuckle at James' face, which is wearing a relieved expression. "Come on. Next stop is the Pantheon. It's quite funny, because we're doing this completely arse-about-face. It made sense at the time, but this is like watching the film backwards as that's where it all started."

"Yes, but that doesn't really matter. We've been bold explorers, had a proper Italian pizza, and seen quite a bit of Rome in the process, so I think you've done brilliantly."

"Why, thank you. I'm having so much fun. Real life seems a very long way away, and it can just stay there as far as I'm concerned."

My map is beautifully accurate (thank you Google!) and soon we're standing in the hot and very busy Piazza della Rotonda. I can't help wondering how many other tourists are following the *Angels and Demons* route, as it's an excellent way to see Rome. It occurs to me that I really wouldn't have known what to look for otherwise. It's free to get into the Pantheon and once inside we're surprised at how roomy and light it is, despite being filled with tourists.

"That's the oculus", I say, pointing up to the hole in the ceiling. "It's 8.8 metres in diameter and it's the only source of light in here, and when it rains the water that comes in drains away from the floor, which is gently sloped for that purpose. Haha. Wouldn't really work in England, would it? I'm paraphrasing, by the way," I say, waving my paper under James' nose. "But, hey, listen to this. The diameter of the dome is 43.2 metres and is in perfect proportion with the actual building by the fact that the distance from the floor to the top of the dome is exactly equal to its diameter. Wow. They knew a thing or two, didn't they? It was designed by Hadrian (who is responsible for many of the beautiful buildings in Rome as well as that Wall) who wanted it as a temple to worship all gods – which is what Pantheon means, apparently. And he said the oculus was so 'prayers would rise like smoke toward that void where we place the gods'. Isn't that a lovely thought? Anyway, all that ended on 13th May 609 when it was consecrated as a Christian Church. Nowadays Mass is held regularly and people can even get married here."

We wander round for quite a while, captivated by the sense of history and the beauty of the building itself, which doesn't really look much from the outside. Eventually, having separated and wandered round in different directions only to meet in the middle, we decide we really do need to be leaving to stand any chance of getting back to the ship in time.

Chapter 23

Safely back on the train and rejoicing in its air conditioning, I'm deep in thought about the last couple of days. They've had an unexpectedly religious theme and it makes me think of Mum and Glastonbury, and how she seems to have found her spiritual home, and is so happy. And I think about all the priests and nuns we saw scurrying around St Peter's Square, probably outrageously happy to be in the absolute heart of their religion. And the Swiss guards, whose devotion is so absolute that they would die to protect the Pope.

"James, are you asleep?"

"You absolutely crack me up when you do that. No, I wasn't actually. I was just thinking about the last few days."

"Me too. What were you thinking about?"

"About how religion either seems to give people a meaning in life or it completely fucks them over. And you?"

"Nothing quite so succinct, to be honest. But kind of similar. Except I hadn't got to the 'fucking people over' bit."

"Well think about it. I'm starting to see that if you come to a place of faith, religion, discipline, whatever, of your own volition, and maybe out of genuine interest, it is much more likely to mean something than if it's shoved down your throat from an early age."

"Which is what happened with you, from what you said the other day."

"Pretty much. Sort of 'my way or no way', and so I abandoned myself to the 'no way' as I clearly didn't fit in with the rest of the family. And I think that's been responsible for a lot of my troubles, to be honest. Not only feeling I didn't fit in, but that I was actually a bad person because of being gay. That doesn't mean I'm blaming my family, just that with nothing to guide me or support me in that sense, I wandered from pillar to post, a bit lost. I was floating free as a fairy in the wind." He hams up the last bit to lighten the sudden heavy tone of the conversation, as only James can.

It works, and I chuckle. "Just think what the world would have missed if you hadn't. We wouldn't have had 'the James Experience.'"

"There's some might say that would've been a good thing," he says, and laughs. "I do know I'm a bit much for some people. But, hey ho. That's the rich tapestry of life. They don't have to hang around me, do they? Anyway, enough of me. What were you thinking about?"

"Well, fortunately for me, I haven't had the 'fucking you over' experience with religion, only a gaping hole waiting to be filled. Which has probably led me to have the same experience, only with people. A person, actually. But I was thinking about how having a sense of the divine, or faith, or call it what you will, seems to give people such comfort. Just look at what happened to us at Montserrat. We went there with completely open minds and yet suddenly we were in touch with something that resonated so deeply within us, and I personally loved that. And you say you've found calmness and peace in meditation. And Mum seems to be so happy at Glastonbury."

"And...?"

"I've never felt that before. And I don't want to lose the feeling. I've started coming out of my shell on this holiday for sure, but I've also discovered something a lot deeper in me, which I really didn't expect – especially on a holiday with you!" I grin and shove him with my elbow.

"That's how I like to be – full of surprises!" he beams at me and laughs. "It's nice to see you kind of waking up after a period of much darkness. You remind me a lot of Dory in *Finding Nemo*. I wonder if you could go a whole day, or even an hour, without going, 'Ooh look!' Which I love, by the way, so please don't stop. And as you said, you should write about all this. For yourself. Under your own name. A bit like Elizabeth Gilbert did with *Eat, Pray, Love*. And then get some Hollywood star to endorse it and get it made into a film. Now wouldn't that be amazing? Doing Ivy's stuff is okay but it isn't really you, is it? I mean, not the new you that I'm seeing right now. And there's a story in all that. Like surviving the difficult relationship and learning to have a bit of faith in yourself again – you don't know where any of that might lead."

"Yeah, I might turn into a hippy and go and live in Glastonbury with Mum!"

"Nothing would surprise me at the moment! And I definitely think you should go and stay there for a while, so she can get to know the new 'you' during hikes up the Tor. You've never gone up there, have you?"

"No, funnily enough, considering how close she lives to it. But if I'm going to do that I'd better get in that gym, cos at this rate they'll have to hoist me up!" I've noticed in the last few days that my clothes are a teeny bit tighter than they were. But there's all that food and drink… so hard to resist. All hail for stretchy fabric.

"Well Sarah certainly spends enough time in there."

"Presumably that's to avoid being with Nick."

"Well I'm going to investigate tomorrow, after Naples. Much too tired today. All this sightseeing is wearing me out. At this rate, I'll be glad of the next sea day. And would you believe it, I'm hungry again."

We're too tired to participate in the forthcoming Sailaway party, so armed with books and swimming stuff we retreat to the quieter pool and bag some sun loungers. After a day tramping the streets of Rome and a hot wait for the shuttle bus to get us back to the port, I'm more than ready to slide into the cool water. And I don't even care about my hair. I've scrunched it into a pony tail, which fans out behind me as I lay on my back, and closing my eyes against the bright sunshine, allow the coolness to seep into my scalp. Aaah. Heaven.

Ouch. I so lose the plot during my floating that my head bumps into the edge of the pool. I come to and get upright in time to see James laughing his socks off. If he was wearing any, obvs.

"Just thought I'd leave you alone as you looked so peaceful. And I was so sure you'd wake up when you got close to the edge." He carries on laughing, so I scoop some water at him. "Nooo! Mercy! Look, I have a peace offering."

Having a quiet Sailaway doesn't of course preclude us from having a drink, so while I've been floating my cares away, James has done the honourable thing and acquired a glass of chilled wine and a plate of sandwiches to help me stave off the hunger until dinner.

One of the lovely things about the Med at this time of the year is that, even at this time in the late afternoon, it's so warm I don't even have to dry off. I just haul myself from the pool to the lounger, and sit in my bikini, wet hair pulled back, sunnies in place, enjoying chilled wine and a bit of food – and in barely no time I'm dry. How much better can it get?

After a while the Captain announces that we're ready to leave, so we wander over to the side and watch the lines being released and the ship's thrusters gently pushing it away from the quay. I never really appreciated how slowly everything happens with ships – obvs because I've never had any dealings with them – and I kind of chuckle to myself thinking what kind of damage too much of a 'left hand down' could do. But on the other hand it would also take ages to make an emergency manoeuvre, which is a sobering thought.

With Civitavecchia disappearing into the distance, we retreat to a jacuzzi. This is rapidly becoming one of my favourite times of the day. After the excitement of the Sailaway, and no doubt tired of their exertions, most of the passengers head for their cabins to rest and get ready for dinner, so we really are left in peace.

I yawn and stretch out in the hot bubbles. "I am SO tired. D'you mind if we eat up here tonight? I feel like just scruffing my hair up in a bun and coming up here in jeans to stuff my face, as I'm also incredibly hungry. Again."

"With you on that one – it all seems a bit too much of an effort from where I'm sitting. We could just come up here to eat and hang out until bed."

In fact, lazy slobs that we are, we missed out the middle stage and just stayed at the Lido until they opened for dinner. The evening was so warm we found an outside table and continued our musings under the lush velvet canopy of the Mediterranean night sky until it was time for an early stagger to bed. Awesome.

Chapter 24

Still seriously tired from our exploits in Rome, we only just make it to the coach in time next morning. Walking down the aisle to the remaining seats at the back, we spot the lovely June, who seems to be very engrossed with her mini-group, and Mrs Grumpy, who is actually talking in an animated fashion to Mr Grumpy, but they both pause to beam at James, as do a few others who recognise him from the tender incident. Sweet. His fan club is growing, and I wonder what will happen at the next line dance class.

I haven't done any research for this port, so settling into my window seat I'm happy to listen to our guide, and to be amazed and stunned by Pompeii, and also Vesuvius, which we will pass on the way. We learn that Pompeii was badly damaged by a massive earthquake in 62 CE, so fortunately it still wasn't fully occupied when Vesuvius erupted 17 years later. Sadly a lot of the people who were there were a bit too interested in watching what was going on and didn't leave in time. Either that or they didn't have anywhere to go, choosing instead to take shelter where they could. It's thought they were killed almost instantly by the waves of scorching hot toxic gases – hence the grotesque postures a lot of them were found in. They were soon buried to a depth of six to seven metres by the hot ash raining from the skies. The fortuitous result of this (for us, obvs), is that the sudden burial of the city and its residents caused them to be both perfectly preserved and also perfectly protected from vandals until 1748 when the city was rediscovered during a survey. So we will be seeing the city and the residents just as they were when it happened.

A couple of hours later I'm skulking in what precious shade there is, as we are slap bang in the middle of the ruins and with the sun literally bouncing off the stones it is unbelievably hot. Fortunately my big floppy hat provides a bit of relief, but I'm hoping we'll be moving on soon. James seems perfectly fine and is hanging around at the edge of the group, lapping up the guide's every word, and is clearly totally transfixed by the whole experience.

Finally we get going again, and as we crocodile our way down the street towards the Forum, he tells me that we'll be seeing some of the 'frozen' figures in the nearby Grain Store, and that they are really plaster casts of the original bodies. Euuw.

"Okay, having a stupid moment here. Do tell me how they make a plaster cast of something that is made out of lava, which is so hard you can't even chip away at it. I did hear her say that bit."

"Yeah, I wondered that too. But the bodies were covered in fine ash, which hardened into a porous shell – and as the contents decayed they were absorbed until literally all that was left was the shell, and possibly a few bones."

Double euuw.

"The director of excavation at the time, somebody called Fiorelli, got the onsite builders to pour plaster into the hollow. They left it a few days then chipped away the hardened exterior and – voila! – the cast of the poor occupant at the moment of death."

Weird. "That sounds a bit sort of irreverent. Like they were buried all those years and are now being dug up so people can gawk at them. Not sure how I feel about that."

"That's what archaeologists do all the time, though, isn't it? Look at the number of mummies and caskets in museums. Guess that's how we learn."

By now we've reached the Forum, the financial and political heart of the city, but what really impresses me is the view of Vesuvius in the distance. I nudge James, "It looks such a long way away. You'd have thought they'd be safe here. You can almost imagine them seeing the smoke pouring out of the top and down the hill, and thinking, 'Woah, look at that! Safe here though – no way that's gonna reach us."

"From what she was saying, I gather it wasn't the raining ash on the first day that did the real damage, although most of the residents left at that point. The next morning the other side of the volcano blew, which is what spewed the burning gases into the air and they travelled so fast nobody would have been able to outrun them. Hence people being 'frozen in time'. Which is a bit of an oxymoron if you think about it."

I don't get the chance to, as at this point we've drawn level with the guide.

"What's really interesting is that the day before the eruption, August 23rd, the residents of Pompeii would have been celebrating the Festival of Vulcanalia, the god of fire. How ironic is that? Clearly he wasn't best pleased by their efforts."

Haha. *This* is what makes a good guide.

The statues are fascinating in a grotesque kind of way. These people were literally caught at the moment of their death by scorching gas. They didn't even have time to collapse or scream or even try to grab a loved one. Life was snuffed out in a nanosecond. There's even a cast of a dog wearing a collar, writhing at the moment the heat hit. I could wander here for hours, lost in some grisly fascination at their final moments – but in the winter! Right now all I want is the coolness of the coach, so I'm delighted when the tour comes to an end and we're herded back to the meeting point to re-join it.

James leads me to one of the seats on the right-hand side. "I want to look at Vesuvius as we go by. We were on the wrong side coming here."

Indeed, as we draw close, an awed silence falls on the occupants as we consider what we've just seen, and contemplate the immense and unstoppable power of nature. Thankfully something the majority of us have never witnessed first-hand.

I'm proud of myself for turning down Luisa's kind offer of wine. Apart from the fact that this lunchtime drinking is getting to be a bit of an expensive habit, I want to go to the gym this afternoon, as in the midst of this hedonistic lifestyle I'm actually missing running. Some of the tours are still out, so hopefully it will be more or less empty.

The atmosphere in the gym is very earnest and subdued even though it's surprisingly busy. I've left James lounging on the top deck with a book, a world away from this air-conditioned temple to the body, where I feel positively fat. These very fit looking people are on holiday FFS, do they have to take it all so *seriously?* There doesn't appear to be anyone on duty, so I wander over to a free running machine and within moments am happily pacing along on the moving belt. I don't usually like running indoors; for me, part of the experience is feeling and smelling the fresh air, which definitely smells different when I'm running as opposed to walking. It also saves me a fortune on gym membership. However, this is free and it's good to feel my heart rate rise a bit at the exertion. It takes a while to get the machine running at the right speed for me, but then I do and for a few minutes enjoy the disorientating experience of looking out at the sea whilst running on the spot.

Very soon, though, boredom sets in, and just for a laugh I quickly whack the dial up by half a mile an hour increments to 11.5mph, which is the speed at which Paula Radcliffe ran to win the London Marathon in 2003. Massive mistake, as I realise almost immediately that if I'm not going to be unceremoniously thrown off into a heap in the corner I have to turn it right back down NOW. It's going way too fast for me to even contemplate touching the dial, so holding onto the side rails I lift up and plant my feet safely either side of the speeding belt. Phew. So embarrassing.

Looking around, I'm relieved to see that everyone else is either too involved in what they're doing to notice, or they've seen it all before and don't care. How the hell did she do that for over two hours? Feeling somewhat inadequate I turn it back down to a saner 7mph, which seems to be something like my normal speed, and get back into my stride.

At this speed I can get lost in thought, which is my favourite part of running. It occurs to me that this holiday is presenting me with the opportunity for an internal journey as well as the more obvious external one of seeing all these amazing places. Yes, they are amazing, but thought-provoking too. As the days go by I seem to be thinking more deeply and enjoying a growing awareness of life. Too long in the dark places, I tell myself. As the endorphins start to kick in, I discover a genuine and very deep sense of peace, and a big smile spreads across my face. Guess this is why Sarah comes up here all the time.

Or maybe not.

A little while later, and still high on the hormones, I grab a cup of water from the cooler and set off out of the gym in search of James. I'm hoping he hasn't moved as the chances of finding him would be about zero. I might be getting used to the ship, but searching for someone is like hunting for the proverbial needle in a haystack. Pushing through the gym door and deep in thought about losing James forever, I come almost about nose-to-nose with a couple of people who are so lost in each other that they also haven't seen me. We stop short of actual physical contact at which point I realise one of them is Sarah – and her meaningful distraction is hunkiness personified. Then, as we kind of laugh and go 'whoops!' and shimmy past each other, she acknowledges me with a nod and a WINK. What? Not quite knowing where to file that little exchange in my brain, I'm so busy thinking about it that I nearly crash into Mia, who's coming out of one of the treatment rooms.

"Hey, look at you! Being on holiday obviously suits you. How's it going?"

"Ah Mia, it's amazing. Every single moment is amazing. The ship is amazing. The food is super-amazing, hence me being in the gym, finally. And James is amazing. Talking of which, I want to do something for him to say a big thank you for arranging all this, and for being such a lovely friend. Any ideas?"

"If he's free now you could get him a hot stone massage at 20% off. They do special offers on port days to drum up a bit of trade. Come on down to the desk."

Discovering that I can book James in for a treatment in 20 minutes if he wants it, I belt excitedly down a couple of flights of stairs and back along the ship to where I left him. Thankfully he's still there, and still awake. If it was me, I'd be in the land of nod by now.

He looks up. "Good run?"

"Lovely, apart from nearly killing myself on the running machine. But you'll never guess who I saw on the way out."

"I'd say the odds are probably pretty high on it being Sarah."

"Yes, that was probably obvious. But she was WITH someone."

"And in your language 'WITH' means…?"

"Totally involved in A.N. Other. Obviously not Nick."

"If they really are apart now, it wouldn't be, would it?"

"Grrr! Don't you have *any* sense of intrigue or anything? Besides, she WINKED at me as she walked past. Like whaaaaat?! Maybe I'm part of her 'secret' now."

"Ah, now it gets interesting. And …?

"Well that was it on that front." Okay, maybe it wasn't *that* exciting. Then I remember my mission. "But when I was up there I saw Mia, and I said I wanted to treat you to something for being an absolute star so she suggested a hot stone massage. Would you like that?"

"Aw Cait. You don't have to do that, you know. Really."

"Well I wanted to. So if you want to get your backside across to the Spa in, oh, the next 10 minutes, you will find either a gorgeous woman or a hunky bloke ready to, er, massage you. They don't seem to do ugly in there. Sorry."

James' eyes light up. "You mean you've already arranged it? Wow. In that case, thank you."

He stands up and gives me a monster hug. "THANK you!"

And belts off to meet his hot stoney fate.

Chapter 25

"HAPPEE BIRTHDAY to YOU!" clap-clap-clap,
"HAPPEE BIRTHDAY to YOU!" clap-clap-clap,
"HAPPEE BIRTHDAY, HAPPEE BIRTHDAY,
HAPPEE BIRTHDAY to YOU!" clap-clap-clap.

The recipient of these rapidly delivered felicitations looks embarrassed as hell, as the hastily assembled waiters smile their warmest wishes and congratulations, hand over a birthday cake then belt back to look after the tables in their area. Big applause from all the diners just about puts the lid on it, judging by the look on her face, which suggests she wants the ground to open up and swallow her. Sweet though, and I kind of like it, as I'm sure she does really. At least the partner/boyfriend/ husband made the effort. Of course, there might well have been hell to pay if he didn't. You never know the subtext of other people's relationships, do you?

"So what would your reaction be if I did that for you? Silly question probably, as I suspect you'd love it."

"Yeah – got used to it at the holiday park, where they did that kind of stuff all the time. The thing is, everyone likes having a bit of attention on special occasions, don't they? Okay, maybe not so public as this, but just a bit of recognition is nice, isn't it? The making the effort bit. How about you? I think I have an idea what's coming."

"Ah, thanks, Sebastian!" My fillet of beef has arrived. We're on a bit of a repeat menu now, so I know it will only have a little trickle of horseradish and a miniscule dot of potato to decorate the three slivers of beef, but that's fine, as I also have my enormous bowl of steamed green veg which appears without me saying a word. I'm well happy and so is James, who loved the lamb so much the first time around, he has ordered it again. Could get used to living on here.

"Couldn't agree more. It was the 'making the effort' bit which was the problem. I was always nervous in those kind of situations as I never knew how he would be. Even if it was a special occasion, if Mr Nasty didn't feel like it, then it wasn't gonna happen. He said it was about doing something special when you felt like it rather than being under pressure to perform. And he couldn't do that either, to be honest. The perform bit. Whoops. Straying into non-restaurant areas there."

Fortunately our lovely waiters are busy, and as Star Trek has thoughtfully topped up our wine, we're safe. It's been a tiring and thought-provoking day but one that has left us surprisingly engaged rather than knackered. Maybe because tomorrow is a sea day and we don't have to do ANYTHING or go ANYWHERE at all. Not that we had to get off the ship at any of the ports, but it would be such a shame to dock at these places and not actually visit them. I thought the massage would have chilled James to the point of horizontal, but he bounced back all refreshed and wanted to get prettied up and show our faces in the Pyramid restaurant; so we did, and I must admit I'm pleased we made the effort. So good to see Sebastian and everyone, who act like we've been gone forever, bless them.

"You can't start a conversation like that and leave me hanging. C'mon. Where's this one going? Full disclosure required. You're amongst friends."

The tables close to us are currently empty, so at least I can't offend anyone. Or use them as an excuse not to answer him.

"Aaargh. Me and my mouth. Okay. The 'performing bit' was about him not, um, rising to the occasion if I was already the slightest bit interested. So initiating anything myself was completely out. Unless it was a blow job, of course, in which case he was entirely up for it, selfish git."

Sooooo. That was a bit unplanned and possibly a touch too much for the restaurant, but I'm on a bit of a roll. "Wanting some mutual togetherness, and even an element of personal satisfaction – noooo – unless it was all his idea. That made me some kind of slag, apparently."

"What?!! You mean you weren't allowed to be horny and want sex? My friends who have girlfriends would LOVE to be jumped on. How could someone as gorgeous as you not be allowed to express that? How could he not want you?"

"That was it. Wanting him turned him off. It was all about the chase.

I didn't find that out for a while, mind you, as for the first few months he was quite attentive. In fact after about the first week he said he was in love with me. I joked that it was a bit soon to be saying things like that, and he said it was all my fault, that I'd 'made him fall in love with me', and that I had him under my spell."

"Whaaaat?! That's creepy. So what did you say?"

"What *could* I say? I didn't say I loved him back, obviously, because I didn't. But the relationship was at that funny, very early stage where you're not sure whether it's going to work out or not, so I didn't want to rock the boat. So I didn't really say anything. and fortunately he didn't add anything else."

"You should have just run at that point, to be honest."

"Well, for a while it was okay, and I wondered if it would actually work out. Then it all went tits-up in some massive screamy rant and the whole sex thing came out. The slag bit and all that. Pretty horrible and a real shock as I thought I was just being normal. After that I realised that the more I didn't want him and pushed him away because he was being so nasty, the more he wanted me and would do ridiculous things to lure me back. He said I was like a bouncy puppy, desperate for attention, whereas a cat is aloof and untouchable – presumably what he wanted. A complete mind-fuck. I can see that now. I've also since learnt that the person who wants the least sex in a relationship is the one that controls it. He certainly did that."

"What an arsehole."

"I know. Can't make up my mind whether he was sick, deluded or just plain nasty. I think for him relationships were all about power. One day I came home to find a gift-wrapped box of perfume for me on the table. It wasn't my birthday, so I had no idea what he was playing at – or how I should react. And it was an expensive one I'd never tried, didn't even know what it smelt like."

"So..."

"Well I asked him if he liked this one. He said he hadn't smelt it. So then I asked if he thought I liked it. He said he didn't know. What kind of guy buys a 70 quid bottle of perfume for someone, not even knowing if they like it? So, knowing how expensive it was – cos all perfume is outrageously expensive – I suggested I try a tester in a shop so he could take it back if I didn't like it and get his money back."

"Please tell me you're kidding. How control-freaky is that?! Were you trying extra hard to kill the moment?"

"No! How can you say that? As ever, it was always on me. He buys me something a) I didn't expect as he was such a tight wad, and it wasn't even my birthday or anything, and b) he has no idea whether I like, and neither do I, so c) all of a sudden it's my fault if I don't like something I didn't even ask for. Are you getting some idea of the mind games going on here? It's hard enough in a close, happy relationship – hah! Not that I've had one of those – to tell someone you don't like what they've bought you, but with someone who kicks off randomly about anything, it's impossible."

"Let me guess, he didn't like your suggestion."

"Amazingly, he said to just try it. So crossing everything possible I did, and by some miracle I actually liked it. Which pissed me off no end, as the relief at liking it sort of spoilt the fact that he'd actually bought me something."

"And consequently he was all smug because he picked something at random and got it right."

"Just about. And I can see now that it was all for him, not me. He did loads of stuff like that as the years went on. Yes, I know... Don't say it. I'm happy to report that I can now see I learnt a lot from that whole horrible episode. And I'm happy to report something else too..." I chuckle excitedly. Then Sebastian appears out of nowhere to take our plates away, replacing them with dessert menus.

"Aw. I think I could just force down some of that lovely apple pie."

"You'll be in that gym with me tomorrow at this rate. Oh, alright then. I'll go for the cheesecake. I swear my stomach is expanding so I can fit more food in. Can you actually see people getting bigger, day by day, Sebastian?"

"Haha, it wouldn't be for me to say, Madam," he grins.

"That'll be a 'yes' then."

"We do find that passengers who stay on board for a long time tend not to have all the courses. They often choose just a salad and the main. We've got one lady who is on here for months at a time as she says it's cheaper than living at home. She just has a salad every evening."

"Jeez, I'd like her lifestyle if this is cheaper than home!"

"Wouldn't we all!" He departs with a big smile and our dessert order, just as Star Trek arrives.

"Ooh look! That's good timing! My bottle seems to be empty. Mind you, I have been very good and made it last a few days. You having some more, James? Why are you laughing?"

"Just thinking I might count the 'Ooh looks' one day for the lols. And yes, please, Star Trek. Is there another Merlot or have we cleaned you out?"

"No sir, fortunately we took some more on board today so you are fine for a few days," he chuckles. "And I have something to keep you amused while I get the wine for you." He lays some matches on the table:

$$6 + 4 = 4$$

"Move one match to make the sum correct," he says and walks away, huge grin on his face.

We both sit staring at it, then look at each other. Then look at it again.

"Surely a primary school kid could do this?" says James.

Yup, not a primary school kid in sight, though.

"Oh, come ON. It's like those silly MENSA tests that only test the left hand side of your brain. Surely we can do this."

We so can't and when Star Trek returns with our wine we beg him to put us out of our misery.

"Sure you want me to? It's so easy."

We both nod.

He takes the vertical match from the 'plus' sign and adds it to the six, making it into an eight. "Eight take away four is four."

"Nooo! That's ridiculously simple! Grrr," we cry.

"I'll show you another one tomorrow," he chuckles, and walks away.

"What were we talking about before all that? Weren't you about to tell me something?"

"Yes. I've been thinking about this since it happened, not knowing what to make of it. But after seeing Sarah with that bloke, I think I do."

James looks puzzled. "Since what happened? I've been with you nearly all the time and I haven't noticed anything happening with anyone."

"No, you wouldn't have done, and that's why I kept it to myself for a bit. You know when we went to the theatre the other night, and I filed in after Nick and before you. And it was all a bit squashed?"

"Oh, the comedian. Yes," he laughs at the memory. "It was pretty cosy, wasn't it?"

"Well first of all our arms clashed on the armrest as we both went for it and there was only space for one. So obviously he let me have it, being a true gent. Was nice though, brushing against someone's bare skin. Then, after we were all laughing and shuffling about in our seats with hysterics, and settled down, his knee and leg touched mine a couple of times."

Phew. Glad to have shared that little morsel, funnily enough.

James is staring at me. "That's it? That's what you've been thinking about?"

"Well yes, actually. It's a pretty big thing having someone I rather like flirting a bit with me. You think I'm making it up, don't you? That's why I didn't say anything."

"No – I just wonder whether you're reading a bit too much into it. We were all squashed up. And he doesn't seem to be the kind of guy to flirt when he's sitting next to his ex."

"Then how do I find out more?"

"I don't think you need to do anything. If we bump into them naturally you can take the opportunity to chat if it arises. He clearly enjoys hanging out with us, and that could well be because of you. I think you should just relax and let it all turn out as it will."

"You are far too chilled for your own good, you know. I'm still getting used to this new James. Can I have some of what you're on?"

"Haha. You're perfect just as you are. Completely nuts and utterly adorable. It just needs the right man to unlock it all." James raises his wineglass and indicates I should do the same. We clink glasses and he says, "Here's a big 'cheers' to you, my lovely friend! Don't ever change."

Aw.

Chapter 26

After dinner we have a refreshing stroll outside on the deck – no warring couples, thankfully – and manage to get round the Prom Deck twice in relative peace and quiet. I could so get into this postprandial walking thing. It really helps me sort my brain out – it's been through quite a lot today.

"Ready to go in?" James waves at the door we're about to pass for the second time. "Or are you training for a marathon?"

"Haha, no. Think I've had enough now, but we could wander round for a bit inside, couldn't we?" Leaving behind the serenity and warm night air of the deck, where the only noise is the sound of the ship cutting through the waves, we push through the heavy doors into a completely different world. Over in the atrium beside the dance floor the pianist is hammering out some show themes with commendable gusto, although no one's dancing. The duty free shops are open, people are wandering around with glasses of wine, and it all seems slightly surreal.

"This is such a strange existence, isn't it?" I ponder aloud, as we lean on the rail, watching people walk across the dancefloor one level below us. "Being on a floating palace in the middle of the Med, every luxury within reach, music playing in the background, drinks on tap – you could quite easily lose touch with reality if you stayed on here for too long. Either that or get really bored."

"I'd imagine with you the boredom would kick in long before you lost contact with reality. Assuming you have any contact with reality to start with!" He laughs and shields himself as I'm about to punch him playfully in the stomach. "Shall we go down to the next floor – looks like the pianist is finishing and they're lining something else up."

Never a dull moment on here, that's for sure.

We carefully make our way down the beautiful curved feature stairway that will deliver us to the edge of the dancefloor, and suddenly I feel like I'm on a film set. "We should be singing 'New York, New York' as we do this", I say, linking my arm through James' and starting a high-ish kick. "Da, da, da-da-da, Da, da, da-da-da."

Ever the performer, and never one to miss a chance to show off, he joins in, with the RIGHT WORDS. How does he *do* that? He always knows the words to whatever I'm humming... I'm loving the courage I get from being with him and really ham it up as though I'm a proper show girl. "Start spreading the news, I'm leaving today... I want to be a part of it, New York, New York..." then sadly we're at the bottom and high kicking straight into the dance teachers, who are the next gig up and making their way across the front of the stairs.

"Oops, sorry," I chuckle, as we collapse into giggles. God that felt good. "Couldn't resist it. Such beautiful stairs – just had to."

Fortunately we haven't caused them any permanent damage, as they laugh and say they completely understand, and ask whether we would like to stay for the dancing that's about to start.

"I think I've made enough of a fool of myself already, so we'll just watch for now," I say, "But thank you." Leaving the dancefloor we move over to the side nearest the shops. "You're so good at all that stuff. Don't you miss it in your new job?"

"Maybe a little bit. But doing it for fun is much better than doing it for a job. Obviously." He twinkles at me. "Sorry I can't dance though – not like they're going to be doing. Do you want to stay around and watch?"

"Yeah, but maybe from upstairs so I can actually see them. Sorry. We'll go back up like normal people. Promise."

"No worries. I did actually enjoy it. Maybe one of the teachers will dance with you?"

"It's okay. I only went to the one class, so unless they do jive I wouldn't know what the hell I was doing, and after our impromptu performance just now I think I need to keep a low profile."

The dance floor is starting to fill up with couples, so we go up the side stairs instead. Not half as much fun. By some miracle there's a table free so we can sit down and watch through the glass barrier as the couples attempt variations on the waltz. To my untutored eye (apart from watching *Strictly* of course) they appear to range from an awkward shuffle that might well be a waltz (but the couple look seriously old, so hats off to them – more than I can do!) to seriously impressive. Knowing how lovely it feels when I get the steps right in the jive, I wonder about going along to the ballroom class tomorrow. Hmm. Or even proper dance classes when we get back home. BACK. HOME.

Oh no. "James, do you realise we're heading back home now? We've reached the furthest point and now we're heading home. Don't wanna go home. Not ready!" I can literally feel my eyes widen at the thought. I haven't felt this good in, oh, maybe ever.

"I think after another – what – five days of this kind of debauchery I might even be lusting after a plain cheese sandwich. Either that or they'll have to evict us. Can you imagine? 'Please *unlock* the cabin, Miss Powell.'"

Haha. "Yeah, guess all good things have to come to an end at some point, or we wouldn't appreciate them. And this is such a good thing. Thank you so much. Again. I know I keep saying it, but it's true. Really can't believe my luck."

The music changes to a cha-cha, and I just have to stand up and prance around in my own version of cha-cha-CHA based on what we learnt in the class. I know. Embarrassing. But safe in the knowledge that nobody on the ship is going to see me again (apart from James and he will be sworn to secrecy), I'm having loads of fun, really not caring who's watching.

"I see the lady likes to cha-cha," comes a voice from behind me.

It's Nick. Shit. Double shit. Fuckety shit. Where the hell did he come from?

"Actually no idea AT all. Just loving the music really." I instinctively look over his shoulder for Sarah, who as it happens, is talking to James. That's handy. "I absolutely can't cha-cha, more of a jive gal really. That's about my limit at the moment. But watching those people – they're really enjoying it – I'm tempted to go to the ballroom class tomorrow. Or Latin. Whatever." I'm gabbling due to being caught out.

"There's certainly something special about dancing."

Waaaaaiiiiiiiiiiit. Maybe he can dance. Men don't usually say that kind of stuff, especially if they're only talking about dad-dancing. Now that would be a result.

The cha-cha-CHA comes to an end and the next song comes on. 'All I

Do is Dream of You', by the fabulous Michael Bublé. They're kidding me. My favourite song. I start bobbing around again and Nick or no Nick, I just have to move.

Nick holds out his hand in the time-honoured fashion. "Not saying I'm any good, but would you like to jive to this?"

My heart leaps into my mouth as I take his hand and all of a sudden I'm really nervous about dancing with him. Uh - grow *up* Caitlin?!!

He leads me, a bit shyly, down the curvy stairs and into the middle of the fray, without me even getting the chance to say that I've had loads to drink so I can't spin. It really doesn't matter, because he can clearly jive and I just follow his lead – he's good and is very gentle on the spins, which is lucky as I would quite probably have fallen over if he wasn't. In fact he's really gentle anyway, which is a pleasant change from being hauled around the floor like a sack of potatoes. Some men seem to forget there's a person attached to the arm.

The handy thing about modern jive is that there's a good variety of basic moves, so even if you've only had a few classes you can dance with a complete stranger. Only Nick doesn't feel like a complete stranger, and I can't help noticing how gorgeously musky he smells each time he pulls me across the front of him to go into a turn. Michael Bublé finishes and we move seamlessly on to 'Slow Boat to China' by Barry Manilow and Bette Midler. No. Are they inside my head or something? Another favourite song. We settle into an easy jive step which is kind of bouncy and funny and we're grinning like crazy at each other, especially when Bette gets to the 'key change' bit. He obviously knows it as well as I do and we start singing at each other in the higher key. As the song comes to an end, the teachers get back on the mike to announce the next dance, which is a waltz. Aaaaw. I'm having so much fun I don't want to stop, but I can't do this one. We look at each other.

"Mmm, maybe not?" I venture.

"No worries. They'll play another one, I'm sure." Keeping hold of my hand he leads me back off the floor, and slowly up the stairs to our table. Which is empty of James and Sarah, as well as my wrap and bag. I'm hoping they're all together.

"Thirsty work, isn't it? Chardonnay with water on the side?" he asks, grinning. Clearly a seasoned jiver.

Chapter 27

My heart rate doesn't seem to have slowed down much by the time our drinks arrive. So grateful for the water, as I know how fast the wine will go down otherwise. I'm loving sitting here with Nick on his own. Maybe James has taken Sarah away so we can dance and chat in peace. I'm SO glad I told him about the theatre thing, even if I did imagine it. Or maybe Sarah dragged him away anyway. Whichever it was, I'm silently thanking the Universe.

Nick asks where I learnt to jive, and we discover we don't live a million miles away from each other, as he's just a few miles into the New Forest. Then he asks how I got into jive. Ah. Completely different kettle of fish. Most people at our local class know Jules brought me along, and there isn't anyone I care enough about or am close enough to that needs to know any more. Still no James, so I need to be all grown up and sort this one out for myself, which is kind of weird. I'm going through the options rapidly in my mind, trying to find one that doesn't make me sound like a) a complete loser or b) I'm desperate to find a bloke so went boyfriend-hunting at a jive night.

"Sorry – didn't mean to intrude." He must have been watching my face as I considered the answer to a ridiculously easy question. Not!

"Ah bless you, no. Was just trying to get my words in the right order. Always a good idea."

I crack a grin as I hear my lovely mum's advice in my head, 'Tell the truth sweetie. Always the easiest option.' She knows a thing or two, my mum.

"Bad relationship break-up, and my best friend Jules dragged me out to save me from becoming a hermit." Bollocks. That definitely came out wrong. Not the message I want to convey AT all.

"No – wait. That came out all wrong. Take two. Post-traumatic stress stemming from the long-overdue breakup of an extremely toxic relationship. Yes, I like that better," and laugh, probably necessary given the weight of the words. I'm sure he wasn't expecting that, but at least it's the truth, and if I'm to forge ahead as the new 'me' I've promised myself, then I'm not going to be hiding anything or apologising for what happened.

Nick smiles. "I appreciate the honesty. And the clever choice of words. Sorry you had to go through all that, but happy that you learnt to jive. It's a great way to relax, isn't it?"

"Absolutely. So glad Jules dragged me along. How about you?" Fair's fair. I don't do shrinking violet any more. Not since about two days ago.

"Nothing quite as traumatic. Sarah and I have been drifting apart for a long time. She was into keeping fit and going to the gym when she wasn't working, so when one of my work-mates suggested jive, I went along and discovered I loved it. I think I always wanted to dance but never had the balls to take myself along to a formal class, especially on my own. Jive ticks all the boxes for me – aarrgh! Sorry. Hate management speak! It's a good way to be out with friends and I'm enjoying learning to dance. And it's the sort of thing you can do anywhere, isn't it? As we just discovered!"

Still no James. God, I love that man.

"So d'you think you might go to the dance class tomorrow? I'm sort of gathering James isn't interested." Nick smiles at me, hopefully.

Crikey. Play it cool, Cait. "Mmm possibly. You're right that James doesn't want to go."

He continues. "No idea what it is, but if you're free I think I would sooner make a fool of myself with someone I know slightly, rather than with a complete stranger. A bit of Dutch courage. It'll probably be heaving, but, whatever." He grins, which I've noticed he does a lot.

I invested in a book on facial characteristics some while back, which is when I discovered that Mr Nasty's nearly non-existent and slightly cruel lips suggested just that about his personality. Non-existent with the potential for cruelty. Ever since I got the book I've taken a lot more notice of people's faces – apart from whether they are good looking or not – obvs. I can't help noticing that Nick has quite full lips, which sort of twitch when he smiles, like he's not completely sure of himself. Cute and kind of inviting. Oh FFS I have got to get out of Ivy's books!

So, let me just think about that question for a nanosecond. OF COURSE I WANT TO GO TO THE LESSON WITH HIM!

"That would be nice, actually. I'd love to." I'm proud of my apparent laid-back calmness, 'cos inside my heart is leaping about all over the place. "James and I tried the cha-cha class on here at the beginning of the cruise, and it was really busy, but they made it a lot of fun. Well, I enjoyed it but it wasn't James' thing. The line dancing was fun too but it was so ridiculously overcrowded I gave up on the second lesson. Sat and watched from the side of the dancefloor while the women swooned around James. In fact I think they were watching him more than the teacher. He seems to have that effect on people. Especially women."

"Sarah's certainly taken to him. They're probably off in one of the shops having a great time."

"I hope so, cos I can't keep up with him. I mean I like it a bit, but he loves shopping so much he could easily make it a career option. I'm absolutely fine with sitting here after what has been an incredibly busy day."

We sit watching the other dancers for a while, then amazingly another jive comes on.

Nick looks at me, eyebrow raised. "Can you face another dance?"

I chuckle. "I think I can just about cope."

Then we see James and Sarah heading back, and I feel all self-conscious, and I think Nick does too. My heart sinks, but James just waves us away, indicates that he's leaving my bag and wrap on the table, and calls out that he'll see me back in the cabin. And then they walk away.

That feels weird.

We look at each other like kids being allowed to stay up late, then rush back down to dance to Robbie Williams belting out 'Mack the Knife,' which is one of the best jive songs ever. We're still on a high when the song ends and the teachers announce the end of the session. "But we'll see you at the quickstep lesson tomorrow at 2.30," they add.

As we get back to our table, I'm just saying how I have no idea about quickstep, when a smart little lady dressed all in black pauses by us for a moment.

"Just wanted to say how well you and your husband dance together. Such a good match!"

And then continues on her way.

Well *that* was embarrassing. Talk about bad timing.

"That has to be the quickest courtship in history," laughs Nick, elegantly diffusing the situation. "So, wife, do you fancy a turn on deck?"

Grinning, I grab my bag and wrap and make my way out onto the Prom Deck for the second time this evening. It's still quiet and peaceful, and we wander along in a companionable fashion, enjoying the gentle sound of the ship moving through the water. As luck would have it we've come out on the port side and that good ole moon is shining at us across the water. Smaller than the other night, but still there, and oh so romantic. Fuck off Ivy – trying to stay in control here!

"So – what are your three favourite things about being on the ship?"

OMG he does lists, just like me! "That's easy. I love doing lists so I've thought about this a lot. Let's assume being at sea is an obvious one and doesn't count as one of the three, yes?"

He chuckles and nods.

"So firstly, I love being able to sit out on our balcony with a mug of proper coffee (we brought our own supplies) and just let my thoughts flow out as far as they can. Which is forever as there isn't anything to focus on at sea, is there? And to sit talking to James out there too, putting the world to rights. Well, my little world. That's all part of the same point, if that's not cheating.

Second is probably water-based again, which is funny. I love swimming, so being in the pool, in the sunshine and open air is just perfect. Followed by some chilled Chardonnay, which I don't have to worry about drinking cos I'm on holiday. So, I'm just free to be me, if I can sneak that one in under the same heading.

And thirdly, being taken to all these amazing ports. I never thought cruising could be so exciting. I thought it would be packed with old people being grumpy, but it's not like that at all. We get just long enough in port to decide whether we want to come back again sometime to do it properly, and so far we've had such amazingly powerful experiences that we want to come back to all of them. Especially Barcelona, so we can go back to Montserrat."

I look across at him, worried that I've gone on a bit long, but he's doing that crinkly smile so I guess all is well. "How about you?"

"I'd say you're a pretty astonishing list-maker, and I'm not sure I can compete. My choices are a lot more basic. Firstly, being able to sit around all day and read and eat and drink. I know, total slob."

"Wasn't going to say a word," I chuckle. "Right there with you on that one though."

"Secondly, not having to think about what to do. Holidays can be really stressful when you have to worry about where to go and what to do, and where to eat and all that. Seems like food's crept in again. Haha. But what I mean is there's lots to do if you want to, like the swimming, as you said.

Hmm. Third. Funny that I started this and now I'm struggling. Okay, the opportunity for a new experience or ten, assuming I can be arsed. Must admit I wasn't hopeful of this holiday being even slightly successful, due to the situation with Sarah, but I'm really enjoying myself on here. I've been able to get some much-needed rest (too much of the day job going on recently), so I haven't really taken advantage of getting off the ship very much. Sounds like you've done a lot more. Tell me about Montserrat."

Tell him about Montserrat! Straight in at the deep end then. Malaga would have been so much easier. Woah. Not sure I can do it justice and concentrate on walking, so I pause by the rails, just where the moon seems to be shining across the sea at us. Funny that.

"You okay to stop here for a moment? It will be easier to talk if I'm not walking. Hey – maybe I'm a bloke, not being able to do two things at once!" Shut UP. That was unkind and unnecessary.

"You're hiding it well," he laughs. "And yes, of course."

I lean my elbows on the handrail, hands clasped loosely in front, and look down at the water speeding by beneath us. Deep inky blue and apparently bottomless, and I feel as if I could get lost in it forever.

"You don't have to tell me if you don't want to. I was just curious."

"No, no, I want to. It's just that this holiday has turned out to be so utterly different from what I expected, and so much more important in the grand scheme of things than I could possibly have imagined. And a lot of that has been because of Montserrat. And the conversations I've been having with James. So…" And so I launch in and describe all of it – the history of the Black Madonna, the way the Basilica grew from small churches due to so many pilgrims coming to visit, the journey up there, the way the statue is protected, the queue, the buzz from touching the orb – and why all of it was amazing.

But it's when I get to thinking about the huge sob and the votive bit (which I'm not planning on telling him about), that it all starts to unravel, and I realise it's very much still A Work In Progress. A wave of emotion rises up from my stomach that I just can't hold back, and suddenly the tears are streaming down my face, just as they were in the Basilica. Just like someone's turned the tap on and wandered off to get lunch or something. Unable to speak any more, I bury my face in my hands to wait for the storm to subside. Thought I'd sorted this. Where's the brave new Caitlin now, huh? Fuck.

And Nick puts his arm around my shoulders, rests his head gently on mine, and holds me close as if he's done it a million times before.

Chapter 28

Thankfully whoever turned the tap on wanders back and turns it off, and I come back to the present as Nick kisses the top of my head and gently strokes the arm that's not pressed against him. We're still standing side by side, facing out to sea, which is pretty handy as my face is probably a complete disaster zone. Hopefully the cool salty breeze will calm it down a bit.

"God, I'm so sorry. It was exactly what happened in the Basilica though, times about a zillion." I'm hiccupping and sniffing quietly but he pretends not to notice, bless him, as he laughs and ruffles my hair slightly. I like that a LOT.

"Can't believe you have an experience like that and you're still articulate."

"Only just. Jeez. I really thought I'd slayed that ghost after the last few days. I've been so much happier and stronger, then it smacks me over the head again, completely out of the blue."

"Sounds to me like what you went through is far more powerful than you realise. You're not going to get over it quickly. Cut yourself some slack."

"Well I thought I was. Grrr. Obviously not enough. Maybe a good move would be to not go round talking about it! Well not the Montserrat experience, anyway."

"Possibly not, but in my completely unprofessional capacity as an ordinary human being, I think you should write about this stuff, 'cos you almost had me in tears there too. Even start a blog. That's what people do now, don't they? Hey, yes! A blog about recovering from shit relationships. Well, getting out of them too."

"It's the 'getting out' bit which is fundamental to it, I think. I know I'm still suffering the fallout from being in such a destructive and toxic relationship – that's a major reason for this holiday – but at least I got out. When your days are spent walking on eggshells and dreading the next outburst, it chips away at your self-esteem and you lose any sense of who you actually are. It's a really horrible mind-fuck, and although finishing it and walking away looks easy to outsiders, it really isn't. Especially if the abuser keeps apologising for their behaviour and promising they won't do it again."

"I can't even begin to imagine what you've been through. There must be a combination of relief at being out of it and lack of confidence from being treated so badly for so long."

"Ha! That much is true. James is such a perfect gentleman but he says that the way he behaves is just good manners, and that I was wrong to put up with the bad manners for so long. See – that's the other thing. After a bad relationship it's very easy to view any 'normal' (I make those silly quote signs just for a laugh) bloke as some demi-god just because he buys me a drink. It's pathetic. Um – present company excepted, obviously." That came out all wrong.

Pressing the back of his hand to his forehead Nick closes his eyes in true drama queen fashion. "I'm gutted. You mean I'm not a demi-god?"

That was lucky. Unwitting full disclosure is one thing, insults are quite another. Poor bloke. In fact poor anyone. My emotions are all over the place – how on earth can anyone keep pace with me?

All of a sudden the long, long day has caught up with me, and I can't stop the most enormous yawn creeping out. "Aaargh – so sorry. Seem to have gone through quite a lot today, starting with plaster casts made from human beings that were blasted to death by scorching hot gas, to nearly killing myself on the running machine, to a fab dinner, to even more fab dancing, then finishing with a complete emotional meltdown. My days can be very busy, you know." I finish with a bit of a grin, hoping I haven't offended him with my monster yawn.

"Think I got off lightly! I also think you're going to sleep well tonight. At least you've got a nice quiet sea day tomorrow in which to do absolutely nothing. Except dance, if you're still up for that?" Nick moves his hand from my shoulder and we turn away from the handrail.

Aw. I was enjoying that. "Yes, absolutely. Think I might just have stirred by then! I'm certainly not going to be rushing up to breakfast."

We wander along the deck until we get to the next door, pausing somewhat reluctantly, as if neither of us want to break the spell. I sure as hell don't. Maybe it's just the moon and the sea air, and I'm imagining it all. Maybe he was just comforting me. Maybe, maybe, maybe. What I do know is there's another yawn brewing.

"Come on, then. A big sleep for you and tomorrow's another day," Nick pronounces cheerily, reaching to open the heavy door. Think he's spotted the incoming yawn, which I'm trying frantically to keep clamped between my jaws.

"Yes, absolutely." With a sudden shiver I realise I'm really cold now, and quite grateful to be inside. Not grateful for the bright lights which are going to expose my tear-streaked features to all and sundry though, so I keep my head down and head for the stairs, as usual. Even if I *am* tired, the last thing I want is to be in a bright lift with a load of people looking at me. As it turns out, there's just about nobody around, and we climb the stairs in a fairly relaxed, nay subdued (on my part) fashion until we reach my deck.

At the parting of the ways, Nick stops and gently puts his hand on my arm as he smiles into my swollen eyes. Everything he does is so *gentle.*

"Just wanted to say that, I know it's been very hard on you, but I've had a lovely time this last couple of hours. Thank you for opening up to me. You're one amazing woman. I'll see you tomorrow."

Then he kisses me gently on the cheek, squeezes my arm, and is gone.

Chapter 29

Ow.

I wake up feeling like I've been crying for England. For several years. Ug.

This emotional stuff is exhausting. What I need is some lovely bloke to bring out all my happy bits and make me forget the past. Oh yes. I think I might know one of those but then I cried all over him about said past and he probably wants to run a mile now. I drag myself out onto the balcony then almost immediately come back in for my shades, which wakes James.

He takes one look at my face and sitting upright points back out to the balcony. "Go. Sit. Crisis meeting in 5, with coffee. Will be there in a mo."

And he is, armed with lovely fresh coffee.

"So what the fuck happened? Thought you'd be all excitable and wake me up at dawn to tell me about it."

"Well it was all going beautifully until he innocently asked about Montserrat, at which point I spontaneously unleashed a torrent of tears all over the poor guy. He said he thinks I'm amazing, but I bet he can't wait to get off the ship to escape me now. Talk about intense."

"I thought I left you dancing. How did all that happen?"

"You did, and it was lovely, and thank you. Some lady even thought we were married as we danced so well together – Hello, embarrassing! – then we went for a walk on deck and that was lovely too, then we talked about what we liked most about being on the ship. It went downhill from there when I said something about special experiences and mentioned Montserrat – he asked about it, so I told him and then started crying again."

"Yes. Intense. Not ideal first date material."

"It *wasn't* a date, and I couldn't help it!"

"True. But you said he was okay about it."

"He was lovely. It's me that's in deep agony. I'm totally fed up with my feelings exploding out all over the place when they feel like it and spoiling things."

"Woah. Now wait *just* one moment. What about the promise you made to yourself at Montserrat? The one about being stronger? And in fact the things you've been saying ever since?"

"Hm. Easier said than done. I can't just flick a switch and become this amazing strong woman who doesn't cry about stuff." That definitely sounds a bit sulky, but, whatever. All I'm remembering from last night are the horrible bits. There must have been some good ones too.

"So what were the highlights then? The good bits? I'm assuming there are good bits." He narrows his eyes. "Not too much detail though."

I swear he's in my head. "How do you *do* that? How do you know what I'm thinking?"

James just looks at me and waggles his eyebrows, which does actually make me laugh. "Years of practice. And because I see you jumping down into the pit and I think, 'Woah, there she goes,' and then I reach in with my big ole hand, and drag you out to the happy lands on the other side that were there all along, just that you didn't see them. There. Now tell me something good that happened."

So after some more coffee and more chatting, my beautiful, wonderful friend has got me back to Happy Land, where I don't feel so silly, and, crucially, my eyes are less puffy. At this rate I might even be able to go up for lunch, which would be good as we've so totally missed breakfast. And I've got to face Nick at dancing. But I'm sure that will be *fine*.

Then I realise we've only covered my side of the evening. "Thanks for entertaining Sarah. Or dragging her off. Or whatever you did. Really, really appreciate it."

"Funny thing was, I didn't have to do much. She was ready to roll... and interesting."

"She seems to be different with you."

"Just as Nick seems to be different with *you*."

"So it really is two people reaching the end of the line. Like they said."

"My guess is that they want different things now. Don't know how long they've been married, but she's seriously into working out at the gym and she's passionate about good nutrition. She also loves clothes and would like to start up her own sports fashion line. Nick just isn't interested in any of that. He loves reading, she'd rather be doing something. All those things that don't seem to matter when you're first in love I guess, but then turn from little differences into gaping great holes in communication further down the line."

"You don't seem to have a problem communicating with her."

"No. I genuinely like her, actually. Plus of course, I'm not trying to have a relationship with her."

"Maybe we've been a bit hard on her. I mean it can't be easy coming away and being in close proximity to someone when you've separated from them, can it?"

"I think she's probably over that bit, and is trying to make the best of it in her own way, which happens to be working out like crazy and staying really focused. Don't think she suffers fools gladly though."

"Does she think Nick's a fool then?"

"Not necessarily. They're just different. Sarah is very quick on the uptake and can be very sharp without actually meaning to be, from what I can tell. Maybe Nick wants someone a bit softer, more feminine." He bats his eyelashes at me. Sadly I haven't got anything to throw at him.

"So did she say anything about Nick – as in the context of me?"

"Um, nope. Sorry. We didn't have that long, you know. I did my best in the time available." Big grin.

"I know you did, and I will love you forever for it. Was just wondering. He seems quite shy. Which is very endearing after my recent experience."

"I would imagine that's where the big difference lies. You can't be shy in her profession. She's used to being in control. Mmm..." His eyes take on a distant look.

"Euuw. Stop it! You can do the S&M stuff in your own time. OMG you're actually thinking about being with a woman and her being in control and all that weird stuff?"

"Possibly. Hmm. Maybe I'll explore that at a later date!" He flashes his gorgeous smile at me. "But now, all this thinking has made me hungry. Everything makes me hungry on this ship. I think they design it that way. Lead me to the Lido!"

I'm looking over the balcony at a bit of a flurry several floors down.

"In a mo. Look at this." 'This' appears to be a seagull that's trapped on someone's glass fronted balcony. It keeps trying to take off but is flying straight at the glass each time. The cabin steward's trying to help by flapping a towel in its general direction, but the bird is getting more and more distressed. Looking around at the surrounding balconies, quite a few other passengers have noticed it too.

"Hm. I've got an idea. Come on." James grabs my hand and pulls me out of the cabin.

Fortunately I have the presence of mind to grab my bag and key on the way or we would be really stuffed. Can't get Chardonnay without the room card, although, granted, it's still early. James leads me two decks down then along the passageway the same side as our cabin. Sure enough, the door to one of the cabins is open, and we can see through to the balcony where the steward is still struggling to release the bird.

James strides in purposefully like he knows what he's doing (he so doesn't), at which point the steward and his very timid assistant look hugely relieved. I'm hovering by the door, not feeling quite right about walking into someone else's cabin. James carefully goes out to the balcony, closing the door behind him. Smart boy. I would NOT want to see a seagull panicking in a cabin. And then, bless him, it all happens like in a film. He turns the little table upside down and gently moves it under the gull, lifting it slowly until the bird is the same height as the handrail – at which point it takes a mighty leap and flies free. Wow! There's a burst of applause from outside, and James turns round and looks up, then waves and bows to the audience who have been watching from above. Job done. So proud of that man.

After busily stuffing my plate with spaghetti carbonara (loads of garlic) and garlic bread (ditto, obvs), and a token bit of salad, I suddenly freeze, revisiting the jive rules in my mind.

James has clocked it. "What's the matter?"

"I'm going to the dance class – don't want to breathe garlic all over Nick."

"Cait, you're dancing with the guy, not snogging him. And he will probably have garlic too. Almost everything on here has garlic in it. If necessary you can go back to the cabin before the class and clean your teeth. Really. You could even make it a conversation piece."

My expression possibly suggests otherwise.

"Joke. But I think you need to relax a bit. Or get another dish and I'll eat this. Anything. Just move. I'm starving."

So, okay, I forgo the garlic bread as that's definitely a bridge too far, but the carbonara is so ultra-tempting it's a must. I hold back from the Chardonnay as a) it really is getting to be TOO regular a habit and b) I don't want to fall over in the dance class. Oh – and it's much too early.

"How're you feeling?" James leans forward to inspect the damage to my face. "You look okay close up. Not puffy at all now. Just a bit tired."

"I totally love your honesty, James, so thank you. I'm just relieved I come up to your high standards. Talking of which, it's a formal night tonight, isn't it?"

"Yes you do, and yes it is. But you probably have around 5 hours to have a wardrobe crisis and the shops will be open, should you be lacking anything, although I don't believe that's possible, given all the stuff you brought. Shall we have a fashion show when you get back from the class?"

I realise with horror that it's gone 2.00 and we've been sitting gassing and eating for ages. I have precisely fifteen minutes to get back to the cabin, clean my teeth, change into some trousers as this skirt will def not go with my jazz trainers, and of course pick *up* my jazz trainers, then fly down about God knows how many flights of stairs and get right to the other end of the ship.

"Yep, better get moving," chuckles James, who's been watching the drama unfold on my face.

"If you hadn't kept getting more dessert and more coffee for us, I would've had more time!"

"Ooh! So not my fault. There's always that 'No' word. Remember that one? Go on, off. You've got loads of time. I'll be in the usual spot up the top. Oh, and remember the new 'you', yes? The happy, non-angsty one."

This last bit of advice is addressed to my back as I pick up my bag and belt down through the Lido to the nearest stairs.

Chapter 30

Feeling slightly sick from eating too much, combined with a heightened sense of anticipation, I tumble through the door of the Copacabana club just as the class is starting. Can't see Nick anywhere, and I'm thinking about waiting by the side of the dance floor when Doug, one of the teachers, spots me and calls over the mike, "Oh lovely, come on in and join the fun. Don't worry if you haven't got a partner, we'll sort you out with one later."

Thanks for that, Doug. Now I've got a big sign over my head that says 'Billy No-Mates'. I mumble that I do have a partner, that he's just not turned up yet, then decide maybe I will join the ladies' side of the room on the basis that it looks a bit less wall-flowerish than if I sit by the side to wait for him. We start off with the men and women facing each other each doing their respective steps. For us it is back with the LEFT, side-close-side, then forward side-close-side – pretty easy but I have my back to the door which makes it hard to keep an eye out for Nick. We get into a big mess at the top of the room so Doug tells us to turn around and do it all the way back down again. Ah. That's better – I can also see all the way along the corridor outside when we go this way.

We go up and down several times until it looks like people have got it right, then Doug asks us to pair up. Still no Nick. A dapper little man who just about comes up to my shoulder asks if I need a partner, to which I say thank you but my own partner will be here in a minute, so he pairs up with someone else. By the time everyone else is sorted out it's clear I'm on my own, so Doug wanders over and says – off mike, thankfully – that he'll dance with me until my partner arrives. It's really sweet of him and somehow he manages to give directions over the mike at the same time as dancing round the room with me. Almost in spite of myself I actually enjoy it for a while, until the disappointment roils in my stomach again as I realise that Nick really isn't coming, and I just want to howl.

For the next set of steps we go back into our lines to learn the lock step, which isn't exactly rocket science but some of the others get in a real mess with it. I find I'm next to Mrs Grumpy, who on the odd occasion I've seen her since the line dance class hasn't actually looked grumpy at all. Maybe she was just having a bad day.

"Are you OK dear?" she asks.

Damn. Thought I was hiding it so well. "Oh, yes, thank you," I reply, smiling brightly. "Looks like he got delayed. Never mind, eh?"

After lots of practice and a bit of sorting out from Doug and Angie, we're asked to pair up again and Doug automatically comes over to me. Yup, officially Billy No-Mates. Angie starts the music, which is the appallingly inappropriate 'A Fine Romance', sung by Frank Sinatra, and we dance several circuits of the room doing the whole sequence, before Doug excuses himself to sort out some people who seem to have forgotten nearly everything we've just been taught. I take this welcome opportunity to slide away and, still in my jazz trainers, hurtle up about eighteen flights of stairs to the top deck where James is sunning himself.

I only just make it before the sobbing breaks out. Dumping my Mary Poppins bag on the sun lounger next to him, I flop down and bury my face in my hands.

"What?! What the fuck's happened now?!?"

"D-d-d-d-didn't turn up," I snivel. "And I felt so s-s-s-stupid in front of all those people."

James moves over to my lounger to give me a monster hug, and I don't even care about his sun block going all over my pale pink t-shirt. It's just good to be held.

"There must be a good reason for it. He said last night he was coming, didn't he?"

"Yes, but he's probably realised I'm a complete head case and has backed off. We didn't exchange cabin numbers or phone numbers or anything, so he couldn't have let me know even if he wanted to."

"By the same token though, he couldn't have let you know if something had come up. He wouldn't just not turn up – don't think he's that kind of guy. Besides, he knows I would probably have to kill him if he did that to you."

I smile gratefully. "Maybe he jumped overboard, knowing that."

"Or maybe Sarah got cross and pushed him."

"Or maybe she jumped and he went in to rescue her."

We're getting more ridiculous by the second, which is doing a brilliant job of cheering me up. Then Luisa appears, as if by magic, which cheers me up even more. She's obviously noticed I'm in deep emotional distress and in great need of a large glass of nice cool Chardonnay. Rifling in my Mary Poppins bag I'm delighted to find that in my crazy dash earlier I did in fact remember to sling in my bikini, sarong and shades. With a nifty arrangement of the sarong, I manage to get into my bikini by the time Luisa is back with our drinks. I'm definitely getting used to this life, even if I am a bit sad around the edges at this point. Taking a great big slurp of my lovely cold wine, and adjusting my sunglasses to cover the worst effects of crying (again), I settle back on the lounger to grab a few rays and continue my recovery from being stood up.

A little while later I'm still thinking about it, though.

"Maybe they've been confined to their cabin with that horrible sicky bug."

"Mmm."

Oops. Probably woken James up so I shut up. Too late.

"Yes, you did wake me up, actually. And I do hope not. I haven't heard anyone talking about it. Talking of stomachs, can we go for afternoon tea soon?"

"You really are incredible. I swear you're eating more as the days go by. Shall I go down and get it for you?"

"Is this so you can have a snoop around for Nick?"

"Possibly. Okay, yes, actually. But I can get you a plateful of goodies at the same time."

"Well on that basis, please do – in the interests of detective work, of course."

After hanging out in the Lido at cream cake time, and wandering round both pools until it became obvious I was stalking someone, I have to admit Nick has disappeared off the face of the ship, as has Sarah. I even sneaked up to the gym, but she wasn't there either. Must be serious if she's not working out.

"Maybe they really have been taken ill," I wonder out loud.

"Trouble is, there's no way of getting in touch with them," says James, collapsing back on his lounger after the effort of eating afternoon tea several times over. "I am so gonna miss the cakes. And the afternoon drinkies – talking of which…" he waggles his glass at me.

"You're going to be sick yourself, at this rate."

"Aw, come on. We've only got four more days after this, and two of those we'll be off the ship for a chunk of time. How about getting top-ups down by the pool and going in the jacuzzi for a while? Then after that we can head back to the cabin for your wardrobe crisis."

By the time we gather up our stuff and get down there, it looks like a lot of people have already left the pool area, presumably to address their own wardrobe crises. James is busily chatting away about something, but I spend most of the time in the jacuzzi with my head swivelling in one direction then another, which isn't that restful, TBH. Or polite.

"You know, it's quite hard to talk to you when you're doing that."

"I don't want to miss him."

"I can't imagine he would try to skulk past. Just relax, huh? Be patient."

"Don't really do patience. My stomach is in knots and I feel all anxious."

"Then let's do a bit of relaxation."

"What? Here?"

"Yup. Nobody needs to know. In fact there's hardly anybody here."

That much is true. "You promise I won't look silly?"

"Promise. Trust me?"

I nod cautiously, like a small child who's got no idea what's going to happen next.

"Okay. So just sit with your feet on the floor of the jacuzzi, and your hands on your lap."

This last bit is hard as they keep floating up in the bubbles, so I giggle a bit.

"Doesn't matter if bits float around, just concentrate on your feet. and allow yourself to relax into the warmth of the water. Feel that relaxation spreading up to your shins, the backs of your legs and your knees."

"That feels quite nice actually."

"Good. Now concentrate on relaxing your thighs, buttocks and hips and then up into your stomach… notice anything that's tense and just allow it to relax...

Moving on up, allow your back, then your shoulders to broaden and relax…

Feel your chest expand, your shoulders drop, and your arms relax all the way down to your fingertips…"

I'm liking this a lot. James has such hidden talents.

"Allow your neck to relax, your jaw to soften, and the space between your ears to expand…

Enjoy the feeling of being completely relaxed, and the warm water and the sunshine on your skin…

Just stay with that for a moment..."

It feels amazing and I could stay like this forever. Several minutes must have passed by.

"So now, when you feel ready, start to come back into your body, feeling the contact with the seat and the floor of the jacuzzi again and notice the sounds around you – but remember that lovely sensation of being relaxed, and know that you can do it for yourself any time you want to. Then when you're ready, open your eyes."

Wow.

Don't want to come back. Ever.

But eventually I do. "James, that was amazeballs! Where did you learn all that?"

"Part of the meditation practice. Good, isn't it? Really helps with stress."

"Woah. No wonder you're all chilled out if you keep doing that. Can we do it again tomorrow?"

"Of course. We can do it any time you want."

"Have you been doing it on here?"

"Yup. When you go off swimming, or when you're in the shower. Doesn't take long once you get used to doing it."

"Thank you so much. And talking of showers, I guess we'd better float out of here and go and get ready."

Chapter 31

After a long steamy shower, I'm sitting on my bed in my lovely fluffy white dressing gown, hair wrapped up in a towel. I still don't understand what happened with Nick, but after several glasses of wine and a relaxation session with James, I'm feeling a bit more mellow and prepared to give him the benefit of the doubt. It had better be a bloody magnificent excuse.

"I'm thinking your slinky black dress with the low back would be good. Is it new? I noticed that when you were unpacking. Then you can wear your hair loose and it will all fan out and look amazing."

Absolutely everyone needs a gay friend in these situations.

"Yes, Jules made me buy it. I'm a bit worried it won't fit after all this food. It was very tight before we even left, so God knows what it will be like now. I'll be hanging out all over the place."

"I'm sure it will be fine. C'mon. Show me."

Some minutes later I've dumped the towel and struggled into what is basically a black, sparkly tube with a bit of a fishtail and half the back missing. I cannot IMAGINE what Jules was thinking when she made me buy it.

"Woah! Fuck me, that looks amazing."

"Thank you – but I can't actually move."

"It's stretchy, isn't it?"

"It HAS stretched. That is it. I have filled it to capacity. There is no more fabric. And I really cannot move."

"Sure you can." James lobs my spiky shoes over – thankfully they're slip-ons so I don't have to bend down and do anything up. "Put those on and see if you can walk. It'll be better with heels."

"How do YOU know? I can't get over the way you know all this stuff. You're not even a girl."

"Comes with the territory," he beams.

Sure enough, my balance changes once I get the shoes on, and the dress starts to feel a bit more comfortable. There still isn't a morsel of stretch left in the material, but it's quite forgiving. Hopefully it won't rip. There's no way I'm going through all the palaver of taking it off to do my hair, so I carefully reach up to tease it into the curls that seem to come so easily on here. "You know, I'm really going to miss the soft water. I hardly have to touch my hair – no sticky products or anything. Love it."

"I think the life really suits you, actually. You're looking happy and tanned and really well. And your hair is incredible. What you need to do is bend over so it all goes over your head, run your fingers through the scalp to lift the hair up a bit, then flick it back over your head again."

Very cautiously so as not to rip the dress or fall off my shoes, I do as instructed.

"Oh that's nice.... Go look in the mirror."

Tottering over to the full length mirror I'm delighted to find that all the blotches from crying (again) have calmed down, and that I really haven't scrubbed up too badly – and it's all my own work this time. As in scruffing my fingers through my hair, obvs. And I haven't even put any makeup on yet.

"So when you start getting book deals, you'll be able to work from a cruise ship, won't you? Have laptop, will travel! If you require the services of a PA you will let me know, won't you?"

"That would be amazing. And yes, always." I can't help the huge grin on my face. I'm just hoping we see Nick. "Come on then, get in the shower – I'm going to have to stand up until you're ready as I'm not sure I can sit down in this. Might be going for the salad option tonight! As indeed might you, given how much you've stuffed your face today."

"Difference is, I can still fit into my clothes, daaarling!" and James darts into the bathroom with a loony laugh just in time to avoid the towel I carefully lob at him.

"Ooh and be careful as it hasn't drained away properly," I call through the door. "Sorry about that. I didn't wee in it or anything though so you should be alright."

The sound of retching issues from within, followed by, "You're gross!"

"Hahahahaha. Think we probably need to tell Marco."

Having chickened out of walking down the stairs and taken the lift, due to only being able to take little steps, I'm surprised there isn't much of a queue when we get to the restaurant. I was expecting a long crocodile of penguins all dolled up to the nines, but we don't even have to wait for our favourite table. Sebastian tells us this is because people often only bother with the Captain's Reception due to the free wine (ah-hem!), and that they are probably lolling around in shorts in the Lido for this one.

I ease myself carefully into my chair. "So what should we do in Cartagena tomorrow, Sebastian?" I haven't done any research on this port due to time constraints – Montserrat and Rome were kind of higher up the list, if I'm honest.

"I like the shopping, Madam! But also, it is very historic and you can go to the Roman Theatre, and up to the fortress if it isn't too hot and you have the energy. But the prices there are very good – especially at the moment as the exchange rate is in our favour."

I look at James. "Got your number then! Two days of shopping – Cartagena and Gibraltar."

"I thought you wanted to see the monkeys!"

"I do, but we might be able to do both. Can we do both, Sebastian?"

The best thing about the restaurant being over half-empty is that Sebastian is much more relaxed and can spend a bit of time talking to us without watching what everyone else is doing. "Yes, if you get off the ship in good time and get the shuttle or a taxi into town. You can then get a bus up to the Rock, or even a cable car if you prefer. If you're not doing all the war stuff in the caves there isn't a huge amount to see, so you should be able to get back down in time to do some shopping. You know they take sterling?"

"Yes, clocked that one," says James. "That will be weird though. Which do you prefer for shopping? Cartagena or Gibraltar?"

"Depends what you want, Sir. Gibraltar is cheap for alcohol and cigarettes, but everything else is a bit more expensive as it has to be imported."

Having made our selections – and yes, I'm having a very light meal of soup followed by fillet of sea bream with salad as I daren't eat more than about five mouthfuls – we have a bit of a chat to Star Trek, who got our wine while we were talking to Sebastian. Wine is of course a completely different kettle of fish as it doesn't fill me up as much as food. I am so going to need a massive detox when I get off here.

"You want another puzzle?" he asks, big smile across his face.

"Go on then. Let's see if we can be any more intelligent this evening."

He lays the matchsticks out like a wine glass, adding a chocolate he's taken out of his pocket.

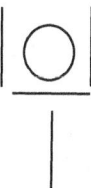

"You have to move two matchsticks to get the chocolate out of the glass," he says, then fills our glasses and walks off grinning his face off.

"Nice to be entertained while we wait. They're such lovely guys, aren't they? We're really lucky – some of the others look a bit grim." I'm watching the other sections where the waiters don't seem to be laughing too much.

"That'll be our sparkling conversation then," grins James.

"Well at least we seem to be keeping it clean tonight. Although it's so empty in here we couldn't upset anyone if we tried. Come on then smarty-pants. Solve this one – I haven't got a clue."

We both stare at it for a while and try a couple of moves, but every option leaves the chocolate in the glass. Eventually I offer to eat it.

"That would be cheating and it also wouldn't move two matchsticks."

It's another fail. How rubbish can two reasonably intelligent adults be at logic games? Very, apparently, as Star Trek appears just before our soup. I usually hate soup, but needs must and all that. The answer is ridiculously simple, which cracks us up and makes him giggle:

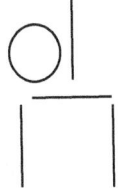

Simply by moving the horizontal match to the right, and the left hand side of the 'wine glass' down and to the right of the 'stem' of the glass, he creates another wineglass outside of the chocolate. He retreats with his matchsticks to leave us to eat, although I feel more like I should be looking at the food rather than eating it.

"I'm sure you'll be fine. It's not like you're going to stuff a plate full of chips, is it?"

"I think I can feel my stomach expanding from all of today's food actually. Maybe I should go for a run in the gym when we get back on the ship tomorrow."

"Good idea. Maybe you'll get an idea of where Sarah is."

"I suppose I could describe her and ask whether she's been in. Say I'm trying to contact her and we keep missing each other. Maybe we just keep literally missing them."

"Nah. We've hung out at all their usual haunts and they haven't been at any of them. Something must have happened."

"Well seeing as we are so beautifully dressed up, I think we should have a bit of a nose around after dinner. Maybe take a wander along through the bars. Just in case." I can't help noticing that James is in fact looking divine in his black evening suit, black shirt, and midnight blue bow tie. His already golden hair has become streaked in the sunshine, and he's managed to gain a healthy tan without burning.

"What?!"

"What do you mean, 'what?'"

"You're looking at me."

"Because you look drop dead gorgeous in all that gear and I'm really proud to be with you."

"Aw, thank you."

I'm staring at him.

"What now?"

"You really have changed, haven't you? In the past you would've shrugged it off. Been sarcastic, self-deprecating."

"Well, I've learnt through one of the monks that leads the meditation group, that we have to learn to appreciate compliments and be kind to ourselves before we can do the same for others. And saying 'thank you' instead of being sarcastic is an important step along the way."

I'm halfway to miming putting my fingers down my throat as in 'new age shit' when the look on his face stops me.

"Try it. You look absolutely beautiful tonight, Caitlin. Possibly better than ever before. And I really mean it." He nods. "Go on. Say it."

It's like pulling teeth. "Thank you."

"And how does that feel?"

"Weird and very self-indulgent. You sure about this?"

"Absolutely. If you can be kind and loving to yourself, it's easier to be the same with other people. As within, so without."

There's a bit of silence while Sebastian whisks away our empty soup bowls and serves up my teensy portion of fish and the usual shipping load of greenery. James has ordered chicken breast in Madeira sauce which is about five times the size of what's on my plate. He must have an elastic waistband.

"How come doing that doesn't make people all up themselves?"

"Firstly because people who are 'up themselves' aren't usually drawn to a lot of introspection, so possibly wouldn't get into that kind of conversation. Secondly, because it's about valuing ourselves. Truly and honestly and properly. And that means accepting ourselves just as we are. It's not like saying, 'oh yeah, I'm the dog's bollocks' when we know that isn't true. In the dead of night, deep inside, we know what's true, and what isn't, so the only person we're deluding is ourselves. So accepting the compliment when someone else says you look nice, is like recognising it for yourself too. It's so easy to say, 'Oh this old thing' if someone compliments you, but that's disparaging them as well as yourself. They think you look nice. The correct response is, 'Thank you'. You would be amazed how many people find that hard to do."

"I could sit and listen to you for hours, you know."

"Thank you."

We both collapse into giggles.

"And you know, what I've found with the monks I've met is that they have such a wicked sense of humour and are full of joy. They smile while they meditate, and their joy is absolutely genuine."

"That's cos they're shut away, not having to deal with the world. I'd bloody smile if I could do that."

"Ah, apparently not. They say that, just like when we go on holiday we take ourselves along too – so for that read all our problems and baggage – life in a community is very similar. In fact it must be worse. Imagine having to join in doing the washing up for a few hundred people when you feel like shit. Or digging up potatoes when it's really cold and you'd sooner be snuggled up reading a book. I don't think it's as easy as we imagine."

"So – going back to the holiday bit, which we're still on – this is all a bit weird, isn't it? I mean you couldn't make it up."

James' mouth is full so he gives me a 'go on' kind of look.

"Well, if I wrote this in a book, nobody would believe it. I get whisked away on a lovely cruise – for very little money (how amazing is that?), by my gorgeous friend – and along the way get quite close to really liking some lovely bloke who is on the ship with his very odd ex-wife, then they both disappear without trace. And as a massive added bonus, my previously decadent and extremely rowdy gorgeous best friend seems to have turned into some kind of budding Zen master. I mean, really?"

"Sounds amazing to me. Anything less would be boring, frankly," he says, grinning. "Sebastian, you're gonna be the death of me."

Our lovely head waiter has arrived with the dessert menus. "Just a little something to keep you going until the morning?"

"You haven't seen all the little somethings I've been eating today!" I say. "I could hardly move in this dress before I ate, so I'm not sure I will actually be able to stand up when I have to."

"I must say you are looking stunning this evening, Madam. Formal night suits you both. For some people it is – er – not so good, but you both really look the part."

We look at each other, then both say "Thank you!" to Sebastian and promptly burst out laughing. He walks away grinning, and shaking his head, completely bewildered by us.

Chapter 32

So after avoiding dessert on account of there not being a millimetre of give left in my dress, we go for a wander around the decks. It's always chilled at this time – a pianist in one bar, a singer in another, the dance teachers running a session in the Atrium… Dancing!

"We need to go to the Atrium in case they're watching the dancing!" I totter off in what I think is the general direction of the Atrium.

"Okay, but you're going a helluva long way about it," chuckles James, gently turning me around and steering me in the opposite direction.

"I'll just about have this ship sussed when it's time to go home. Oh. Not saying that word again as it makes me sad."

The dance session is just starting. I check out everyone I can see as we casually cover the whole area, and apart from a nod from Mrs Ungrumpy and a surprised look from the lady in black from last night – who obviously thinks I have more than one husband – we don't see anyone we know. We do, however, end up walking past DDG photographer and his sunset backdrop. He's obviously having a quiet night as nobody's queuing to be snapped in their posh togs, and he's looking bored as hell.

"Ah, hi! Good! Some lovely people to photograph. How lucky am I?" Ooh. Smarmy.

"Quiet night then," says James. Shall we?" He gestures for me to take my place next to him in front of the sunset. I'm delighted to oblige.

"No – people don't seem to be that interested tonight. It's always a lot busier on a Captain's Night. Free booze and all that. Nice to see people dressed up though – makes a bit of a change, doesn't it? Can you turn and face him, Madam, hand on his shoulder please? Then look to the camera. Lovely."

He's obviously still not clocked we're not a couple, as he gets us doing all the lovey-dovey sort of shots, which is actually a good laugh. We ham it up a lot as there isn't anyone else waiting.

"So what are you guys up to tomorrow?" Still snapping away.

"Shopping, I think. Possibly a walk up to the fortress. Anything you recommend?" James is shamelessly playing to the camera. I can't wait to see these photos.

"Cartagena is great for artisan shops, and really interesting to wander round. A bit further out of town there's a shopping centre with all the big brands you see in England like Zara, only a lot cheaper than at home. Also some good coffee shops, and you can walk straight off the ship into the town, which is handy."

"Yeah, we heard that," says James. "Then Gibraltar, then two days and we're home. Can't believe it's gone so quickly!"

"Can't wait, personally. I'm finishing after this cruise."

Ooh, that's not quite the holiday spirit, is it? Bad day at the office, perchance? "Oh, why's that? Have you been on here for long?"

"My first contract actually, but I miss home too much. It looks amazing and flashy, swanning around in dinner suits and doing everything from port pictures to weddings, but I want to have my own business and develop the wedding side myself – have a bit of creative flair – which you really don't get the chance to do on here. And I miss my partner too much."

Woah, wasn't expecting that! So is it a 'him' partner or a 'her' partner? I really am nosy as hell. I look at James, wide-eyed, and dig him in the ribs on the side away from DDG.

He's good. We're such a team.

"Oh, that's a surprise – you look all smiles when you're out with the punters. Will it take you long to set up?" He's all innocence and light.

"My partner is in IT so the pay is good. I might just have to be a kept man for a while," he smiles.

But it's actually a sad smile and all of a sudden I feel a bit sorry for him.

"Can you work from home to build the business?" asks James. "Sounds like your partner might be able to help you. It's all digital now, isn't it?"

"Sadly not. She's more on the sales side – so good bonuses but no technical knowhow – haha! But it will be good to be home."

Well THAT'S a surprise. I was absolutely sure he was batting for James' team. And what was all that flirting about? "Well thank you for making it all such fun. I usually hate having my photo taken," I say, meaning it. "And I can't wait to look at this little lot."

"Come to the desk tomorrow night and I'll go through them with you. You're really lovely – you should have more confidence." This is to me and I can feel my cheeks starting to blaze in response. Fortunately another couple have arrived to get snapped, so we say our goodbyes and thank yous and I totter off with a big smile on my glowing face.

"Soooooooooo! *That* was a surprise."

"Just shows, you never can tell," says James, pulling out the ship's daily newsletter from his jacket. "Strange that under all that flirting he's really quite sad. Guess he has to be 'up' when he's out the front, just like we had to be at the holiday park. God, I hated that. Tears of a clown and all that stuff. Anyway, I had the astonishing foresight to bring the newsletter with us, so we could wander along to one of the shows, if you like."

After all that standing still and posing, my feet are starting to throb.

"Okay. I fancy a bit of a sit down so my feet can recover. Where do you want to go?"

"I was thinking about the theatre – they're doing old movie themes – Fred and Ginger and all that. Thought you might like it because of the dancing. And I love that music."

"You dark horse. I'm up for it, but it might be a slow shuffle. That's the other end of the ship, isn't it? Eek. Come on then."

By the time we get there, bearing in mind the theatre is the other end of the ship, I feel like I've walked for miles and sink gratefully into the first seats we find. Slipping my shoes off, I stretch my toes out on the carpet. Aaah. Bliss. But not for long. The music turns out to be okay, but the dancing isn't great, and after a couple of numbers I catch James looking at the newsletter again. Oh no.

"This isn't very special is it? How about the comedian in the bar? It's a different one from the other night – we haven't seen him yet."

Like the dutiful companion I am, I stuff my throbbing feet back into my shoes and hobble halfway back down the ship and up a floor to the piano bar, which is currently hosting a comedian doing a truly filthy set. There aren't any seats left so I lean against a convenient pillar to ease my feet.

"Take your shoes off?" suggests James, clocking the pain on my face.

"Can't. I do have standards you know. And it would look awful. As would the dress, remember?"

"This bloke's horrible. I can do dirty, but this is unnecessary. How about the Sky Bar?"

"Are you fucking kidding me? I can hardly walk! Have you got ants in your pants or something?"

"Um, lift?" offers James apologetically. "I promise I'll stop then. Love it up there. Just wanted to try out some of the entertainment, but I don't think we've missed out on much."

He guides me slowly towards the lift which *should* take us to the Sky Bar. I'm not completely convinced it will, as the Sky Bar is stuck right at the top of the ship and is only accessible from one stairwell. We get in and discover this lift will deliver us one stairwell along from where we need to be. Which actually means down two flights of stairs, along the deck and up the next two flights of stairs.

"Next time you suggest big girl's shoes, I'm saying no. Life is so much easier in flats. I am so not having fun."

We've come out of the lift and are slowly descending two lots of steps. I can hold the handrail here so it is much easier.

"But you do need heels with a dress like that. Just wouldn't work with flats." This comes absent-mindedly from James who is now examining the deck plan they so thoughtfully put up next to every exit. "Quickest way is along the outside deck. Are you up for that?"

"You have no idea how much they hurt. You never, ever wear heels. Not as far as I'm aware, anyway! And yes, okay. Outside."

I am so angry.

Actually, it's amazing out on deck, and the beautiful balmy evening does a bit to dispel my sudden bad mood. What's that about? It's not exactly a disaster, is it? Why am I so angry? Ah. Carefully buried memories leech up to the surface and suddenly all becomes clear. I grab James' hand and pull him to a halt, conveniently near some loungers that have been forgotten in the day's tidying up.

"Come. Sit."

He does, like a confused child.

"I need to apologise. I'm sorry for kicking off about my shoes. Oh – that's quite funny actually, isn't it?"

Suddenly I realise how ridiculous it all is.

James goes to reply.

"No. Let me speak. 'Healing in progress' alert." I do those silly speech marks which makes us both smile. "I just realised something. This is an echo of what happened to me in the past, and I took it out on you. And it's my fault not yours. What used to happen is that I would get coerced into wearing something I wasn't really comfortable in, then because I felt miserable and was often in pain from ridiculous shoes, I didn't look or behave like the sexy siren-like model he had in mind. So then he'd sneer at me and for the rest of the evening I'd get the silent treatment while he paid attention to every pretty woman in the room, ignoring me. And of course it would get worse once we got home where I'd be berated for not being a proper woman and not having a clue how to be seductive. And what I should have done, apart from dumping the little shit, obvs, was to tell him where to stuff his tarty dresses and killer shoes. But I didn't have the courage to. I'm so sorry James. You didn't deserve that tantrum. Hey – look! No tears!"

I turn to look at my dearest, loveliest friend, who is now grinning widely in relief.

"You know what, I think you're making progress! But it was also a good wakeup call for me. I wasn't any better than him in encouraging you to wear something you didn't really want to. And yes, I wouldn't necessarily think about your comfort – which is completely wrong and very chauvinistic."

I pull my wrap more tightly around me as the wind picks up. "Thank you. But I'm not sure where one draws the line. Where does encourage-ment to wear something become coercion?"

"I'd say when the other person gives you grief for not wearing what they want you to wear." James stands up, offering me his arm. "Come on, you're cold. We can continue this inside."

Impressed that he's noticed, I stand up too and lean on his arm as we walk slowly towards the Sky Bar.

"And I would suggest men are worse at it than women – as far as the comfort part goes," he continues. "With men it might just be the girlfriend nagging him to wear something different from jeans, but with women it's a different story. It's the whole package, isn't it? Some of my friends love their girlfriends dressing up and wearing loads of makeup and ridiculous shoes, others like them more natural."

"Mr You-Know-Who used to say that men like pencil skirts and stilettoes because it stops women from running away. Talk about belittling women. Christ. There are so many things I wish I'd said, right at the beginning, instead of just pandering to him. But at the beginning you make those little adjustments because the relationship is new and exciting, don't you? Well at least, I did. Maybe that's the problem."

We successfully negotiate the stairs up to the Sky Bar, and as we walk into the warmth I'm delighted to see there are comfy seats over by the windows. And there's also a duo singing quietly away in the corner, so maybe we'll get a bit of entertainment after all.

"Maybe something to bear in mind is how that decision feels inside. Being more in tune with what you want, rather than worrying about what will make them happy," suggests James. "I do honestly believe that if you were with the right person a lot of this stuff would disappear. Or at least, you could talk about it openly and maybe even agree to differ. What's wrong is someone imposing their will on you to make themselves feel good. Dressing up for someone because you want to is completely different from feeling obliged to because otherwise they'll throw a hissy fit."

"So true. I remember one time he lost the plot because I felt like dressing up a bit more smartly to cheer myself up. Think we were going out to the shops or something – nothing major. He'd already decided to be the scruffy end of casual and was in the garden waiting for me to get ready, and he expected me to match him. His face completely clouded over when he saw me. And ironically I was in something he'd liked the week before. That sulk lasted the whole day before I could get out of him what was wrong, then he screamed at me that apparently it was always only about me, and I didn't take him into consideration at all. It was insane, and so was I by the end of it."

"I think I've said this more in the last 10 days than ever before, but thank GOD you're out of that one," says James. At this point our drinks conveniently arrive, so we have a(nother) bit of a toast to the future and things being different.

"One thing I did mean to tell you, on the shoe front, was something one of the girls at the office is doing."

"You talk to the girls at work about shoes?" I laugh. But actually, why am I surprised? James talks to anyone about anything as far as I can tell.

"It just came up one day. I sort of earwigged what they were saying 'cos it sounded really interesting. You know the current fashion for ridiculously high shoes? And the way most women stick their arses out in order to be able to walk in them?"

"Or totter, like me?" I add, helpfully. Where on earth was this one going?

"One of the girls is going to lessons with someone who teaches women how to strut their stuff – properly. Maybe you could go one time when you come up to London. She's all about women looking amazing whatever they're doing, and being completely empowered, rather than wearing sky high shoes and looking stupid in them. Which quite a lot of women do, in my opinion. This girl at work absolutely loves the classes and she certainly looks good in the shoes. I think there are Youtube videos too, so you can get a sense of what she does. But anyway, the whole point is that you wear what you want on *your* terms rather than to please anyone else."

"Hmm. Might think about that. Hopefully in the future I won't be so ready to compromise everything due to the fear of losing someone."

"If that's what it takes to keep someone, they're definitely not worth it. Even Nick. I wonder where the hell they've got to."

"Well, tomorrow's another day. Maybe they'll come out of hiding. Can't wait to hear his excuse for standing me up."

"Haha. Me neither. Better be good."

And so it turns out that after listening to a bit of music, drinking (yet) more wine, and a lot of gazing peacefully out the window into the blackness beyond, I totter back down to our cabin on James' arm in a much better mood than when I tottered up. I love that guy.

Chapter 33

As we leave behind the coolness of the ship for the searing heat of Cartagena, I'm already pretty sure this escapade will involve either a) long hours in a coffee shop, or better, b) long hours in other, much nicer shops, as I'm up for a bit of retail therapy and it's way too hot to do much else. The ship is moored up really close to the town so we wander in the shade as much as possible towards the town centre.

"You know, I don't mind going up to the fortress as long as we can keep to the shady bits," says James. "Seems a shame not to."

"And I don't mind either as long I can have a shower when we get back. Hopefully Marco will have got the shower sorted. It hadn't drained away at all by this morning."

Shade or not, my floaty hippy dress still feels like several layers too many, and I'm already thinking about the pool and a glass of well-chilled Chardonnay. That's pretty decadent at 11.00 in the morning, but do I care? Nope.

The pathway up to the fortress is thankfully well-shaded, and the trees are spectacular, with their roots curling over each other above the ground. It's kind of circuitous, and we get lost a couple of times, but when we get to the top the views are amazing and well worth the schlep up the hill. Can't say the fortress does a lot for me though, as it's more for defence than a pretty place for kings and queens to come and stay (way more my thing), but we can see most of the bay, and the sea looks so pretty, sparkling in the sun. Thankfully we remembered our water, and pause to take a much needed break in the shade.

"I'm thinking it would be better to do this kind of stunt much earlier rather than at almost midday – which it nearly is now. Mad dogs and all that stuff."

"Yeah, but we can't get off the ship until all the trips have gone, so we're a bit stuck with that," says James, tipping his head back to pour some water on his face. "Plus you wanted to hone your stalking skills at breakfast, and that took a bit of time."

"Well I can't believe they've just disappeared. We *always* see them around, especially in the Lido. If we still haven't seen them by tea time I'm going to the gym to ask if they've seen Sarah. I mean, something awful might have happened to them."

"If it was something awful in their cabin then the steward would have found them. Like a joint heart attack or something. Or murder, haha. And if it was out of the cabin then surely someone else would have found them. Whatever the reason, they clearly can't get to the usual places and have no way of communicating with us."

"Funny that we started out not knowing what to make of them, and dreading seeing Sarah, and now all that's changed. I miss them!"

"So do I. Hopefully we'll see them when we get back and the mystery will be solved. Come on. I think we can see the amphitheatre on the way down, then we can go and find some nice cool shops."

We stop to admire the magnificent view of the amphitheatre on our way back down the hill. It looks somehow incongruous, tucked in amongst the more modern buildings and shops beyond it. In fact we get such a good view of it that I don't see the point of buying a ticket to go in and actually walk in the ruins, especially as there's no shade whatsoever. In the funny way that it's always quicker to get back from somewhere than when you're trying to find it, we're in the town centre much sooner than expected.

"Ooh look! Pink boots!" Stopping outside one of the most gorgeous shoe shops I've ever seen, I've got my nose pressed up against the window. "And only 55 euros. Wow. Wonder if they're leather." I raise my eyebrows at James. "D'you mind?"

"Be my guest. It's the first bit of retail therapy we've done, and at least it'll be cool inside."

Swooping joyfully into the shop, I head straight for the pink Coronel Tapiocca boots which turn out to be the softest suede and possibly the most impractical footwear I've ever considered buying. Pale pink? Moi? A beaming shop assistant is already on her way to serve my every whim, and miraculously she speaks some English so we establish I need a six and a half if possible, or seven if not, which is a 40 in their sizing.

James, meanwhile, has wandered over to the men's side, and funnily enough, is trying on the same make for men but in a deep tan.

"So sorry, only 40 in pink. But these in half size smaller," she says, presenting me with a tan pair. Euuw. Tan absolutely does not go with my usual pink/purple/navy palette, and quite frankly, I don't see how it could, even if my feet *are* a million miles away from my upper regions.

"Oh, okay. I'll try the pink." Slipping the stockingette socks over my embarrassingly sticky feet, I pull on the gorgeous pink boots and stand up.

"Oh. Too big. Oh. That's sad."

The assistant proffers the tan boots. "Just for size. You see. Or buy socks for bigger one," pointing at the pink ones.

I slip on the tan ones which fit totally perfectly. Oh. Bollocks. Don't want tan, I want the pink ones to fit.

"You here tomorrow? Can get size for then."

This is torture. "Ah no, we're on the ship. Only here today."

James wanders over in his boots. "Crazy to be buying boots in this heat, but they're lovely, aren't they? Think I'll get these. Really good price, especially with this exchange rate. How are you getting on?"

"Stuck between the tan ones which fit but that I don't like, and the pink ones which I love but are too big."

"Thick socks or innersoles?"

"Guess I could, but the tan ones fit so perfectly. I'll try the pink ones again." I do and they are definitely too big. But could I cope with them being too big? Would probably need innersoles AND socks, but maybe they look too big anyway. They certainly look ridiculous with my floaty hippy dress.

I ask if they sell socks. They don't but the assistant points down the street to indicate there's a sock shop down there, although I can't imagine anyone needing socks in a country that gets this hot. I mean, does it ever get cool enough to need them? James buys his boots, and we leave, saying we will buy socks and come back.

"I'm gutted. So want those."

"Well let's go buy the socks and then you can come back and try them on again."

The sock shop turns out to be a few hundred yards away and is of course filled with very lightweight summery socks due to the fact it's summer. Obvs. Tucked away in the corner are some muted stripey and very soft socks which aren't at all what I would choose at home, and they're ten euros. I usually buy three pairs for that price in Sainsbury's, so I'm not overly excited.

"They're only socks, Cait. You'll always need socks."

"Yes, but I could end up buying expensive socks I don't really like, and the boots might not even fit. Let's look a bit more." The assistant speaks a little bit of English but not enough for me to explain why I need the socks in this heat. It's all becoming faintly ridiculous.

"Seems like they're the only ones. Anyway look, they're 50% cashmere. And with the exchange rate they'll be a bit cheaper so you'll actually have some lovely soft and very luxurious socks even if you don't end up with the boots." James flashes his trademark grin.

I give in. "Ice to the Eskimos. How do you do that?" I hand over the money to the relieved assistant.

"Desperation. And coffee. I want coffee. And food, actually. And we've still got to go back and go through the whole trying on thing again. Is shopping with you always this hard?"

"I'd say this is a tough call. I'm not used to buying expensive things in another country that I won't be able to take back if I change my mind."

"Good point. But I think they'll be fine."

We go back up the hill to the shop, where the assistant gets the box out from under the till, bless her. She really did think we were coming back, so now I feel almost obligated to buy the boots. All the walking up and down the hill to get the socks has made me hot all over again and I'm ready to expire as I pull on the cashmere mix socks, then the boots.

"Hmm. Still a bit big." I stomp up and down the shop. "And my feet are hot so they've swollen a bit. So the boots will be even bigger when my feet are cold. I don't know what to do!"

I could howl. Everyone is looking at me now and I feel really silly. Is it really that hard a decision?

"Leave them then. See if you can get some at home."

"I really want them. And I've never seen anything like them at home."

"Then buy them. Considering the ship leaves in about two hours and we've still got to have lunch, it would be helpful if you could make a decision soonish."

"Oh fuck it. Guess I could always sell them on eBay if they really don't fit." To the relief of everyone present I do that universally understood thumbs-up sign, and hand the boots over. Can't even begin to describe what a relief it is to get the socks off.

Ten minutes later we've discovered not only a nice looking restaurant with seats in the shade, but Mia, sitting with some of her friends from the ship. There are big hugs and smiles all round as we join their table and tell them excitedly about our adventures, then get quite a few laughs when I relay the trauma of buying the pink boots. My coffee becomes a Chardonnay as of course it's way too hot for a warm drink, and also because it goes much better with the paella James and I are sharing. For the next hour or so, we relax happily with our new friends, finding out more about life on the high seas. The atmosphere amongst the crew seems to be akin to boarding school mentality – you either love it or hate it. These girls seem to love it, and are intent on enjoying every minute, especially their days off.

With lunch finished and the clock ticking, we wander back to the ship together, and Mia hangs back a bit to talk to me. "You're looking better every time I see you. More relaxed."

"That would be the sunshine, the wine, and being with James, I reckon. I'm absolutely loving it, and I'm going to be SO sad to get off the ship. It's amazing to be whisked around all these beautiful places. And the lifestyle… and… and… well, you know, I guess. You must hear it all the time from your clients. I can't imagine having a land-based holiday now. That would be so boring."

"Sounds like you've got the bug. People either love it or hate it – there's no in-between. Either completely addicted, or not! By the way, would you like me to put your hair up for the last formal night? I need a bit of practice for a wedding on the next cruise so I can do it a bit cheaper, especially as there won't be any cutting involved."

"That would be amazing! Thank you! I'd like to make an extra special effort, as it's the last chance I'll get to dress up for God knows how long. This isn't my usual lifestyle, sad to say." And I'm thinking that just in case I do get to see Nick again, it would be fun to pull out all the stops and show him what he's missing. "Shall I call in to make an appointment later?" And sneakily check on Sarah's whereabouts in the gym, at the same time.

"Either that or phone in. Whichever works for you, but sooner rather than later so I don't get booked up."

Result. And I'm going to plan my wardrobe so I'm comfortable as well as drop dead gorgeous. The pain is never, ever worth it as far as I'm concerned – as was clearly shown by last night.

Chapter 34

Happily back in the air-conditioned interior of the ship, we realise we're just in time for afternoon tea. Not that I can eat a lot after that paella, but I could definitely force down a cake and some coffee. And it's a perfect place to continue our hunt for Nick and Sarah. I'm not so much cross at being stood up now, as genuinely curious as to what's happened to them. When we get back to the cabin Marco is i
n the corridor, looking very troubled.

"Ah, Sir, Madam, my manager wants to see you about your shower. Will you be here for a minute or two so I can phone him to come down?"

We assure him we're not going anywhere just yet and sink gratefully into the coolness of our cabin. Sure enough, in no more than three minutes there's an authoritative tap on the door. We open it to find Marco with his manager, the scary looking Ice Man from the Captain's Reception. Up close he is terrifyingly perfect. His blond hair is buzz cut to within an inch of its life, and he smells as though he has literally just stepped out of a shower. He probably has. His eyes are indeed a piercing blue, and I know instinctively that I would be scared shitless working for this person. Having introduced us, Marco slides gratefully away.

We invite Ice Man into the cabin, where he apologises for the problem with our blocked shower.

"I'm very sorry to say that Maintenance have been unable to fix it yet. It involves several cabins and is a blockage in the pipes below the floor, so it is a bit more complicated than they first thought. They have absolutely assured me it will be fixed by ten o'clock tonight, but of course that will be too late if you wanted to shower before dinner."

I bet they will have it fixed too. I absolutely wouldn't want to be the one to tell him it wasn't. James and I look at each other. I was so looking forward to a nice shower after the sweatiness of today.

"We could shower up by the pool, I guess," James suggests.

"I was thinking you might like to use the showers up in the Spa. I'll leave your cabin number at the Reception so they give you free access.

I think you'll find the facilities up there will more than make up for the inconvenience, although I am of course very sorry for all this."

Result! That is so cool. Pink boots and a pass to the Spa, all in one day!

"Thank you! That will be really welcome as it's been so hot and sticky today. We climbed up to the fortress, then did some shopping, so a nice shower would be good." I'm gabbling. I always do in the presence of authority. And I bet he doesn't even know the meaning of hot and sticky – I bet he was born in ship's whites and has stayed pristine ever since.

He smiles, says he is sure we will enjoy the Spa experience, shakes hands with both of us then departs, leaving a fragrant trail in his wake.

"I bet even his shit smells of roses," says James, laughing. "God. Can you imagine working for him? Woah."

After a speedy reorganisation of my Mary Poppins bag to include swimming stuff, a book (obvs) and supplies for the shower at the Spa in case I don't like their shampoo (unlikely), we leg it up the eight flights of stairs to the Lido. Amazing how cream cakes focus the mind. I have absolutely no idea how I'm going to cope with ordinary food once I get home. Talk about spoilt.

The Lido is heaving as all the trips are back and people are panicking that they haven't had their full calorific quota for the day so far, and the Sailaway party is due to start. Like I'm one to talk. By some miracle we find a table and James agrees to guard it while I go on cream cake patrol. In spite of not being so cross with Nick any more, I *am* a bit apprehensive about seeing him again, so with that in mind I decide it's easier to go and do something useful like get the cakes, rather than wait like a sitting duck for him to walk by. Or not. Maybe they're confined to quarters with the sicky bug after all. I plunge into the fray, and frustrate quite a few people by spending more time looking around me than choosing cakes. Unable to prolong my stay any longer, I add the coffees to my tray and make my way back through the crowds to the table.

James is still alone, and once I sit down I realise I don't really want the cakes after all.

"You know what, I'm still full from the paella," I say. "Euuw. You're just disgusting."

James has already sunk his teeth into a chocolate éclair so is unable to respond. As soon as he can speak, he tells me that it would be a terrible waste if they weren't eaten.

Yeah, like. "Well – there's a helluva lot more back where that one came from, if you feel that bad about it. I wonder if I'm going to be really hungry when I get home. I haven't done any exercise for ages. I was going to swim every day and run. Ooh. We could wander up to the gym and ask if they've seen Sarah. AND..."

"We can go in the Spa," James adds, finishing my thought. "Might as well make use of it, if it's free. At least I assume we can use the whole lot. I can't imagine they'll follow us into the showers then throw us out when we're done. I'll just finish this little lot."

And he does. Truly disgusting.

So after a quick visit to the gym (which was totally empty, so we couldn't cross-examine anyone about Sarah), and a stop by the salon to book my appointment with Mia, we find ourselves received like royalty in the Spa.

"Shame we didn't come back earlier – could have made a lot more use of this." James lies back against the rails in the hydropool. "Aaaah. Amazing how tiring it is being on holiday. If you slide down a bit the jets catch you just on the lower back." James closes his eyes in ecstasy.

I slide down further into the water too, and it is indeed amazing. We're completely alone in the suite; I assume people are either stuffing their faces in the Lido or bopping around at the Sailaway.

"Funny how we've gone over to the quiet side; as opposed to the noisy, party side, I mean. The Sailaways were fun at first, but what I like now is that they leave the rest of the ship pretty empty.

"We're getting old, that's what it is."

"Possibly. Or maybe it's a state of mind. Some of those people that rock around the pool are way older than us. In fact they put us to shame, so tomorrow we must give it a go. I bet it will be a good one as it's the last port day. Noooooooo! I feel like my life has only just started. Something way down deep inside is finally stirring, and I'm so not ready to go home yet."

"Now it's started, it won't stop – you can continue to allow the process to unfold at home. Just be aware, and don't let yourself slide back into old habits. Granted, it won't be in a hot tub under a sunny sky, but it will still be there for you. As will the memories. And me."

"Aaw. Stop it, you'll set me off. One of the things I'm going to miss most is sitting in the jacuzzi or pool having these lovely talks with you. Will you be my guru?"

"Haha. Yes, the water helps, doesn't it? And no. Even though you're joking. A few good books, conversations with like-minded friends, that really is the way it works. It's an internal process, and the more you get that 'Oh, wow!' feeling when you get some revelation or other, the more progress you make. And I've also found that some of my friends have dropped off along the way as they're not especially interested in self-development. It doesn't mean it's all I talk about, it's just that I have a deeper and clearer focus, and don't necessarily want to do all the stuff I did before.

All that partying was just a cover for me being a bit lost, and now I'm not so lost I don't need to party so much. Anyway, the holiday isn't over yet – we've got Gibraltar tomorrow, then another two days at sea. You might be ready to go back by then."

"True. But the days are galloping by now, aren't they? Haven't heard from Aiden actually, so I might send him a message when we get into port tomorrow. Just to make sure the flat is still there. And Titan. I do sort of miss him, actually. He follows me around like a little ginger shadow, so it's quite strange being away from him for so long."

"See? And the holiday will have given you a new perspective. I bet when you get back you'll see it all with different eyes. D'you fancy the thermal suite yet?"

"Yup. I've cooled down a bit now. We can do the steam room and the showers, and everything. Don't think I've ever been so clean in my life!"

Some time later, and so squeaky clean I can't believe it, we emerge from the Spa. "I think that when I come on a cruise again, which I absolutely definitely will, I'll get a pass to the Spa so I can come in whenever I want. It's a truly magnificent experience."

"Absolutely. To be followed by a celebratory glass of wine, yes?"

"Always."

We wander slowly back down a variety of outside stairways until we reach the Lido level, where we make our way to the back pool, which is now almost deserted. This is our favourite place to watch the port slip away into the distance. Being short-sighted as hell, I don't clock the fact that someone else is there.

James pauses, and nudges me. "Do you see what I see?"

"Um, no?" I say, squinting.

He turns towards me. "Nick. And Sarah. In a wheelchair. What do you want to do?"

"Holy fuck. Which one's in the wheelchair?"

"Sarah."

"Oh my God. Come on…!"

As we get close to the table, Nick sees us and stands up. "Oh, are we pleased to see you guys!"

Wasn't expecting that. Sarah has her back to us so we walk round in front of the table into her line of vision. She looks really pale.

I bend down to give her a hug. "What on earth happened? Where have you been? We were getting a bit worried – in a non-stalkerish kind of way." Probably didn't need to say that last bit.

"Completely stupid. Turned round to talk to someone as I stepped off the running machine and literally fell off it, ripping various muscles in the process."

Now, I wonder who that could have been? I have a truly evil mind. But I do feel sorry for her – what a horrible thing to happen. At that point I notice that her left leg is swathed in a thick bandage from just below the knee to right down over her foot, and she's wearing one of those wrap around support braces.

"Thankfully nothing is broken. What an arse. Guess this is what holiday insurance is for, huh? So poor Nick has had to look after me, which is a fate worse than death. Sorry he missed the dance class with you."

I look at Nick in surprise, but then I guess he would have told her – he's that kind of bloke. I'm ridiculously happy to see him again.

"I was literally on my way to the class when I heard a call for me to contact Reception. When I did, they told me to go straight down to the medical unit as Sarah had had an accident in the gym. So I couldn't get to you to let you know what had happened and then afterwards I didn't have a way to contact you. I am so, so sorry. You must have thought I was really flaky to let you down."

Oh, way worse than that, mate. Flaky doesn't come close. "Well, I was hoping I hadn't upset you so much the night before that you turned into a no-show," I say, grinning and hugely relieved. "I told James you'd probably have an excellent excuse, but I'm so sorry it had to be this, Sarah." She's looking tired, and must still be in a lot of pain.

"The divine irony is that we're separated and came away determined to survive the holiday by spending as little time together as possible, then, because of this, Nick virtually becomes my carer and has to look after me 24/7. I'm surprised we haven't killed each other."

Can't help thinking that if this was one of Ivy's books she'd have them falling in love all over again. I close the door firmly on that idea.

"We thought you had, actually. We were trying to decide who'd thrown whom over the side. Or maybe there was poison involved and nobody had discovered your bodies yet." Not quite true but it sounds good, and we all laugh.

"The most important question is whether the pain relief allows for alcohol," asks James, wearing his pretend serious face.

"Absolutely. I checked that. In moderation, of course," chuckles Sarah.

"Ah, that's the first time I've seen you smile since it happened," says Nick, grinning at her. The last 24 hours must have been tough on them both.

The pool area is so quiet that one of Luisa's colleagues is glad of a bit of action, and our drinks arrive in what seems like seconds.

"Well here's to finding you again! Mystery solved!" jokes James, as we clink glasses. "We were seriously considering our next move if we didn't see you this evening – like going to the Reception desk and insisting they track you down in case you were trapped somewhere. Or had been left behind. Or something. Whatever…"

"Well I certainly need rescuing now, and so does Nick. I think we've discovered that we can tolerate each other in a situation of extreme need, and for a limited amount of time, but that's as far as it goes. And we have a serious case of cabin fever. Now the pain's under control a bit more, I can at least be out and about a bit – so long as someone can push me around. "

We sit chatting for ages about this and that, and I'm surprised how easy it is. Sarah is clearly impressed that Nick has stepped up to the mark, and even feels guilty that he's had to look after her. Several glasses of wine turn into dinner in the Lido as it's much easier to manoeuvre the wheelchair and we don't have to worry about any kind of dress code. We manage to get a round table where Sarah can be comfortable and have quite a laugh going up to the buffet for what looks like a whole ton of food, as of course some of it is for her. Yes, she's actually eating.

"So how did you guys manage with food over the last 24 hours?" James always thinks of his stomach first.

"Room service. They were brilliant. I was in so much pain I couldn't even think of moving, so Nick kept me company and we got the food delivered. Dinner, breakfast, lunch… so he didn't get off the ship today, or even out of the cabin until just before we saw you earlier. And that was because we were in desperate need of company and fresh air. What are you guys doing tomorrow?"

James and I look at each other. It seems a bit churlish to talk about zooming round Gibraltar when they're stuck here. But she did ask.

I go first. "Well, James wanted to do a bit of shopping…"

"And Cait wanted to see the monkeys. So we were going to see whether we could squeeze both in. Maybe do the monkeys first as that's further away. Dunno. We'll see."

"You wanted to see the monkeys too, didn't you?" asks Sarah, turning to Nick. I wonder what's coming. How would she cope if the three of us went off together? Unusually for me, I keep quiet.

"Yes, but I can come back another time. I'm not leaving you for the whole day."

"You don't have to," pipes up James. "How about I take you out shopping? It'll be good fun wheeling you around. We can get a taxi into town and just have a wander. Then these two can go do the monkey thing on their own." He turns to look at me. "I'm honestly not bothered about seeing them."

"Brilliant idea, James. If you can bear it. Thank you." Sarah turns to look at me too, so then I look over at Nick, who kind of shrugs helplessly and raises his eyebrows at me.

Why's everyone looking at *me*?

James has now raised his eyebrows at me too and nods, imperceptibly. Like, go on then…

Chapter 35

"I can't believe how all that fell into place. It was just like you and Sarah had it all planned between you."

"Pretty cool, huh? Couldn't have worked out more perfectly, could it?"

We're eating an early breakfast in the Lido, where Chinese chef is rushed off his feet, but he still had time to give me the thumbs up from a distance and produce two beautifully poached eggs by the time I'd loaded up with mushrooms and beans and made my way down the buffet to him. These guys are *good*.

"Well I also can't believe that a) the excursion desk was still open last night, b) that there were still spaces on the monkey trip, and that c) Nick insisted on buying my ticket to make up for missing the class."

James is laughing at me.

"What?"

"Your lists. They're brilliant."

"It's become a bit of a habit. They used to be just in my head, but they seem to be sneaking into my conversations as well now."

"Nothing wrong with a public display of OCD. What?!"

I'm frowning at him. "Are they really silly? Maybe I should stop while I still can."

"It shows you are a logical thinker. And it's very endearing – I really wouldn't worry. All set for your exciting day?"

"It's all a bit weird. I feel totally set up and kind of awkward, like I'm borrowing someone's husband for the day. And, like, I got all upset and angry when he didn't turn up for the class, and now I'm spending virtually a whole day with him."

"You know what? Firstly, you need to finish your breakfast as time is moving on, and secondly, I think you should just relax and enjoy your time with him. No pressure. Just have a good day. What?!!"

I'm totally scowling at him. "You're taking the piss – doing lists."

"I learnt from the best," James grins. "But I mean it. Don't spoil today worrying about tomorrow. You have a lovely man all ready to be your companion for the day. There may be a future in it, there may not. Does it matter? No. Just enjoy it. And really... we do need to get going."

In the quick flurry of organisation last night, we agreed to meet at the entrance to the theatre where we get our tour stickers, so that James and Nick can do a bit of a handover and a rundown of how the wheelchair works. I thought it was pretty obvious actually, like push to go and, erm, stop, to stop. But after several glasses of wine I clearly hadn't thought that one through, as obviously it will need to be folded down to fit in the back of the taxi they'll be taking into town. So much for my sarcasm.

By this morning Sarah is feeling a lot better. She's sorted it all out herself and knows exactly what folds down where and then – more importantly – how to put it back up again, as she directs operations from a chair nearby. In stark contrast to her razor sharp mental processes, all I've been capable of is deciding to wear my patterned gypsy skirt (new) with a dark blue vest, so that almost any colour sticker will go with it. (Orange, in this case – euuw.) Sad, but there it is. I usually slum around in jeans at home, and I'm enjoying rocking the floaty/hippy-like stuff for a change.

Nick looks lovely in chino shorts and a navy t-shirt, so quite by co-incidence we look very co-ordinated. Ooh. He also has a rucksack with water and fruit which he thoughtfully brought for me too, just in case I didn't have time. *So* not used to that level of care. It used to be that if I forgot anything, it was tough shit. Either that or suffer evils from you-know-who if he had to give me his jacket because I'd forgotten mine.

With wheelchair logistics sorted out and arrangements made to meet up later, somewhere in Gibraltar, we wave goodbye to James and Sarah and wish them a fun day shopping (Sarah) and pushing (James), then join the crocodile of passengers leaving the ship.

"It's gonna be a hot one," says Nick, squinting up at the sky. "I'm glad we're on a trip as opposed to doing it independently. Not sure I could cope with the heat and the stress of doing it all in time."

A bit of research and a chat with the assistant on the sales desk last night had revealed that we could do an awful lot more by joining the excursion. The cynical part of my brain knows she would say that, but I also didn't fancy worrying about getting back to the ship the whole time we're out. And once we get onto our air-conditioned coach we absolutely know we made the right decision. It's comforting to see some familiar faces, which include Mr and Mrs UnGrumpy, June, with some of her friends, and surprisingly, the dance teachers. As we walk past them to our seats, I point behind me to Nick, and can't resist saying, "He did turn up eventually," to which I get a big smile and a thumbs up from Doug.

"Good," he replies. "Maybe see you at the class tomorrow?"

"Hope so," says Nick, from behind me, making me jump.

"What *he* says," I add to Doug, smiling to myself. I'm still stunned about today – hadn't even got round to thinking about tomorrow!

With everyone settled into their seats, the coach sets off and our guide, Josie, introduces herself. She's a very feisty older lady who was born in England but moved to 'Gib' as they call it, with her parents in her teens, and hasn't looked back since. I have to say that on first impression it's a weird and not especially pretty place, and I gather its most popular attraction is the monkey – or is it ape? – population, followed by its importance in the war. Oh, and the fact everyone speaks English and the currency is sterling. So actually a fair bit, when you think of it like that.

Josie tells us that the Barbary macaques are often called apes but are actually tail-less monkeys, and that although they may look adorable and tame, they are wild animals which will scratch and bite if approached. Under no circumstances should we pose for pictures with them.

"Treat them like rampaging toddlers and you won't go far wrong," she chuckles. "Zip up any bags or they will go in for a rummage. To them, bags equal food, so leave all food on the coach. Although with the amount you lot must be eating on the ship, I can't believe you'd actually need to bring any with you." A trickle of laughter from the happy campers. She's not wrong there. "Likewise keep a tight hold of cameras and phones as, just like toddlers, those are their special favourites, and they will run off with them if they can."

Hmm. Glad I brought my rucksack, which will stay firmly strapped to my front at all times. She goes on to tell us that the macaques are the only free-roaming primates left in Europe and that their population has now reached around 230. They are closely monitored and cared for by the Gibraltar Ornithological and Natural History Society, who from what Josie says, seem to be pretty much on first name terms with all of them. Lucky them. The monkeys sound fascinating and I can't wait to see them.

Before we know it, the coach has pulled to a halt at the cable car station from where we'll go up to the Rock itself. Josie wanders down the bus looking at what people are proposing to take with them.

"You don't want to take that love," she points at a bag overflowing with God knows what. "I'd take a bit out then zip it up if you can. You're not staying overnight you know."

The owner reluctantly puts it down and starts to unpack it. Do people really not listen? We wait (im)patiently while she sorts it out as she's blocking the aisle for the rest of us, then finally she's ready.

Nick is first off and turns round to help me off the coach. What lovely manners. He seems to be the exact opposite of my previous experience of men – James excepted of course. Then he lets go, which is only proper, I guess, but it reminds me again how much I miss physical contact, and that I'd love someone to want to be with me enough that they'd stroke my arms and nuzzle into my neck. When I tried that with Mr Nasty as a kind of clue to what I'd quite like done to me, I got shouted at for being clingy and too touchy-feely. What was too much for him wasn't enough for me. Hmm. Moving on…

We're spewed out at the top of the Rock, where it is actually pretty chilly, especially in the shade, where we're standing, so I sneakily move into a patch of sunshine where I can still hear Josie talking about the Rock's history. *So* glad I brought my shawl, which Nick helps to wrap around my shoulders – the sun might be out but that wind is sooo cold. Not surprising considering that the tip of the Rock is over 400m high. Once our party start to investigate the top area the monkeys appear, no doubt eager to see what goodies the new visitors have brought. The ones with babies clinging to their backs or tummies are SO cute. So cute in fact that one of the women just cannot resist sidling close for a photo.

Really? After the lecture we just had? I look up at Nick and just shake my head. "Why?"

He bends down close to whisper back, "Dunno, but there's always one isn't there?" He grins and his eyes do that lovely wrinkly thing.

Fortunately the woman escapes with everything intact and Josie points out the border with Spain, the other side of the runway that cuts across the road separating the two countries. She tells us that many locals go to shop in Spain, which is surprisingly cheaper for most things.

"That's not going to go down well," says Nick. "Sarah was thinking it would be cheap here, and she would absolutely mop up."

Josie goes on to tell us that certain things are cheaper in Gib, like alcohol and cigarettes, and possibly perfume, but everything else is probably more expensive as it has to be imported. Just as well I got my pink boots in Cartagena then! After some chilly sightseeing where she points out the Rif Mountains of North Africa and the Sierra Nevada over the Costa del Sol (both stunning) I begin to understand what a key position Gibraltar holds as the gateway between the Med and basically the rest of the world.

Thankfully we start our descent down to St Michael's Cave, which we're informed remains at a constant 18 degrees C whatever the weather or rainfall outside. It feels positively balmy compared to outside, so I'm very happy to wander around in there even though caves aren't generally my thang. The acoustics are astounding, especially in the Cathedral Cave which is so-called due to the rock formations that look like organ pipes. It has tiers of seats just like a concert hall, and is hired out for all kinds of events. Josie tells us it was initially thought that the caves were bottomless, and there were rumours that they ran all the way to the coast of Africa, 15 miles away, and that that's how the monkeys came across. Not true, but spooky all the same. She points down some very narrow tunnels and tells us that the network of caves are still being explored.

"Used to work with someone who went pot-holing at the weekend. Sometimes he'd come in on the Monday with his face all scratched up," says Nick.

"Oh, there's no need for that." I shudder at the thought. "Didn't he wear a helmet?" You definitely wouldn't get me doing that.

"When he first went down, yes. But apparently the most fun was when they got further in and the tunnels became too small to wriggle through with helmets on, so they took them off. Hence the scratched face."

"Sounds horrible. Sometimes I have nightmares about having to squeeze through small spaces to get somewhere. It's always like jagged rock or something – never smooth walls or doorways. Everyone else in the dream can either get through perfectly fine or they find a way to go round. I'm always at the back and there's that feeling of being left behind, so I have to overcome the fear I'll get stuck and try to get through."

"And do you?"

"Interesting question. Just realised I usually wake up at that point feeling really frustrated and stressed."

"I read a fabulous book once called *Dreaming Reality*. Can't remember who wrote it, but the authors spent years researching dreams, doing stuff like setting the alarm so they woke up at specific points in the sleep cycle. The conclusion they came to, having also interviewed loads of other people, was that dreams are usually a residue of the experiences of the last few days, and if you think through what's been going on, you will usually find it played out somehow in your dream."

Wonder what that says about me and my narrow passageways then.

"So it's sort of symbolic of what you've gone through, rather than symbolic in a symbolic kind of way?" I grin at him as I realise how stupid that sounds. "Sorry. Massive attack of playing with words. That and making lists are hopefully my worst points."

"Funnily enough though, it does make sense. Like if you dream of a flock of birds taking off and flying across the sky it might symbolise freedom or aspiration, or whatever, according to those interpretation handbooks, but if you recall events over the last few days it might be that you noticed a flock of birds taking off and it registered in your subconscious, so it comes up in your dream. So not especially meaningful, as far as these guys would see it."

"I think you've just destroyed a whole section of the Mind, Body, Spirit market in one fell swoop, to be honest," I chuckle. "And how about if you trawl through your memories, and there isn't a rational excuse for the dream?"

"Ah, well, maybe it could be considered to be divinatory when that happens, but taking what we've said into account, I'd imagine it's not going to happen very often."

Can't help thinking that I've had more interesting conversations on this holiday than I've had in possibly the last ten years.

Chapter 36

Before I realise it we've left St Michael's Cave and are now being led into the Great Siege Tunnels, which are absolutely bloody freezing. They extend for 34 miles and were created over the last few hundred years. Josie (who's only wearing a T-shirt but doesn't look at all cold) leads us deeper inside, whilst telling us that The Great Siege was an attempt by France and Spain to capture Gibraltar from the British during the American Revolutionary War, which lasted from 1779 to 1783. Their guns faced each other across the patch of land that now has the runway cutting across it, but the British garrison were unable to cover a blind angle on the North-East side of the Rock, thus leaving themselves open to attack. That side of the Rock was inaccessible because of its steep terrain, and the only option appeared to be to get a gun onto the spur of rock called The Notch; the then Governor offered a prize for anyone who could think of a way to do it.

"I can't begin to imagine how they got the guns up here, even to the accessible bits," I wonder out loud. "Those poor men."

Josie leads us further along the network of tunnels and stops in an alcove which is open to the elements and houses a whacking great gun, pointing out through a gaping hole through which the most perishing wind is blasting. She doesn't even seem to be aware of it. The mannequins 'tending' it are laughably lightly dressed for the temperature – a bit of poetic license there methinks. She tells us that a bright spark called Sergeant-Major Ince suggested blasting the Rock from within and excavating up to the Notch so that guns could be placed inside, so the blasting and excavation by hand began. The workers soon began to suffer from the poor air quality inside the tunnels (imagine Health and Safety getting their claws into THAT one), so in the interests of keeping them alive it was decided to blast some holes upwards to create air vents. In a massive stroke of luck it was discovered that the holes and ledges created during the blasting were perfect for siting the guns, and consequently the push upwards to the Notch was abandoned in favour of lower tunnels. That must have been excellent news for the poor workers. All in all, an amazing feat especially considering this was in the late 18th century. We move away from Josie to look at the rest of the exhibition pieces in that section, which would probably be fascinating if I was wearing the correct clothing and could concentrate properly. In my humble opinion correct clothing would be a thick fleece, warm trousers, and boots with thermal socks. But they didn't tell us that in the Newsletter. I'm standing shivering in front of one of the displays, when Nick unzips his rucksack beside me and pulls out a jumper.

"C'mon, slip it on. I know it's massive but you're frozen." He pulls it over my head and down over my shoulders and body as I lift up my arms like a child being dressed; he gently disentangles my hair from inside it, then vigorously rubs my arms up and down to get some warmth back into them. How much better can life get? I've obviously crash-landed in one of Ivy's books. It feels amazing, and the jumper, apart from being navy, thus co-ordinating perfectly with my own wardrobe, smells lovely and musky. Good musky, not stale musky BTW.

I know that a huge smile is lighting up my face, because I can feel the glow from way down deep in my stomach. "Ah, thank you. Any chance you've got thermal socks in there too? How the hell did they cope with the cold? And this is summer!"

"I know. Unbelievable isn't it? And no, sorry. Clean forgot the thick socks when I was packing the rucksack this morning. Can't imagine why."

Josie is now telling us that the Tunnels were extended in World War Two using much more sophisticated machinery, and they contained what amounted to a small city, housing over 5300 people at one point. The ratio was 5000 men to 300 women, most of whom worked outside the Tunnels during the day, only returning inside for safety at night.

"Not sure a ratio of around 17 to 1 constitutes 'safe', are you?" Nick chuckles.

I turn to look at him. "Woah. So you just worked that out in your head?"

He laughs, a bit embarrassed. "Um, yes? Seems to be the way my brain works – probably similar to you and words."

At which point Josie adds that the women's quarters had locked gates to protect them. Seems like they had more to worry about than bombs dropping on their heads.

"I rest my case. Have you seen enough? I'm more than ready to get out of here."

For some unimaginable reason, considering the cold, some of the party linger in the caves, but we head for the exit and some sunshine, which takes a surprisingly long time. Didn't realise quite how far we'd come, but when we finally get outside the warmth is very welcome. We head for a bit of wall to sit on that is in bright sunshine, and I finally start to defrost. Not ready to let go of his lovely jumper yet though.

There's a part of me that wants to have a massive conversation with Nick, as this is obviously the longest time we will have together away from the others until the end of the cruise. I want to ask him how he feels, does he really like me? Would he like us to see each other again? All the questions that I've been attacked for asking in the past as being 'too intense', so my confidence is shot to pieces and I have no idea what is appropriate any more. I bring to mind what James said about enjoying myself and the moment for what it is. Consequently, and after much internal struggling, I decide to just relax and enjoy Nick's company for as long as we have together. I don't want to spoil it by forcing a conversation he's not ready to have yet.

The rest of our party have finally wandered out of the caves and as we crocodile our way back to the coach I'm wondering how we'll meet up with James and Sarah, although I'm not at all ready to. I want to savour every beautiful moment with Nick as he's so easy to be with, but the minutes seem to be speeding by way faster than I would like. Then my mind goes back to my conversation with James, and I realise I'm being all control-freaky again, and it isn't my responsibility to organise everything. So I do actually let go a bit. It feels weird, but nice. I'm not quite sure what to do with this, because I've always organised everything into virtual oblivion – unless Jules is around of course, as she leaves me standing on the organisation front. When does organising become controlling?

"Penny for them?"

Hmm. Not sure I want to share this as I haven't explored the whole thing yet. But maybe that's being control-freaky too.

"Didn't mean to intrude – you just looked very thoughtful."

"For once I'm not sure of the right words, but it's about me trying to control every situation by organising it in advance instead of letting it unfold naturally. I've been told in the past that it stops other people being spontaneous, and that I'm a complete control freak."

"Haha. Oh, trust me, you've got nothing on Sarah. In fact I'd say you are positively laid back compared to her. If she hasn't got the whole week planned out in advance, she's unhappy – social as well as work. Comes from being in the legal profession I guess."

"I think with me it comes from fear. I'm not good with spontaneity unless it's me doing it. And that really is being controlling, isn't it? I don't want to just go with the flow if I haven't decided where the flow is going."

"So give me an example. Maybe I can help."

Ah. Bollocks. This will lead to me having either one of the conversations I decided *not* to have. And this is me not being controlling. How is this shit supposed to work, then?

Deep breath, here we go then. "This is so funny. There's me trying to go with the flow, and in doing so I'm going to have to tell you what I was thinking about. So I will end up saying exactly what I wanted to avoid saying."

Thankfully I'm let off the hook for the moment as we're back at the coach, where the air conditioning isn't quite as welcome as usual given that I have only just warmed up. On the plus side it means I'm still not letting go of the jumper.

It seems like a few party goers had near misses with the monkeys. The lovely June had one clamber onto her rucksack but fortunately it wasn't able to undo the zip and leapt off again when it spotted another target. The lady with the massive bag who was forced into removing half the contents is deeply grateful for that advice and is somewhat subdued, since the monkeys still attempted a smash and grab. Fortunately they were also foiled by the big fat zip.

Once we're all on board and Josie has counted the heads, she announces we'll be stopping in the main shopping area and that those of us who want to get off and walk back to the ship are more than welcome. I'm still determined not to bring up the subject of James and Sarah.

Nick breaks into my thoughts as the coach sets off. "I'm not really ready to meet up with the others yet. Do you fancy a coffee somewhere?" YES. "Oh, thank you – yes. Not quite defrosted yet. That would be really nice." And hopefully it will be in the shade and I can keep the jumper on. I know. Shameless. The journey down takes what seems like just a couple of minutes, during which I'm hoping Nick doesn't want to continue with his question.

As the coach pulls to a halt, Josie counts us off and tells us to keep walking in the same direction for about a mile to get to the ship. I cheerfully chuck a couple of pounds into the little basket thoughtfully left by the exit for tips. She was good fun. Nick helps me down the step again, even though I don't need it. I mean, if I was on my own I could so totally do it myself. Why do I let a man help me down a step which is, oh, two feet off the ground? Because I want him to, dear reader. Simple. I hate it when he lets go.

It's much warmer back at this level, so it's with great sadness that I take off his jumper and hand it back. "Thank you. Life saver, really. I cannot imagine how anyone lived up there either. Thank heavens we're back in the warmth and daylight."

Nick points out a nearby coffee shop, where we can sit under the awning but still be in the sun, which is good. It's now after lunch time so we order sandwiches too. After all the food on the ship I can't even begin to think about anything complicated, but I am a teeny bit hungry. It feels really uncaring to not think about James and Sarah and how they're getting on, but knowing that the new grown-up James can deal with anything, I practise another bit of letting go. This is seriously weird.

"So back to my original question. I think I might be able to help a bit, because there's something I'd like to talk about and it might be the same thing as you were trying to avoid. So I can do it for you." Nick takes a big slurp of Americano, served with warm milk on the side, just like me.

That would indeed be a massive help. "Go on."

"Well, I really, *really* like you. But, especially after what you've been through, I don't want to mess you around, and I'm already feeling bad about having let you down at the dance class."

"That was unavoidable. And anyway, I'm having such a good time now that I've forgiven you," I beam a big smile at him.

"Glad to hear it, and thank you. I want to be really honest with you. You know I go all over the place for work… that's because of what's been happening with me and Sarah. I deliberately took on contracts abroad to get away and have a break from what was a very difficult situation. Contracts that stretch out for at least the rest of the year as I wasn't expecting to meet someone anytime soon that I would want to spend time with. So, in the words of many fine songs and quite a few films, 'it's complicated', because in spite of all that, I do want to see you again." He's looking at me anxiously and a bit sadly. "Is that anything remotely like what you were trying not to say to me?"

I have to laugh. Bless him. He's even more sensitive than me, and that's going some. "Pretty much word for word, only from the other point of view. So thank you, yes. And I want to be honest too. I was in a really bad way when James booked this holiday, as you know, and it has been an absolute joy to get away from my everyday life and all the things that were holding me in the past. With his help, the sunshine, a ridiculous amount of alcohol and a good haircut I've started to look at myself differently, and I sort of want to explore that when I get home. I'm also hoping it won't fade with the tan."

Nick grins and starts to say something, but I'm on a bit of a roll so carry on talking over him. Oops. Would have got a stony-faced response to that, way back when. "I would also say I'm probably not a good bet when it comes to relationships at the moment. So although, yes, in an alternate reality it would be lovely to meet up after the cruise, the universe has kind of made it difficult, hasn't it? Crikey, just listen to me. I'll be leading some chanting next! But what I mean is it takes the pressure off us so we get time to recover a bit from what we've been through."

"That was a pretty impressive summing up, actually," says Nick. I'm relieved to see he's smiling, so I haven't upset him.

"So what I was thinking, in my newly control-free state of mind, is that we should just enjoy ourselves on here, and if, at some point in the future we get back in touch, great. But no pressure. Let's just continue as friends and have fun. If that's not being too bossy."

At which we both smile stupidly at each other at the huge release of tension, and go on to enjoy our lunch with no elephants in the room, or under the awning.

Eventually Nick leans back and yawns, saying, "Guess we should make contact with the others. No doubt James needs a bit of relief from Sarah by now. Shall we have a bit of a wander and see if we can find them? Then if we can't we can text, but it would be more fun to track them down."

And so with some hilarity we take bets on which shops we think they will be in and go hunting for them. We agree we're not allowed to ask if a tall good looking man pushing a woman in a wheelchair has passed this way as that would be cheating.

After quite some time we've drawn a complete blank. "They seem to have disappeared. We've probably covered just about every likely shop and restaurant, especially considering the wheelchair."

"Dunno about you, but all this haring around has made me thirsty," says Nick as we wander past a wine bar. "D'you fancy a glass of wine before we go back on? Maybe they've gone ahead. It can't be easy being in a wheelchair in this environment. And definitely not easy pushing it."

I've just taken a slurp of cold wine when my phone beeps.

"Have got taxi back as the shops were rubbish and Sarah was a bit bored. Meet us in Lido when you're back. They're getting ready for one mother of a sailaway party here, Jxx"

Which serves a sharp reminder to drag ourselves out of our cosy bubble of togetherness and get our arses back to the ship. Aaw. Could have happily sat there for hours.

Chapter 37

Apparently the last Sailaway of the cruise is several notches up from the others in terms of excitement and entertainment, and there's an atmosphere of expectation amongst the party-goers up in the Lido. We finally track down James and Sarah at a table close to the handrail, from where we'll be able to watch the ship slip her lines for the last time, as well as enjoy the party.

"Good table. Well done," says Nick, shaking James' hand and bending down to give Sarah a hug. "How did you manage that?"

"Pity party. It works brilliantly," grins James. "I just have to ask people to excuse me, wheelchair coming through, then they see Sarah's leg and they're full of sympathy and they can't wait to clear the way. Some lovely couple insisted we have this table as they can go somewhere else to watch the ship leave port."

"Amazing. Every home should have one," I chuckle. "And how are you feeling?" I ask, turning to Sarah.

"Actually, I'm pretty good. We had a mooch around the shops, and everyone was lovely. Really friendly and all agreeing it was a bummer to get injured on holiday so they were extra helpful."

"Did you get anything?" I don't see any bags around.

"Nah," says James. "I think the shopping in Cartagena is better. Okay for the usual duty-free stuff, but I'm not really interested in that. We had fun though, didn't we Sarah?"

"I defy anyone not to have fun when James is around. He's like a mobile party and I think the people in the shops were very sad when we left. He played up shamelessly."

Nick's managed to attract the attention of a waitress and is busily ordering drinks.

"Yup. That's what life is for. Having fun and making the most of every moment," says James, a big grin on his face. "And how did you two get on with the monkeys?"

"Ah they're adorable." I grab my phone to show them the pics. "I wasn't very brave and stayed well back, but a couple of the people on the coach had near-misses. Thing is, the monkeys are so cute, especially the babies, and it's so hard not to reach out and stroke them. Our guide was really good though and very strict. Guess it's not in her interests to bring back wounded tourists."

"The tunnels were amazing too," adds Nick, who has now re-joined the conversation. "Apart from being perishingly cold of course, but the sheer ingenuity of what they achieved is amazing. And the tunnels are still being used by the military. Apparently we only get access to about 1% of what is actually there. Imagine how creepy it must be in the rest – love to know what goes on there. It would make an amazing adventure film – like James Bond or something."

"Must admit I'm glad to be out of there and back in the warm though. But so sad this is our last Sailaway. I could get used to this."

"Ah, well, I ordered something to cheer us all up," says Nick as our waitress approaches, carrying a silver bucket, four glasses, and with a blindingly white tea towel draped over her arm.

Ooh – bubbly, by the shape of the glasses. How sweet of him. He must be loaded to order a bottle on here.

"Well, it seems like we've all had a good day, and it *is* the last Sailaway, so I think there is cause for celebration," he says, winking at me with a big smile.

And far from being sad that we haven't arranged to see each other again after the cruise, I feel liberated that it was me that made the decision. Woah. The girl is changing.

The speakers crackle into life. "Ladies and gentlemen, I'm happy to announce that we now have our full complement of passengers aboard and are ready to slip the ropes and start our journey back to Southampton – where we will dock at about 6.00 AM on Saturday morning. We're looking at a calm smooth passage out of Gibraltar, and if the weather gods don't change their minds, hopefully all the way home, so your wine glasses should stay safely on your tables at all times. Talking of which, I understand there's a huge Sailaway party starting on the Lido deck, so as soon as the youngsters get this ship safely out of port, I'll be coming down to join you. Enjoy the rest of your time aboard the Titania."

As the ship starts to move away from the quay the Captain sounds three short blasts on the horn and the entertainers start the party with that Rod Stewart classic, 'We are Sailing'. There's a sneaky little lump in my throat as I unexpectedly pick up on the emotion of it all, and of course there's the thought of the holiday coming to an end. And judging by some of the faces around me, I'm not alone. But then Nick pops the cork on the bottle, and the general hilarity of trying to get the bubbly into the glasses without it spilling out over the top takes my mind off it.

"To new friends!" says Nick, looking mostly at me.

"To new beginnings," says James, looking mostly at me.

"To new everything," laughs Sarah, looking directly at me.

"You lot are stitching me up! Thank you all for a fabulous holiday… and I'm going to shut up now or I'll get all silly." Too late. We share hugs and kisses which nicely distract from my brimming eyes, then enjoy a few slurps before turning to watch the ship leave port. There are a couple of other cruise ships still moored up, and the Captains share a sort of hooty exchange, just like they're talking to each other. It's a brilliant end to a brilliant day in port.

Fortunately Sarah has a good view from where she's sitting, and isn't left out as the rest of us lean over the side to watch the ship move out into the bay then turn to head south on her journey out of the Med and towards the Strait of Gibraltar. It's at that moment I realise I haven't sent a text to Aiden, or called my mum, but there weren't any messages on my phone when we docked, so clearly they don't actually need me. And why would they? As everyone has been telling me, it's only two weeks. But two weeks that have pretty much changed my life.

A warm arm leans next to mine, and a familiar fragrance wafts over me.

"Good day, huh? You came back looking really happy."

"Ah James, you are such a sweetie. Thank you for making this possible. Yes, we had a lovely time. No pressure, a bit of chatting and a lot of fun. And you?"

"Same. Genuinely nice day. Hey, listen. They've started a line dance. Shall we?"

And indeed the effervescent Laura, clad in her blue polo shirt and perfectly pressed white shorts, has got the people nearest the pool doing the Macarena. Must have missed that one, but no worries as of course she's calling the steps.

"WIGGLE, WIGGLE, WIGGLE, WIGGLE. THAT'S IT, GET WIG-GLING. So it's RIGHT with palm DOWN, LEFT with palm DOWN, the RIGHT UP, LEFT UP. Brilliant. And again.

We're just getting good at this when Mrs UnGrumpy wangles her way past me with a big grin, and into her place next to James.

"Good times, huh? Don't mind if I push in, do you? Need to follow your man."

James and I carry on wiggling and shake our heads, chuckling. She really is something else.

"RIGHT behind ears, LEFT behind ears, RIGHT on hips, LEFT on hips. WIGGLE in a circle and JUMP! You're all really GOOD at this!"

And we are. The sunshine, the bubbly, the dancing, it's all going straight to my head as the music gets faster, and by the end of it I'm ready for a sit down. Staggering back to our table and laughing like crazy we sink happily into our chairs, where Nick presents us both with freshly topped-up glasses. How much better can life get?

By the time we've got to the end of the bottle the entertainers have exhausted the traditional British songs (and us – flag waving is *tiring*), and have started the Americanos line dance on stage as their finale. Completely nuts, and I've got no idea how they can do it so fast. They are fully entitled to collapse into little blue and sparkling white heaps at the end amidst much clapping from the grateful cruisers. I will be back. I'm totally hooked on this lifestyle.

Chapter 38

I'm lying stretched out under this lovely white duvet, totally relaxed and immobile, due partly to a just-about-bearable hangover and partly because that's just how I feel. Opened out and happy. Is life good or is it good? Moving an arm, very gently, I catch the tantalising hint of an unfamiliar scent. Mmm.

"Oh. My. God. Who'd have thought it?"

"Not sure who would have thought what, but you're a very different girlie from the one that boarded, that's for sure," answers James, still snuggled into his pillows. "You seem much more at peace now."

"Yup, that's true. It could also be due to the ridiculous amount of alcohol in my blood of course. I think for most of this cruise I would still have been over the drink-driving limit at breakfast."

"But no worries on that score as instead of driving, you are being ferried around on a multi-million pound, state of the art, floating gin palace."

"Well if you put it that way…"

"A lovely one though – don't get me wrong. But I'm totally spoilt for camping holidays from now on."

"I don't believe you've been any closer to a camping holiday than I have to the International Space Station."

"Well even if I had, I wouldn't now. Not even glamping. I mean, what the fuck is that all about?"

"Dunno, and I have no intention of finding out. Anything that involves going outside to the toilet in the middle of the night is off the menu for me. Anyway, I've found my spiritual home on here, and I'm not planning on going downmarket if I can possibly help it. And that champagne was pretty damn good. Generous of Nick to splash out on it. The perfect end to a perfect day. Well, that part of the day, anyway."

"Good. I'm glad it all came together for you."

I love the way this isn't a cross examination. One way or another we didn't get much of a chance to talk last night, so if it was me I'd be asking loads of questions – but James is leaving it all open so I can say what I want. I appreciate that, and funnily enough, just for once, I can understand how Mr You-Know-Who found it both irritating and intimidating to be quizzed by me. Never thought I'd be agreeing with him on something. Or anything, TBH.

"Yeah, so am I. It was a very odd day. We managed to have a really good chat before we got back on the ship, but there were points before that where I really did want to just drag him off to a room. Thankfully there weren't any available in the Siege Tunnels. Well, not any I would have wanted to bunker down in." I'm laughing at the thought. Then I shiver. Imagine being locked behind that grille for the night – protected from the male residents but cut off from the world, with very spartan facilities and no proper fresh air. Euuw. Not a pleasant thought.

And anyway, who had the key?

"So what changed?"

I need to sit up for this, so I do, wrapping my delicious duvet around me, and getting another waft of that lovely perfume. "What *is* that scent?"

"Tom Ford Black Orchid, if I remember. You do remember being in the duty-free shops…"

Suddenly it all comes back to me. More wine after the bubbly, segueing into dinner in the Lido with Nick and Sarah, then downstairs to check out the duty-free shops where I think we were probably a bit badly behaved, then dancing, then more wine. Oooh. No wonder my head's a bit fragile.

"Ah. Yes. Now you mention it. Moving on swiftly, er, what was your question again? Obviously killed off a few million grey cells too."

"So what changed?"

"Oh yes. I suddenly realised that much as I desperately want a loving and totally hot, sex-fuelled relationship, I also want to have a period of recovery, to explore new ideas and new experiences without being accountable to anyone. The very fact that Nick is away a lot is actually very helpful, as we couldn't leap into a full-on relationship even if we wanted to. So talking about that helped. Not the sex-fuelled bit, obviously, but he was worried about messing me around as he's going away on contracts for ages. I think he was really relieved that I wasn't up for a full-on relationship. Maybe something to consider further down the line, but talking to him made me realise all of a sudden that it isn't what I want right now. And it seems like he doesn't either. How'd it go for you?"

James sits up too. I like this snuggled-into-duvets sort of talking.

"Interesting. Sarah is a lot of fun and really easy to be with. Well, for me, but then there's no risk of a relationship, is there? I don't think she would be at all easy as a partner."

"She seems to have taken the accident really well."

"Yeah. She likes the attention, and she's had that in spades over the last few days. Apparently the medical staff were amazing and stunningly good looking, so that kind of made up for not going to the gym to get her usual fix."

"Yeah – did you find out any more about that mystery admirer?"

"Not really. She just said she would miss seeing the usual people and that she felt a bit stupid for falling off the machine, so she's probably not desperate to go back."

"I bet she fell off it talking to Mr Hunky."

James lobs his pillow at me. "You're impossible. Is this because of Ivy's books?"

"Mmm, possibly? No? Haha. Why is my voice going up at the end of my sentences? Maybe I've spent too much time listening to the entertainers?"

"I think you're right? Aw, stop it." James yawns massively. "These Sailaways are killing me. How'm I gonna get back to the nine-to-five grind?"

"No idea, cos I don't do it anyway. Well, maybe I do, but in pyjamas or whatever, with a pause for a run or something whenever I feel like it. But it will still be hard. This lifestyle is nuts. Talking of which, I'd better see what I can fit into today. Shall we go up to the Lido or down to the restaurant? Or we could sit on the balcony and have coffee. We'll lose the sun in the morning once we start heading up the coast of Portugal." I peer out onto the balcony and realise it's in shade. "Oh. That's sad. We already have. Homewards to the Northern climes then."

"Ah, but we'll be able to have evening drinkies as the sun sets."

"Hey, Mr Brightside, you're lovely, and indeed we shall. Okay, how about duvet coffee? Then we can stay as we are until we're hungry. I'll get it." Stretching my way out of my lovely white duvet and grabbing the kettle I head to the bathroom. "Just as well we're nearly home. We're almost out of coffee, and that would be terrible."

Chapter 39

After grazing my way through what's left of the morning, then into lunch, there's only just time to go back to the cabin to change into something a bit more suitable for dancing in – something I didn't take into account earlier on. My organisational skills are rubbish with a hangover. Thank heavens for elasticated waistbands, cos I feel like a beached whale. Nick suggested meeting me in Reception to avoid the possibility of another wallflower episode, which is very sweet of him. And he's already there, as I come flying down the stairs. Bless.

"Hey, you look lovely. And see? I'm here," he smiles at me, pulling me close and giving me a peck on the cheek.

He smells lovely. Not like just-out-of-the-shower lovely, which is sometimes a bit overpowering, but just right, and in spite of our mutual agreement yesterday I am very much looking forward to being in his arms for the next forty-five minutes. Walking into the Copacabana club together we catch the attention of Doug, who smiles and gives us a thumbs-up. One less person for him to worry about then.

"Ladies and gents, take your sides please. We'll be learning the Slow Rhythm, otherwise known as the Social Foxtrot. It's a nice slow smoochy dance for later in the evening and also for when there isn't a lot of space."

Oh goody.

"We'll be practising the steps without partners first as they are identical, then getting back together when you've got it."

Guess that bit had to happen – hope they all get it quickly. For a good five minutes we shuffle across the room doing back-back-side-close-forward-forward-side-close until I could scream. How hard IS this for fuck's sake?

Finally we get to join our partners and sliding happily into Nick's arms we start the slow shuffle around the room again. There's a lot of laughter (in general) as we learn the rocking bit, and some embarrassment (from us) as we both rock forward at the same time and bang thighs, although everyone else seems to manage it perfectly well.

"We'll be able to do this tonight as well as the jive then," says Nick, close to my ear. "Looks like we need a lot more practice."

"Oh definitely," I smile back, all innocence. Not sure how successful this wanting to stay single thing is as far as he's concerned, TBH. That was yesterday, and this is very much today.

There's much hilarity as we continue our practice and several couples back into each other and generally cause a massive mess on the dance floor.

Doug and Angie think it's brilliant. "Okay, everyone who trod on someone else's feet needs to stay after school for floorcraft class. Seriously though gents, when you step backwards please check the floor is empty, and yes, you do need eyes in the back of your head. Ladies, if it isn't and he keeps going, please stop him. This is the only time you are allowed to tell him what to do, so enjoy it! The rest of the time it's the man who leads, however bad he is at it."

"Haha. This reminds me of a card I saw once," I chuckle. "Ginger Rogers did everything Fred Astaire did, only she danced backwards, *and* in heels. Ta-da!"

"Yeah, but I have to lead. And that is so hard you wouldn't believe it. And think about the next steps so I can lead you into them."

"Wow. Multi-tasking. Wonders will never cease – eek!" This last because Nick squeezes me tightly round the waist and laughs.

Sadly Doug was only joking about staying after class and we're chucked out to make way for the Zumba class which follows. It's lovely to chat as we wander slowly back through the casino and lounge and even more slowly up the stairs (the class was quite tiring, truly), towards the back, where James has parked himself. Honestly, if he wasn't in more or less the same place every day I'd be searching for him forever.

"Good class? You're just in time for tea." James leaps up, clearly starving.

"Oh, heaven help me. Okay, just a couple of small ones then and a coffee. To make up for all the calories I haven't burned in the class. But I want a swim first."

Nick says his goodbyes as he's off to check on Sarah, but not before we agree to meet at the bar outside the Pyramid at 7 o'clock. While James flies off to quadruple today's calorific intake, I do a nifty change into my swimwear and plod up and down the pool a few times, just to show willing. I haven't done a millionth of the exercise I was going to, but I don't actually care. I suspect I was running a lot before to work out the anxiety and raw emotions that were still belting around my body – right up until the point I came on the cruise. I drip my way back to the sun lounger and sit quietly enjoying the warmth and the opportunity to take a slow wander through my thoughts.

"Penny for them?" James is back with overflowing plates and mugs of coffee. Glad we're eating a bit later tonight as those cakes look too good to miss. They're much better if you get in first, something James discovered a few days ago. Who wants to be left with Madeira cake? Yuk.

"Hm. A couple of things really. I think, despite what we decided – or me, to be precise – I do actually fancy the pants off Nick and it will be hard to say goodbye. But the other thing I was thinking about, which is almost more important, is that I don't actually remember how to have a normal relationship with someone. With my chequered career I might not even know."

"Just be yourself and you'll be fine."

"Thank you, but not true – being myself caused all kinds of problems before. After the initial happy period of, oh, a month or two, it seemed that bit by bit my friends weren't appropriate, and all my decisions were wrong and selfish, and why would I want to go out without him, and so it went on. Oh yeah, and something I haven't told anyone else about, fairly early on he helped me put iTunes on my mobile, then showed me how to install the 'Find Your Phone' app. 'Ooh that's kind,' I thought. 'How useful.'"

James pauses, cream cake halfway to his mouth. "Oh no. Please not. I've got a horrible feeling I know what's coming."

"Yup. I must have had 'stupid' branded across my forehead, because it didn't occur to me that by installing the app he could track everywhere I went. And he did. Sometimes he asked why it took so long for me to get home from somewhere, and it took me a while to wonder why."

"Jeez. What a low-down bastard. If you don't have trust in a relationship, you don't have anything. Didn't you think of taking it off and changing the password?"

"Too scared by then. Looking back, it would have been an obvious thing to do, but there would definitely have been some kind of payback when he realised."

"Well trust me Cait, that is not normal behaviour – from either partner. I'm so sorry you went through all that – as well as all the other stuff. Just as well I didn't know, as I would have been tempted to meet him in a dark alley one night. And not for sex, I can assure you."

As ever, my lovely friend brings a smile back to my face, and we continue with the important task of filling our faces. Again.

"Come and sit down. I'm looking forward to this."

"So am I. Close-run thing though – time just seems to disappear on here!" And indeed catching a few more rays and enjoying a cool glass of Chardonnay took way more time than I realised, especially as I needed to do the whole showering thing before I went up to the salon. Blagh. Feeling ever-so-slightly sick with all the rushing around. At least, that's *my* excuse.

"Have you decided what you're wearing? And your nails are still looking amazing. Are you wearing something to match them?"

"Ah thanks. That's 'cos I'm not doing anything with my hands – happily there's nothing to do on here except relax, is there? Oh, and eat, of course. Anyway – after the way the last formal night went, I want to be comfortable. I ended up wearing a skin-tight dress which needed heels I can't really walk in, so it wasn't a good evening, to put it mildly. And poor James got it in the ear for being the one to suggest it."

"Aw dear. Poor James! But men don't realise, do they? Bet if they had periods and had to give birth and wear heels – not together obviously – they would have either found a solution in the case of the first two or refused in the case of the third."

"I think it's because we're scared to say 'No, not doing that.'"

We're at the basin now where Mia is giving me a gorgeous head massage. This could definitely turn into a lifestyle choice when I get home.

"What I've come to realise, now that I've got some distance and different surroundings, is that we all compensate like crazy at the beginning of a relationship, because we want it to go well. Nobody wants to be the one to cause the first row or fall-out. Or say, 'Actually I don't want to do/wear that'. Then having done it once we do it again, don't we? So saying 'No' becomes more difficult. My not-so-charming ex used to get really cross on the rare occasion I said 'No'. I remember towards the end I did actually tell him that I can also say yes, but he wasn't asking the right questions."

"And I bet that didn't go down well." Mia combs some luscious conditioner through my hair and stands back for a moment to let it sink in.

"Correct. But now I do feel stronger. And James apologised, which was really sweet. He didn't realise he was doing the same kind of thing. Until I told him of course. So tonight, Mia, I will be elegant, beautiful, and COMFORTABLE!"

"You go, girl." We have a good laugh at that thought. "So, what I need to know is whether you are wearing halterneck, long or cocktail. And do you want to look sophisticated, sexy or romantic. Sorry for all the questions!"

"Hm. I do actually have all three. Haven't worn the cocktail dress yet. But that's tight, so probably a no. I've got a long halter-neck I borrowed from Jules that could work – haven't worn that yet either. It's a very deep purple and very elegant and not tight. At least it wasn't two weeks ago! And I could wear flats with that couldn't I? And sophisticated hair please. That will be new for me!"

"Sounds lovely. Okay, I have an idea – and it will look good when it's down tomorrow too. Trust me?"

"Absolutely. When I was a kid I used to love my mum playing with my hair, so I'm in heaven right now."

"Splendid. Your hair is a good length for this."

Back in the chair, Mia is drying my hair into poker-straightness, which is a miracle in itself. Then I watch in fascination as within minutes it's transformed into a French plait which goes from the front to the back of my head.

Mia holds up the plait to show how she's has finished it off.

"When you go to bed tonight just take the pins out and the plait will stay in place until you take this band off. It should last for a couple of days at least."

I am silent in the face of such expertise.

"Ta-da!" Mia steps away to pick up a mirror then shows me her handiwork from all angles.

Oh. Wow. The style she's chosen really sets off the shape of my face, and even without makeup I'm looking tanned and well. Standing up to give her a big hug, I can feel a huge smile spreading across my face.

"Having a session with you is way more than just a hair appointment. It's a complete therapy in itself."

"We aim to please," smiles Mia, "And thank you for being my model. I've got a lady next week who wants something similar, I think."

"How do you know that? Do they book the hair do in advance?"

"Yep – they book the whole package way in advance and there's an option to have hair styling too. Looking forward to it actually. A wedding at sea is pretty special, isn't it? One of my colleagues did the hair for a bride today, so you might see her in the restaurant later."

"I'll look out for her. Thank you so much." We share another hug, then I realise as I walk out of the spa – getting some sweet comments from the girls on Reception as I do so – that this posh hair do even makes me walk differently. Maybe I can actually be elegant after all!

Chapter 40

Marco's in the passageway as I reach our cabin, which shouldn't have come as a surprise as he always seems to be around somewhere. He works so hard, but he's always ready with a nod and a big smile.

"Good evening, Madam. You are going to the formal night?"

"Yes, we're looking forward to dressing up tonight. Just hope I can still fit into my clothes."

"I am sure you will, Madam. Enjoy!"

Sweet. I'm definitely walking taller and feel like a bit of a grown-up with it piled up like this. The most I ever do at home is scruff it into a scrunchy to keep it out the way, but this is way more fun, if a bit more effort. Well a lot, probably. And a bit of contortion to see what I'm doing in the mirror. Anyway.

James is freshly showered, judging by the lovely scent coming from the bathroom, and is sitting in his white fluffy dressing gown enjoying the evening sun on the balcony. Can't help noticing he's cradling a glass of Merlot.

'So? Whaddya think? A new me?"

He turns and scrutinizes me, which is quite unnerving actually as he usually just comes right out with it. After several moments of this he finally utters his verdict.

"Really, really sophisticated. Not what I expected at all. You look really different... sort of preppie. Yes. Do you like it? It looks very intricate."

"Yeah. It feels kind of weird being all pulled back so tightly – like the Bride of Frankenstein only flatter – haha. I'd better not let myself down tonight. Talking of which..." I look pointedly at his glass.

"Oh, shit! Sorry – yes, of course I got you one – it's in the fridge all ready for you. Thought we could sit here and enjoy the evening sun for the last few minutes before we get changed, so I brought them down from the bar at the Lido.

"You know, you really are God's gift." I sidle my way back to the fridge, then nip back out onto the sunny balcony.

"Why thank you," James manages to grin and sip at the same time. "I like to think I try."

It's completely addictive sitting here, gazing out to sea as the sun gradually sinks lower towards the horizon. I can't lean back on my lounger properly as the ballerina bun gets in the way, so I have to tilt my head to one side or the other, and before I know it, I've nodded off.

"Methinks thou hast had too much happy juice." James' voice breaks into a dream in which I'm whizzing round a dance floor with Nick. "Sorry to disturb you, but we should probably start getting ready."

Opening my eyes and stretching, I realise he could be right as my mouth is as dry as the bottom of a budgie's cage. But then again maybe not. "Nope, not too much happy juice, too much happiness. I'm really, really happy, for the first time in a very long time. Happy right down to cell level. Or even molecule level. Whatever."

"I'm so pleased. And you know you can keep that happiness in your heart, just like that lovely peaceful feeling from the meditation, and take it out whenever you want to. Now you've experienced it, it won't go away."

"That's a nice thought, thank you. I was thinking I'd quite like to try some meditation when I get back. How can I do it on my own?"

"I've got some good CDs at home. Or you can download the tracks – one of them guides you through the relaxation and then the actual meditation, which is a real help when you first get started. Everybody gets side-tracked, and the discipline of regular practice helps you to become less distracted and focus more on just being in the moment. Just allow the thoughts to rise up as they will – if you don't pay any attention to them they just fall away. Thich Nhat Hanh likens it to sitting by a flowing stream without paying attention to the movement of the water. In fact any of his books are excellent, as he writes very simply and very clearly. I'll email you some links when we get home. I can also find out from my lot if there's any groups near you, as meditating together is really powerful. But for now, lovely lady, we really do need to get ready to par-tay!"

I am SO much more comfortable like this. My black ballet flats go perfectly with Jules' dress and I feel almost regal. And also a bit like I'm dressing up, and in a minute someone's going to come and tell me to take it all off. Only they're NOT, haha! All it needs is elbow-length gloves and I'd be well into Audrey Hepburn territory. James meanwhile is rocking his black dinner suit with black shirt and black tie.

Wowza.

Standing in front of the long mirror together we beam at each other and giggle like overgrown children, wondering what the people at home would make of us. This really is another life.

"C'mon, let's go. Think I need my phone ready to take a pic of Nick's face when he sees you."

"He knew I was having it done, but no more than that. I do love all this dressing up, don't you?"

"Hell, *yes*! What gay man wouldn't? I'm in heaven, darling! You know we need to get some of those photos, don't we? As evidence, more than anything, as this is all going to be just a memory in a few months."

"Oh don't. I don't want to think about that. But maybe we can get a group one, if Nick and Sarah are up for it."

"Smart girl. Good way of getting a pic of Nick too. Hey, that rhymes! Haha."

It's really easy to trot down the stairs; have I finally seen the light? Never, ever going to get talked into wearing something I can't walk in again. Most of the penguins are queueing for lifts, but maybe that's out of respect for their ladies who possibly can't walk in their shoes either. Maybe I'll start a flattie rebellion to liberate women. I'm lost in such thoughts and almost go down too many flights of stairs.

"Woah! Come back!" James has stopped and waits while I climb back up to his level. "Where were you? It looked very serious, judging by your face."

"Oh, I was busy liberating women from their stupid killer shoes and getting sort of angry at the pressure they face to wear them. Nothing major."

"Well bear in mind that some women want to. That's what those classes are about – learning to look fabulous in them because they want to."

"True. Maybe I'm being a bit judgmental. Might try one just to see… Look, they're already here."

Nick and Sarah have indeed got a table at the bar closest to the Pyramid. Sarah is looking better every time we see her, so maybe the pain is a bit more under control now. She also manages to look really elegant, even in a wheelchair, having chosen a long black, sparkly skirt and rich blue silk vest. And Nick? Aaargh. Just gorgeous. He's gone all out with an ivory dinner jacket, crisp white shirt and black bow tie, which looks suspiciously like a seriously grown-up one that you tie yourself.

He stands up to shake hands with James, then I get a lovely whiff of musky aftershave as he pulls me close to kiss my cheek. "You look absolutely gorgeous. Your hair really suits you like that – we should get a picture of us all together as a memento."

Aha! So he wants a picture of me too. Can't help thinking we've kidded ourselves a bit (a LOT actually) that it will be easy to say goodbye. It so definitely won't be – not from where I'm standing anyway – but I'll worry about that when it happens. For now I just want to enjoy the moment, as James keeps telling me to. The joy of this dress is that I can sit down comfortably too – wonders will never cease – so I plonk myself down next to Sarah for a catch-up and a bit of people-watching while the men sort out the table buzzer and drinks. I can't help thinking that life on this ship is like a complete world within itself, and I bet the staff watch with amusement as the dramas unfold on each cruise. And I wonder if they talk about us to each other; I'd love to be a fly on the wall in the crew area. I'm brought back to the moment by the arrival of our wine.

James raises his glass. "Well cheers to the posh togs. I could get used to this!"

"Absolutely," chime the rest of us, curiously in synch with each other. Who'd have thought it? Two weeks ago we didn't even know these people and now they feel like old friends.

Happily, James asked for our favourite area when he got the buzzer, so we're seated at a round table just up from our usual patch. With a bit of shuffling, Sarah gets herself comfortable.

"They've given me crutches too, but they'd be lethal on here, to be honest," she says. "Even the slightest pitch of the ship upsets my balance, so rather than risk another accident it's easier to be pushed around. Sorry Nick – you didn't sign up for that."

"Haha. No idea what I did sign up for, but no worries. Just sorry it happened."

Yeah. That must be weird. The whole thing is weird, to be honest. Coming away to share a cabin with your ex-wife, then ending up having to care for her. Guess they must have made their peace with each other to do that. You can't be snipey when you're relying on someone else to push you around, can you? Just imagining Nick leaving Sarah stranded somewhere on an upper deck because she was rude makes me smile. But then she seems to have mellowed a bit. Maybe that's the James effect.

"Madam?" Sebastian jolts me back to the present by offering me the menu.

"Ah lovely, thank you. I can have proper size portions tonight because my dress is nice and loose. Yay!"

"In that case you should try the lamb," says James. "It's beautiful – really melt-in-the-mouth beautiful. In fact I'm going to have it yet again on the basis that in a couple of days I'll be back to beans on toast in my little bedsit in London."

I can't resist it. "Thank you, I think I will. And I'd imagine you have enough calories stashed away to keep you going for a while, so I wouldn't worry about starving." Then realise that could be a bit hurtful rather than funny, but it's too late as I've said it now. Me and my mouth.

He doesn't even pause. "Yup. And I'm planning on adding as many as possible before I get off here too. Life's too short. Let's eat and drink and party while we can!" Haha. Water off a duck's back. That was lucky.

"Well after the last few days of sitting around doing nothing, I'm going to keep it light," says Sarah, "otherwise I'll weigh a ton by the time I get back in the gym."

I don't say anything, but yes. I haven't done anything on here apart from that one run and I'm pretty sure I do weigh a ton.

"Hmm. Thinking about the swordfish. Or maybe beef fillet," says Nick.

"Lovely but tiny. You might need several plates of that to fill you up." Oops. That wasn't very polite either. Think there might be a tiny bit too much wine going on here.

"That's okay. I go for quality rather than quantity," and winks at me. Tart.

Star Trek excitedly brings the wine list, which is completely unnecessary as we all know what we want. Sarah and I have Chardonnay and the men share a bottle of Merlot. Thankfully he also tops up our water glasses as I'm really dehydrated. Too much sun, food and booze, and not enough water, I think.

Suddenly there's a bit of a kerfuffle over by the entrance and we're treated to the arrival of a bridal party. Aww. The bride looks stunning in a white sequin-covered fishtail style dress with a long train, and her husband is sporting a morning suit with a deep pink corsage, as are the other men in the party. Looks like they have both sets of parents plus a couple of other people with them, and as they make their way across to the big round table by the window everyone starts clapping. What a brilliant way to celebrate getting married. Once they're seated, the waiters deliver glasses of bubbly then all the servers gather round and start singing 'Congratulations', in a style which has absolutely nothing to do with the way it was made famous by one Sir Cliff. Double aww.

DDG photographer is busily snapping them, and then he starts to make his way around the room, and of course eventually ends up with us. "Would you like a group photo? Last formal night and all that? Hey – LOVE that up-do."

This last was to me, obvs and annoyingly I can feel my cheeks warming at the attention. I hate it when that happens and hope they calm down a bit by the time he takes the shot.

"It's probably easier if we come over to you two, isn't it?" asks Nick. So he and James come round to squat down by me and Sarah and DDG steps back to get the shot, or shots, as he seems to be taking a few.

"Lovely. You'll be able to see them tomorrow, and obviously you will need to buy them then too as by the end of the day they all get taken down ready for the new lot coming on board."

"Thanks. And tomorrow is your last day, isn't it?" I bet he can't wait.

"Yup. Really, really can't wait. Since I made the decision the days seem to have dragged, but it's finally here. Yay! Okay, gotta do all the rest of 'em so I'll catch you later."

"He's a nice guy," says Sarah. "You seem to have got to know him well."

"Yes – well – he was flirting outrageously with both of us when we got on, and we couldn't decide which camp he was in, mine or James', and whether he was really flirting, so we sort of kept chatting to him. But in the meantime we discovered that the crew can't have relationships with the passengers anyway, so it was all just a bit of fun. And then he told us he was getting off at Southampton and going freelance as he misses his partner too much. A female, as it happens – that was a bit of a surprise."

"Oh, didn't know that. About the crew and passengers. Interesting."

I swear her cheeks have gone a teeny bit pink. I look at James who's spotted it too and registers it with an almost imperceptible raise of his eyebrows. So maybe the hunky mystery man was one of the gym staff after all.

At which point our main courses arrive and effectively stop that particular line of conversation. Shame. There seems to be a huge amount of food on my plate, whereas Nick's looks like they've forgotten half of it. And then my dish of greens arrives.

"Oh look Sarah – it's your main course," jokes Nick.

"That's what you'll be on when you get home if you have any sense. I really don't know how you can eat so much all the time."

Still spiky then. We all start tucking in to what is our second-to-last dinner on board.

Nick's obviously used to it. "Yup. I'm with James. This is the feast and the famine starts when I get home, so I'm making the most of it. Although actually I'm off again fairly soon, to New York, so it will be American-sized portions for a few months."

My heart sinks even though I knew he was going away again.

"Sounds amazing." I'm trying to be cheerful but inside I'm fighting the urge to beg him not to go. In private of course. With lots of kissing and naughty stuff involved so he couldn't possibly tear himself away from me.

Write your way out of this one, Ivy.

Chapter 41

James pauses in our slow amble around the Promenade Deck, tilting his head slightly upwards and closing his eyes, as if he's savouring every last moment.

As am I, actually. "Smells good, doesn't it?"

He sighs and opens his eyes, looking far out into the darkness. "Yup. I want to remember this for a very long time."

We wander over to the handrail to watch the sea racing by, knowing that with every second the ship is taking us closer to home.

James leans his warm arm against mine. The night is still balmy despite the hour and I don't even need my wrap.

"What's made it special is you, Cait. You're so easy to be with and so much fun. And completely on my wavelength. There hasn't been a single moment when I've regretted coming away with you."

Gulp. "Same for me too, you know. And I've been through a fair amount of stuff while we've been on here. Stuff I really didn't expect to come up. And you supported me through all of it."

"It's easy. I want to protect you, and your happiness has come to mean so much to me. It's like, I dunno..." he says, looking away from me for a moment as if the intensity is too much. "It's like," he turns back to face me, "It's like I'm more of a *man* with you around. You bring out the best in me. And I'm going to miss you so much when we get off here."

This is just like a beautiful ending to one of Ivy's books, where James' next move would be to kiss me passionately, then sweep me off my feet and carry me away into the sunset. Except her heroes aren't generally gay and the heroine isn't pining to be carried off by someone else. James' eyes are very bright and sparkly, like he's only just holding back the tears, and the expression on his face is so earnest it breaks my heart.

"So, um," now I'm fighting the tears too, "that's really lovely. When you say you're more of a man, do you mean like, as in being interested in a woman?" That was rubbish. Most of my usually vast vocabulary seems to have deserted me in my hour of need.

"Yes, I do. Right at this moment I know exactly what I want. And if it was any woman except you I would probably close in to try a kiss, which would be a first for me. And that's why I'm gutted. You seem to be everything I didn't know I wanted, but I couldn't kiss you."

"Er, why not? Just out of interest, of course."

"Because we're too close and we go back too far. It would be like kissing my sister. But it doesn't stop me loving you like crazy."

Bit of a mess then, Ivy, isn't it? I truly feel his pain, but I think I'm also a bit relieved. I love James like crazy too and think he is the most gorgeous man to walk the planet, but I'm right up there with the brother/sister thing. So looking up into the depths of his beautiful, glistening eyes, I say, "Oh... just give me a big, big hug, you lovely, lovely man, or we're both going to be in tears."

And he folds me against his beautiful, scented chest and we have the most massive hug ever. At first I can feel his heart pumping fit to burst, but as I gently stroke his back he gradually calms down and his heart rate slows to something approaching normal.

Pulling away but keeping hold of my hands, he says, "All a bit of a mess really."

My thoughts exactly.

"I've been more open with you than possibly anyone else in my life," he adds. "And I definitely feel closer to you than anyone else in my life. But even if we weren't almost brother and sister, it still wouldn't work, because you're in lust with Nick."

Oh. Well, if you put it *that* way...

"So really, we've got two lots of unrequited love going on here."

"That's a brilliant bit of summing up, James." I'm glad to see his eyes aren't quite so shiny any more. "Couldn't have put it better myself. Just as well we're not on here for longer or we would be in no end of trouble."

He smiles a sad smile.

"But thinking about it in a more positive light," I continue, "What this means is that you have crossed that line – in terms of feelings, not sex (yet) – so if you can feel that way about me, you can feel it about someone else. If that's what you want."

"Hm. Guess so. You wouldn't happen to have a cousin, or anyone very like you that I could be introduced to?" More smile, less sadness.

"I don't think so, but I promise I will give it a *lot* of thought."

"Thank you. But what about you?"

My heart lurches. Didn't really want to pin my turbulent feelings down with words.

"As in?"

"Nick. You're quite clearly nuts about each other. Watching you dancing together after dinner, I don't think I've ever seen you smile so much. You were glowing, and so, so happy."

"Well, there isn't anything I can do. We agreed we wouldn't start anything because he's working away and I'm in recovery." We've started walking again now, in the same direction as the ship so it looks like we're belting along.

"But what if he's *part* of your recovery? Maybe you don't need time apart."

"Same applies. He's working away. And I'm not going to put any pressure on him. He's got contracts he can't get out of, at least until Christmas. It's his call. And I'm not planning on sitting around pining for him. Having said that, though, it's not going to be easy."

"I guess we're both in situations we just have to sit with and meditate upon. There isn't an easy answer for either of us, so that's what we have to be with, and make our peace with, in the knowledge that things will untangle themselves when they're good and ready."

"God, I wish I had your patience. I'm really not good at that stuff."

"Then tomorrow we will do a little meditation together so that we are nice and calm for when we leave. I think I'm emotionally wrung out for now. Are you ready for bed?"

"Yeah – all that dancing and laughing and lovely wine and lovely company has worn me out. It's also ruined me for life back home. C'mon."

When we get back to the cabin, Marco has turned our beds down (like, can't people turn back their own duvets? So weird.) and left the usual chocolates (which I have been stashing away to cheer me up when I get home), but he's also left tickets for disembarkation and instructions about when our cases have to be ready and left outside the door. I don't even want to think about getting off here. But when we open the big white envelope placed carefully next to the chocolates, I can see it's probably a good idea that we are.

"Shit. Oh. My. God."

"What?" James is struggling out of his shirt, which is so new that the buttons are still stiff.

"This is our on-board account. We've basically drunk enough to sink a battleship and now we have to pay for it."

Arms now free of his shirt, he peers over my shoulder. "Ooh. Yeah. What you said. Shit. Oh well. I s'pose it's about what I thought it would be. I sort of kept a mental check as we went along."

"I didn't. Dearie me. My dad's money just about covers it, thank heavens. How to piss away money, huh?"

"Yeah, but it's really good quality piss and we had a good time doing it, didn't we? And I don't know about you, but I'll be asleep about ten seconds after my head hits the pillow. All this emotion is just too much for me."

Yeah – what he says. With bells on.

Chapter 42

So this is it. The Last Day. The day that seemed so far away when we boarded two weeks ago. According to the disembarkation instructions we need to be out of our cabins by 8 o'clock and off the ship by 9.30 tomorrow, so it's the last morning I can luxuriate in this beautiful downy duvet. And the last day I can twist round to look out onto the balcony and the sea beyond. And the last day I'll see Nick. Possibly. But then I can't see how that's going to happen. I also can't see how we can ever have a relationship. So much I can't see. So thinking along the lines of my discussions with James, what I need to do is try to stop thinking, and let everything turn out as it will. Yeah. Like that's going to be easy.

Ah. Yes. James. He's still fast asleep. Either that or he's pretending. Either way, he looks adorable and my heart goes out to him, as last night's baring of the soul must have been so hard for him. I've been uncertain about a lot of things in my life, but never, ever my sexuality, and I can't imagine how he deals with it. But, hey, on a positive note, he isn't just restricted to half the population, like me. A small smile creeps onto my face, which doesn't go un-noticed. While I've been lost in thought his eyes have pinged open.

"D'you know, I've never known you be so thoughtful, or quiet, as in the last few days. And now you're smiling that smile. What is it this time?"

So not disclosing that last bit. "Last day kind of stuff, you know. Last morning snuggling into the duvet, last day enjoying the ship… And thinking that tomorrow night some lucky bastards will be in here, sitting on *my* bed and putting clothes in *my* wardrobe and getting all excited about where they're going."

"Where *is* the ship going next?"

"Dunno, and I'm not torturing myself with even finding out. The thing is that now I know I love cruising it's opened up a whole new part of my mind. Granted, I've probably destroyed a few brain cells in the process, but I would never had tried it if it wasn't for you. Dad went on about it endlessly, but I kind of assumed I'd have to be over 70 to enjoy it."

"Well I guess you could come on and not drink. That would save a lot of money."

I can't help looking at James as though he's grown another head.

"What?!" He's trying the innocent look. Doesn't work for a nanosecond.

"You have to be joking. Imagine the warm sunny afternoons without a cold beer, or those lovely meals without a glass of merlot. Or Sailaways without bubbly. Or sitting in the jacuzzi without a drink."

"Hmm. Okay. Well maybe not us, but some people seem to cope."

"Possibly, but in spite of the cost I've really enjoyed myself, and I'll worry about my drinking at another, less tumultuous time. And definitely not on the last day of our holiday."

"Ah. That's what they all say."

"Who?"

"People who are trying to give something up. It's always tomorrow, never today. I know that myself, because when I hit rock bottom that time it was very tempting to stay there for another day. But anyway, I am having the most fabulous time on here, and I agree. Today we party. So – we're awake early enough to do the line dance class. You up for it? Seems a fitting end to the holiday."

Which is how I found myself down in the Atrium a couple of hours later, amongst all the regulars who of course wanted to snuggle up to James. Aah.

Laura bounds onto the stage and I can't help wondering if she's on something to be so happy and bouncy all the time. Whatever it is, I want some.

"So good MORNING. Have you all had FUN?

"YES!!!"

"Are you ready to go HOME?

"NOOOOOOO!!!"

God, we're well trained. We're also grinning from ear to ear, and for once I don't mind that we're jammed in like sardines, because this really is so much fun.

"AAAAH. I'm going to MISS you all. You are the BEST class so far. So I thought we should PARTY and do all the fun dances you've been learning. So let's start with the Macarena as you were all so BRILLIANT at the Sailaway. Are we READY?"

"YESSSS!!!"

"OKAY." She starts the music. "And, WIGGLE, WIGGLE, WIGGLE, WIGGLE. RIGHT, LEFT, RIGHT, LEFT…."

She's so good. The entertainers certainly know how to get the party started, even at 10.30 in the morning. Of course, loads of people have forgotten it, or weren't paying attention on deck and the usual level of mayhem follows. James is doing it perfectly of course and his harem are following his every move, rather than Laura. Catching my eye over their heads he gives me a massive wink and a big smile. Mrs Ungrumpy is right next to him and is grinning her face off, so presumably the first few days of grumpiness were just her unwinding. Hope they enjoyed their wedding anniversary.

The Macarena comes to an end amid much laughter and we move on to The Lemon Tree, which has become a personal favourite of mine. Maybe I'll look at finding some line dance classes when I get home. Most of us are coping right up to where it gets to POINT, CROSS, POINT, CROSS, POINT, POINT, POINT, when we end up in a tangle. Mrs Ungrumpy is doing it all wrong then turns the opposite way to the rest of us, facing towards James just like she did before. But knowing that she is really quite a sweet person after all, I just smile and watch as James patiently turns her round to face the right way. Again. And every time, actually. Aaah.

After much hilarity and another couple of dances we come to the end of the class, and people hang around chatting. June wanders over – didn't notice her earlier on. Her pretty face is glowing and she looks really happy.

"You're looking good. Glad you came?"

"The best thing ever. I was really worried at the beginning, but everyone has been so nice, and after several years of stress and worry, it has been *so* much fun. Found a 'me' I'd forgotten existed. I'd definitely come again. I've made some really good friends on here. How about you? Your hair looks good."

Mia was right. After unpinning the ballerina bun last night, my hair has stayed in the plait just as it was, and I love it.

"Really good, and thanks. I needed to get away and this has done me the world of good. And I've got a new hairdo to go back with. And about another stone in weight!"

"Definitely agree with you there. I don't think I've ever eaten so much! Oh, hello!" June turns as a snowy-haired gentleman joins her.

"Did you have fun?" he asks.

"It was lovely. And by the way, this is the lady I was telling you about. Caitlin, meet George."

George extends his hand for me to shake and in smiling and saying how pleased I am to meet him, I can't help noticing he's got exceptionally sparkling eyes. Good. Just what June needs to cheer her up. They go on their merry way just as James comes over, having escaped his fan club for the last time.

"Woah. That was hard work. Just like being back at the holiday park!"

"You're just a babe magnet, that's what it is," I say, chuckling, and pointing over at the coffee bar add, "We haven't tried the coffee over there yet. Or the cakes. Shall we indulge? Can't believe we've been on here all this time without paying them a visit."

"So much to do, so little time. Probably just as well looking at those," he says as we draw close to the cabinets.

"Ooh. Chocolate covered strawberries! Never had those before. And I've completely stuffed the budget, so I'm just going for it anyway."

Finding a table by the window – a rare thing, I suspect – we contemplate our bounty.

"It seems nuts buying food and coffee when it's free upstairs," says James, preparing to dig into the biggest cream cake I've seen in my life.

"Different clientele, I guess. They wouldn't dare churn out the same cakes down here – nobody would buy them – so they must have another chef for this. Or make different cakes. Like yours, fr'instance. That's totally ginormous."

"Gotta be done. It would only go stale if I didn't have it."

"Interesting relationship you have with food."

"Yes, and possibly unusual in that it's uncomplicated. I enjoy it. End of. No faddy diets, no angst – it's there to be eaten and so I eat it. Just like this," he says, carefully inserting an over-laden fork into his mouth. His eyes close in rapture, and I take the opportunity to sink my teeth into one of the four chocolate-covered strawberries that cost the same as James' cake.

Silence reigns for a few precious moments while we concentrate on the delicious explosions of flavour in our mouths. Some things in life need total focus and this is clearly one of them.

I'm free first, as James is busily wiping the cream from around his chin. "Whoever thought up that combination deserves a medal. Wowza. Wonder how easy it is to do at home. I'm picking up some seriously bad habits on here. How're yours?"

"Utterly delightful."

"I'm ruined for afternoon tea now."

"I would imagine so. And we've got lunch soon. The meals are all morphing together. Aargh."

"Before we go up to do whatever we're doing next – which is a whole lot of nothing, I suspect – d'you mind if I just nip into the duty-free shop? I want to try that lovely perfume again. If it's as nice as I remember, I might buy it before we get off. The chances of me remembering it and being arsed to go and find it when we get home are about zero. Anyway, it seems the right thing to do. New me, new perfume, and all that."

"I think I can just about waddle that far."

"You've got all those stairs to climb to the Lido as well. At least, I presume that's where you want to go next."

"Sadist. Or should that be masochist, as I can't believe you enjoy it either. Or maybe both. Wonder if you can be both. Maybe someone who's both enjoys everyone suffering, including themselves. Sometimes I think I'm so naive."

Leaving him to ponder his own peculiar thoughts, I head for the perfume shop and the Tom Ford stand. Fortunately no one's around so I have a liberal spray of Black Orchid. Mmmm. It smells divine – deep and musky with a sharp edge – completely unlike most of the other perfumes on offer which are way too sweet for my taste.

"Yup – that's the one." James appears behind me. "Pleeease can we take the lift?"

"Nothing to stop you taking it. I want to walk up, as I've managed every time except when I had those stupid shoes on, so it's kind of a personal thing."

"Well if you're going to drag your huge bulk up all those stairs, I guess the least I can do is keep you company."

"It'll never be as huge as yours, so let's go," I say chuckling. I'm going to miss the banter. Life at home with me, my laptop and Titan is going to seem very, very tame after this.

In view of the fact that I will need more than four chocolate strawberries to get me through the dance class (with Nick, yay!) I do find a bit of space for some Thai green curry and a few noodles when it gets to lunch time. And a big pile of veg to balance it out. Then, being mindful of garlic breath, there is the obligatory schlep back to the cabin to clean my teeth. Yes, I could have chosen quiche and salad, but, erm no. Not on holiday, and probably not ever, TBH. If I was ever on *Room 101*, quiche would be very high up the list.

"Aw, you smell gorgeous." Nick is in Reception before me and closes in for a kiss on the cheek and a hug. "And your hair survived. Looks nice down too."

"Um, not used to quite so many compliments in one sentence! Thank you. I went back to test the Tom Ford to make sure it was the one I tried before, and it is. Thankfully James remembered which one as I was somewhat away with the fairies at the time. And yes, Mia said this would last for a few days, so I'm loving the temporary new look. Let's hope that we don't have to do any turns or I'll be lashing you in the face."

"It'll be worth it – and I can always duck if I need to," and he smiles his lovely crinkly-eyed smile.

When we get to the class it seems we are doing a sequence dance. We could just be walking around the room hand in hand – I'd still love it.

Doug gets on the mike. "This is a fun dance that often comes up on social nights. It's called the St Bernard's Waltz and it's very easy and a great way to finish the cruise. We'll be learning it in hold, so please take your partners."

Which I now have. Yes!

This is the kind of dance to ham up like crazy – and we do. How can you do SIDE, CLOSE-SIDE, CLOSE-SIDE, STAMP-STAMP without a huge grin on your face? You can't, looking at the people around us. In a way, today seems like even more of a party than the Sailaway, as everyone is doing stuff for the last time, and loving it. Moving on to the SIDE, CLOSE-SIDE, CLOSE-SIDE, then the back, back, forward, forward bit that comes after it, naturally causes chaos as some people appear incapable of going BACK when Doug tells them to. We get through it, however, and I even manage to do the lady spin without my plait smacking Nick in the face. Possibly not a hairstyle for jive nights! The fast little Viennese waltz bit is a dream, maybe because we are used to moving together in jive, then it's back to the beginning.

"Are you free for a coffee after this?" asks Nick when there's a brief pause.

Ooh. "Absolutely. The only thing I've got to do is pack. I'm meeting James back at the cabin at 4, as our suitcases have to be outside the cabin by 5. Sob. Can't believe we're at the end."

My sadness is interrupted by Doug taking us through the sequence again.

"By Jove, I think we've got it," laughs Nick as we time our STAMP-STAMP perfectly. Doug happens to be passing at the time and nods in agreement.

The class comes to an end way before I'm ready.

"So, ladies and gentlemen, you will have the chance to practise this tonight, for your last dance session. We'll see you in the Atrium at 10."

Chapter 43

Funnily enough, Nick leads me to the table James and I were occupying just a few hours earlier. Now way too stuffed with noodles and Thai curry and with a touch of indigestion, I opt for peppermint tea, which seems a bit of a shame as the coffee was really quite good, though not a patch on ours, obvs. But if I want to stand any chance of eating dinner, I'd better try and calm my poor tummy down. I foresee a very long fast when I get back. Tomorrow.

"You're very thoughtful," says Nick.

I wonder if I've suddenly become thoughtful, as James keeps pointing that out too. Was I not able to have a thoughtful face before? Or maybe I just didn't think much. How odd. Maybe I always wore a vacant look before because there weren't any thoughts going on. Maybe it's all part of the new me. Who knows?

"It's quite funny you say that. James has been saying it a lot recently too, so I'm beginning to wonder if I looked like an idiot most of the time. Or talked all the time. Which I guess is equally possible." I'm gabbling. Possibly because I'm a bit nervous and wondering why he wants to stop for a coffee, although I'm loving every extra moment of being with him. Maybe I'm over-thinking again. "Just last day stuff, you know. How fast it's gone, and how lovely it's been. And thinking I probably won't eat for a very long time once I get off here."

"Yes, you've got a point there. I can't even think about getting back to normal life after what's being going on here over the last two weeks."

"Well, your life isn't exactly normal anyway, is it?" Oops. That sounded a bit fierce, or even slightly envious. "I mean, you're off to New York soon, which isn't quite like going back to a run-of-the-mill day job ..." SHUT UP.

"No, you're quite right. It isn't normal or mundane, or any of those things, which is partly why I chose it – to escape from an unpleasant situation. But now I'm finding that in us agreeing not to stay in touch, what I appear to be doing instead is backing away from what could be a wonderful situation. So that's occupying quite a lot of my thinking time."

He's not alone on that one as my resolve has all but crumbled. So where's the strong decisive 'I want time on my own' Caitlin now, huh?

"But it seemed like you did the best thing at the time, didn't it? And from what you said, you don't have any choice about it, as you're on a contract."

"True. But I think I would get through it a lot better if I could be in touch with you occasionally. Like the odd email. Or text. Just a bit of a 'Hi, it's raining on the coast, how are you?' sort of thing. I know that's not what we agreed..." He peters out and gives me some pretty convincing sad eyes.

Um. Right. Honesty is probably best here. I can hear my mum in my head again.

"So, by the same token, can I email you and say, 'Hey it's so hot here on the South Coast'? In fact, probably hotter than where you are? Has been known. You know, I like to stay positive where I can." I'm grinningly stupidly, because, let me just think for a moment. Do I want to be in touch with Nick? Hell, YES!

"You're brilliant." The grin goes from ear to ear. "Is that a yes from you?"

"It's a 'Yes' from me, to be sure, and it sounds like we've really got to stop watching those crappy talent shows." And I'm laughing too.

So amidst more chatting and laughter we exchange email addresses and mobile numbers, and rather than feel sad at the thought of leaving the ship, I start to feel a tiny bit excited about the future. And that hasn't happened in about a century.

"So, I reckon I can take all of this back and get a refund."

I've dumped the contents of my wardrobe and drawers on my bed, and having packed all the stuff I've worn, am faced with a big pile of stuff I haven't.

"Really? Don't you want to keep it?" James is aghast that there could be clothes I don't want to keep.

"Well, to be honest, this one was Jules' idea." I'm holding up a luscious fuchsia pink cocktail dress which is totally gorgeous and seemed such a good idea at the time. "And yes, it is beautiful, but it cost a bit and

I can't see me wearing it anywhere else. I mean, a cruise ship is about as posh as it gets, isn't it?"

"Okay. Possibly right on that one."

And so I plough on through a pile of clothes, none of which I've worn and all of which still have the price tags on.

"I can't believe you did that."

"What?"

"Left the tags on."

"Well I packed in such a rush – a lovely rush, mind you – that I just chucked everything in, tags and all. I've only been taking them off as I wear them, which is actually quite clever, isn't it? No point in keeping things I won't wear. How about you? Have you got loads of stuff you didn't wear?"

James' bed is army-style orderly, much like his side of the bathroom. While my shampoo, conditioner and all that cleansing lark were lobbed anywhere I could reach, and stayed there, all of his toiletries were organised in one corner. So wish he could move in with me and organise my life.

"I think I probably brought less than you. And, to be honest, as you erm, 'pointed out'..." he does those silly inverted commas we both hate, "I didn't have as much to worry about as you. On either the wardrobe or the footwear front."

Ouch. He remembers. "I'm so sorry about that. I didn't mean to make you feel bad."

"Stop it. No apology needed. And although at the time I was a bit confused about what had happened, I'm really glad it did. You just carry on doin' that stuff and don't let anyone tell you what to do."

"Hmm. It's interesting you say that, because I think I used to be like that before, and it got whittled away by the constant picking and sniping."

"Yes. Thinking back, I always saw you as a strong woman who knew her own mind. Not in a bossy way, but just, I dunno, strong. Strong and funny and a bit scatty, but definitely not a pushover. Which is why it was so surprising that you slowly changed into someone different."

"Well, Mr Shit-for-brains used to tell me that he loved the fact that I was working freelance and in control of my own life – like – not in a day job. He said he admired me for that as he liked strong women, but looking back he was obviously threatened by it, which is no doubt why he used to scream at me – that it was all about me, and what about him? He used to say that I was so high-and-mighty and so up myself that I didn't have time for anyone else, when in fact I would go out of my way to involve him and try to get him to make decisions and stuff, as well as dressing to please him, even if it made me feel uncomfortable. Like wearing these, for instance."

I'm still clutching the high shoes I'm about to lob into my case. "So these are for the charity shop. Or maybe eBay, which I know nothing about, but I'm sure I can learn."

"Good idea – they don't even look as if you've worn them. Sorry, didn't mean to start all this off again on the last day. You don't have to talk about it if you don't want to."

"No worries. It does actually help to talk it out when things crop up. I never really told anyone what went on – as you know – because I was so embarrassed and ashamed. But after this holiday I'm feeling a lot prouder of myself because I managed to get out of it, and because I've told you some of it. It's not a box of horrible experiences locked away in my memory anymore. In fact there's one more thing I want to tell you about because I'm extremely proud of it, then I will shut up and get this packing thing done."

"OK, go on."

"Well while I was figuring out how to get him out of my flat, I had to find a way of controlling his horrible outbursts. I suddenly hit on the idea of recording him on my phone, then threatening to send the recordings anonymously to his friends, who had only ever seen him as cool, calm and gracious. Nobody would have believed me if I'd told them what he turned into when we were alone. So one day when he was being really nasty I grabbed my phone and pointed it at him and said that I was recording it and would send it to his friends so they could hear just how horrible he really was."

"Wow. That sounds a bit dangerous. He could have just grabbed it and smashed it – and possibly laid into you too."

"True. But his rages had never been physically abusive – in fact he just used to flip in a second into this horrible verbally vicious personality – so I guess it didn't occur to me that he might do that. Amidst all the psychological abuse there was still an element of respect, which I know sounds completely mad. But I practised in secret how to record him, so I could also set it off without him knowing if I needed to. Just looked like I was checking my phone."

"And did it make him calm down?"

"Yes, fortunately. Because I was really scared I would get chucked out of my flat. Nobody wants to hear arguing, especially the kind of screaming he did, and I was really worried one of the neighbours would make a complaint about us to the management company. Which is why of course I had to be careful about getting him out with the minimum fuss. If it was a rented flat I would have just gone. No kids to worry about – I really would have just gone."

"Well thank heavens for small mercies. Imagine if you'd had kids with him."

I shudder at the thought. "Don't want to even go there. Firstly because it would have been such an awful environment and a rubbish example of a healthy relationship for the child – having a bully for a father isn't a great role model, is it? But also, imagine perpetrating those genes. Eek. Whatever's wrong with him, it shouldn't be carried forward into another generation. Perish the thought."

We're interrupted by a knock on the door.

It's Marco. "Good afternoon, Sir, Madam. Just checking your cases will be ready for 5 o'clock as we will need to take them away then."

It's gone 4.30. Eek.

"Yes, of course they will. Sorry – we were just talking. Thank you for reminding us." Closing the door James looks at me with puppy eyes and we fall into a huge hug. That's at least three this cruise.

Pulling back I put my serious face on and say, "Okay, being practical because time's a-ticking here, I'm lobbing it all in and it can get sorted out when I'm home. Then I think we should go up and indulge in a glass of wine and watch the world go by. For the last time."

Miming a sob I throw myself back into James' arms and we pretend to cry our eyes out for a moment into each other's shoulders. Anyone listening outside, like Marco for instance, would be absolutely convinced that we're nuts. And they wouldn't be far off the mark.

Chapter 44

It's surprisingly warm out on deck as we speed ever closer to Southampton, but of course nothing compared to roasting in the Med. As a result of waving goodbye to my suitcase at five o'clock, I had to choose what to leave out that would do for this afternoon, tonight and tomorrow morning, bar a couple of bits that would fit in my outrageously stripy overnight bag. This was complicated – for me, not James obvs – as we want to eat in the restaurant. I know the dress code is smart/casual but my new hairdo (still intact) begs for something more than my best jeans. So it's smart navy cropped trousers with a slinky black vest, and a stunning pink and black wrap Jules encouraged me to buy but I haven't worn yet. I've come to realise that a girl can never have too many wraps or scarves, something she mentioned several times during our short but intense shopping trip, but didn't really sink in at the time.

The mood up on deck is pretty subdued as I guess people are starting to think about that Real Life Thing that awaits them tomorrow. James decided he has finally reached his limit with cakes so we've settled for a glass of wine at a table in the sunshine instead.

"So, I haven't asked, what are your travel plans tomorrow?"

James has been hiding behind his shades, presumably gazing out to sea, which is sort of what we did when we first came on here, two weeks and a whole lifetime ago.

He turns to face me, shades still down. "Um, getting the first available train back to London I guess."

"You're welcome to come back to mine. I suspect Aiden will be belting back to his friends in Glastonbury so there will be a bed free, and possibly even some clean bed linen, if you'd like to stay over."

"Ah thanks, but I might as well get back into the fray. Sort the washing out and all that stuff. Plus with the engineering works they always do on Sundays it could take me forever to get home. You could maybe drop me at the station though."

"Of course. It's going to be weird, isn't it? I feel like we're leaving a whole lifestyle behind – and people we've got to know, like Sebastian and Star Trek and Marco. Oh and Laura. Just think, they have to crank it all up again tomorrow for the new people. I so couldn't do that. And then there's all of us going back to our lives. I wonder if Mrs Ungrumpy is usually grumpy or usually not. And I hope June keeps up with that twinkly-eyed gentleman. People shouldn't have to be on their own after their partners die. That's so sad."

"That's where the benefit of those clubs comes in, meeting similar people, maybe with no expectation of anything more than friendship. Talking of which, here come Nick and Sarah."

Amidst all the frenzy of packing and stuff, I realise I haven't told James about the recent upgrade from 'friends-but-not-keeping-in-touch' to 'there-might-be-sthg-here', but I guess it will come out at some point.

"Yo there," smiles Sarah, as she manoeuvres herself up to the table and reaches over to hug me. Who'd have thought it?

"Hey, you're getting good at driving that thing!"

"Had to. Nick must be getting sick of pushing me around. But it stays here when we get off, so I'll have to get used to using the crutches then. At least I'll be a bit safer with them on dry land."

"I wouldn't bank on it, based on your recent attempts," chuckles Nick, bending down to kiss me on the cheek. He's gone for the casual jacket with a navy t-shirt and pale chinos look. I can't imagine him ever looking less than gorgeous.

Sarah glares at him, obviously immune to his gorgeousness. So not all sweetness and light then. "I suggest you get me something to eat to redeem yourself or I might be tempted to savage you." Then she grins. Borderline savage then.

"Hey, good idea," says James. "You?"

"You mean me? The me that in our cabin said she wasn't going to eat until at least eight tonight?"

"The same. Is that a yes?"

"Jeez. A bowl of crisps maybe, to soak up the wine I'm planning on drinking!"

Chuckling like two old mates, Nick and James wander off, leaving me and Sarah to discuss how the hell she's going to cope at home on her own and What Happens Next in terms of her recovery. Can't help thinking she's not planning on doing a lot of resting.

Continuing with the list of what's weird today – haven't quite stopped doing lists – is knowing that we don't have to go back to the cabin to change. There is nothing to change into. What I'm wearing now is more or less what I'll be wearing when I walk through the door tomorrow to greet Titan. Oh and Aiden of course, haha. I'm assuming he will actually hang around to say hello, probably followed by a pretty speedy goodbye. Okay, I did leave out clean underwear and a warmer t-shirt as I'm not a complete slob, but in essential terms This Is It.

"Earth calling Caitlin." James is waving his hands in front of my face.

"Don't tell me I'm doing that thoughtful thing again. I did it before too, just that nobody was interested enough to notice. If you see what I mean." That came out all wrong.

"Well, no matter," says Nick, smoothing my ruffled feathers. "We were saying that maybe before dinner we should go down to look at the photographs to see if we want any of them. This is the last chance."

"Good point. We haven't checked them for ages, have we?" I say, looking at James. It will be an interesting experience, as we've both come a long way since the day we boarded.

Seems like everyone else is panicking too when we get down there, as the photo gallery is busy, but this is where Sarah comes into her own.

"Oh, I'm sorry, could I just get through to have a look?" she says, looking up at the person blocking our view, with big eyes I definitely haven't seen before. She's shameless. The guy who's been hogging that section for ages steps back, all apologies, and we move in to check it out.

Aw, bummer. "Sorry mate, but we're not actually in this bit after all". Moving as a foursome we investigate the other displays and soon accumulate a pile of photos.

"We really can't afford this lot!" I whisper to James.

He agrees and we cut the final total down to about four, which even without proper frames still amounts to a small fortune.

"Okay. The picture with the Captain is rubbish. Sorry. Nice bloke, but very false picture. Not us, Cait."

So that's three.

Then there's the pic of all of us, in which Nick looks totally gorgeous so it's a no-brainer.

"Don't forget I can scan anything we want so we both get a copy."

Okay, that I can cope with.

Nick and Sarah don't have any such problems, obvs, as they hardly want pics of each other at this stage of their non-relationship. In fact they just buy a copy each of the four of us together. Hmm. Maybe she thinks more of James than I realise. Or Nick. Or maybe I should just stop over-thinking.

So, deal done with DDG photographer who is on a complete high as he gets off tomorrow, we make our way to the Pyramid restaurant for the last time. It seems like most people are slumming it in the Lido as the place isn't exactly busy. Either that or they don't want the embarrassment of the tips fiasco. James told me that the tips would be added to our bill automatically, but that we could also choose to reward particular members of the crew if we wanted to. Having mutually decided we did want to, James has several envelopes containing cash stashed in his jacket. Empty restaurant or not, we're determined to enjoy our last night on board and to show our appreciation for Sebastian and co. for being so lovely.

It's interesting that as the cruise has progressed, I've realised I don't have to eat all the courses. But the choice and variety have inspired me to try a bit harder when I get home, should the opportunity of entertaining rear its dusty and long-unused head. Soup. I could probably do soup as I've got one of those whizzy hand-blender things, also dusty and unused. Oh and I can do a mean salad as that's one of my favourite meals. I'm not really a dessert person, which cuts it down from five to four courses, so if you have the salad as a veg it's back down to three. Which I could passably manage. I just need to find a willing victim. I'm roused from my reverie by the deafening silence of my dinner guests.

"What?!"

They're all looking at me, grinning their faces off.

"Don't you dare say I'm looking thoughtful again! I'm actually very thoughtful, very often. Just that you haven't had much opportunity to witness it."

Nick can't stay quiet any longer and bursts into laughter. Not the kind that makes you go pink with embarrassment and anger, more a sort of gentle, kindly laughter.

"We just wondered how long it would take you to realise we'd stopped talking," he says. "You were so lost in your own world that it was kind of fascinating watching your face. Sorry. That was probably a bit cruel."

At that moment Sebastian comes back to see whether we've made our menu choices and they all look at me as everyone else appears to know what they want.

"Would you like a bit more time to think about it, Madam?"

"Um…"

"NO!" they shout, drawing surprised looks from the other diners.

"We'll be here all night if you ask her that," says James. "Any ideas Cait?"

Amidst much chuckling I make an on-the-spot selection and Sebastian takes our orders away with a big smile on his face. I like to think he'll miss us.

Chapter 45

We're all having a dessert as it's the last meal. Even Sarah. Amazing what you can force down when you want to, and I have to say my lemon drizzle cheesecake is heavenly. A few more diners have been dribbling in while we've been here, so there's a bit of a happy buzz going on, and those that are leaving before us are handing envelopes to Sebastian, who excitedly stashes them in a drawer at the serving station.

"You've got ours, haven't you?" I ask James. Pretty sure he has, but it would mean a schlep up to the cabin if he hasn't.

"Yep," he pats his pocket in reply.

"Ah," Nick puts his fork down, finishing his caramel flapjack with Chantilly cream with a satisfied sigh. "Well, annoyingly, I haven't, so do you guys want to get coffee while I nip back?"

"I thought you did!" Sarah's not impressed. "Didn't you put it in your jacket?"

"No. I meant to, but I left it on the side. No matter. I'll get the lift so I won't be a moment."

Sarah raises her eyes heavenwards. She's very close to the edge, that one, capable of going from nice to nasty in an instant. A bit like somebody else I know.

"No worries," says James. "Brandy or anything to go with it?"

"Thanks, but no. Might have a bit more wine later though. Back in a minute," and he's gone.

My poor stomach is really complaining now, so I go for the peppermint tea, especially as I want to dance later. The thought of a long day eating almost nothing when I get home is very appealing. Nick is back almost before we know it, so we sit in companionable silence, sipping our drinks as they cool down and watching everyone enjoying their last night too. It feels very different in here from the first night, when it was all abuzz with the excitement of a new ship to explore and new adventures to be had. Tonight you can tell that people have kind of disembarked already in their heads, thoughts moving more towards filling up the fridge, doing the washing, and wondering what the hell the kids have been up to while they've been away. Or in my case, Aiden, but I'm probably being unkind as I'm sure it's all been fine. It'll be good to see the ginger ninja again though.

Drinks drunk, petit-fours nibbled (that would be James), there's no excuse to hang around here anymore. Sebastian and Star Trek come over to say goodbye and we share genuine hugs, and the guys hand over the envelopes which are very well received. So glad we did that. It turns out to be quite an emotional moment and my eyes are ever so slightly misty as we make our way towards the exit, Nick expertly manoeuvring Sarah's wheelchair amongst the tables. James puts his arm gently round my shoulder and gives me a squeeze. When I look up I can see his eyes are misty too.

"Aw. You too? It's been so good, hasn't it?"

"Yep, sure has. Although it's not over until the fat lady has sung. Or danced in your case."

"Oh you're so rude! I'm sure you must have put on a ton of weight too!"

"Possibly," grins James, pulling himself up straight to his full height and running his hand down his ridiculously flat stomach. "But you won't catch me admitting it. Not in public, anyway."

We're walking past duty-free and I suddenly remember what I was going to buy. "Ooh. Can we just pop in there a minute? I want to get that perfume."

In the background I can hear an announcement and it looks like the dancing will be starting in the Atrium any minute. The panic clearly shows on my face, as I'm tortured by indecision.

"They stay open really late, so you could get it afterwards. They probably want to get every last penny out of us they can," he jokes. "And besides, you'll worry about leaving it somewhere if you get it now."

"True. Shall we find a table and have another drink?" I've given up worrying about either my liver or combining spinning and drinking. I'm pretty hopeful that Nick will catch me if I totter. And while I've been fannying around he's already got us a table on the balcony looking down on the dance floor.

"Good evening ladies and gentlemen, and welcome to the last dance session of the cruise. Aaaah!"

Doug milks it as we all join in.

"So assuming you can still move after all the food they give us on here – and yes, isn't it amazing? – you must feel for us, as we're on for the next one too. I know, but someone's got to do it… Yes, anyway, as it's the last night there's no particular structure so you can ask for your favourite music, and if we've got it we'll play it. We're starting with something slow as no doubt you've just finished eating."

It turns out to be a slow waltz which we can't do, so it's an opportunity to settle down and order some wine, as we were surprisingly abstemious over dinner. We've got to be up early tomorrow, but, hey, whatever… so it's Merlot for the boys and Chardonnay for me and Sarah, as a final celebration.

"How are you going to manage when you get home? I mean, shopping and everything?" From our conversation earlier on it sounds as though Sarah doesn't have a lot of backup, so I do wonder what's going to happen.

"The first thing I'm getting is an x-ray and a second opinion. I'm sure the doctors on here are amazing but I'd like to see a specialist. Need to get back on my feet as soon as possible. And actually the pain is a lot better, so I think it might not be as bad as they say. Once I can get some arnica on it and do some icing, I'm sure it will heal quickly. This was really just damage limitation from their point of view, I think."

She sounds so organised. As if the very universe unfolds according to her vision of it, as there is no leeway as far as I can see. The men are deep in discussion, but as the music changes to 'Save the Last Dance for Me' by the lovely Michael Bublé, Doug comes on the mike telling us this one is for everyone who's met someone special on this cruise. Nick apologises and breaks off from talking to James and stands up.

"I think we need to dance to this one, don't you?" he says offering his hand in the time-honoured fashion; and having taken mine, pulls me down the steps to the dance floor. There's a part of my brain that thinks this is all a bit weird, dancing to a track like this right under Sarah's nose, but I just have to trust that he knows she's alright with it.

Down on the dance floor Nick is singing his heart out as we jive to the song.

"... laugh and sing,
but while we're apart
don't give your heart to anyone..."

All with a big grin on his face. With emotions apparently more or less out in the open, it gives me an idea for a request for later on.

As the music fades, Doug gets back on the mike. "Here's a little test for everyone who was at the class today – we're going to see just how much you remember of the St Bernard's Waltz," and as he turns to start the music, James appears by our side.

"I'm taking Sarah to one of the shows, then we're turning in for the night. See you back in the cabin." Then he's gone. We look up to see Sarah giving a thumbs-up and a wave, and it feels just like the parents have allowed us to stay up late again.

The St Bernard's Waltz turns into a complete mess with everyone turning the wrong way. The fast Viennese Waltz bit in the middle makes me a teeny bit dizzy, but thankfully Nick keeps a firm hold, and as it comes to an end there is much laughter and fanning of faces.

"Wow, I need some water after that!"

"I'll sort it out – probably need another glass of wine too," Nick says, leaving me at the edge of the dance floor to chat with June and her new man. This is the perfect opportunity to make my request, so after a few words with them I make my way over to Doug, who is more than happy to oblige when the right moment arises.

"Think we need to slow it down a bit after that, so here's a social foxtrot so you can get your breath back. It's Frank Sinatra and 'I've got you under my skin.'"

Hell, is he in our heads or what? Or at least mine.

"Fabulous choice of music tonight, isn't it?" says Nick. Glad he's clocked it too.

"Yeah – I was just thinking the same thing. D'you s'pose they always do this for the last night, or is this a special one? Maybe they've noticed a few people, erm, getting together on the ship. Like June. She came on all unhappy and a bit fearful and look at her now." She's on the other side of the balcony talking avidly to her very attentive partner and looking as though she's really, really happy. "And Mrs Ungrumpy. She came on all bad-tempered but she seems happy now as well."

We've talked through a couple of slow tracks, then Doug announces the first request of the evening. "A lovely song for being at sea, under the light of the moon. How much more romantic can it get? Here's Van Morrison's 'Moondance', which is for Nick from Cait."

I look at him anxiously, hoping I haven't overstepped the mark. "Love the moon, love the dancing, thought it was a touch relevant… hope you don't mind."

"Ah, not at all, it's brilliant. One of my favourites."

Down on the dance floor I'm singing away as we jive like crazy, when I suddenly realise how inappropriate the lyrics are. Eek. 'I just wanna make love to you to-night' is a bit heavy for our current non-relation-ship status.

Nick notices my embarrassment and grins, shaking his head in such an endearing way I just want to hug him.

"No worries from my side!" he says, winding me close into his waist before expertly unfurling me into a turn. This guy is a good dancer. One beautiful song follows another as all the requests segue into each other, and there's precious little time to get my breath back except for one very quick toilet break. Back at the table, where Nick has thoughtfully refilled my water glass, I'm just about to sit down when Doug comes on the mike again. Surely not the last dance already!

"I have to say you people have excelled yourselves in your choice of music tonight. This is the perfect end to a lovely cruise, and we wish you a safe journey home, and many happy hours of dancing in the future. Here's 'Beneath your beautiful' by Labrinth. And Nick says it's for the very beautiful Caitlin."

Nick stands up, and gently takes hold of my hand, bringing it slowly up to his lips where he kisses it softly. "Because you are. Inside and out. You just don't realise it yet."

And with tears threatening to spill out of my eyes he leads me down to the dancefloor, where we abandon all pretence of doing a social fox-trot and just smooch around in a circle with my head buried into his shoulder. When I trust myself to look up, I can see several other couples have done the same, including June, who gives me a massive wink and a smile as we pass each other. With Nick holding me close, his head leaning gently against mine, bodies moving together, I'm starting to feel that yes, maybe I could let this man in, and I need to give myself and him a chance. The question is, dare I?

The music finally comes to an end and everyone's clapping and smiling. What a beautiful evening.

"I think we need a walk on deck, don't you?" Nick says, as we reclaim my wrap and his jacket from our chairs.

"Ah yes. Don't want it to end..."

"Well it isn't going to yet. We have a bit more time, in fact we have as much time as we want."

The air outside on the Promenade deck is surprisingly warm, and the sky is surprisingly bright, filled with twinkling stars you don't see when the moon is up. After a slow wander hand in hand to a secluded spot by the handrail, Nick pulls me to a halt to face him.

"You know, I can't believe how my life has been turned upside-down in the last two weeks. I came on here just hoping to survive being in close proximity to a woman I no longer love. I thought if we could just get along well enough to cope without destroying each other, it could be regarded as a success."

"Well, considering the circumstances, I think you've excelled yourselves."

"Yes. I think you're right, and I'm happy that we did cope. But having carefully barricaded my heart behind big walls so I would survive the experience, I find that the reverse has happened, and that all my defences have been blown away by meeting you."

Gulp.

"That's why I cried at the Labrinth song – you couldn't have chosen any better. We're both scared and unsure and wary. But I feel so close to you. Not like we only just met." Despite myself, I can see that as a line straight out of one of Ivy's books.

"I know. And when that song suddenly came into my head, I was so pleased. So yes, I absolutely do want to see you again when we get off here, but for now, I want you to have something to remember me by."

My heart jumps. Is he going to kiss me? I'm panicking as I'm a bit out of practice, but instead of moving towards me he reaches into his coat pocket and brings out a package, wrapped in pretty pink paper.

Putting it carefully into my rather shaky hands, he says, "Go on, open it."

Fortunately it's one of those quick release kind of arrangements, probably designed for just such an occasion, and the paper falls away to reveal the really cool gold and black box of Tom Ford's Black Orchid.

"Oh my God! OHMYGOD! Thank you. How did you know about this? Oh, thankyouthankyou." Shut up Cait, once is enough.

"I asked James when we went to get the food earlier up in the Lido. Then I went to get it when I said I was going to get the envelope for the tips."

"Ah, that is so sweet. I wanted this one so much. Thank you."

I'm busily looking down at my present, not knowing what else to say because at every moment he just blows me away.

"You're more than welcome. But I want to have something to remember you by too."

I'm just lifting my head to ask what that is when I find out, as Nick's hands gently frame my face, and his lips come down to meet mine in a kiss that blows the stars right out of the sky.

Eat your heart out, Ivy. This one's for real.

THE END